AN EVIL TALE I HEARD

Seán Haldane

Rune Press Limited

Published in 2022 by Rune Press Limited, London, UK.
www.runepress.com

The author acknowledges that the land where this novel is set is the traditional Mi'kmaq territory of the Lennox Island – L'nui Mnikuk First Nation and the Abegweit – Epekwitk First Nation. He acknowledges their culture and traditions and their impact in the writing of this book.

Printed and bound in Great Britain by TJ Books Limited, Padstow, Cornwall.

Cover design and typesetting by Peter Keighron, London, UK.
Cover photograph 'Eel Spear, Prince Edward Island, 19th century', by Christina R. Haldane, Moncton, Canada.

Research and editing assistance by Ghislaine Lanteigne, London, UK.
Proofreading by Maeve Haldane, Montreal, Canada.

ISBN 978-0-9574669-9-9

To Ghislaine

Mo nighean donn a Cornaig…

My brown-haired girl from Cornaig,
you were golden and beautiful,
my brown-haired girl from Cornaig.

It was an evil tale I heard
on Monday after Sunday …

… your hair was trailing down your body,
and your finely woven shirt in shreds,
and your smooth white breasts
spouting blood together.

From the Gaelic, Outer Hebrides.

Translated by Sorley MacLean.

1

'*Abegweit*, the Injuns call it. *Cradled on the Waves.*'

At least one thing was the same at the other end of the continent of North America: people called the original natives 'Injuns'.

We were looking north out of Tatamagouche Bay between two headlands to the blue, calm waters of Northumberland Strait. The coast of Prince Edward Island, a low stripe of green, occupied the horizon between the headlands. Cumulus clouds were moving steadily across the sky in the prevailing wind from west to east – the direction in which we had come.

We had left the other island, Vancouver Island, without sorrow. Our two years in Victoria had been hard, as we attempted to make a living in a world we had loved and which now seemed to hate us. We had certainly loved in that world, at Orchard Farm where our son Will had been born, and where Lucy and I had embraced in our bed under the eaves of the wooden house surrounded by its garden and orchard, with its stables, hen coop and pig pen, within a fringe of forest. Close behind the farm was the blunt and once volcanic cone of Mount Douglas, and in front of us, twenty miles away to the south and across the strait of Juan de Fuca hidden by forests, was the blue-grey serrated line of the Olympic mountains in Washington Territory.

No mountains here. What they called mountains in Nova Scotia were crags of ugly black basalt with scrubby trees on stony slopes, and Prince Edward Island had only low hills, I had been told, none higher than 500 feet. *Abegweit.*

The man who had said the word, the stagecoach driver, was waiting for a tip. He had unloaded our trunks onto the quay. I gave him a 25-cent Canadian 'shinplaster' banknote. Two boatmen began loading the trunks into the schooner we were about to board. I took Will by one hand, Lucy took him by the other. We often walked like this, a little human chain of three. Will was only sixteen months old, still proud of being able to walk, and tending to run off and trip and fall. We looked out at the sea and the island.

'I wonder how long we'll stay over there,' Lucy said.

'Not more than a month or two, I hope. Then we'll be on our way.'

But what was our way? From the Pacific to the Atlantic, so far. We had handed over Orchard Farm to a new tenant in April. The apples and pears of the orchard were in full blossom, which somehow made the pain worse. But it was not a pain at leaving. It was a pain for the dead. And as we distanced ourselves from that beautiful place, our pain lifted. We had taken a ship to San Francisco where we had avoided calling on the only people we knew there, the Quattrinis. Mrs Quattrini, formerly Mrs Somerville, was our landlady at Orchard farm but we communicated by letter. The Quattrinis did not approve of Lucy – the former Lukswaas, sister of the Tsimshian chief Wiladzap who had led Mrs Somerville's eldest daughter Aemilia to her doom – massacred by another tribe of Indians. They would not have approved of little Will – named after his dead uncle. Lucy and Will. Lukswaas and Wiladzap. Lucy did not mind the change of name, or any other change. She adapted, and enjoyed learning a new role as Mrs Hobbes, wife of the retired police sergeant. In effect this was a pre-emptive retirement. I would have shortly been sacked, on account of my marriage to an Injun woman whom I had met and seduced or been seduced by in the course of an investigation. The investigation had been successful, and much to the credit of the Victoria police force and of the magistrate Augustus Pemberton and ultimately of the Chief Justice of British Columbia, Matthew Begbie.

Mr and Mrs Pemberton and Matthew Begbie were the only friends Lucy and I had.

We were on our way to 'England, Home and Beauty', as the phrase goes. We had crossed America on the transcontinental railway, from San Francisco to New York. Next, we would take a ship to Queenstown, in Ireland. At Queenstown we would pause for a few weeks, to see Ireland as Pemberton had recommended. He had confided excitedly to me that he hoped I might like Ireland. Yes, England was home for me, but we both knew how rigid and conventional it could be. Ireland was more free and easy, he said, an untidier and friendlier version of England. And they had extensive police forces which needed to expand further. There could be a place for me there with my unusual skills as an Oxford graduate in jurisprudence and as a police detective. And, frankly, Lucy might find it easier in Ireland than in England – not only because of the frequent rain that would no doubt remind her of her childhood up where British Columbia reached Alaska.

I knew what Pemberton meant, and I gave him permission to write to his friends in Ireland about me, but my heart was set on going home to England and walking with Lucy and little Will over the Downs of Wiltshire with the larks singing and the grass rippling in the breeze. I knew my parents would welcome Lucy. As for other people, to hell with them! And since there were no Injuns in Europe, surely the instinctive disdain at Lucy would not be there. Even in the States, we had noticed, she was not always recognised as an Injun woman. Tall, slim and elegant, with golden-brown skin, raven hair and slanted eyes, she could also have been taken for another kind of 'Indian' – a Hindu I imagined.

Prince Edward Island, 'cradled on the waves', was not yet in Canada. British Columbia had held back for a while but was due to join Confederation by the end of this month, July 1871. Begbie was adapting to the idea of Canada, and had begun to argue that although in a way he would have liked to become an American, because he admired the US constitution with

9

its emphasis on individual liberty (with the cruel exception of the Indians of course), he preferred to stay British and to administer the law in the name of Queen Victoria. I had hardly heard of Prince Edward Island and had no idea where it stood about joining Confederation. But I assumed it was 'British' in the same way British Columbia was.

Two telegrams had been handed to me as we disembarked from the transcontinental train in New York, by a uniformed messenger who had alerted the police to make sure we did not proceed out of the station. I had read the telegrams on the station platform:

> *My homologue in Prince Edward Island Sir Robert Hodgson has written to me about a criminal case of great importance for the island. Having heard of our case Victoria 1869 he requests your help. You will hear from him. Please accept this Chad.*
>
> *Ever yours. Begbie*

Typical of Begbie to use a word like 'homologue,' meaning no doubt that just as he was Chief Justice of British Columbia, Sir Robert Hodgson was Chief Justice of Prince Edward Island.

The second telegram:

> *Urgent criminal case requires attention from very experienced investigator to assist Attorney General Brecken. You are very highly recommended by my friend Justice Begbie. Realise delay your return England but we need your help Charlottetown soon as possible. All accommodation will be provided you and family.*
>
> *Robert Hodgson*

I telegraphed my acceptance and New York hotel address to Sir Robert, and later that day I received a further telegram from the Attorney General of Prince Edward Island who had the magnificent name, fully spelled out in the telegram, of Frederick de St Croix Brecken. He also spelled out the financial terms which were indeed generous, provided an itinerary to Charlottetown, and telegraphed separately ample funds in American dollars to cover travel expenses.

We took a ship from New York up to Halifax, a voyage of four days. Luckily the sea was calm, we had a large cabin, a wide deck to walk on, and good food. Then from Halifax we travelled by train sixty miles to a town called Truro. This took over five hours on the slowest train I had ever been on, through a dreary landscape of rocky basalt hills, forests of low conifers with stumps of felled trees and piles of timber 'slash', and then across farmland with wooden houses and barns like almost anywhere in North America (which I now felt I knew well after the transcontinental journey). We had stayed in a simple but clean hotel in Truro, then we travelled in a hired buggy some thirty miles to Tatamagouche, another five hours, arriving around noon. The harbour was in a sheltered bay and there was a dockyard where schooners were built using timber from the Nova Scotia forests.

The Fair Isle was a schooner which had been sent especially from Charlottetown to Tatamagouche to pick us up. Soon our trunks were on board and we stepped from the wooden dock over the gunwale of the ship, me first. I reached back to take Will from Lucy's arms, then to help her onto the deck. I knew she hated the awkwardness of her long dress of grey silk and her tightly laced boots over white silk stockings that were glimpsed briefly as she stepped forward. She would have been more comfortable in a pair of leggings and a man's shirt such as she often wore at the farm. Or half naked. But as always, she was poised and very much, as the English would say, 'a lady'. She even tended to look down her nose, literally, at people. Now one of the sailors was addressing her in French. She smiled: 'I'm afraid I don't understand.' Her accent was, inevitably since she had learned English from me, very English. The sailor looked startled and apologised in English, glancing at me for help. The ship's Captain appeared, a ruddy-faced man with a half-uniform of naval jacket with brass buttons and a peaked cap, but oilskin trousers and heavy boots.

'Welcome on board *The Fair Isle*. I'm Captain Munro. Sir, Madam, if you would like to come this way, I can show you the cabin.'

'Can we stay outside?' I asked. 'We'd like to see the view, and the weather looks fine.'

'Of course. The crossing will take about five hours.'

We were in the well between the cabin and the stern. He pointed out a sort of park bench screwed into the deck, facing the gunwale. The sailor who had spoken French ran to fetch some blankets we could put over our knees.

'I gather you are coming to help us with our local scandal,' the Captain said with an expression of what looked like resignation.

'I gather you don't think the scandal will go away quickly. But I know nothing about it yet.'

'Well, I'll not be the man to tell you', he said, not unkindly.

Now we were tacking out of the bay with only one sail up, into a fairly stiff but steady breeze from the west. We broke out into the open sea – Northumberland Strait – and went into a series of long tacks. Luckily it became calmer, with a light breeze (the schooner was now using two main sails and a jib) and warm in the sun. The boat leaned to one side or the other and occasionally pitched but we could hold onto the arms of the bench. For a while Lucy nursed Will, then he lay asleep across her knees. We could see blue mountains, real ones, in the distance across the sea to our right, on Cape Breton. Ahead of us Prince Edward Island revealed itself as a series of pink beaches and low red cliffs with a green landscape behind. I had not seen this colour in rock and soil since as a boy I had visited Devon, in England.

I knew next to nothing about Prince Edward Island, and although I had looked for books about it in Halifax there were none. The owner of the bookshop said the island was best known for its exports of potatoes, lobsters and oysters, and there were three languages spoken there: English, Gaelic, and French – in that order. Oh yes, and the Mic Mac Indians (he did not say Injuns) had their own language, but there are only a few hundred of them. And speaking of language, he said, I shouldn't be surprised at the bad language of people there – even the children. It had come from British sailors. Charlottetown had lovely houses and a deep harbour, although not as big as Halifax. But so far, in 1871, the island had refused to join the Dominion of Canada, and as a result – in the bookshop owner's view – was flat broke. I had heard that statement before, when I had arrived on Vancouver Island in 1868. Although British Columbia was now joining Canada, it was certainly not broke, and my friends there thought it would contribute more to Canada than it would receive.

One of the sailors came and asked us to lunch with the Captain, so we followed him into the cabin. There were padded benches built into the walls, and an oval table with its legs bolted through brackets to the floor. Places for the three of us had been laid around one end of the table, and as we sat down a sailor brought in platters of cold meat – ham and chicken – sliced cold potatoes, bread, and fruit. There were jugs of water and of light ale. I don't like ale but I sipped it politely. Will sat on Lucy's knee and she mashed some potato to spoon-feed him. The Captain paid attention to him, commenting on how good-looking he was, and getting up and coming back with some clean rope ends Will might like to play with. He was indeed a good-looking boy, sturdy and with my blue-green eyes although they were slanted like Lucy's, dark hair from us both, and bronze-coloured skin with ruddy cheeks. He was learning to talk and pointed to things announcing: 'plate,' or 'cup,' or 'table'.

As we ate the conversation was light. The Captain described how the Northumberland Strait froze over completely between December and early May, and the island was cut off from the mainland except for transport by ice boats – huge sleds with sails which were driven by the wind where the ice was flat, but had to be lugged and pushed over the rough stretches. There had been some ice floes on the water until mid-May this year. It was now early July. The potatoes were in flower. Although rain was regular on the island, the soil was porous and well-drained, and the constant breeze prevented any buildup of damp to cause fungus or disease. Besides which there were a lot of Irish people on the island who knew all about potatoes.

The Captain described himself as a Lowland Scot, although born on the island. We chatted about how, by contrast, almost everybody on Vancouver Island, apart from the native Indians, had been born elsewhere. The English there sounded English, the Americans sounded American. But the Captain said that Prince Edward Island had an accent of its own. Certainly his own accent was unusual to me but he spoke very clearly. He looked politely at Lucy and said she looked like some of the Acadian French on the island, which was why the sailor had addressed her in French. She explained she was entirely a Tsimshian native or Indian.

'It's true,' the Captain said, 'that you look not unlike some of our local Mic Mac, but they and the French have intermarried. Otherwise our different communities are quite separate. The island with its fields, as you'll see, is like a great patchwork quilt, and so is its society. The main places I travel to are in the Boston States, and the people there seem more at one than we are – all free-born Americans, as they would say. The island is a real madhouse of differences. It was called New Ireland for a while, but there has never been a majority of Irish. The English are usually Anglican and Conservative. The Irish and the French are Catholic and Liberal. The Scots are usually Presbyterian, but they split into sects according to differences in how they read the bible. And there are Lowlanders like me who speak only English, and Highlanders who speak only the Gaelic' (he pronounced this as *Gallic*). 'There are more of us Scots than anyone else, but we are divided among ourselves.'

I clarified some of this to Lucy – in English. I don't speak much

Tsimshian. By now her English is excellent for everyday purposes. But there are whole areas of English-speaking life about which she knows next to nothing. She knows where Scotland is on a map, but I had to explain to her 'Lowland' and 'Highland' and 'Gaelic'.

'Our biggest division at present,' the Captain resumed, 'is about the railway. It will run from end to end of the island. Many people, including myself, think it will just throw us into debt and then we'll have no option but to join Canada. The Railway Bill was passed a few months ago. It's said that the cost of an Assemblyman's vote in favour of the Railway Bill was £200 – a small fortune. You'll soon get to know what we call "the island way".'

He paused with a sudden change in his facial expression from bonhomie to something like despair.

'I said earlier that I wouldn't be the man to tell you about the scandal, and I won't. But I'm catching myself in the way I talk. On the island we talk a lot about politics. The scandal that the authorities have asked you to investigate is a political affair. But behind it is a bloody murder. A lovely young lady beaten to death. And nobody knows by whom.'

We were at the end of our meal. The Captain was now looking blankly at the table. He then gathered himself, looked politely at Lucy and said, 'Mr Hobbes and I will have some things to discuss, and I have a couple of maps the Attorney General, Mr Brecken, gave me for him. If you'd like I can send tea or coffee to the other cabin, or out on deck if you prefer.'

I realised with a sinking feeling that this was the official world that Lucy and I had managed to avoid at Orchard Farm. There we had worked together, man and wife, sharing everything, working together. Now it would be assumed that only I, the man, would need to know about the wider world, especially as I was now a sort of freelance police officer. But I felt like delaying this development.

'I'd prefer my wife to stay with us,' I said. At least until we discuss

15

anything about what you call the "scandal".'

'Of course, you're welcome, Ma'am,' said the Captain, and called for coffee and tea. 'You'll hear the story of the scandal from Mr Brecken,' he said.

We went on to discuss the landscape of the island. Will was getting restless and after coffee we went out on the deck and strolled back and forth for a while on the side away from the wind. Then Lucy went to the cabin with Will to lie down for a rest. I stayed outside on the deck and looked out at the sea.

The island was now so close that I could see a pattern of fields and patches of woodland on gentle slopes and low hills behind promontories of red cliffs and the pink-grey sands of beaches. Captain Munro had explained that this was the sheltered south side of the island. Most of the harbours were in the south or east. The sea was much rougher along the north shore which was wide open to the Gulf of St Lawrence, and various sandbars made harbours impossible. He said the whole island was made of sandstone. There were various rivers and estuaries, as I discovered from the maps Captain Munro had given me.

I had some time to sit down and study these maps. The island was not only cradled on the waves, it was shaped something like a cradle, the east and west ends reaching more to the north than the middle – a crescent lying on its side, some 130 miles long and varying, from the map scale, between ten and forty miles wide.

By late afternoon we were approaching Charlottetown. Lucy and Will had come out on deck again. I held Will in my arms as we looked ahead. We could see that behind the clifftops there were scattered houses painted white or in light blue, green, yellow or grey, with unpainted wooden barns. We entered a narrow gap between two headlands, one with a lighthouse, and came out in the irregular wide bay of Charlottetown Harbour. There were larger houses now, with long vegetable gardens reaching down slopes towards the shore of pink sand and low red cliffs, several churches in white wood with small square towers, and then in the town itself two church spires rising not very high over streets of brick and wood buildings sloping gently down to the harbour and its quays. There was a mass of ships of all sizes, including a few naval vessels.

We were approaching a series of unusually long wharves stretching from the harbour quays out into the bay towards us. The Captain, standing beside me, said they were up to a hundred yards long, and they had to be, since there was a thirty or forty yard stretch of tidal mud from the shore until the harbour suddenly became ten fathoms deep. The schooner was now under only one sail, which was taken down with a rush and a bang from the boom as we approached the end of one of these wooden wharves, with the usual rushing of sailors on the ship and men on the shore to make the ropes fast, as the ship slid with a squealing sound along the edge of the wharf, padded with leather.

We disembarked and stood on the planked wharf, as a couple of young men in blue dungarees clambered onto the ship and began to unload our trunks. One was heavier than the others, as it contained my books and papers. 'Careful with this bastard,' said one of the men. 'She's a heavy fuckin' bitch.'

2

A reservation had been made for us at the St Lawrence Hotel, a building of new pink brick facing over Water Street across the quay to the wharves packed with ships. The hotel had an all-purpose air, with people milling in and out. What may have been the best rooms had been reserved for us on the first floor up – a sitting room and bedroom and our own bathroom and water closet. We also had a maid assigned exclusively to us, a young woman by the name of Katie who oohed and aahed over Will and immediately made herself useful to Lucy, helping her unpack our travelling trunk and ordering dinner in the room. Katie already knew I would be going out.

Two sealed letters awaited me. The first was from Frederick de St Croix Brecken. When I opened it, before reading it I held it out in front of me at arm's length to get a general impression – a habit I picked up from my father who as a country clergyman received many letters from parishioners he had not met, and enjoyed as a sort of game, predicting their personalities. Brecken's letter was a square patch of handwriting with wide margins on all sides, no corrections, in a typical university hand, small and neat. He invited me to dine with him that evening at eight o'clock. He would send a man to escort me. It was now past six o'clock.

The second letter, from the secretary of the Governor, William Robinson, invited me to a meeting at Government House the following morning at eleven o'clock.

Mr Brecken's man turned up promptly at a quarter to eight. He introduced himself as Sergeant McNulty. His police uniform consisted of a dark blue jacket with grey waistcoat and trousers, a peaked grey cap, and no badges of rank. He had a hard-sounding accent I recognised as from the North of Ireland, and a grim expression. He was rather small for a policeman, but lean and brisk. We walked quickly side by side without a word, heading slightly uphill from the harbour, left and right through streets at right angles to each other. The commercial area of Charlottetown behind the harbour seemed to be designed on the New York or San Francisco system of a grid. But we were now entering an area of wider streets at more pleasingly irregular angles which the silent McNulty said, when asked, was called Brighton. There were large new-looking wooden houses painted in cream or grey or light blue or even light green or pink, with open porches and balconies with the elaborate fretwork and stained-glass window panels which I knew from the Pacific coast as the 'gingerbread' style. The houses were set in large gardens with shrubs and mature trees – oaks, limes, maples, silver birches. I remarked to McNulty that the leaves were of such a fresh light green it still looked like spring.

'They've only been out for six weeks. Trees here don't come into leaf until the end of May. The cold winds across the frozen sea hold them back. Summer arrives all at once, then the leaves cling on for a long time in the fall. Then we're back to our six months of ice.'

He went quiet again. We reached a domain of about half an acre surrounded by a wooden fence and with a wide gate that McNulty opened. There was a huge lawn with a few scattered elms and oaks, and clusters of rose bushes in full flower sending out their scent in the dusk which was now beginning. Shrubs in dark red blossom which I recognised as quince bordered the front of an imposing house, double fronted with a central Georgian doorway but a classical pillared porch and peaked Gothic gables – an agreeable mixture of three styles. The house was made of beautifully layered overlapping clapboard, painted a gleaming light blue.

A manservant let us in. On each side of the hallway were wide double doors, one open on my right to a large dining room where I could see an elegant mahogany table, the one on my left to a room of the same size, a library. Here Frederick Brecken greeted me, and gestured for McNulty to leave us together. We sat opposite each other in leather armchairs, with glasses of sherry. Brecken was younger than I had expected − forty-two, as I later found out − of medium height, dark haired, blue-eyed, with a short well-trimmed beard. Not unlike me, in fact. I had had no time to unpack and dress for dinner but at least I was wearing a suit and a necktie with a white ruffled shirt − as he was too.

'Sir Robert has exchanged telegrams with Mr Begbie,' he said. 'He got in touch with him because he had heard about the events in Victoria two years ago when Mr Begbie and the local police, following the lead of yourself, had resolved that notorious murder of the mad-doctor by the Marine officer. Sir Robert has reported the main details to me. It was obviously a sensitive case in which many people's reputations were spared.' He smiled. 'I dare say I want my own reputation spared, Mr Hobbes, but it's not on the line in this case − at least not so far. But I do need an experienced police officer to take charge of solving what seems to be a very complex case beginning with the murder of the wife of a prominent politician. And there is such a network of relationships here, with almost everyone known to each other personally or by reputation, that an investigating officer "from away", as we term anyone from "off island", will be needed.

'Charlottetown has a local police force who can be on hand for serious offences in the whole of the island. It consists of only six men − five constables and Sergeant McNulty whom you have just met. Luckily, McNulty can be relied upon to be neutral in political matters, being, as we say, from "over across" in Nova Scotia, and an Irishman well used to trimming his sails according to events.

'There are smaller police forces covering each of the two other counties: four constables located in St Eleanors for Prince County and three constables located in Georgetown for Kings County. There is no central legal authority apart from myself, as Attorney General. I am a one-man band. My role is to ensure that the administration of justice proceeds under the law from policing to court. And there is of course the court process with Sir Robert as the Chief Justice. Given that this murder happened over a week ago, a start to an investigation is overdue. I have consulted with colleagues at the Executive Council and I am minded to appoint a Superintendent who can coordinate investigations with the help of the police forces from the three counties if necessary. Why operate this way? The former Marshall for the Charlotte-town Police Force has recently resigned. There is no one on the island who has enough experience for the job. Furthermore, any island appointment could be seen as having a political dimension. The three counties – Kings to the east, Prince to the west, and Queen's in between, including Charlotte-town – would each want to provide the successful candidate. It is better to find someone "from away". Sir Robert thought of consulting his "homologue" as he puts it, Justice Begbie, on the Pacific Coast over three thousand miles west of here, and Begbie put him onto you, and here you are! Furthermore you are on your way home to England. There is no danger, unless you become irredeemably attached to this remote island, of your digging yourself in here and taking things over. I should say, though, that our lack of preparedness for a case like this has alerted us to the necessity of reforming our current police forces.

'That's enough, I hope, for the background picture, but don't hesitate to ask me any questions that come to mind. Prince Edward Island is a young and small place, and its future is unclear. While you are here no doubt you will become part of the general discussion of this future. But back to this case! What have you heard about it?'

'Not much. Captain Munro described it as a "scandal" but preferred not to say anything more about it, other than that a young woman had been murdered.'

'Just over a week ago the wife of a member of our Legislative Council was savagely beaten to death at their summer house near the North Shore. She had just given birth to a child which had disappeared. It reappeared in a remarkable way – floating on the water of a pond a short distance behind the seashore, about twelve miles to the north west of the house – in a wicker-work cradle. "Cradled on the waves", you might say, like *Abegweit* itself. And miraculously alive. A baby girl.' He paused.

'The scandal is who the murdered woman's husband is, and in a lesser way who she was. The marriage was odd from the start. And now the husband will have to be questioned by the police and possibly led before a court, although on the evidence so far, he is not under suspicion.

'A further dimension – a further ring expanding outwards in the water from that miraculous cradle – is that the husband of the murdered woman is an advocate of confederation with Canada, and many others on the island – such as myself – are not. I'm in favour of the island keeping its independence. We're in a squeeze, you see. You know the children's game called "Piggy in the Middle"? The island is Piggy. On one side are the Canadians urging us to join them. And on the other side are the British Colonial Office urging us to join Canada – or else! Their latest move is the petty one of stopping the pay of the Governor – their own man here – so that we have to pay him. And his mission here is to make us join Canada. He has just recently arrived in post, but the husband in this murder case is *his* man. Certainly not mine. Yet I am the incarnation of justice here. In the event that I decide to send the dead woman's husband before a judge, it's quite possible that they would be on opposite sides of our current over-heated political debate – or on the same side. Any judge will be damned if he does, damned if he doesn't. I don't think I'm biased myself. I've been Attorney General for this island for several years now and before that a barrister, and it's my job to uphold justice while bringing people to trial when they may have broken the law. But who knows what other people may think of me?

'So apart from helping us solve the crime, that's another reason you are here. You are an outsider who will ensure that I, the Attorney General, and the police who work with me, don't have a chance to show bias, and that we don't refer anyone in error to a court – where a judge might then show bias. Will you accept the job?'

'I wouldn't have travelled from New York to here if I had any doubts about that. I'm curious, and I'd like to help.'

'It will be worth your while financially. My secretary will make the arrangements. I have no idea how long your mission will take. I hereby formally appoint you as Acting Superintendent of Police for Prince Edward Island, accountable to me as Attorney General. I must admit that as I look at you I'm surprised to see – in the light of your reputation as described by Matthew Begbie – how young you appear. But don't tell me your age! I don't want to know! I say "Acting Superintendent" because you are "from away" and no one knows if you'll stay here. But we need strong direction of the police to solve this crime and resolve the scandal. We don't need a large police force on the Island. We almost never have felonies here, only misdemeanours. But we do need a more structured police force, and I hope that your working with us here will help the force improve.

'The prison and lock-up here in Charlottetown, for Queens County, is known as Harvey's Brig, and the police work from there. In St Eleanors and Georgetown, it's similar but the buildings also house the courts for Prince and Kings counties. The Brig is, I'm ashamed to say, a horrible place. The prisoners are a wild lot, and not in jail long enough to settle into a routine. We very seldom have to send people to jail for long sentences. The Brig is bursting at the seams with a constant turn-around of people picked up drunk and disorderly or in brawls, or even in riots although we haven't had a major riot since 1865. It was about tenant rights and absentee landlords – who live mainly in England – and we simply didn't have any means of stopping the disorder. So Sir Robert who was Administrator when the Governor was absent at the time, sent for British troops from Nova Scotia. Over a hundred of them. They put the riots down with only a few injuries and no deaths.'

I was becoming used to Brecken's accent. Like Captain Munro, he had a flat and even intonation which from my little knowledge I associated with the American of New England. But he pronounced 'I' as 'Oi', and 'island' as 'oiland' – as in the English West Country. And 'a' sounds became a long 'e': 'scandal' became 'scendel,' and 'man' became 'men'. Then some 'e' sounds became 'i', so that 'send' became 'sind,' and 'when' became 'whin'. Yet at the same time he sounded quite English, his articulation crisp and precise.

'By the way', he said, 'it's a pleasure to meet someone who attended Oxford. I know it quite well, having studied Law at the Inns of Court in London where I made friends with a number of Oxford men.'

'I'm afraid reading jurisprudence at Oxford provides one with little experience in everyday law. We studied court cases but we had no contacts with courts or the police. Vancouver Island soon made up for that. But I envy you your experience at the Inns of Court.'

'It was invaluable. But there is something special about an island – I mean a smaller island than Great Britain of course. I learn more about humanity every day, in my own native town in this remote part of North America, than I learned in London. You get closer to people on an island... Or is it that you can't escape them?'

Brecken stood up and we went into the dining room. A simple dinner of nicely rare roast beef with roast potatoes, after the usual vegetable soup. A good French Burgundy – Montrachet, Brecken remarked – from a large decanter. And afterwards cheese and fruit with port – one glass each. I am not a great drinker, and nor apparently was he. But our tongues loosened a bit as he provided more details.

'As I said, the victim's husband is John Harris. A simple English name – like Hobbes! Anyway, our man Harris, of English background, goes and marries a French woman. By which I don't mean from France, or even from Québec: I mean local French, "Acadian". More a girl than a woman. She was not yet twenty when she died. Her name was Marie Évangéline. You know the poem *Évangéline* by the American writer Longfellow?'

'I'm afraid not.'

'The poem came out in 1847 and took North America by storm. It's about an exiled Acadian girl called Évangéline. Nobody really knows where the name "Acadian" comes from, but it's used for the French who settled in Nova Scotia and in New Brunswick, and also on this island – originally called *Île Saint-Jean*, St John's Island.

'After the Treaty of Utrecht in 1713, England controlled most of the territory on the East coast of North America, apart from a few posts such as Louisbourg and Île Saint-Jean, which still belonged to France. Most of the Acadians living under the control of England were in Nova Scotia and they were eventually asked to swear an oath of allegiance to the King of England, which they refused to do. It was a shame since they were an entirely peaceful people, and were known as the "Neutrals". But neutrality was not good enough for the British, so in 1755 plans were made in Halifax to deal with them. The British – us! – shamefully deported most of them back to France, where almost none of them had been for generations. Others of them were deported to British colonies along the East coast of America, and even to Louisiana where they are now known as "Cajuns" – their pronunciation of "Acadians".

'After the fall of Louisbourg in 1758, Île Saint-Jean also came under the control of the British Crown, and the deportation of the Acadians here was ordered soon afterwards. Around fifteen hundred of originally four or five thousand Acadians escaped to elsewhere on the mainland, and the rest were deported, except for a few hundred who hid in the woods. For some reason the small village of Malpeque was forgotten – it seems that some English officer didn't have it on his map. Acadians from Malpeque stayed in the area, hiding in the surrounding woods.

'Of those deported many died on transport ships. But in the following years a good number of the survivors made their way back to this island. And now their population is creeping back. And a fine people they are too. They have lived off the land here – building houses, keeping pigs and cows, clearing the forest, planting crops. The Acadians are survivors.

'Longfellow's poem is a pathetic and lugubrious story, in which the girl Évangéline is separated from her suitor Gabriel and deported into America, then becomes a nun and eventually meets Gabriel as he is in middle age and dying of a disease, and she cares for him until his death. I suppose I should find Longfellow's poem moving. People cry when they read it. But I find the sentimentality disgusting. In the rage for the book, some Acadian families began calling their girls Évangéline – to the priests' displeasure, since there is no Saint Évangéline. But almost all Acadian girls are baptised Marie as well as their usual name.'

'So the murdered woman was Marie Évangéline.'

'Yes. A beautiful girl – and wild, or at least very spirited. Her father is a notary called Honoré Gallant. He is a close friend of John Harris, and also a member of the Legislative Council. Gallant's father was a prosperous fisherman and he was sent "over across" to study in Quebec and became a notary. He works all over the island, but mainly in Charlottetown and in another practice in Georgetown facing Nova Scotia where he goes often – to Antigonish and Chéticamp. He is involved in the import and export of goods, for which he provides notarial services. You might think, in English terms, that this entails a conflict of interest, but given the small scale of things here, many people have their fingers in many pies. Gallant and I are not on the same side of the political fence. Like Harris he's a liberal. I'm a conservative.

'I call the poor murdered girl Évangéline "wild" not because her behaviour was improper, but because although she was so beautiful she was also a tomboy and an enthusiast for boating: she could row and sail like any man. At the same time she was a bookworm in both English and French. Perhaps this led to an affinity with John Harris, who is a great reader. But possibly he only managed to marry her because he was a political ally of her father.

'There are rumours. One is that Harris killed his wife in a fit of rage on discovering that the baby was not his – that someone else was the father. Another rumour is that she was killed by an unknown intruder "from away" – meaning the mainland in Nova Scotia or New Brunswick. This is very alarming to the populace – a murderer at large on the North Shore! Another is that she was killed by one of Harris's political enemies. I have no doubt that the Legislature harbours murderous thoughts, but I doubt if these thoughts are acted on to such an extent.

'At any rate she's dead. What remains of her is in the care of the Queens County Coroner, Dr Reid, awaiting your investigation. He proposes you attend his post-mortem tomorrow afternoon. Ascertaining the cause of death will not be difficult: she was very badly beaten and it seems slashed by knives. And she had just had a child – as was known – a few days before. It was gone. Until it turned up cradled on the waves.

'Unless the person who killed Mrs Harris confesses, or a witness implicates someone through a statement for the court, Dr Reid would have to continue to an inquest and call various witnesses. And he would have to come to a conclusion about the circumstances of the death. On current knowledge, he would have to conclude the murder was "by persons unknown". No one was caught standing beside the body with weapon in hand. But there are the rumours. In complicated circumstances like these, a coroner examines the body, releases it for burial, then sits on his hands until the legal process has gone through to complete his report. I believe there was a recent English case where a coroner took two years to conclude on his investigation. Dr Reid is too scrupulous for that.'

'So I shall attend the coroner's post-mortem of Mrs Harris tomorrow afternoon. When exactly did the death occur?'

'Over the night of Friday the 30th of June, and Saturday the 1st of July. But the body has been preserved, as you'll see – on ice.'

'Following tomorrow I'll interview Mr Harris and Mr Gallant, and anyone else whose name emerges at the post-mortem. And as you have already mentioned I am invited to meet the Governor tomorrow morning.'

'That's why I thought that it would be best for you to hear about this case from me as the Attorney General responsible for the investigation and possible prosecution – not from the Governor, Mr Robinson who has just arrived in post. There are many secrets on this island, most of them open. It's known that when the Governor's post became vacant last year, Sir Robert let the Colonial Office in London know that he would like the position for himself. They appointed Mr Robinson. So it's widely thought that Sir Robert is resentful. I suppose he is. But not, I think, from personal ambition. He likes being Chief Justice. And a knighthood under the sword of our great Queen Victoria is enough for any man's pride. But he wanted the island to have a governor, for the first time, who had been born on the island. The Colonial Office were not moved. They know Sir Robert too well. They want to get rid of this island, and to hand it over to Canada. That's the plan. So they appointed Mr Robinson. An Irishman, by the way. He is married to the daughter of a Bishop – Church of Ireland, a version of Anglican: they attend St Paul's Anglican Church here. He's an impressive man, and she's a lovely lady. He was previously Governor of the Falkland Islands, God help him.'

'I take it as given that I may interview anyone as I think I need to.

Can you suggest anyone in particular?'

'I believe the baby is being taken care of by the victim's mother, Mrs Gallant, in North Rustico, in East Queens, where the Gallants have a house. There are hundreds of Gallants by the way. It's a common surname among the Acadians here. Do you speak French?'

'Almost none.'

'Nor do I. Few English Islanders do. As for others to interview, *if* there is a political dimension, there are Harris's political allies. And I suppose his enemies.

'There's a House of Assembly of thirty Assemblymen, elected for a four-year term by all men of adult age. Then there's the Legislative Council of thirteen Councilmen, elected only by the holders of landed property. The Council is elected for an eight-year term, which makes it very hard to budge. And it can block legislation proposed by the Assembly. The Councilmen are therefore by far the most important people on the island.

'John Harris and Honoré Gallant are both Liberal Councilmen for Queens County. The Council is finely balanced, and with a membership of only thirteen, a change in position by even one Councilman can be crucial.

'One of the island's open secrets is that Gallant in his trading business is involved in smuggling. If you look at the stores in Charlottetown you will see cloth and wine and spirits and fancy goods from all over the world. We import a lot of goods. And we export potatoes and lobster – now even canned lobster – and Malpeque oysters on ice, some in season, some not. We are not within the Canadian tariff. Goods come to here from Europe or from the West Indies, quite legally, by sea in the summer months. Much more goods than we need ourselves. And of course it's tempting to avoid even our own tariffs which are low for most things – 5% for wine, for example. One of the highest tariffs is for books – 20%. But although I can't vouch for whether or not the full tariff was paid for every book in this library, I doubt if book smuggling is very profitable. Tobacco is almost as heavily tariffed as books, and there is certainly profit in smuggling it. Smuggling is a double game: smuggling *in* to the island and smuggling *on* to Canada. But most of us don't smuggle on. The books in this library shall stay here. At any rate, it's in the interest of smugglers to keep Prince Edward Island out of Canada.'

'But if smugglers want to stay *out* of Canada, why would they support men like Mr Harris and Mr Gallant who want to be *in* Canada?'

'I ask myself the same question, Mr Hobbes.'

Sergeant McNulty must have been drinking with the kitchen staff. He did not look quite so severe, and his cheeks were red. He escorted me along the deserted streets almost jauntily. But in one particularly dark stretch – there was only the occasional light from a house, and there was no visible moon – he paused and held up a finger. I listened but could hear nothing.

'I believe we're being followed,' he said quietly, pulling a revolver out of his pocket. He made a gesture with his other hand and we walked on, with him glancing back from time to time. Suddenly he held up a hand again and we stopped. I could hear nothing except a vague noise of the town – of distant voices, cartwheels rumbling, a horse neighing. The hotel was around the corner, so we hurried on and reached it.

'I'll be staying here overnight,' he said. 'In the room down the corridor from you. Lock your doors and use the bolt. Have you a gun?'

'In one of my trunks.' This was an American Colt revolver and ammunition I had acquired with the Victoria police.

'Keep it handy.'

He said no more, as we were admitted to the hotel and went upstairs to our rooms. Lucy – my Lukswaas! – and our son were asleep in the double bed. I slipped in behind her and held her gently, my nose in her thick, oily hair, black as the night we were in.

3

We had breakfast served in our rooms. Oranges, scrambled eggs, bacon, toast, and coffee. Will was still nursing but also eating some solid foods, so he gnawed at pieces of toast dipped in water. We then went out for a walk. McNulty was waiting in the lobby, and he insisted on accompanying us, walking a few steps behind. I had not yet bothered to unpack my revolver. I asked him how we could contact Mr Harris to see him tomorrow afternoon. He informed me that the mail from Charlottetown reached a post office twice a week near Stanley Bridge where Mr Harris had his summer house. A note if sent today by noon could reach him by mid-morning tomorrow. I quickly prepared a note for him to drop at the post office since he told me we would pass in front of it.

It was a bright morning, with more heat from the direct sunlight than in Victoria, since Charlottetown is a few degrees further south. We had arrived on a Sunday – the 9th of July. Now it was Monday and the streets were already busy. Apart from the grid system of its streets, Charlottetown was something like Victoria in size and in architecture, with the same mixture of wooden and brick houses and storefronts. But the people – unlike in Victoria where as well as people of European or North American origin there were Negroes, Chinese and Indians – were all white-skinned, some formally dressed, most men wearing working clothes: dungarees, canvas trousers with checked shirts. Some women were as elegant as in Victoria, but most wore practical country clothes. In a word, it was less pretentious. To my surprise there was a smell of sewage here and there, and the wood of the plank sidewalks was rotten in places.

The road surfaces were of packed red-brown earth which in wet weather must become muddy.

The centre of the town was a large square, Queen's Square, dominated by the Colonial Building, well-proportioned in the Georgian style and built of grey stone. I turned and asked McNulty about the stone, and he said it was called Wallace sandstone and imported from Nova Scotia.

'They say here that on the island "there's not stone enough to throw at a dog". The island is made of sandstone but it crumbles. We have bricks, but almost no stone for building.'

At one end of the square was St Paul's Anglican Church with a white wooden tower and a small spire, and at the opposite end was a huge two storey enclosed market building of brick, called the Butcher's Market. Horses and carts were loading and unloading and we had to pick our way around steaming horse dung. Inside were the stalls of butchers and other provisioners. It was noisy and smelly and jostling with people, so we retreated outside. There were impressive shops and stores along the streets. I thought of what Mr Brecken had said about the low tariffs and the smuggling. Robertson's Custom Tailors had a display window with bolts of Scottish tweed, cashmere, and worsted wool. Mason's, for ladies, had Irish lace and linen, French merino wool, Maltese lace – all labelled proudly. Bremner's stationers had books, vellum paper, artists' drawing paper, a variety of pens and pencils, easels, and bookrests. And the bizarrely named MacEachern's Italian Warehouse had a window stacked with jars of olives and figs, along with bottles of Champagne and vintage port, and casks of French wine, red and white, from Burgundy or Bordeaux.

People stared at us. Perhaps Lucy looked out of place. But in the hotel the servants had told her they thought she was English. Perhaps they were thinking of some other British colony in the Indies. And in the streets, we heard women talking French who looked something like her – very dark hair and eyes, and high, rather Indian cheekbones. Perhaps the staring was simply because we were unknown – 'from away'. We went and sat for a few minutes on a bench in a small park, as McNulty loitered nearby. Lucy remarked that she did not like towns very much. Nor did I. We were used to Orchard Farm, with occasional trips into Victoria. We had both found San Francisco and New York filthy and crowded. Charlottetown was small, with about 8,000 people according to Captain Munro in our conversation, but it was still too big for us.

Lucy said, 'I asked the hotel maid, Katie, whether there might be somewhere in the country, outside town, with a hotel. But she said there were almost no hotels although often there are rooms in taverns. People travelling have the habit of knocking on the doors of houses and asking to stay overnight. She said this was a custom because the winter was so dangerous that travellers caught in a storm would simply go to the nearest house until it stopped. Being "storm-stayed", she called it.'

I gestured to McNulty and he came over to us.

'Are there any hotels outside Charlottetown?'

'Or even *in* Charlottetown,' he said in his usual dry manner. 'For a town this size, it's amazing there are only guesthouses and the one hotel, the St Lawrence. I reckon the best hotel on the island is a brand-new one out at North Rustico, on the North Shore – the Ocean House. We'll be going that way after you interview Mr Harris. He's at his summer house – the house where… Then I imagine you'll want to go to North Rustico to see Mr and Mrs Gallant.'

'How do we get to the North Shore?'

'By wagon or by two horse buggy. But do you ride, Sir? It's only a few hours by horseback.'

'Yes I ride. That's good.'

So Lucy would be stranded from tomorrow on in the St Lawrence Hotel. At least the rooms were large, and she had Katie to help. They could take walks together.

I left Lucy and Will back to the hotel and set off on my own to Government House. I had reassured McNulty that I would carry a loaded revolver in my pocket, and we had arranged to meet between midday and one o'clock at Harvey's Brig in Pownal Square, just around the corner from the Butcher's Market. We would then go together to the coroner's.

I had been directed to walk west along the quays and past them until I saw Government House. The road crossed a bridge between the harbour on my left, and a pond on my right, then there was an avenue lined with chestnuts and limes leading to a large Georgian-style mansion in a park. But unlike in England where such a grand building would be brick or stone, it was made of freshly painted white timber, and the windows had black wooden shutters. It was two stories high and with a covered porch or deck along the front overlooking the lawn and driveway. There was a soldier in a red jacket, unarmed, guarding the gate, and another at the entrance to the house. They were expecting me. A servant in a black uniform led me to a huge drawing room in the front of the house. A dark, slim, rather sensitive-looking man in a grey linen summer suit held out his hand.

'Mr Hobbes. Delighted to meet you. I am William Robinson. Can I suggest we go and sit outside? It's such a lovely day.'

'Of course.'

He led the way out of the room and along a hallway to the side of the house, where a smaller, more private open porch looked out onto a side lawn where I noticed some children's toys – a wooden rocking horse and brightly painted little wooden wagons with handles for pulling. They were full of various dolls and stuffed animals.

'I have three children – so far,' Robinson announced. 'They'll turn up eventually I imagine. They are now in what we call the school room.'

We sat on wicker chairs with flat blue cushions – in the shade of the porch roof but looking out into the sunlit park.

'What a lovely house,' I said dutifully, but meaning it.

'The nicest so far,' he said. 'The Colonial Office have got it into their heads that I like islands. Perhaps because I am from the rather large island of Ireland. So far they have sent me to Monserrate – a tropical paradise from which any governor is lucky to escape alive. Most succumb to yellow fever or malaria, so there is a quick turnover. I survived. Then I was sent to the Falklands – the fag end of the world, with many more sheep than people, constant rain even by Irish standards, almost no trees, and perpetual raw cold. And now I am here – with my wife. We arrived here in May and since then I have been paying visits to towns and villages across the island from one end to the other. It has been a frantic time. My wife has been working hard too. A "Strawberry Tea Reception" here in this garden is imminent. But by comparison to the other islands I've been posted to, it's more than lovely. And for a while, until 1799, it was even called New Ireland! I feel quite at home here when I am out among the horse farms and the potato fields. I'm from the middle of Ireland – Meath. The Emerald Isle! Same colour of fields here, sloping down to cliffs above the sea. Although the cliffs here are red, as in Devon.'

'I look forward to seeing it all,' I said politely, somewhat bowled over by this informality – very un-English, although he sounded as English as I did.

'I confess I know something about you. I've received two long telegrams from Augustus Pemberton.'

'Ah! I might have guessed you would know him.'

'I've never met him, but our families know each other. I understand he is now a member of the Legislative Council of British Columbia.'

'True. He seems to enjoy the possibility of applying his mind in the political arena.'

'So I know you are very competent and brave and that, as Pemberton put it simply, you are a gentleman. I see you smile. As an Englishman, part of being a gentleman is not to mention being one. In Ireland it's different. "He's a gentleman" means "he can be trusted". I should like very much to hear your account of that extraordinary murder case you solved in Victoria. But you will have questions for me. And first I want to put my cards on the table. I always do. Again I suppose it's the Irish way. It may not be good in diplomacy, but so far I've survived. Diplomacy is a polite version of what the Americans call horse-trading. And my method is to state my price and stick to it.

'You are investigating the murder of Mrs Harris. I suspect there are as many secrets to be discovered here as there were in Victoria. But I know that Mr Brecken has got in before me and you had dinner with him last night. So you will know some secrets already – insofar as secrets exist on the island. One semi-secret is that I have a mission from the Colonial Office to push this island into the Dominion of Canada at all costs. Currently the horse-trading is about getting the Canadians to pay the possibly ruinous costs of the island railway which, according to the interests of various land-owners, will snake its way here and there across the island from village to village rather than in the desired and economical straight line.

'Another semi-secret is that Mr Harris is a strong supporter of my mission. He is in the coalition government and he is a campaigner for union with Canada. So if he falls, this is a setback. And he will certainly fall if your investigation incriminates him. Rumour has it that he murdered his wife – his young, wild, and possibly unfaithful wife. Yet he was in Charlottetown with associates when the murder occurred. So did he arrange the murder? It's not out of the question. He and his colleague Mr Honoré Gallant have disreputable acquaintances. Mr Brecken may have told you about his concern that at least some people in the smuggling industry – it is an industry – are for some reason supporting these two supporters of Confederation. Which makes no sense.'

'Yes, Mr Brecken did tell me.'

'A number of well-positioned people do not support joining the Dominion of Canada. For instance Sir Robert is known in some circles to have such a position. Like Mr Brecken and I, we are on opposite sides of a fence. His family were big landowners – part of what was known as the Family Compact that ruled this island for a century and still partly does. And in 1865, when he was Administrator, acting in this post, he brought in a force of soldiers – over a hundred of them – from Nova Scotia to crush riots in favour of tenant rights. This pretty much destroyed the Tenant League and Sir Robert's reputation among some of the population was hurt. The Colonial Office is not happy with the sequel, which is that the cost of deploying the troops was £5,000, but the island refuses to pay. Of course, land rights are the issue of our times. The Scottish Highlanders who have settled in this island had their crofts burned down and were cleared off their native land to make way for sheep, and had to emigrate. In Ireland we have the Land League fomenting rebellion against the Union, and we are the source of the Fenians who want Ireland to become a republic. You know about them?'

'Manchester, in 1867.'

'The "Manchester Martyrs". Three Fenians were hanged for having killed a policeman. But there were extenuating circumstances. Things are never black and white. You will also know that the Fenians from America staged two invasions of Canada in 1866, the first into New Brunswick, which is of course our neighbour here, and the second into Upper Canada, what's now called Ontario. Both invasions fizzled out. Then a Fenian assassinated a cabinet minister in Ottawa of Irish origin – in fact a former Fenian! – D'Arcy McGee. The Irish here favour Confederation because it will loosen the ties between Prince Edward Island, "the small protected by the great" as its motto explains, and Britain. But I'm told that Fenian ideas are circulating here. Does all this make your head spin?'

'It makes me glad I'm not in your position. Or in any political position. I have a crime to solve. Will I be obstructed?'

'You call a spade a spade, Mr Hobbes. My answer is: not by me. And to put another card on the table: I am not a personal friend of John Harris. I don't know him well. We have begun to work together, that's all.'

During this discussion a servant had brought us tall glasses of iced lemonade which we now sipped in silence for a moment.

'Mr Pemberton writes that you are an Oxford man,' Robinson resumed. 'I went to "the other place" – Cambridge.' Then after another pause: 'Please tell me something about that case in Victoria.'

I told the story of the case of the murdered mad-doctor, in broad outlines. Robinson was attentive. He could listen as well as talk, and his occasional questions were to the point. When at last I could, I turned back to my current concern:

'Now that we have been discussing these horrors, does anything come to mind about this new case? It begins equally dreadfully, with a mutilated corpse and a possible suspect – in this case Mr Harris. Can you tell me more about him?'

'I'll allow myself to confide in you that he is a rather slippery character. I was surprised to hear he had a much younger wife and that she was an Acadian. I suspect it was a political alliance. He is pretty thick with the Acadians. He speaks French, which few non-French Islanders bother to learn. As for the murder, perhaps it's a crime of passion. But what I don't understand is the cradle on the waves. Was somebody making a political point? It staggers the imagination.'

We were interrupted by the sound of children's voices. A small boy and a more grown-up girl were running across the lawn to the toy wagons which they began pulling here and there. Behind them a woman with golden-brown hair flying loosely, without a hat or cap, but wearing an elegant sky-blue silk dress and a white shawl, was approaching us. We stood up.

'This is Mr Hobbes. My wife, Olivia.'

She held out her hand, gloveless, and I shook it gently.

'I've heard something about you from the Pembertons via William,' she said. 'And about your wife. I hear she is from a Tsimshian tribe. They are from up near Alaska, are they not?'

'Almost that far,' I said in surprise.

'Pemberton mentioned this in one of his telegrams,' Robinson interjected, 'and said we should be sure to meet her.'

'And you have a small son.' This was Mrs Robinson again. 'Are they stranded in the St Lawrence Hotel while you rush here and there on your investigation? Would they like to come to tea? I can send someone to bring them here.'

This was unexpected. Mrs Robinson sounded a touch less English than her husband – Irish like Pemberton, in fact – and her manners seemed free and easy.

Robinson added, 'Olivia would be very happy to meet your wife. I wish you and I could be more sociable. I can't even invite you to lunch, I'm afraid. Given your investigation and the appearance of possibly taking sides, we shall have to keep our distance. But I'm sure there would be nothing remiss in your wife and son visiting Olivia here.'

'Thank you both. You're very kind.'

'What's your wife's name?' Mrs Robinson asked.

'Lucy. At least that's her English name. Her original name is Lukswaas. It's Tsimshian for a sudden shower of rain.'

I don't usually share this information. But I liked the Robinsons.

4

I found my way to Harvey's Brig to meet McNulty. It was a square, high wooden building with three floors. The windows of the upper two floors had bars. As we talked in a small police room on the ground floor, we could hear the shouts and banging doors of the prison overhead, and even the ground floor had a smell of unwashed people.

I had to get something clear with McNulty.

'Who are you protecting us from? Who do you think was following us last night?'

'I don't know. And Mr Brecken wouldn't know either. But Mr Harris is obviously in the focus of our investigation, and he has dangerous friends.'

'Mr Brecken spoke of smugglers.'

'Well yes, they may be involved.'

'But how? Even if Mr Harris is doing business with smugglers – for example accepting money from them to persuade the Council not to investigate smuggling too closely, or some such thing – it's hard to imagine they would kill his wife. Why?'

'To send him a warning? Perhaps he has let them down in some way.'

'It would be a very costly way to send him a warning – if they are caught. Smuggling is not a felony like murder. You don't hang for it.'

'I don't fully understand it, Sir, and I admit I am speculating. I look at Mr Harris and Mr Gallant and I find myself thinking *Arcades ambo*.'

'Virgil. "Two innocents", or "two rogues", depending on how you translate it. If you don't mind my remarking on this, Sergeant, you sound to me like an educated man.'

'I spent a few years at a Jesuit school, Clongowes Wood, in Dublin. I'm from the North, however. A place called Ballybofey, in Donegal.' He pronounced the name with a stress on the last syllable – Bally-bo-*fey*.

'I was brought up as a Presbyterian', he said 'But I was always a bit of a contrarian. So I became a renegade, in the strict sense of the word: I abandoned my own sect and took up with another. I "turned", as we say in Ireland. At the age of fourteen, I convinced my parents I needed to convert to Roman Catholicism, and I did the exams for Clongowes and was accepted. I then decided to become a priest and attended the seminary at Saint Patrick's College, in Maynooth. Then, having got the habit of moving on to new pastures, once I had been ordained I asked to be moved to the Diocese of Nova Scotia where they were in need of priests. Irish people were arriving in droves there. In 1847, I landed in Halifax where the Bishop assigned me to the parish of Antigonish. I was a parish priest there for a few years. Out of the frying pan into the fire! It was just like Ireland – constant splits and struggles. Antigonish was splitting from Halifax to become a new diocese which would be Gaelic speaking – while Halifax would be English-speaking. But the Gaelic speakers of Antigonish were Scottish while the English speakers of Halifax were Irish. And I was a Gaelic-speaking Irishman. Where was my allegiance? I solved that problem by falling in love with a parishioner who was an Acadian – French-speaking. So I was defrocked. For fornication. With the woman who became my wife. Technically that makes me a renegade yet again. I had left Protestantism for Catholicism and left my new sect and took up with a woman, not another sect. But I transferred my faith to her. Would you agree that qualifies me as twice a renegade?'

'I don't think so. The woman you fell in love with was not a religion. But you are surely still a contrarian. And you seem to have an ironic way of looking at the world.'

'I should add', said McNulty, 'that I am no longer with my wife, which makes me perhaps a triple renegade.'

What a peculiar man! He seemed to be running himself down, or was this just his sense of humour?

'I believe you are not a renegade,' I said, 'unless you leave one faith for another. It's not enough to leave a faith and then drift. You were a renegade the first time, when as you say you "turned", abandoning Protestantism for Catholicism. But not the second time, in abandoning Catholicism but not for another religion. And certainly not for a third time. You have not now become a Jew or a Mohammedan. You are only a one time renegade: you left the Protestant church and became a Catholic.'

'That's a relief. No new wife yet, Sir. Sorry for bothering you with my personal history, but you should know who I am.'

'Thank you. But to get back to our case, if smuggling turns out to be a red herring, who do you think committed this murder? Any suspicions?'

'If smuggling is a red herring, it's a very large fish on this island. I have an open mind. My job is to protect you. And to keep my eyes open. If I see anything of interest, I'll report it to you. That's my duty.'

'All right. This afternoon Mrs Hobbes is going for tea with Mrs Robinson who is sending someone to escort her and our child. Is that safe?'

'As houses.'

'And you will show me the way to Dr Reid's office. Am I right in thinking it's in effect the morgue?'

'Yes. There is no morgue as such here. There is not even a hospital – none on the island. There are just medical practitioners who in some cases offer hospital services in their own offices or houses. Dr Reid, the Coroner, is a surgeon. He trained in Edinburgh. Very highly thought of. He has a sort of morgue in a barn behind his house. I believe the corpse is on ice.'

We stepped outside the Brig. I was relieved to be in the fresh air.

McNulty paused. 'In this square, two years ago, what I hope was the

45

last public execution in British North America took place. A chap called Dowie. He was a sailor who knifed another man in a brawl in a tavern. The first time they hanged him, the rope broke. But he had fainted. They brought him back to the Brig and revived him. He is reported to have thought he had died and that he was waking up in heaven – although the Brig is more like hell, I would say. An hour later they hanged him a second time, and this time the fastening to the rope broke. At which point the crowd protested and the guard unsheathed their bayonets, so the crowd shut up. After another delay they hanged him for a third time, and the rope held and that was it!'

'Horrible.' I could not help thinking of my struggle in Victoria to save Wiladzap, Lucy's brother, from being hanged, in the same year, 1869. And the excitement there at the prospect of one of the last public executions.

We set off to walk to Dr Reid's. He lived, like Mr Brecken, in the area behind Government House called Brighton. His house was large and built of brick, in the Georgian style, surrounded by a huge garden with an orchard. To one side in the garden there was a wooden house, equally large but somewhat lower, with a surrounding porch and deck chairs, overlooking a lawn and a lily pond. Dr Reid came out of the brick house to meet us, springing energetically down the steps. He was a small rotund man with healthy pink cheeks, wearing a straw hat.

'Welcome,' he said. 'As you see I have a whole establishment here. This is my house, and the other house is a sanatorium. And behind the house we have the morgue.'

He led us between the houses and lawns along a path of the usual packed red earth. 'I'm very proud of this morgue,' he said in a soft Scottish voice as we entered a low wooden building, like a stable. 'We'll only stay in here a few minutes, given that we're not dressed for winter.'

There were no windows. In the dim light from the doorway an

attendant reached up with a pole which had a slow-burning rag on the end and lit two oil lamps. The golden light revealed a rectangular pit in the floor in which the first thing to be seen was a layer of sawdust.

'In the usual morgue, in a hospital – where such institutions exist,' Dr Reid explained, 'the bodies are kept in embalming fluid. It turns them brown and soggy, and by the time of the funeral they are repulsive to look at, and in an autopsy the knife cannot cut cleanly. But here in winter the sea freezes through the whole Northumberland Strait to the south, and to the north the open sea of the Gulf can freeze as far out as a hundred miles. During the winter, close in shore, people cut through the ice with huge handsaws and transfer it in blocks to icehouses. Almost every farm has one. A pit in the ground sheltered by a hut with a door, and with a layer of sawdust over the ice. Blocks are taken out one by one and stored under more sawdust in another hut which becomes a cool larder in summer until the block melts and they go for another one. So I thought, why not use ice for a morgue? The temperature in this room is always below freezing – about 10 degrees of frost. And we have a smaller room over here in which it is 20 degrees of frost.'

He opened another door for a moment and in the light from the doorway of a small windowless room with a similar ice pit I could see a table with a human form lying on it, covered with a layer of sacking.

'When we are ready to do a post-mortem, we take the body out and we let it thaw.

'There are almost no murders on the island, so my work rarely entails criminal investigation. But sometimes bodies are washed ashore after a boat has capsized, or some poor devil is found frozen stiff on the street after falling down drunk in winter. I have even tried to interest our local undertakers in this method. But they want to lay the body out, saturated in embalming fluid then smeared with oil or wax, so that the family can come by to say farewell to a wax doll. This won't work with our method. You'll see. If you come with me to my laboratory in the house, I have the young lady in there.'

His manner was, to say the least, professional. I had no idea what his personality might be. He had taken his hat off, revealing a balding pate, as we entered the barn – in respect for its contents I supposed. McNulty and I already had our hats in our hands.

We walked out again into the suddenly dazzling sunlight across a stretch of lawn to a wing of the main house, through a door into a porch, and into a room well lighted by tall windows, in the centre of which was a sort of table. I say 'sort of', because it was more like a high box bed in which instead of a mattress within the box was a mass of ice chips, and on top of it was a body, lying on its back – a young woman, stark naked. Her hands were by her sides, and clenched. Her legs stuck straight out with the soles of her feet facing me.

A young man who was already in the room was introduced by Dr Reid as his assistant, Dr Simpson. We moved close to the dead woman, me on one side standing next to Dr Simpson, Dr Reid on the other. Her hair, which was dark brown and matted with blood, was gathered behind her head and was probably shoulder length if I imagined it uncoiled. She had a small triangle of hair of the same colour at the base of her belly. Her breasts were swollen – she had been a nursing mother – with a gash mark on the right breast, where streaks of dried blood were visible. Her eyes and mouth were closed.

I am forcing myself into this basic description. It leaves out two things, each of which contributed to a frisson which I felt go down my body, and a half-held gasp of my breath.

The first thing was her colour – a ghastly blue-white-yellow like the skin of a chicken whose feathers had been plucked long ago and which was beginning to decay.

The other thing was that she had been battered and torn. There were streaks and patches of thickened and hardened blood, now a dark crimson verging on black. There were gashes on her thighs.

And her face! Her nose had been broken, smashed to one side, and her right cheek was bruised, almost black.

There was a slight butcher's shop smell of blood, and the ice around the body was turning pink in places. She was thawing out...

'I shall now start the post-mortem examination,' said Dr Reid in a formal tone.

McNulty and Dr Simpson, produced notebooks and stood at the ready.

'I shall first state that this body was brought here ten days ago, in the early evening of the 1st of July, in a covered wagon from Stanley Bridge where it was discovered that morning in the house of her husband, John Harris, on the floor of a library room. The lady was identified to staff here by one of the men who brought it – an employee of Mr Harris by the name of Edgar Aucoin – as Marie Évangéline Harris, aged nineteen, almost twenty. She had been transported wrapped in sheets, on a layer of ice blocks. Unwrapped from the sheets she was naked. She was wearing three rings which I cut off her fingers and which were subsequently given to the police.' Dr Reid looked at McNulty.

'I have them,' McNulty said.

'When I first saw the body, it was in rigor mortis. Rigor sets in a few hours after death and it can persist for as much as forty-eight hours. When I examined her first thing in the morning of the 2nd of July, she was no longer in rigor. This helped in examination, in that I could test fairly easily for broken bones by moving her limbs. There was some lividity on her left side where her body had sprawled on the floor.

'Since the cause of death was, I might say, "external" – that is to say she was beaten and slashed to death – she did not die from an illness. I won't thaw her out and cut her up to see if there is a cancer somewhere or a swollen heart or whatever. A swollen heart because of something in her life, I will not rule out, but I cannot detect that.

'Going from the head down, I should first note that when she arrived, she had some signs of salt in her hair – a very fine dried out powdery coating. It is no longer visible, because of the effects of the ice. We verified that it was dried sea salt. She must have been in or very near the sea shortly before her death – perhaps swimming. More probably she was splashed by sea water rather than immersed in it. I could see no signs of caked salt on her skin. As I ascertained by turning the body on its stomach and pushing on the back, there was no water in her lungs.

'Now, starting this examination at the head, she has contusions on both temples. Her nose has been broken. She has a bruised right cheek, and a fracture of the skull on the right side. That there is more damage in the right side of her face and this and a wound on her right breast suggest that blows were struck by a left-handed man, using a heavy object, perhaps a club or a weighted stick.'

He reached forward and carefully peeled up the left eyelid. The eye was like a blue-grey marble.

'Blue-eyed,' he remarked. 'Unusual among the Acadians. Either of these contusions to the head, and especially the skull fracture, could have been fatal. Her neck has not been broken.'

Here, Dr Reid moved the head up and down with two hands. The body had thawed out enough to permit this.

'Now, look at the mouth, Gentlemen.'

He pushed the chin down gently with one hand and with the other he pulled the upper lip up slightly.

'Note the discolouration in the corners of the mouth.'

The corners were purple, darker than the lips themselves which had gone pale.

'I wonder if she might have been gagged.' He paused.

'Her thighs have been gashed and bruised.'

He paused again.

'The question arises: were these injuries inflicted by one person or more than one? Either is possible.

'Did she fight back? Look!'

He took the woman's right hand in his own left hand and held it up a few inches while with his right hand he gently pried the fingers apart.

'There is dried blood under the fingernails, and one of them is broken. But look at this! You see this ring of blue-black marks around the wrist. And the other wrist.'

He went to the other hand and lifted it.

'And now look at the ankles.'

He moved down to her feet and held each of them in turn up a few inches – presumably her flesh had been frozen, as the legs were stiff. Around each leg just above the ankle were rings of similar black-blue marks to those on the wrists.

'You see? It seems she must have had her hands and her ankles bound together. She was bound and gagged. But when she arrived here there were no cords or gag.'

He turned back to the head.

'It is to be hoped that one or other of the blows to her head either killed her or stunned her before the other injuries were inflicted.'

He now stepped back to the level of her hips and he reached forwards and with his bare hands separated her legs slightly.

'You will note that her sexual organs are intact. You will also note that her abdomen has stretch marks. They are obscured by discolouration, but look. You will see these faint white striations. They are a result of pregnancy. Looking again at her breasts and nipples, you can see, in spite of the wound on her right breast, that both breasts are engorged. She was ready to feed her baby. She was a nursing mother.'

51

He beckoned to Dr Simpson, who put his notebook down on a chair and came over to the body. One on each side, they reached forwards and carefully turned the body over on its front, on the ice. The girl's buttocks and thighs were criss-crossed by long slashes and gashes, black with dried blood.

'These gashes would have been red,' Dr Reid said, 'and as you can see the skin has been broken in places apart from the gashes. But here on the buttocks and thighs, in contrast to the front of her body, some of the gashes are parallel.'

He paused again. The effects of these pauses were dramatic, but seeing the tension in his face – almost a mask of clinical indifference – I found myself thinking he was effectively but rather desperately holding in any possible signs of emotion.

He turned to a side table where there was a towel covering a large shapeless object. He lifted the towel. On a grey cloth on the table was a sort of trident without a handle: four sharp curved metal tines about six inches long on a short steel tubular base. The steel was slightly rusty with faint black streaks.

'Do you know what this is, Mr Hobbes?' Dr Reid said, turning to me.

'No. I've never seen anything like it.'

'It's an eel spear. You can see the tube of the base has drilled holes. It's nailed or screwed onto a pole. A short pole of four or five feet long for an eel fisherman in long boots standing in the water, or a pole ten or even twenty feet long for when the fisherman is standing on a wharf or a rock, or in winter is standing out on the ice and stabs the spear down through a hole cut in the ice. You plunge it straight down, then pull it up sharply. It hooks and spears the eels from underneath. As you can see the tines are razor sharp and curved like the barbs of a fish hook so the spear can pull the eels up and out of the water without them slipping off. Eel spears are very common on the island, and some people claim they were invented here. The various estuaries and bays, where sea water and fresh water from rivers mix, are thick with eels.

'This particular eel spear was found on a chair in the library room where the corpse was lying. It was brought here with the corpse. There were dried blood stains on the spear, and I could perceive more of them when I examined the blades with a magnifying glass.

'As you can see from its shape, this eel spear would make slash marks if applied to human flesh, and since the tines are parallel the slash marks would often be parallel also. I say "often" because, depending on the angle, in some slashes only one tine point will have been applied force-fully. When the murderer or murderers turned her body onto its front, they raked her buttocks and thighs with the eel spear.

'Then as if the slashing and piercing of her buttocks by the eel spear was not enough', he went on, 'she has also been heavily – brutally – beaten there with a belt. There are even marks from a buckle. See?' He pointed at some crossed marks where the skin had been cut open deeply.

He moved forwards and, as delicately as he could, he pulled the legs apart again slightly.

'This is as I suspected. As the body has thawed out, blood has seeped onto the ice below. But note, this blood is dark red, probably not from the vagina, but from the anus. Excuse this, Gentlemen,' he said, and he inserted a finger. 'It is ripped on one side.'

He withdrew his finger. Dr Simpson came to his aid with a basin of soapy water and a nail brush. He scrubbed and washed his hands, and dried them on a towel. He looked at me but spoke to us all.

'I think, Gentlemen, that this woman was violently buggered.' He paused. 'Whether before death, or after, I cannot say. Mr Hobbes, I hope you find the man or men who did this, and I hope that man or those men will hang! Although hanging is too good for them!'

His jaw was quivering. He turned away for a moment then looked back to me. He was back in control.

'I must inform you that following her husband's wishes, I shall now release the body to her parents for burial. They are in North Rustico I believe. I shall advise the undertakers to do their best to prepare the body to show less signs of injury, and to obtain clothes from the woman's parents. As Coroner for Queens County, under certain circumstances I can hold an inquest to complete my findings. Now I know the police are investigating the circumstances of this death, I may not need to engage in such a process. We already have the information from this post-mortem examination which you have witnessed. With the help of my colleague here, I shall write a summary of the findings and keep it in my records. After your investigations are completed, whether or not I proceed will depend on the report from the Attorney General.'

McNulty and I walked back into town.

'What about the three rings?' I asked.

'I was waiting until you had seen the body, to give them to you. I have them in my pouch.'

He stopped and reached into a pouch on his belt and pulled out a small brown envelope and handed it to me.

'Mr McNulty – Sergeant McNulty – thank you for your diligence, but please don't do this to me again. From now on, if you learn anything whatsoever about this case, I want you to tell me about it at once. No waiting.'

'I will, Sir. I apologise.'

'Is there anything else you have not shown me?'

'No, Sir.'

We were walking along a road beside a park on our left and with a view of the bay on our right. Small pleasure yachts were tacking here and there, white sails shining in the sun. There were benches overlooking the water. We went to one and sat down, side by side. I tore the envelope with my fingernail and tipped the three rings into my palm. Each had been clipped through, I assume with a sharp pliers, and slightly bent, to get them off the woman's fingers. One gold wedding ring, one silver engagement ring with a diamond, and one bronze signet ring with a small round capsule on it.

'Have you opened this? And by the way two of these rings are very valuable. Why have you been carrying these around?'

'I don't trust my colleagues, the other constables.'

'McNulty — I'll stop calling you Sergeant at this point — I trust your instincts, but again, please don't hide things from me. I think we need to have a long talk together about all sorts of things that you know and I don't know. But meanwhile, have you a knife to open this capsule on the ring?'

McNulty produced a folding pen-knife with a sharp pointed blade. I managed to pry open the capsule from an indentation between its halves. There was no spring, but it fell open from a tiny hinge. In it was a tiny piece of folded parchment. I opened it — four folds. In miniature letters in black ink there was a phrase in a language I did not know. I held it up to the sunlight.

'I have a magnifying glass,' said McNulty, and produced one from his pocket.

'You're a gem.' In truth I could only marvel at this strange man.

I examined the text through the glass. *Mo nighean dubh, mo chroí, mo rún.* 'What language is this?' I said, handing glass and text to McNulty.

'That's easy. It's Scottish Gaelic — or as they pronounce it "Gallic". I know Irish Gaelic, since I grew up in Donegal where many people still speak it. And since the Donegal Gaelic is closer to the Scottish than to the Gaelic of the south of Ireland, I can usually understand it. In the Irish this would mean "My black-haired girl, my heart, my love". But we would spell *n-i-g-h-e-a-n* as *i-n-í-o-n*.'

McNulty, the scholar, seemed as interested in languages as I was.

'But this young lady was not Scottish or Irish,' I said. 'She was Acadian French. And her husband was English.'

'A suitor, Sir? Or a father? A god-father? In the Irish, at least, *iníon* means either a girl or a daughter — as in English when a father might refer to his daughter as his "girl". Even "My heart" is a term of endearment, something like "Darling".'

'Have you got children, McNulty?'

'I have a son, grown up now, "over across" in Nova Scotia.' He smiled grimly, as if afraid of being sentimental.

'But this girl's father is French,' I said, returning to professional matters. 'And presumably a god-father would be too, although we can check that. And her hair is not black.'

'You have a point, Sir, but *dubh* is sometimes used loosely for "dark". Another point: *rún* is an interesting word. It means "love" – in this case "my love" – but it also means "secret". So, "my love", or "my secret love", or maybe even "my secret".'

We paused to consider this. Suddenly I saw again the girl, slashed and beaten, on the bed of melting, blood-stained ice.

5

Again Lucy and I had a simple meal served in our room – over-cooked lamb chops and soggy roast potatoes. We felt daunted by the idea of seeking out a restaurant with our rather active son. And after having gone to tea with Mrs Robinson, Lucy had an idea for getting us out of this.

'The Ocean House. It's a new hotel on what they call the North Shore. It's by the sea. Olivia is keen on going there for some weeks with the children, and her husband William can visit from Charlottetown. She grew up by the sea, in a place called Waterford. Her father then moved to the middle of Ireland as a new Bishop, near where William's family were living in a huge house which was falling to pieces with leaks in the roof. William's elder brother is an Earl or something, but the family has no money, and William has to earn a living like anyone else. She and William fell in love. Her father objected that she was too young. Then William went to England. Then Olivia's father died, and William came back to Ireland and they got married.'

It was oddly pleasurable to hear Lucy talk like this, in her very precise English, almost as if she were suddenly part of 'society' – after the two years we had spent together in Victoria in isolation, apart from visits with our friends the Pembertons. Mrs Pemberton was another Irish woman. Pemberton had once told me that in Ireland they had their own tribes, like the North American Indians – groups of families, and religions. Anyone from outside could not be placed in a tribal or family category, so was simply accepted. I supposed Robinson was now in another tribal setting, the Colonial Office.

'I liked William Robinson,' I said. 'Very clear-minded.'

'Olivia says that his favourite things apart from work are playing with the children and playing the piano. He loves music.'

'That's a good sign! But is Mrs Robinson serious about this project of going to the hotel by the sea?'

'That's what she called it. A project. She is at least ten years older than I am, but we get along well. And she has a son about Will's age. They don't exactly play together but they play alongside each other, with different toys. And the elder of her two daughters is very nice with Will. The younger daughter is a baby girl whom Olivia is nursing. She is absolutely exhausted by the whirl of visiting the island with William as he makes himself known, and she wants to get out of Charlottetown. She says that once she gets the Strawberry Tea Party out of the way she will have fulfilled what she calls her "social obligations" for a while.'

'I'm going to the North Shore tomorrow. I'll have a look at the Ocean House if I can. I may have to stay overnight somewhere. If so, you'll be alone here tomorrow night. It's not ideal.'

'I'll see Olivia again tomorrow. She's discussing the "project" with William.'

From Charlottetown to the main stretch of the North Shore was about thirty miles – a day's travel by trap or wagon, half a day on horseback. (I use the English word 'trap' for what they call on the island a 'buggy'). From the map I could see that North Rustico, site of the Ocean House, was only about twenty miles north of Charlottetown on a small irregular bay separated from the sea by what looked like a sand bar. Stanley Bridge, where John Harris lived in the house where his wife's body had been found, was further west, on New London Bay – a larger bay with another sand bar. McNulty said there were no more than three hundred people in the villages of New London and Stanley Bridge, although there were farms and small hamlets in the area, and there was a lobster cannery in New London.

We rode. We could trot or even at times canter for a stretch. The road surface was packed red or pink earth with occasional shale, and lined with drainage ditches, although McNulty said the roads could become impassable with mud in heavy rain. The weather was now dry and sunny, with a gentle cool breeze although the sunlight was hot.

It was a landscape of rolling low hills with river valleys, neatly maintained patches of woodland, and a patchwork of neatly farmed fields – some for pasture, with cattle or horses, and others of wheat or hay. The wheat was a fresh light green, and the hay was darker green and dense with the pink and blue flowers of clover and timothy. Fields were separated by fences of wire on posts, or by zigzagging fences of poles stacked alternately on each other at the joints. In Vancouver Island these are called 'snake fences,' but McNulty told me that on this island they were called 'French fences.' Along them grew wild roses and various flowers I had not seen before. McNulty knew their names. 'Devil's Paintbrush'. 'Pearly Everlasting'.

We stopped for an early lunch in a tavern at Hunter River where the river cut through a valley and we crossed a covered bridge – a wooden structure with a peaked roof along its entire length. There was a grey wooden church with a square tower, and houses along the river banks, painted in bright yellows and blues or pale green or grey. The tavern was a larger house, with a roofed porch on which we sat at a table and ate sandwiches of cold meat and cheese. We drank iced water and coffee. I suggested to McNulty that we should take a brief walk and have a look at the covered bridge as the decorated wooden arches were said to be unique.

The road north from Hunter River led towards North Rustico but at a hamlet with the ambitious name of New Glasgow, we took another road north west across farmland where the fields became larger and the slopes longer. After about an hour the road crossed over a ridge and we could see the blue bar of the sea to the north, under lighter blue skies with small cumulus clouds. In spite of our gloomy mission, my heart lifted. Eventually we descended a series of gentle slopes, at a canter, to the village of Stanley Bridge where the road continued towards New London across a bridge over the Stanley River. On a hill overlooking the village was a cluster of houses and barns, including a prominent white house with out-buildings and stables. This was the local tavern and guesthouse where we would stay the night. Just before we reached it we turned right, clattered across another short bridge across a stream, then turned left and northwards again onto what turned out to be a low peninsula with the sea on both sides and a view straight ahead to the north across a few fields then the bay to a long line of dunes along a sand bar. 'New London Spit,' McNulty shouted, pointing it out.

It was now about three o'clock and the sun was still fairly high in the sky across the sea on our left. Up a slope on our right was an imposing large house – white clapboard with black trim and shutters and the usual porch – like a smaller version of Government House. There were out-buildings, and a paddock with horses. We rode into a short driveway. A roughly dressed man, young and muscular but with such sparse hair that he seemed almost bald, appeared and took hold of the horses' reins as we dismounted, then led the horses away. He uttered no words of greeting and seemed to avoid looking at us.

We walked up the porch steps and McNulty banged a large door-knocker of black iron. The door was opened by another rough-looking man, big and tousle-haired, wearing black trousers and a white shirt. 'Mr Harris is expecting you,' he said, and led us to the back of the house along a wide hallway with a polished wooden staircase to one side. We came out of the house again onto the back porch. A man was standing facing us, silhouetted against the blue of the sea. His face looked dark at first because of the light behind him, but close up his skin was pale. He was clean-shaven. His eyes were grey-blue, not unlike the marble eyes of the woman on the bed of ice – his wife. His hair was straight and smoothed to his head, a grey-blond colour. He was probably aged in his early forties. In contrast to the men we had just seen, he was slight in build, and his face was narrow and boyishly handsome but with a severe thin-lipped mouth. He held out his hand to me, then to McNulty.

'Welcome to Stanley Bridge,' he said. 'Such a lovely day too. I'm John Harris.'

His hand had been slightly clammy, and cold. His voice was light and agreeable, his accent more English than usual on the island. He was un-smiling. But then this was not a cheerful occasion. I introduced myself and McNulty.

We sat on wicker-work chairs on the porch, rather as I had with William Robinson at Government House, the three chairs making a semi-circle facing north over the porch railing to the azure bay and the high sand dunes of the spit, pink in the light of the sun which shone over the house from the west. The house was in the middle of the base of the peninsula, with sea on three sides, but closest on the east side where the shore was only fifty yards or so away, and farthest to the north where the peninsula widened out for half a mile or so, with fields and patches of woods and scattered houses.

The tousle-headed man, whom I assumed was some sort of butler, appeared with a tray with three tall glasses of ice tea with mint. We each took one. The man went back into the house.

'The message said you were Superintendent Hobbes,' Harris said abruptly to me. 'I didn't know there was a new Superintendent of Police. What a surprise. I made enquiries and I hear you have been employed by Mr Frederick Brecken, the Attorney General, to investigate the murder of my wife. I hear you have come to the island with your own wife who is possibly some kind of Indian. Where have you come from? And why you?'

I explained briefly. The name of Mr Justice Begbie seemed to make an impression, as well as perhaps the fact that I had dined with Mr Brecken and already spoken with the Governor. Harris now became emollient, and almost eager to help. He seemed capable of quick changes.

'Ask me anything you'd like Mr Hobbes. You can understand I'm in a huge state of shock. I wake up every morning – when I have managed to sleep, that is – in a state of dread. I cannot explain what has happened, and I have no idea who could have done such a frightful thing – to my dear young wife – and to me!'

'If you don't mind, I'd like to start at the beginning by asking you something about yourself, as you have asked about me. I know little about the island, even, and nothing about you except that you are a Councilman for this area, and known as a supporter of Union with Canada.'

'Even that, Mr Hobbes, may not be quite right. I do hope the island can become part of the new Dominion, and share British North America with our neighbours, but always assuming the conditions are favourable. And we have a unique system here. The Legislative Council is elected by landowners only, and they tend to be Conservative. But they also tend to hedge their bets. So in Queens County we have two Conservative and two Liberal Councilmen – Mr Honoré Gallant and I. You will note that Mr Gallant is Catholic, and I am Protestant. Protestants and Catholics stand side by side for pairs of council or assembly seats. It has been called an "incestuous" process.'

'And you were born and grew up here?'

'I was born in Charlottetown. I attended school there at Prince of Wales College, then I studied Law at Dalhousie University in Halifax. Then I came back to the island and practiced law for many years. My father had a string of farms and businesses, and recently I took over management of all of them and I'm in the process of closing down my legal practice. And to anticipate your next question, or the next but one, I was leading such a busy life that only recently did I get around to marrying.' Here he suddenly looked gloomy, almost tearful. 'My darling Évangéline,' he said in a low voice. 'A lovely girl, twenty years younger than I, and the daughter of my colleague Honoré Gallant.'

'And you have a child,' I said.

'She is with Madame Gallant, in North Rustico. Not doing well, I hear. The poor mite! She was found floating in a wicker basket in a pond behind Thunder Cove which is a wild and often stormy beach. It's a long way away from here – about twelve miles by sea, longer by land. Someone must have placed the baby there, to be found. Some angel? Or the brute or brutes who killed my wife? Mr Hobbes…' Here he brandished a fist, or actually both fists, which made the gesture somehow ineffectual. 'Please find those brutes!'

For a moment I could say nothing. To undertake to find 'those brutes' would be to admit I believed 'those brutes' did not possibly include Mr Harris himself. I was not going to rule anyone out.

'Please tell me everything you can about that day your wife was killed, and how she was found. You might start, if you can, with the birth of your child – I believe it was only a few days before.'

'I'll do my best,' he said, his voice trembling. 'Our child hasn't even got a name! We had decided to wait until we knew whether it was a boy or a girl, and then to let ourselves be inspired by his or her appearance. The birth went well, with the assistance of our local doctor, Dr. Kelly, along with Évangéline's mother, Madame Gallant from North Rustico, and Modeste Aucoin, our domestic help. Both women have been midwives, informally, for many years. The birth was upstairs here in the spare bedroom. I waited down here, pacing as nervous fathers do, until I heard the baby's cries and rushed upstairs. And there at my wife's bosom was this lovely little girl! We were so happy! Madame Gallant stayed on for the next few days. The baby was feeding well. I thought we might call her Sophie, but Évangéline wasn't sure. We decided there was no hurry to make up our minds about the name until the christening, in a few weeks.

'The baby was born on Sunday the 25th of June. The following Friday, the 30th, I had to go into Charlottetown. I have regular meetings there usually every two weeks and need to stay the night. I rode down

63

there after breakfast as always, had a meeting in the late afternoon with some associates, then we all went for dinner at the St Lawrence Hotel. I should have mentioned, we have a house in Charlottetown, with a couple, Mr and Mrs. Palmer, as housekeepers, and there I stayed the night. I was just starting doing paperwork on the Saturday morning, assisted by my secretary, Mr Johnson, when a telegram arrived from Edgar Aucoin, who also works for me. Edgar's telegram said that Évangéline had died suddenly and the baby had been found near Thunder Cove. It's miles away. He and Modeste were by then in Malpeque on their way to fetch the baby. I set off home right away, on horseback, and got here in less than four hours. By then Edgar was back here. He told me where Évangéline was, so I ran upstairs to the library. I was horrified.

'Edgar told me that in the early morning around seven o'clock, a man by the name of Matheson had knocked on the Aucoins' door. He gave Modeste a note for me from Calum MacKinnon in Darnley and asked her to pass it on to me. He said it was about a baby found in a wicker basket on a pond near Thunder Cove which MacKinnon thought could be Évangéline's child. He was on his way to Summerside and left in a hurry. Since I was in Charlottetown, Modeste decided to open the letter. She then ran straight here. She called to Évangéline but there was no reply. She went upstairs. Then she saw… She saw bloodstains on the hall floor towards the library. She felt afraid and she ran to fetch Edgar. And in the library they found Évangéline, on the floor, unclothed, and covered with blood. She was cold. She was dead.'

He bent forwards with his face in his hands and began to sob noisily. After a while he took away his hands and looked at me. There were tears on his cheeks. 'I'll never get her back!' he said desperately.

'You mean she was alone in the house when this happened? Don't your staff live in?'

'No,' he said, quite sharply. 'We like our privacy. The Aucoins live about fifty yards away just up the road in a house I own. They are what you might call my factotums. They help me with everything. Our other servants live "handy," as we say here, meaning close by in Stanley Bridge. If we need immediate help from the Aucoins and they are not in this house, we ring a bell. The houses are out of sight of each other because of a clump of trees along a fence. We all like our privacy! But there is a bell on the fence which can be clearly heard by the Aucoins. There is a cord to it in a steel pipe. We pull a handle in the kitchen.'

'But your wife had just had a baby…'

'I know, Mr Hobbes, I have been reproaching myself. Madame Gallant had gone back earlier in the morning to North Rustico. Évangéline had told her mother and me she would be well on her own. She knew the Aucoins were close at hand, and she wanted, she said, a quiet time with her baby. She trusted and liked Modeste who would come in and see her in the morning and as needed by Évangéline whenever she rang the bell. How could we have known? Nothing happens in New London! There are no bad people here at Stanley Bridge, or within miles.'

'Can we please have a look at the library?'

'If you wish. I have not been into it since that terrible first day when I came back and saw her! Lying on the floor naked, covered with blood.'

'And she was left lying on the floor?'

'Dr Kelly – who had been called in the morning of course, and upon my return – insisted. He said that since it was a crime, the authorities should observe the scene. But frankly, the poor man was not thinking straight in the shock of it all. What authorities? There are no police here! I wasn't going to leave my wife to rot on the floor! I ordered Dr Kelly – yes, I ordered him and I take full responsibility for it – to see that the body was transported to Charlottetown right away. I'm not a criminal lawyer, but I know the law, and I knew that she would have to go to Charlottetown for a coroner's post-mortem followed by a police investigation. What a scandal! So Dr Kelly arranged for her to be transported on ice – knowing that Dr Reid uses all the latest methods, including preserving the body on ice. But I left the library as I found it. The door is closed. No one has been in there since that dreadful event. I certainly cannot go in there. I couldn't bear it. So I must ask you to go there without me. I shall stay here. The library is opposite the staircase, facing the back of the house.'

'You say no one has been in there since the – the event. So nothing has been taken out?'

'Not that I know of.'

'What about the eel spear?'

'What eel spear? I know nothing about that.'

'It was used in the murder of your wife. The men who brought her body to Charlottetown brought it with them. I assume they found it in the library. Did you see it? It looks like a sort of trident of sharp blades. Or anything else left there? Items of your wife's clothing? Anything unusual?'

'I don't recall anything. But I hardly looked. I could only look at poor Évangéline! Of course I know what an eel spear looks like. Everyone around here has them, since the estuary is full of eels. We have several here in one of our sheds.'

'Perhaps we could have a look at them, in case one is missing.'

'I wouldn't know! I don't know how many eel spears we have. It's like asking me how many shovels or axes we have. They are a common item. And I must say I'm too confused in my mind to recall anything about our eel spears. The only thing in my mind now is Évangéline's body on the library floor! Like an item in a chamber of horrors!'

'When is the last time you used an eel spear?'

'I haven't used one for years. I don't fish for eels, although as I say most people around here do. If an eel spear was used in this murder of my wife it could have been brought in. Everyone has them. But that would surely be very clumsy, given that eel spears are commonly ten to twenty feet long – which is why they are kept in barns or storage sheds. Or you mean just the head of the spear? It can be detached.'

'This one was detached. But now, with your permission, can Sergeant McNulty and I examine the scene?'

'Of course.'

McNulty had been sitting on a chair beside me on the porch but he had said nothing. I looked at him and we all stood up.

There was a rather grand circular staircase to the upper floor. McNulty and I found ourselves in a broad hallway with several closed doors. With a look at me, McNulty stepped forwards and opened the door facing us. 'Christ!' he said. I followed him in. The room was a shambles. A rug had been thrown against the bookshelves. The wooden floor was spattered with darkened thick blood stains. Some of the books were lying, open or closed, on the floor. A chair was lying on its back beside an escritoire which was itself covered with blood stains, by now brown. The only neat thing in this chaos was a pile of neatly folded clothes, on the floor in one corner. Between the shelves were two high windows, both closed. The room smelled stuffy and perhaps of blood, although this may have been my imagination. We stepped forward, McNulty and I, and each opened a window. The room was along the back of the house. To the left was a clump of trees with the roof of another house – the Aucoins' I supposed – partly visible. From that side, the west, the sun poured its golden light over fields and water. To the right there was a lawn sloping down to a little wharf with two small sailing boats moored to it with shipped oars and masts with furled sails.

I turned back into the room. Now a fresh breeze ruffled the curtains – blood-spattered at their bottom ends, except for one which was torn down and lying on the floor.

McNulty and I did not speak to each other. I did not want to be overheard by anyone in the house, and I suppose he thought similarly. We occasionally pointed at things of interest. In particular the top of the escritoire. It was of dark green leather and at one end it had a large pad of blotting paper near an upset inkwell. The blotting paper was streaked with a black ink-splash, and a patch of dried blood had a curved imprint in it that might have been from the base of a hand, as if someone had leaned on it. The leather on the other side of the blotting pad had different coloured stains – whitish. McNulty pointed to this and wagged his finger as if asking me to remember it. I nodded. He then took a tape measure from the pocket of his uniform jacket and measured the distances between the various stains and marks on the table, jotting them down in his notebook.

We then went and looked at the clothes in their neat, incongruous pile. At first glance they were a man's – or a boy's, as they were rather small-sized. Blue dungarees, a checked work shirt, thick grey socks, a pair of boots – also small-sized. A pair of short white cotton drawers – a woman's – lying on a camisole. Both garments were clean, but the dungarees were streaked with white. Salt. There were a few streaks of blood on the shirt and dungarees. From her broken nose? And there were buttons missing with small rips where they would have been.

We then went and looked at the half-rolled up rug and spread it out on the floor. Here was another large stain, though not blood. McNulty bent down, raising the rug with one hand, and sniffed it, wrinkling his nose.

'Urine', he said.

After a final look at the room, we went out and closed the door behind us. We went downstairs.

Harris was where we had left him, sitting looking out over the bay.

'The boats down there,' I said. 'Who uses them?'

'Mainly Évangéline. I don't sail. They are quite heavy – skiffs with centreboards – but Évangéline could row and sail them on her own. She was an expert with boats. A tomboy! That's one of the things I liked about her! She even wore boys' clothes when there were no people around, since she could then row a boat. The bay is usually calm here, and we can row across to the spit and walk along the sand. Or we could!' he exclaimed.

I remained standing. 'What's your own theory?' I asked, 'About who these brutes, as you call them, were?'

'I've been agonising about this!' he exclaimed. 'They weren't robbers: nothing is missing. Were they political enemies of mine? But anyone will tell you I haven't got any enemies. Were they old enemies of Évangéline's? She had no enemies I know of. All I can think of is that it must be a sexual assault. Tell me! I can bear it! Was she raped?'

'Dr Reid could not say,' I said as noncommittally as I could manage. 'She had recently given birth to a child, after all.'

'I know I can't offer a reward to the police!' he exclaimed. 'But whoever else provides any information, I can assure you they will be rewarded.' Then, in a sudden shift of subject: 'What are they saying in Charlottetown? I was there for a meeting and a dinner with associates. And of course my housekeepers the Palmers know I spent the night in my house. People know I was in Charlottetown when this crime occurred, don't they?'

'If you mean, do people suspect you of this, I can't really say. Forgive me, but we naturally have to consider every possibility. By the way, was your father-in-law Mr Gallant at the dinner in Charlottetown?'

'No. The associates I mentioned were former friends of my father's. I assume Mr Gallant was in North Rustico or in Georgetown where he transacts a lot of business these days.'

'As a lawyer, Mr Harris, you must know very well that marital conflicts can be bitter. Did you have any conflicts?'

'None! What do married people argue about? How to bring up their children, perhaps. But we weren't yet at that stage. Money! But we had a marriage settlement we were both happy with. You can see it at the notary's in North Rustico. For the sake of propriety we chose the young notary, not Honoré Gallant. Religion? No. She was Catholic, and I am Anglican, but on this island the most acute religious antagonisms are between Catholics and Presbyterians. We were married in the Catholic church after obtaining a dispensation from the Bishop in Charlottetown, and I was happy with that. I speak French, and we would speak either French or English to each other. So language was never a contention. Politics? Certainly not. I may as well admit that some people have pointed to this marriage as a political alliance between me and Mr Gallant. But an alliance is an alliance! It pre-existed. He and I agree on most things.'

'And the child was yours?'

'What? How dare you ask that?' He jumped to his feet, looking agitated.

'It's my job, Mr Harris. I have to ask.'

He became calm suddenly. 'Of course, of course. Forgive me, I lost my temper. It's such an outrageous idea. You forget how young Évangéline was. She had no experience of that kind, and may I say, she was very strictly brought up.'

'She has been described to me as "wild".'

'By whom?'

'I can't say. But I don't believe there was any implication of misconduct. I think the person who used the word may have been suggesting that she was a spirited young woman.'

'Yes, she was spirited! That's why I liked her! She had a mind of her own. Yes I know she was brought up by strict Catholic parents. But one reason we liked each other was that we could talk to each other. We could discuss these things I have mentioned – religion, government, languages – and not have to be on our guard. We saw eye to eye! And now she's gone.' He sat down in his wicker chair abruptly and slumped low in it, putting his face in his hands again.

'Thank you, Mr Harris,' I said. 'You have been very kind to talk so openly with us. You have all our sympathies. And now we shall take our leave. Would you mind if we came back briefly tomorrow morning to talk to Mr and Mrs. Aucoin? I'll go and knock on their door and set a time. We shall also have a talk with Dr Kelly. And we'll go to Thunder Cove to view where the baby was found.

'I'll also ask Mr and Mrs. Aucoin about their visit to Mr MacKinnon in Darnley. And then, I suppose by the day after tomorrow, we'll go to North Rustico to talk to Mr and Mrs Gallant. I'm informing you of all this, so as not to keep you in the dark.'

'Thank you, Mr Hobbes. You will appreciate this has been difficult for me. But of course I shall be available for further meetings as you see fit – either here or in Charlottetown.'

We took our leave. Outside, Aucoin was standing with his back to the house – on guard, as it were. He turned when he heard us, and I proposed that we would pay him and his wife a visit at half past nine the following morning, 'to check details'. He agreed with an unsmiling nod. He turned to face to the side of the house and called out 'I-Guess!' A young man appeared leading our horses – the man who had taken them when we arrived – strong-looking, clean shaven – or was it simply that he had no beard or whiskers? When he had appeared and taken the horses from us when we arrived, I had thought he must have extremely short hair, but I could now see that he was almost completely bald, with just a little fuzz above his ears like a monk's tonsure, yet with a round baby-like face. It was hard to tell his age. The sleeves of his checked shirt were rolled up, and his arms were strongly muscled. Without a word he handed us the reins of the horses.

We rode back to the guesthouse. A groom took our horses and led them to the stable.

I was hungry, but I wanted to talk with McNulty in private, not in a dining room, even an ostensibly private one. Luckily there was a wooden table with chairs outside on the lawn facing the setting sun, and the air was warm. 'Can we eat dinner outside?' I asked the landlady.

'Certainly. We have lovely fresh lobster, if you'd like that – and of course potatoes. And we have some nice white wine from France called Macon.'

That was a surprise. We sat down in the warmth of the sun and the landlady started us off with a jug of the Macon sitting on a dish with a bed of ice. Ice again! I could not feel cheerful under the circumstances, but I found I was worn out with the horror of the story so far, and I had very little emotion left.

'All right,' I began. 'I understand why Mr Brecken and you have left it to me to find out for myself the history of Mr Harris. But at this point, I'd like to have *your* point of view.'

'Always respectfully, Sir. If you wouldn't mind sharing your observations with me first, I think it would be best. You see, we who live on the island will have all sorts of preconceptions and prejudices, and we have heard all sorts of gossip and stories. You know how to ask questions, and also being "from away" – as we describe an outsider – you will have a fresh view. Then, I can check it against the facts in the background, which of course I'll know more of.'

'I bow to your sense of method, McNulty. All right. No holds barred. But let's start with observations. In the library. The urine stain on the rug. Your measurements on the writing table.'

'The urine would have been voided in panic I suspect', McNulty said. On the writing table I believe the whitish stains at one end were breast milk. That and the partial hand print on the blotter

72

suggested to me that the woman was forced over the table on her front, and raped from behind – or more precisely, to use Dr Reid's word, buggered.'

'I thought the same thing. And there was every sign in the room of a vigorous struggle. Which makes me think that at least at that time her hands and feet were not bound.'

'Agreed. But when were they bound?'

'No evidence yet. Before the struggle in the library. After the struggle, she was dead. And those were her clothes. She must have been stripped in the library. Salt stains on the dungarees. Dr Reid noticed salt in her hair. Had she been in the sea? Was she in a boat and splashed by spray from waves? We need to find out.'

'Agreed, Sir.'

'And Mr Harris? I had the impression he shifted between the truth and a degree of obfuscation, and I had no way of telling one from the other. A certain person I spoke to described him to me as "slippery".'

'Again agreed, Sir. He has a reputation for being every man's friend, yet he lets people down. He shifts very quickly from one point of view to another I suppose. Apart from what you call obfuscation, which as you know means literally a darkening of the truth, he comes close to lying. "There are no bad people in New London". Well, there are bad people everywhere. And one bad one is Wedge – or Edgar Aucoin. He's known to us as a smuggler although we can't prove it. I'm told he was seen in Charlottetown the other night – when we were followed. Then, Dr Kelly was "shocked". Nothing could shock him, he's a former military surgeon from the British army who was kicked out of it – "cashiered" I believe is the military term – and found refuge here, where medical licensing is very much no questions asked: all new immigrants welcome! Then, Mr Harris has "no enemies". All politicians have enemies. Then, he and Mr Gallant agree. Perhaps, but if so it's in the context of a political marriage of convenience. Yes, he expressed his love for his wife, but this was another marriage of convenience, and widely spoken of as one. Furthermore, I wonder about Madame Gallant going home so soon to North Rustico. I find it hard to believe a mother who had also been the midwife could leave her daughter and baby granddaughter alone in a house a few days after childbirth.'

'We can ask Madame Gallant.'

'She too may obfuscate. Her husband and Mr Harris are so intertwined.'

As the sun became lower in the western sky it sent ripples of light across New London Bay, bringing out the pink in the sand dunes of the spit. McNulty and I sat eating the freshest and most amazing lobster I had ever tasted. There was one huge one each, and we each had a pair of pliers for cracking the shells, and a large napkin to tuck around our neck. We discussed theology and Darwin's theory of evolution.

6

The next morning after breakfast we walked along to the peninsula and to Harris's imposing white house, then past it about fifty yards up the road to a smaller house, with grey clapboard siding, faded by wind and sun, where the Aucoins lived. It was indeed largely out of sight of Harris's house because of the clump of trees – some kind of scrub oak – between, with a 'snake fence' of overlapping wooden poles running through it. When McNulty knocked on the door, Edgar Aucoin, followed by his wife, stepped outside. We stood and talked on a path of red packed earth. This was not a forthcoming couple. They waited to be asked questions, and answered them abruptly. Mrs Aucoin was indeed called Modeste. McNulty, as ever informative about language, had told me that it was an Acadian Christian name that could be given to either boys or girls. And Acadians with the surname 'Aucoin' – meaning they lived 'at the corner' – if they turned English-speaking called themselves 'Wedge,' a wedge being something that fits in a corner. Edgar Aucoin was also known as Edgar Wedge.

I had asked McNulty to start the questioning. 'I think we may have met before,' he said to Aucoin. 'Or I may have seen you in Charlotte-town.'

'We often go into Charlottetown, doing errands for Mr Harris.'

'Do you prefer "Aucoin" or "Wedge"?'

'Either.'

'How long have you been living here?'

'Three years.'

'The two of you?'

'Yup.'

'Children?'

'Two. A youngster aged ten, and a grown up of twenty-one. They live "over across" with family in Antigonish.'

'How long have you known Mr Harris?'

'For about three years'

'And you, Mrs Aucoin?'

'The same. Edgar and I have always worked together. We help people of property to manage their affairs.'

She was a tall and rather striking woman, slim, and with keen, sharp features – not beautiful but with penetrating small black eyes and thick black hair partly contained by a headscarf. She was wearing a shawl over a dress, but with rubber Wellington boots.

'And you keep house for Mr Harris?'

'We don't do the housework. We manage things.'

'All right,' I interrupted, fearing this exchange of brief phrases would go on for over. 'First, Mrs Aucoin, please tell me when and where you found Mrs Harris's body, and what you observed.'

'I wouldn't call it observing. After Mr Matheson told me about the baby having been found in Thunder Cove, my first thought was that something must have happened to Marie. Edgar was still sleeping. I quickly opened the letter he had given me for Mr Harris and I ran over to the house. I went in and called for Marie. She did not answer. I ran upstairs.'

'The library door was open?'

'Shut. Her bedroom door too. I knocked on it, then opened it. She wasn't in the bedroom. She hadn't been in bed either, it was still made. Then I knocked on the library door and opened it. She was lying naked on the floor, sprawled on one side – sort of crumpled, as if someone had thrown her there – and there were gashes on her body, with dried blood. I knew she was dead but I knelt down and touched her side. Ice cold. I gave the poor dear a kiss on one cheek, then I got up and ran and got Edgar in. He glanced at the scene then went running for Dr Kelly. That's all.'

'You mentioned Mrs Harris's bed had not been slept in. She and Mr Harris slept in separate bedrooms.'

She looked at me with a quick, penetrating glance.

'Yes.'

'Since the birth of the child?'

'They have never shared a bedroom so far as I know.'

'That's unusual, don't you think?'

'It's none of my business.'

'Mr Harris said that you saw blood stains on the upstairs hall floor, then you went to get your husband, and you both went into the library.'

'Poor Mr Harris, he probably thought it was that way, since I'm a woman, and I suppose he assumes that the moment I saw blood I went running for Edgar. But it was as I said. I didn't notice blood in the hallway.'

'When you found Mrs Harris in the library, were her hands or feet bound?'

'No.'

'Her clothes had been neatly folded and placed on the floor in a corner. Did you notice that?'

'It was I who folded them.'

Mrs Aucoin showed no sign of being upset. On the contrary, she was completely self-controlled.

'It was a horrible scene,' she said calmly, 'and the poor dear's clothes were scattered across the floor. It was the least I could do to pick them up and fold them and put them on one side. There was dried blood on some of them. I wasn't thinking of possible evidence for the police. But there would have been none. As I say, her clothes were scattered here and there at random. And she was completely naked. Full stop.'

She stared straight into my eyes. Her own almost-black eyes were expressionless. But I thought I could see tears in them.

I turned to her husband.

'Anything to add, Mr Aucoin?'

'No.'

'No sound in the night?'

'No.'

'No ringing of that bell I understand can be sounded from Mr Harris's house?'

'No.'

'What about the baby? You both went to Darnley to pick it up. How did you know it was there?

Mrs Aucoin interjected, 'Since Mr Harris was in Charlottetown, I thought it was all right to open the letter brought in by Matheson. It said the baby was being taken care of by Calum MacKinnon. He's the headteacher of the Gaelic School in Malpeque, and he's also a lobster fisherman.'

'I'll get the letter,' Mrs Aucoin said. She walked briskly into the house then came out again almost instantly with a letter.

> *Darnley*
> *1 July 1871*

Dear Mr Harris,

>*A baby has been found floating in a cradle on a pond near Thunder Cove. I fear this could be Mrs Harris's baby. Is she all right? I am looking after the baby. Please come here as soon as possible.*

>*Yours sincerely,*
>*Calum MacKinnon*

'Why would this Mr MacKinnon recognise the cradle – or the baby?'

'I don't know,' said Mrs Aucoin. 'But those cradles are made up that way by the Mic Mac. Anyway, when we arrived in Malpeque, before going to Darnley we sent a telegram to Mr Harris. We also sent another telegram to Madame Gallant in North Rustico. She arrived in Darnley shortly after us. She told me that Mr MacKinnon had already sent a telegram to her husband, and she and her housemaid had set off straight away in a two-horse buggy with a driver. So she took the baby back to North Rustico and I went with her.'

'Did he say how he recognised the cradle? Or the baby?'

'No. He didn't have to. Madame Gallant and I both knew the baby. She was the midwife at the birth of the baby, with my assistance. We were in too much of a state to sit asking Mr MacKinnon questions.'

'Did you know Mrs Harris well?'

'I've known her and her mother since she was a girl. Edgar and I have worked for Mr Honoré Gallant, her father.'

'When Madame Gallant arrived at this man MacKinnon's house, did she know her daughter was dead?'

'Certainly not! On her way to Mr MacKinnon, she had stopped by the Harrises' house in Stanley Bridge but we had locked it on Dr Kelly's orders. I had to tell her what Edgar and I had seen. I tried to get away with saying only that Marie had been killed by a blow to the head. Which may have been true. I hope so. But Madame Gallant is no fool and she questioned me until she got the truth out about Marie's wounds. It nearly drove her crazy. What do you expect?'

'On the way back to North Rustico did you and she discuss who might have attacked and killed Mrs Harris?'

'Yes, but we couldn't make any sense of it. Neither of us had any idea at all.'

'When did you last see Mrs Harris alive?'

'In the morning of the day before, at the house. She and the baby were well.'

'Who is I-Guess?' I said to Aucoin.

'He's called Zénon Cormier. He helps around the place.'

'Is he here?'

'Yup.' Aucoin turned towards the house and yelled: 'I-Guess!'

'*Ouai!*' I-Guess came out of the door, half-bald, plump but muscular. He looked at us blinking as if he had been pulled out of a dark space and was not used to the light.

I hardly knew what to say. 'You're I-Guess.'

'I guess,' He looked at me, then Aucoin, his piggy eyes shifting.

'Were you here when Mr and Mrs Aucoin found the body of Mrs Harris?'

'I guess.'

'You stayed outside?'

'I guess.'

'That's all he says,' Mrs Aucoin said.

'What do you mean?' I looked at I-Guess again.

He looked blank and said nothing.

'How long have you been living here?'

He said nothing, so I rephrased the question. 'Have you been living here long?'

'I guess.'

I realised what was happening. All he said was 'I guess'. And he said it only in reply to questions he understood. Otherwise he was bewildered.

'Do you like living here?' I said lamely.

'I guess.'

I turned to the Aucoins. 'Does he say more in French?'

'Rarely,' said Mrs Aucoin. 'He understands simple phrases in English and French.' She turned towards him. '*Tu comprends ce que je te dis, toé?*'

'*Shpanss-ben.*'

'That's the Acadian for *Je pense bien que oui*, meaning "I guess".'

End of interview. I told the Aucoins that if requested they should be ready to provide a statement about what they had told me. And I might want to talk to them again.

Dr Kelly's house looked rundown for that of a doctor. Weeds in the flower beds where a few violets were showing. An uncut stretch of grass. McNulty knocked on the door with his fist – there was no knocker. Eventually the door opened. A fat man wearing a soiled grey cotton suit – a suit something like mine, for that matter, although mine was clean. A blast of alcohol breath hit me as he opened his mouth and said, 'What do you want?'

'I'm Superintendent Hobbes, and this is Sergeant McNulty. Police.'

'Yes? About the Harris girl?'

'We call her Mrs Harris.'

'What do you want to know?' His accent was that of an English gentleman, although the consonants were blurred.

'When did you find the body?'

'Shortly after eight o'clock in the morning. Wedge came and got me.'

'What did you find?'

'A corpse!' He looked at me contemptuously.

'Cause of death?'

'Beaten to death. Slashed and cut. Some maniac.'

'What maniac? Who did you think of when you saw her?'

'Nobody. I just saw her and I said to myself, "Some fucking maniac".'

I was taken aback by this expression, then remembered about the bad language of Islanders. It must be catching, even to English gentlemen.

'Did you know her?'

'No. I saw her occasionally. She would walk into the village here and pass the time of day with anyone she saw. An amazingly pretty girl.'

'Did you visit her at her house?'

81

'No. I'm no friend of Mr Harris.'

'An enemy?'

'I said I was no friend. That's enough, Goddamn it.'

'What are your thoughts about this crime?'

'None. As I said. Some fucking maniac.'

'You're not curious?'

'Why should I be?'

'Because you're a doctor. You are supposed to be curious about unexpected deaths. Don't you know that?'

'Well, I'm not curious.' He turned his back to us, walked back into the house, and slammed the door.

I went up to the door and banged on it vigorously. It opened, and Kelly was standing there glowering.

'I have more questions,' I said. 'About the birth of Mrs Harris's child. And if you don't answer them, I'll arrest you for obstruction of justice.' This was nonsense, of course. I had no idea whether such a cause for arrest was legal, on the island or elsewhere.

'What about it? She gave birth, that's all. I was there because Mr Harris wanted a doctor there. Childbirth doesn't interest me. Midwives can take care of it very well. They don't need help from doctors unless something goes wrong. Nothing went wrong. I read in some of Harris's library books – a good section on military history. Battle of Waterloo. Some *very* interesting French books.'

'What do you mean by that?'

'Go and look for yourself. Books about the night life of Paris, and the sorts of things those dirty bastards the French do. The kind of thing I might guess Mr Harris would like.'

'What do you mean by 'the kind of thing'?

'Ask him.'

'And apart from reading these interesting books?'

'I did nothing. It was all in the hands of Mrs Gallant and Mrs Aucoin.

82

They knew what to do, and besides, the girl was Mrs Gallant's daughter. The birth was normal. The baby was normal. A little girl – a very *dark* little girl, I might say.' He stopped and reached to close the door again.

I stuck my foot forwards and stopped the door. 'How do you mean, *dark*?'

'Ask Mr Harris! Hah!' This was a sharp laugh. 'He's fucked!' Kelly turned away into the house, leaving me ridiculously blocking the open door.

I withdrew my foot and closed the door.

McNulty and I walked down the road to Stanley Bridge. We leaned over the wooden railings of the bridge, side by side, looking north across New London Bay towards the Spit. Now it was pink again in the morning sun from the east.

'Some time, Sir, you should go for a ride along the Spit. You can go out along the inward side, then when you round the point you cut back on the ocean side, along a strand with the ocean waves breaking.' He paused, perhaps embarrassed at his own enthusiasm.

'All right,' I said. 'Let's sum it up. Just thinking of the people we have met so far. I find there's nothing wrong with speculation, provided it's checked against the evidence. It gets the mind going. And the mind is going anyway. I find myself wondering if the "brutes", to use Harris's term, who killed Mrs Harris, were Aucoin and Cormier – "I-Guess" – either together with Harris or on his instructions. I don't think Mrs Aucoin would have known. Or Harris did it all on his own after Madame Gallant had left, then rode like hell to Charlottetown to put in an appearance in the late afternoon.

'Of course such speculations are based on the idea that if this baby was suspiciously dark, it may not have been Harris's child, and he took revenge on his wife. We do know that Mr Harris didn't mention a word to us of what Dr Kelly mentioned. More covering up. If as Dr Kelly says,

Mr Harris is "fucked", this is not what he conveyed to us. He conveyed only grief – which seemed genuine, by the way. His tears were real. Or were they tears of remorse? Yes, he is slippery. We should know more about his journey to Charlottetown. Can you find out whether Harris was seen on the road?'

'Before you arrived I talked separately with four men who had been at a meeting and dinner party with Harris on the 30th of June that took all evening from about half past four o'clock until after midnight – just as he described. And I talked to his housekeepers, the Palmers, who confirmed he had spent the night there. To get to Charlottetown for the meeting he would have to have left here at the latest after an early lunch.'

'So if Dr Reid's conclusions are accurate about the time of the murder, Mr Harris has an "alibi" in criminal law – meaning literally that he was "somewhere else" when the crime occurred. Sorry, I was forgetting you know Latin. Then, what about the baby? Found "cradled on the waves". It's almost like a separate story, but it must fit in the same story as the murder.'

'Agreed.'

A droll man, McNulty. Economical.

'And the baby was *dark*. Any Negroes on the island?'

'Not that I know of. Some of the Acadians are quite dark complexioned, and of course there are the Mic Mac, but most of them are quite light-skinned.'

'I want to know more about the baby. So do we ride north west and talk to Mr MacKinnon, and look at the place where he found the baby? Or do we ride east, to North Rustico, and talk to Madame Gallant? No. That doesn't feel right. We'll keep to the sequence of events. North west first. Thunder Cove then.'

'Agreed.'

> *Lucy, my Love,*
>   *I miss you and Will. I am near the North Shore, in a place called*

Stanley Bridge, with Sgt McNulty, and we are now going towards
Darnley − further north west. I hope we shall return eastwards and be
in North Rustico tomorrow − Thursday. There are people we need to
interview in North Rustico.

I hope the 'Project' is going well. If so I'll see you soon in North
Rustico! When I'm there I shall be staying in some guesthouse or other, but
I'll be able to visit you if you are at Ocean House.

I hope you don't have to wait around in Charlottetown. If you do I'm
sure Mr Brecken or Mr and Mrs Robinson can be of help if you need it.

I love you as ever − kisses to you and Will,

Your Chad

I sent this letter to Charlottetown, using the horse relay postal system of the island. Lucy and I had never been apart a night since we had come together almost two years ago. Now after only one night I longed for her. And if the 'project' came to fruition, she would be at Ocean House sooner or later. But McNulty and I were on a job. When we went to North Rustico, we would be best to stay at a tavern or guesthouse. Certainly not the fashionable resort that Ocean House was apparently aspiring to be. Perhaps I could sneak in to see Lucy. But I could not stay with her. Besides, I sensed that her friendship with Mrs Robinson was good for her. She and I had been so close that no other people mattered. But other people do matter, in the wide world.

McNulty and I rode west in the late morning, across Stanley Bridge itself, to New London, a cluster of prettily painted houses above a busy little harbour with some surprisingly large cargo schooners, and a long wooden shed − the lobster canning plant. Various small boats were being rowed in and out, with strings of lobster pots attached to their sides or stacks of them in the stern. When I commented on them, McNulty told me they were not called pots here, but traps. More language learning… We crossed another bridge and rode north along the shore of the bay.

The fields were sometimes small and irregular, but many were narrow at the road and stretched back inland for up to a mile. McNulty explained, as we paused to look at the view of the sea from a hilltop, that the log cabins or eventually farmhouses of the first settlements were close together along the road with their lands behind. Some of the original sixty-seven lots of the island had been divided by surveyors into strips extending backwards from the farmhouses. Many of the lots were still owned by absentee landlords in Britain. 'As in Ireland, only worse,' he said. 'At least in Ireland some of the landlords live on their land. The absentee landlords who own these lots here, or own subdivided parts of them, are titled people living in high society in London, and they have never bothered coming here. They just collect the rents.'

Most farms looked prosperous, with grazing cattle or horses, occasionally sheep, and strips of wheat or clover. The farmhouses were often quite large with surrounding porches, the paint on the clapboard of houses and out-buildings was fresh, the gardens neat, the people we saw seemed cheerful – the men in dungarees or overalls, the women in smocks or long skirts, raising their straw hats to us or calling greetings across the fields.

We passed through a hamlet called French River where along what McNulty called the 'creek,' thousands of lupins of all colours were coming into bloom. As if an English garden had escaped into this spacious landscape with its vast sky and small white clouds scudding across it in an increasing breeze as we approached the shore.

We came to the crest of another quite high hill and in front of us to the north across the slope of fields lay the gulf, sapphire blue and seeming to extend to infinity where it blended with the sky. Although there were no high hills or crags or cliffs, I had seldom seen such a dramatic view.

We paused and let the horses drink from a stream, while we sat on a grassy bank eating bread and cheese we had bought at Stanley Bridge, washed down with water from our flasks. Then we continued down towards the shore where the road turned to the west again. We could see the blue of the gulf down on our right above a varying line of low cliff tops and headlands, with occasional dips and glimpses of pink beaches and sand dunes. Occasionally there were sandy laneways leading down through fields and then the dunes. After another hour's ride we came to the laneway to Thunder Cove. McNulty recognised it because the track was a deeper red than the others so far, and the Cove was renowned for the rusty red colour of the cliffs. The sand of the beach would be soft and the horses might have trouble in it, so we tethered them to some small trees where they would have at least a little shade, and continued on foot. I could hear a distant roar of waves. We approached the shore along a lane of pink sand lined with coarse grass – marram grass, McNulty told me – and there were occasional clumps of flowers with white plate-like blossoms. They reminded me of cow-parsley in England, but McNulty said they were Queen Anne's Lace. We came out onto the beach through a gap in a row of sand dunes, themselves covered patchily with tufts of grass.

The waves were dazzling white and foamy, advancing in parallel lines and crashing on the beach. Terns shrieked and plunged into the swell between the waves, seagulls stood in clusters around tidal puddles, and plovers ran here and there along the beach making piping noises. We walked through a stretch of soft powdery sand then came onto the hard tidal sand in front of the waves. The tide was going out, and the sands gleamed wet to our right, the water making them a darker red, as they stretched westwards along the shore to a headland with an unusual sandstone formation – a low cliff with an arch through which the sea pounded sending up clouds of foam. Perhaps over time, the sea had gouged the arch out. The headland was like a crooked finger with its tip in the sea. As we approached the arch the beach was crossed by a narrow creek fanning out in a delta of streamlets onto the sand, and we followed this creek up to our left along a path that meandered parallel to it with stretches of marram grass on each side. After a hundred yards or so we broke out into where the creek spilled out of a huge pond – I would have called it a lake – through a boggy area of reeds. The pond's waters were almost black in spite of the dazzling blue sky.

'This is it,' said McNulty. 'I've heard it called McKay's pond, after a farmer near here, but I don't think the name is used much. People refer to it as the pond behind Thunder Cove, or the Thunder Cove pond.'

The pond was still, except for when birds scudded along the water here and there splashing brief white tracks. The sound of the waves behind us on the shore was no longer a crashing, but a steady calm swishing.

'The baby was not exactly cradled on the waves then,' I said.

'It wouldn't have survived on the sea. I'd like to see that crib, or whatever it was. A tightly woven wicker basket could float safely enough on this pond – for a while.'

It was difficult to walk along the edge of the pond. Our boots squelched in reeds and mud, and I could feel water seeping through the leather. We could see no sign of tracks or marks among the reeds. On the opposite side from where we had come, another path headed off to the west, up into fields.

'This path leads off towards the Darnley Basin and Malpeque Bay,' said McNulty. 'I wonder, Sir, if we are on wild goose chase. All we know about this baby cradled on the waves has come from Harris and from Mr and Mrs Aucoin who are, after all, his employees.'

'Well, there are two other people to talk to. This man MacKinnon in Darnley, and Madame Gallant in North Rustico.'

We retraced our path to the shore and its thundering waves.

Riding west again we came down into Darnley Basin, a tidal estuary and bay with small boats dragged up onto pink muddy sand and attached by long lines to buoys and by anchors to the ground. There were fishermen's huts, and piles of lobster traps. I knew next to nothing about lobster fishing. 'You mean those delicious lobsters come from a muddy place like this?' I asked McNulty.

'Not at all. The traps are put down outside the Basin, along the North Shore where the water is cold and always moving. But this harbour provides shelter for the fishermen. And oysters! You've heard of Malpeque oysters, surely. They are exported all the way to Montreal and to Boston – in season or out.'

A tall ruddy-faced man came to meet us from one of the huts, wearing knee-high rubber boots and leaving deep tracks in the mud. 'Good day!'

'Good day,' I said. 'We're looking for a man called MacKinnon.'

'Calum MacKinnon,' said the man. 'He has a boat shed here, and a croft on the other side of the Basin. He has the school over in Malpeque, but the scholars will be out by now.' He gestured across the brown muddy water to a low peninsula.

'If you go that way and cross the bridge towards Malpeque, then take your first road east, you'll come to the croft.'

We introduced ourselves.

'I'm Duncan Matheson,' said the man. 'A lot of us are Highlanders around here, and we still have the Gaelic. Our neighbours are mostly French. We rub along OK. Some of us are Catholic like them. Not that Calum is. He's a Presbyterian if he's anything. A great man, though a modest one. I can tell you, since he won't himself, that he is a great poet in the Gaelic.'

'A poet? And a crofter. And a schoolteacher. And a lobster fisherman,' said McNulty. 'What does the man *not* do?'

'*Nyee poega ay duh hone,*' the man said – or something like it.

McNulty smiled. '*Guh mannee jeea gitch a hara,*' he said.

The man smiled back, with a slight pout of his lips. 'We'll speak English for the man here,' he said. 'I could tell you must be Irish. And your Gaelic is that of Donegal. As is your accent in English.'

McNulty turned to me. 'What Mr Matheson said to me about Mr MacKinnon when I asked what did he *not* do was: "He won't kiss your

89

arse". I replied with a blessing for Mr Matheson.'

'Well, at least we've got that clear. Mr Matheson, what do you know about this business of the cradle on the waves?'

'I thought you might be looking into that. It was I who found the cradle. I went down past the pond at the crack of dawn towards the shore at Thunder Cove where I was going to dig for clams, then I noticed something in the reeds, and there it was! The wee bairn was whimpering a bit. I tucked the blanket around it tightly, and I carried it in the basket back here. Of course I wondered who might have left the bairn there but I could see no tracks. The ground there is boggy but you can't see it for the reeds. Then I thought of Calum, since he is a man who knows what to do in any sort of a fix, so I walked on to his croft. When he saw the bairn he said in our own tongue, "My God, that must be Mairi's baby. What in the name of God has happened to Mairi?" He then asked me if I could go right away to John Harris's house in Stanley Bridge to deliver a letter by hand about where the wee bairn was. I told Calum I could go since I needed to go to Summerside anyway to buy some netting for my lobster traps. He was in a right state. But since his housemaid was due to arrive shortly, he hoped she could help with the care of the bairn. And after all he has fresh milk from his goats. I left right away to get as fast as I could to Stanley Bridge. When I got there, I first knocked at Harris's house but nobody answered. Then I went to the house next to it. A woman answered the door and she told me she worked for Mr Harris. I gave her the letter, and told her a bairn had been found. I asked her to give the letter to Mr Harris and said it was an urgent matter. I then went on my way to Summerside.

'I heard later a lady from North Rustico came to Calum to collect the bairn. But he'll tell you all this. He never lies. Just go and ask him. He'll only tell you what he wants to tell you, but he'll never lead you false. Just follow the road and take the next road east once you cross the bridge. I can tell you no more. Good Fortune on your way!' He turned back towards his hut, plodding across the mud.

On horseback again, we followed the dirt road around the bay where there were vast areas of shallow water, though separated from the sea by sandbars and low ridges.

'They call this the *barashay*,' said McNulty. 'It's from the French *barachois*, meaning a shallow bay protected from the sea. As you can see Darnley Basin is sheltered, it's also shallow. Hence the oysters.'

We rode past a farm and then across a long wooden bridge where a river emptied into Darnley Basin. A silver metal church spire far ahead across the fields was presumably in Malpeque village, but we turned east along a sandy road, with the river basin on our left and small farms on our right – small because the fields themselves were smaller and not in strips, more of a patchwork, and there were stretches of woodland. The croft was recognisable if only because it was made of stone – as if in Scotland I supposed – beautifully layered pink sandstone which must have been imported at some expense from Nova Scotia. There was a slate roof and a little white-washed chimney. Next to the house were small fields with snake fences, and in one of them goats and kids, and behind the house were woods. There was a clucking sound from a large hen coop. One of the hens must have just laid an egg. The late afternoon sun bathed the land in golden light. A grey rough-haired terrier came barking out at us. A man followed, calling it off as we dismounted and tethered our horses to the snake fence of the goat field. He was middle-sized with energetic movements, a shock of grey hair, a ruddy, tanned face, short grey beard, piercing grey eyes, a questioning expression.

'I am Calum MacKinnon,' he said, shaking hands with first me, then McNulty. 'I can guess where you are from. Charlottetown. Police. I've been expecting you would turn up. Please come in.'

Inside, the house was quite spacious – a large room with an open fireplace in the end wall and at the opposite end another chimney with a cooking range, and a hall corridor down which I could see doors to rooms. In the main room there was a long table, at one end of which were notebooks and papers and an inkwell and pens. The walls between the windows were lined with bookshelves, all full. There were low armchairs around the fireplace. Neither it nor the range were lit. The late afternoon was warm outside, and the room was pleasantly cool.

'I can offer you tea or coffee. Or a dram of whiskey – or all three.'

We chose the coffee. MacKinnon put a pan of water on a hook which swung over the fire, fetched a jar of ground coffee from a shelf, spooned some into a large brown ceramic jug, and poured the boiling water onto it. Then he decanted it through a sieve into three porcelain mugs. We sat in a semi-circle in the armchairs facing the fireplace.

'You'll have questions for me,' he said.

'I'm Chad Hobbes. I'm assisting Mr Frederick Brecken, the Attorney General, in the investigation of the death of Marie Évangéline Harris. This is Sergeant McNulty.'

'I'm pleased you call her *Marie* Évangéline. I think of her name as the Gaelic *Mairi* – or the French *Marie* – they are pronounced almost the same. Évangéline is what her father, Honoré Gallant, calls her. Her mother calls her Marie. Or called her.' He looked at the floor for a moment.

'And she called herself?'

'Marie.'

'You know them well?'

'Well enough. The Gallants used to live near here, in Malpeque. They moved to North Rustico before Mairi was born, so that Mr Gallant could open a new practice. He's a notary – and now a Councilman as you'll know. Malpeque has been losing its French population. There are now more French in North Rustico, and it's closer to Charlottetown. Other French have moved out of here and further west, past Summerside. One of the island's famous sixty-seven lots has been set aside for them. Do you know the island history,

Mr Hobbes? I don't want to tell you things you already know.'

'I'm learning. What you say is useful. And the Scots?'

'I would call us the Gaels. We keep the word "Scot" for Lowlanders. Malpeque was one of the earliest settlements here of Gaels. They too are moving elsewhere, as is natural – the island belongs to us all – but there are still enough of us here to have children going to school in Gaelic, and for us to sing the old songs when we are moved to do so.'

'Leaving history aside, if I may, can you please tell me the story of the baby they are describing as "cradled on the waves"?'

'I can but I won't.'

'Why not?'

'I have reputations to protect. That's all I can say.'

'You sent a telegram to Mr Gallant. You also sent a friend of yours, Mr Matheson, whom we just met in Darnley Basin, to Stanley Bridge with a letter for Mr Harris about the baby. How did you know who the baby was?'

'I won't say.'

'Was there something particular about the cradle that made you think it was Mrs Harris's?'

'I won't say.'

'In the letter, you seemed quite upset at the thought that something could have happened to Marie Harris. Why?'

'I won't say.'

'Mr Matheson told us that you never lie. I find myself wondering if you're choosing to be silent because you cannot lie, and the truth must not come out.'

'More or less, Mr Hobbes. I don't lie, that's true. Because sometimes I am moved to write poetry. And poetry never lies. If it were to lie, it wouldn't be poetry. And if I were ever to lie outside poetry, I wouldn't be a poet – insofar as I am one.' He pronounced the word 'poetry' in a rather old-fashioned English way, as 'poy-etry'. Otherwise his accent was un-English, not Scottish as I would recognise it – I was used to Lowland Scots, I supposed – but rather lilting and sing-song.

'Mr Matheson described to us how he found the cradle with the baby and brought it to you', I said. 'And he said that later it was fetched by a lady from North Rustico.'

'Madame Gallant. I sent a telegram to her husband asking her to come. And also to Mr Harris, but his tenants the Aucoins came. That's all I'll say.'

'But if no one talks to us, we cannot solve the crime. And it's a horrible crime.'

'It is. A crime from hell.'

I fished into my pocket, beside my revolver, and took out the envelope with the rings, opened it, and showed him the ring with the locket.

'Do you know this?' I asked.

'I can't say.' He looked at me with a straight gaze, his jaw slightly clenched I thought.

'What about this?' I sprung the clasp with my fingernail, took out the tiny piece of parchment, unfolded it, and passed it to him. He did not take it. He just looked at me.

'*Mo nighean dubh, mo chroí, mo rún,*' McNulty said quietly from beside me. 'Do you know what that means, Sir?'

'It means "My dark girl, my sweetheart, my beloved".'

'My secret beloved,' McNulty said.

'Not necessarily. But that's one possible meaning.'

'Did you write it?' I said.

'If I did I wouldn't say.'

'Would you mind showing me your handwriting? You must have something with it on your table.'

He got up briskly, moved across to the table, picked up a piece of paper, and gave it to me. It was a poem in Gaelic. It even began with the same two words, *Mo nighean*, but the line went *Mo nighean donn a Cornaig…*

'It's a traditional poem' MacKinnon said. 'From the Isle of Tiree, in Scotland. About a girl who is murdered on the moors. I was thinking about the murder you are investigating, and I got out a book which this poem is in, and I copied it out. It's what I do when I want to get close to a poem. Although God knows why I want to get close to this poem. It kills me.' He clenched his jaw again, and a tear began to trickle down one cheek. He reached into his coat pocket for a handkerchief and wiped the tear off.

The room seemed to fill with a sense of grief. I might have cried myself.

'Can I see the poem?' McNulty asked quietly.

MacKinnon handed him the piece of paper. McNulty sat for a moment reading it. 'The girl's breasts are losing blood,' he said.

'I know,' MacKinnon said. 'That's why the poem reminded me of the woman who was killed.' He seemed to be speaking carefully.

'Were you there when Marie Harris died?' I asked.

'No. I was not,' he said simply.

'You saw her dead?'

'No.'

'Someone told you what state she was in?'

'I was here in this room when the woman from Stanley Bridge, Modeste Aucoin, told Madeleine – Madame Gallant – all about it.'

'You call Madame Gallant "Madeleine"?'

'Not usually.'

'You mean you do when you're alone with her.'

'I know you are a good Peeler, Mr Hobbes, and you are doing your job. But I won't say.'

There was a silence. I did not want to go on questioning him and to get the same answer in the same tone of despair.

'I do think, Sir,' said McNulty to Mr MacKinnon, 'that your handwriting resembles that on the paper from the ring.'

MacKinnon said nothing.

'*Iss shkayul broenach,*' said McNulty softly. 'It's a sad story.'

'*Sha*. It is. But you'll not have it from *me*.' MacKinnon raised his eyes and looked at us steadily.

'Perhaps we'll have it from Madame Gallant,' I said. 'We're going to North Rustico tomorrow.'

'I beg you,' MacKinnon said. 'Don't hurt her. She is almost broken by this.'

'I promise I won't hurt her – not deliberately. But I'll ask her questions which may hurt. I have to. There are dangerous people at large, don't you think?'

'I do. I assume you are armed.'

'We are. Can I change the subject and ask you for some basic information?'

'Of course.'

'You live here alone?'

'At present, yes. I have a maid who comes in. I have two sons, they are aged thirty and thirty-two now. They are in Summerside, in a printing and book business. It's called MacKinnon and MacKinnon, naturally. I brought them up here. We came over here in 1850. The ship sailed directly from Tobermory, on the Isle of Mull where I am from, to Charlottetown – although we had to make a brief stop on Cape Breton at which a hundred or so people got off. They couldn't stand it even for two days more. There were almost four hundred people on that ship when we started from Tobermory. Crowded in the hold most of the way, lying in great wooden bins, like hogs. There was no room for us all on the decks. Fifty or so died of this or that fever. One was my wife, Sheila. That's spelled S-í-l-e. Síle. I don't like the English spelling. The fever got her. She was buried at sea – as were many others – pitched over the stern with a few prayers, wrapped in a sheet with a weight. I arrived in Charlottetown with my two bairns. We came here, and I brought them up. I have had women in my life. If I don't tell you that, someone else will. But never one living with me here.'

'Do you have a private relationship with Madame Gallant?' I had to ask this.

'Mr Hobbes, you are back to your old subject. And I will go back to saying nothing. But use your reason. I would not make a private relationship public. And Madame Gallant left Malpeque for North Rustico soon after I arrived to live here. Now you will ask, "What was she doing here last week?" Again, use your reason. I sent her husband Mr Gallant a telegram, and she came here to collect her grandchild. Now we are back to the cradle on the waves. And I'll say no more.'

'All right. But if you say nothing, I will say something. From a position of relative ignorance, of course. But it's not simply a coincidence that the baby in her cradle turned up in a pond not far from here – but miles away from where she was born which was where her mother was murdered. Someone brought the baby to the pond. It may have been her mother, Marie, before she was killed. We discovered she had salt in her hair when she died, and she knew how to sail a boat. Her voyage must have been in secret – otherwise, why make it? And there is some sort of connection between her and you, or between her mother and you, or among all three of you. She was wearing a ring with a line of Gaelic in it, in what looks like your handwriting, which may have been addressed to her, or to her mother. But I respect your delicacy. You want to protect reputations.'

'As I said. And I'll not say whose.'

'Mr MacKinnon, I take it you are not going on any travels?'

'No. I trap lobsters during the season which is now. And I have a croft to look after. I'll be here.'

'I'm fairly sure I'll be back here after I've spoken with Madame Gallant.'

'It could be so. You will be welcome.'

'One more thing,' I said, standing up. 'Are *you* armed?'

'You may be sure I am.'

98

7

We left the croft and rode into Malpeque where we found a tavern to stay in. We dined there on oysters, served on beds of ice, again with French white wine although not so good as Macon, drawn from a barrel into jugs which were placed in bowls of ice. And of course we had potatoes again, referred to by the landlady as *pommes de terre*, but by the serving maid as *pataques*. I was enjoying these evenings with McNulty. We did not get drunk, but we were definitely more at ease in spite of the horrors of our findings, and talkative.

'That poem is relevant,' said McNulty, taking it out of the pocket where he had kept it after MacKinnon had handed it to him. 'In English it's something like:

My brown-haired girl from Cornaig,
you were golden and beautiful,
my brown-haired girl from Cornaig.

It was an evil tale I heard
on Monday after Sunday …

… your hair was trailing down your body,
and your finely woven shirt in shreds,
and your smooth white breasts
spouting blood together.

'Cornaig must be somewhere in Scotland,' McNulty went on. 'Gaelic Scotland. I take MacKinnon's point there, he is a Gael, not a Scot. But the gruesome death of Évangéline – whom he calls Mairi – reminds him of it. The brown-haired woman. And his handwriting here in transcribing the poem is definitely the same as the handwriting on the parchment in the ring. So he knew Évangéline.'

'Let's call her Marie. Only Mr Harris so far calls her Évangéline. But how did MacKinnon know her? If she is his *nighean*, she is his "girl" in either sense of the word as you have explained it. Is she his beloved mate or his daughter? Unless he has had a recent love relation with her, she is his daughter. If not, and he did have a love relation with her, can he be the father of the baby who Harris thinks may not be his? It doesn't seem possible. The baby is apparently dark-skinned.'

'Marie's hair is not black,' said McNulty. 'I wonder is Madame Gallant's? If so we have the mother of his daughter, and his inscription in the ring is to the mother.'

'The hair is not enough evidence, given as you said that the word *dubh* means dark as well as black. And why does the supposed daughter have the ring? I've been thinking along the same lines. But as I said to MacKinnon, all I know is there is a connection between the three of them: MacKinnon, Marie, and Marie's mother.'

I realised that in my heart and my guts, so to speak, I was angry. McNulty and I were polite with each other. Not so much like policemen as two university professors discussing points of scholarship. But I realised that I wanted, badly, to discover who had killed this girl and to see him or them hang. I would stand beneath the gallows and grimly rejoice. But behind any murder there is often a whole net of evil – not just the evil of the perpetrator. I had learned this on Vancouver Island. Behind each evil act there is a play of evil relations and deception – a play of social forces as well as personal ones. What was going on in pastoral Prince Edward Island to allow such an atrocity? Were people what they seemed? I had a sense that no one was telling all they knew. At least MacKinnon was forthright about his refusal to speak. How about the Aucoins? How about Harris? What more did they know than they were saying?

The next morning, we rode back the way we had come, to New London and Stanley Bridge where we paused for an early lunch at the tavern where we had eaten lobster. Lunch consisted of lobster sandwiches made with freshly baked bread. Then we rode eastward along the North Shore road, with sand dunes and glimpses of the sea on our left, and fields on our right, until in early afternoon we arrived at North Rustico. It was an attractive harbour with boat sheds and jetties along the shore, facing a bay with an outlet made narrow by a sandbar, something like New London Spit, only with a narrower gap. This helped the bay stay calm, although McNulty said that just around the corner from the entrance to the bay was a stretch of wild ocean along the North Shore – something like at Thunder Cove, but golden pink rather than rusty red. Ocean House took advantage of the scene – a huge and brand-new three storey wooden building on a hill overlooking behind it the wild North Shore in the distance, and in front an inlet of the peaceful harbour. We stopped there and I strolled into its luxurious wood-panelled vestibule – all carpets and armchairs and sofas – and asked if a party under the name of Robinson had arrived. I was told the party was expected shortly, this evening – two families by the names of Robinson and Hobbes. I beat a retreat and McNulty and I sought out and found a modest tavern to stay in, the Seagull, further back into the bay near a cluster of boat sheds.

The town had only two or three streets, lined with widely spaced wooden houses, some of them shops with display windows, others offices – insurance, two doctors, a builder. The names were about half and half English (usually meaning Scottish or Irish) and French. For its small size it was busy. There were quite a few tourists who seemed to be

American – more flashily dressed and prosperous compared to others who looked more like Islanders out for the day. Here and there were placards advertising boat trips or 'surf bathing'.

We found a small detached house with a sign saying 'Honoré Gallant, *Notaire* - Notary', and I rang a bell pull. A young man greeted us in French, then finding we did not understand him he switched to English. I explained that we were from the police and would like to speak to Mr Gallant. We were asked to wait until his current appointment was over. After a while two men came out of a room at the back. One of them was Edgar Aucoin, looking as rough as ever. The other was a stout, dark-haired man dressed in black – in mourning. Although he had discarded his jacket in the heat, he wore a black waistcoat. McNulty and I had discarded our waistcoats at the tavern, and were wearing cotton jackets with canvas shirts and trousers. I was hot.

Aucoin passed us by without even a nod and left the house. We were now facing Mr Gallant. I explained who we were and he showed no surprise, ushering us into his office, a large room with book shelves full of leather tomes, a long table with the usual green leather top, and leather chairs.

He indicated chairs on opposite sides of the table and after we had sat down, he sat at the table end. He fixed us each in turn with hard black eyes.

'We are here about your daughter,' I said.

'You are intruding on our grief,' he said sharply. 'This is a family affair and nobody's business but ours.'

This annoyed me. Perhaps it was the long ride in the sun. 'Mr Gallant,' I said, 'You have legal training and you know that is not a tenable position. And we both know that even though you are an eminent man on this island, and a Councilman, you are bound to answer my questions. I am an officer of the law which we both uphold.'

I noticed beads of sweat on his forehead. He changed his tone. 'We are all going mad with this affair,' he said. 'It's inexplicable. Why would anyone murder an innocent girl like my daughter, a few days after she gave birth? The world has gone mad. Mr Aucoin, as you have seen, has been here. He said you and your colleague – he glanced sourly at McNulty – had been offensive in your questioning at Stanley Bridge, and rude and abrupt with him and his wife. And my dear friend Mr Harris has been here and told me you were absolutely relentless in your questioning. What gives you the authority to behave like this?'

'Our office, Mr Gallant. The fact that we are working under the instructions of Mr Frederick Brecken, the Attorney General of this island. And in any case, I deny that either I or my colleague Sergeant McNulty were in any sense rude to anyone at Stanley Bridge.'

'Mr Brecken's position hangs in the balance, Mr Hobbes. In a year or two at most he might not be in government and we will be part of Canada. I don't know where *you* will be. You have blown in from afar, and no doubt you will blow away.'

'You never know. I find I like it here. And I doubt if Mr McNulty will blow away easily either.'

'Mr McNulty is hanging by a thread, believe me.' He scowled at McNulty who was looking as meek as the seminarian he had once been.

'Who killed your daughter, Mr Gallant?' I asked.

'If I knew, I would kill *him*.'

But this was just bluster, and he must have known it, so he changed tack. 'I will answer your questions,' he said, 'within reason.'

'Who killed your daughter?'

'I don't know.'

'Who might have wanted to?'

'I don't know.'

'You have no theory?'

103

'No.'

'Are you taking any steps to find out?'

'That's your job. Do it, and leave us to our grief.'

'Where were you on the night she was killed?'

'At my office in Summerside. I also have offices here in North Rustico, in Charlottetown, and in Georgetown.'

'Where was your wife?'

'At home, here in North Rustico.'

'Do you have homes in all the places you have offices?'

'Of course not. Only in North Rustico and in Charlottetown.'

'Where is your wife now?'

'At our home here.'

'With the baby – your granddaughter?'

'Yes.'

'We'll need to talk to her.'

'You won't talk to her. She's exhausted. She will see no one.'

'Mr Gallant, we shall go – now – to see her.' I stood up, and so did McNulty.

'You can't,' Gallant said. 'She is under guard.'

'What?'

'Mr Aucoin and his man, Mr Cormier, are looking after her and the baby – to prevent intrusion.'

'Mr Gallant, we are the police.'

'You cannot enter the house without a warrant.'

'Actually we can, under Common Law, if we suspect a crime.'

'You can't enter on account of a crime at Stanley Bridge two weeks ago. What new crime do you suspect?'

'From what you say there is a possibility of forced confinement.' Here I was improvising. 'Unless I hear from Madame Gallant's own mouth that she is not being confined, I will break the door down.'

I had made a mistake. Glancing at McNulty I could see his face was like a stone.

'Well then,' said Gallant. 'I will accompany you there and my wife will tell you through the window or door that she is not being confined. Then you will kindly leave us alone.' He got up briskly and indicated the door.

We walked out of the building in front of him. He stepped in front of us and led the way along the main street, one side of which was open to the wharves and the sea, and then he turned inland along a road with a few large wooden houses. We walked silently for a hundred yards or so. The last house on the road was immense, with a large garden, and maples and limes for shade. The house was faced with grey clapboard, and had the usual surrounding porch. We stamped up the steps and faced the door. I expected Gallant to open it, but he knocked. The door did not open, but a downstairs window did. Aucoin looked out at us.

Gallant spoke to him in French. I interrupted. 'In English please.'

'*Mr* Aucoin,' Gallant said, as if imitating me. '*Would* you please be inclined to ask Madame Gallant to come to the window and assure the policemen here that she is a free woman and not forcibly confined in her own house?'

Aucoin disappeared. We waited several minutes. A woman came to the window. A surprisingly beautiful woman with thick black hair pulled up in a bun, a suntanned golden face and, in contrast, violet blue eyes. She was wearing a black silk blouse with a clasp of black wood, perhaps ebony, in the shape of a flower, at the neck. She was expressionless. But her pupils were dilated with anxiety – as it was possible to see in those blue eyes.

'Madame Gallant,' I said. 'Please forgive this intrusion. I am Chad Hobbes from the Charlottetown Police, and this is Sergeant McNulty. May we come in and talk to you?'

She stared back. 'I would prefer not' she said quietly and slowly. 'The baby is asleep.'

'Would you be free to step outside for a minute and have a word with us?'

'I would prefer not.'

'Are you free to do so?'

'Of course I am,' she said quietly.

I felt defeated. 'Is the baby well?' I asked.

'No. She is dying. She won't feed.' The woman began to cry. Her shoulders were shaking. She wiped her eyes.

I turned to Gallant, standing beside me. I looked for emotion in his face but saw none.

'I think you have to let us in,' I said to him.

'Yes. I see. But there is a mortally ill baby in this house. And our daughter's body is at the undertakers in the village. There will be a funeral tomorrow. We don't want it to be the funeral of two people – a mother and her baby. We don't have time for your investigations.'

'We are officers of the peace, Mr Gallant, and we shall keep the peace, I assure you.'

'Yes.'

'Madame Gallant had been listening to this. She said, 'You can come in', and stepped back into the room.

The door was opened by another woman – Modeste Aucoin. She too was wearing a black dress, but with a white apron. Madame Gallant was standing behind her, and Mrs Aucoin stood aside.

What a beautiful woman Madame Gallant was! Younger than I had expected, not much more than forty or so. There were a few grey flecks in her hair. She was slim, and elegantly dressed in her black mourning silk. As she looked directly at me I could see anxiety and exhaustion.

'I can talk to you, Mr Hobbes,' she said. 'With my husband. Not your colleague. He is welcome to sit in a separate room, but I could not sustain a general discussion.'

'Of course.' I glanced at Gallant who now had a resigned look. 'That will be acceptable,' he said.

McNulty said he would wait outside.

Madame Gallant led the way through a large reception room into a small sitting room with tall windows that were open directly to the lawn: the porch did not extend that far along the back of the house. She sat down in a sofa and Mr Gallant sat next to her, close but not touching, and there had been no sign of affection between them. I sat in an armchair facing them.

'I am concerned with what you say about the baby,' I said to Madame Gallant. 'I suppose she has been seen by a doctor.'

'Dr Arsenault. He is very concerned. The baby is not feeding well. She is now almost three weeks old and losing weight. She cries weakly. We have tried gruel and warm milk. Sometimes she takes this food, sometimes not. We do succeed in pouring a little water down her throat. She needs a wet nurse, but this is only a village and there are no women who are nursing their own babies and at the same time clean. One village woman has tried to nurse our baby but the baby rejected her. Dr Arsenault has now made enquiries in Charlottetown, but he doubts if the baby will be able, at this stage, to feed – to "latch on", I believe is the term in English. He predicts that she will fade away in a few days. It's heartbreaking. I hold her and carry her on me, and wipe her lips with a damp cloth, and this calms her at times. She is now asleep, with my housemaid, Liliane, sitting watching her. Modeste also has been helping me day and night.'

Mr Gallant had said nothing and showed no signs of wanting to speak.

'Madame Gallant,' I said. 'Why the protection against intrusion, as Mr Gallant has described it. Are you afraid?'

'After what happened to my daughter, Yes! Mr Harris has now sent Mr Aucoin to watch over us. He arrived yesterday.'

'And before that? Were you not afraid before yesterday?'

'We were too shocked by events to be afraid for ourselves, and then there was the worry about the baby.'

'Madame Gallant, I must ask you about the discovery of the baby. I understand you went to Darnley to bring the baby back here with you. How did this occur?'

'Mr MacKinnon sent us a message – I mean addressed to my husband – saying the baby had been discovered. I went there immediately, by wagon. The Aucoins were already there, having been informed by Mr Matheson, a friend of Mr MacKinnon. They had also sent me a telegram when they arrived in Malpeque but I was already on my way to Darnley by then.'

'Did you go on your own?'

'No. I brought Liliane with me.'

'Could I speak with her if I have questions for her?'

'Yes, but she doesn't speak English. Do you speak French?'

'Only a few words I'm afraid. You know Mr MacKinnon?'

'Not very well, but we knew him when he first came to Malpeque – poor man, just widowed with two boys. He did so well! We and others in the village, in particular his fellow Gaels, helped him with the boys, but he was soon independent. He started a Gaelic school.'

If in front of her husband she was covering a relationship, even a friendship, with MacKinnon, I would help her with silence.

'What's the baby's name?' I asked.

'She has no name.'

There was a silence.

'I have already spoken with Mr MacKinnon,' I said. 'We were in Darnley yesterday.'

'What did he say about the discovery of the baby?' Mr Gallant interrupted.

I felt stumped. I did not want to get MacKinnon into trouble by describing his refusal to answer questions – similar to the refusal of the Gallants, for that matter.

'He and a friend, a Mr Matheson, have lobster traps out that way.

The friend found the baby in her cradle floating in the pond, rescued her and brought her to Mr MacKinnon. Then Mr MacKinnon got in touch with you and with Mr Harris.'

'Why?' Mr Gallant interrupted. 'How did they know whose baby it was?'

'I must admit I didn't ask Mr MacKinnon,' I said, improvising. 'I am not from the island but I know news travels quickly. It will have been known all along the North Shore that your daughter Évangéline had just given birth to a baby girl.'

I was using my imagination here, but it seemed to work.

'That's what Mr MacKinnon told me,' said Madame Gallant quickly. 'He couldn't think of anyone else whose baby she might be.'

There was a pause.

'One thing,' Mr Gallant said suddenly, as if waking from his sullen silence. 'It is causing us embarrassment, and you will hear of it sooner than later. No!' He raised his hand to stop his wife from objecting. 'Mr Hobbes will have to know this, painful as it is.' Then turning back to me: 'The child has an unusual feature. A purple spot in the small of its back – about the size of the palm of a hand. The rest of the skin is normal – pale because the child is now ill. But there is this spot. My wife was present at the birth, as you know. In fact she assisted as midwife – as she has done in births here, working with Dr Arsenault – which is one reason we know he is a competent doctor. At Stanley Bridge there was Dr Kelly.' He paused. 'A rough sort of man. Formerly in the British army. He pointed out the spot right away…' Again he paused, as if lost for words.

Madame Gallant spoke. 'We know this kind of spot,' she said. 'Occasionally babies are born with it. It fades and goes away in a few years. But on this island it is known widely to occur from time to time among the Mic Mac. In fact it may also occur among us Acadians, since we intermarried with the Mic Mac in the last century. I explained that to John Harris and he was reassured.'

There was a silence.

'However,' Gallant said. 'It seems the possibility has been raised that Mr Harris is not the father. Mr Harris is my friend and colleague. He's an honourable man. He must be very upset.' Gallant paused.

'My husband is being very tactful,' said Madame Gallant. 'In fact Dr Kelly came down the stairs from the bedroom and announced – I heard him through the open bedroom door – to John – Mr Harris: "Your wife has had a daughter. But she's an Injun."'

'There was no need to tell Mr Hobbes that,' said Gallant in a cold voice, turning to his wife.

'You raised the subject. And as you said, Mr Hobbes will know sooner or later.' Her voice was equally cold.

'If nothing else,' Gallant said, now in an angry voice, 'because Mr Harris will be suspected of killing his wife – our daughter – on account of her apparent adultery with an Indian. I know you may conjecture that our ancestors intermarried with the Mic Mac, but most of them did not. *We* are pure French *de souche* – "in origin" – we would say. You see what a disaster this is?' He was addressing both his wife and me. 'This honourable man, this friend of ours, this eminent member of our government, may be accused of a horrible crime – the murder, in a jealous fury, of his wife, the daughter of his closest colleague, myself!'

'Please!' I interrupted. 'As you must know, Mr Harris was in Charlottetown on the night of the murder, in the company of others who have confirmed his presence there. Yes, the possibility he was somehow linked with the murder is under consideration – along with other considerations. It has to be. You will have to trust me and my colleagues to discover the truth.'

'You are not even from this island!' Mr Gallant said angrily.

'Think of it the other way around,' I said. 'I'm not from this island and I have no prejudices. Everything I learn is new. I can conduct a forensic investigation and remain objective.' Or so I hoped. 'This is why Mr Brecken has employed me. I have no axe to grind here.'

'Then find the murderer!' Gallant almost shouted.

I could see a quality of the bully in the man, as I had in Harris. Was this what politicians were like? I had met almost none in my life. Politics bored me. I was uncomfortable with it. But I realised I was not uncomfortable with murder. I was coming to understand it. I *wanted* to understand it.

'I shall find the murderer,' I said. 'But now I'm most worried about the child. Your daughter's child. Your grandchild – no matter who the father was.' I turned to Madame Gallant. 'My wife is arriving in North Rustico this evening, with her friend Mrs Robinson, the Governor's wife, to stay at the Ocean House. She's called Lucy. She's from British Columbia, and she grew up in a native tribe where nursing children was practised for the first several years of life. She is nursing our son now. You must as a woman and a midwife know a lot about nursing. But could I ask my wife, Lucy, to visit you tomorrow morning? Perhaps this is grasping at straws. She is certainly not a doctor. But she is closer to nature than many of us are. Who knows, she may be able to offer advice about the baby. Would you accept this?'

'Yes, readily,' Madame Gallant said. 'We are at the end of our tether. Tomorrow afternoon will be the funeral of Marie, and I don't know how we'll be able to endure it. But the baby comes first. I don't want to lose this child…' She gave in to a sob and wiped her eyes with the back of her hand.

'You mean your wife is an Indian?' Gallant said.

'Yes, from the Tsimshian tribe, north of Vancouver Island.'

'Is she well educated?'

I suppressed the urge to reply that this was none of his business.

'She is extremely well educated,' I said – a white lie, considering that I myself had been the main source of her education in the ways of the civilisation which produced men like Gallant and Harris and, God knows, I-Guess...

'I hope she can help,' said Gallant abruptly.

I had no clear sense of this man. No more than with his friend Harris. I felt slightly guilty at having dropped the name of Mrs Robinson but, as I had hoped, it may have helped in introducing the possibility of Lucy talking with Madame Gallant.

I stood up, and Gallant stood up too. He escorted me to the door. I went out into the low golden sunshine and the soft air which seemed to accompany the approaching sunset. McNulty was waiting for me in the street. We walked into North Rustico.

8

Before dinner I walked from the tavern to the Ocean House, and asked for Lucy. She had arrived. A boy in uniform went to fetch her. I waited standing in the lobby. She appeared, coming down the stairs, carrying Will in her arms then setting him down on the carpet so that he could toddle towards me. I picked him up and kissed him, then put him down again. Lucy was lovely in a new summer dress of peach-coloured cotton and muslin, with a filmy white shawl. Her hair was pinned up elegantly. We embraced and I held her against me for an instant.

We sat on a sofa, with Will between us. Lucy explained that she and Olivia, with Olivia's three children and her maid from Government House were occupying four rooms on the first floor up. She was excited by the sea air and the beauty of the place, and she was learning a lot from Olivia: they were telling each other all about their lives.

I explained about Marie Harris's baby, without background details, simply the bare bones of the situation.

'Of course I'll go there tomorrow morning,' Lucy said. 'I'll ask Olivia to come as well. We can leave the children for an hour or so with Olivia's maid and one of the maids from the hotel. There is a huge sandpit for them to play in, down the lawn at the edge of the sandhills. That poor woman! The murdered woman of course, but I am thinking of the woman's mother, Mrs Gallant. She must be distraught. Among our people, she would start to give the baby her own breast. There would be no milk at first, but after a day or two it would come – at least some, and the baby would benefit from the sucking, if nothing else. I can offer suck too. You know the way it is with Will. I have to keep him to one breast at a time, otherwise I will become what the midwives call "engorged" with too much milk.'

'But here it's like Victoria. It's Puritan.'

Lucy knew what 'Puritan' meant, from many angles. We had often discussed the 'Puritanism' of the people she had suddenly found herself among two years ago – us British and Europeans. We were not much less bloodthirsty and violent than her own people, but we were more 'Puritan.'

'I understand,' she said. 'It's all a question of how Mrs Gallant, or *Madame*, as you call her, sees the situation.'

Lucy knew no more French than I did. As for myself I was annoyed at not knowing more. Here I was, capable of speaking elementary Tsimshian, the West Coast trade language called Chinook, classical Latin, and some ancient Greek – but no other modern European language than my own.

We said goodbye. I was longing to make love to her, as we often did, just like that, at any time of day. But this was not the time!

I walked back to the tavern, my mind clogged with thought. I had been evasive with Madame Gallant in front of her husband about why MacKinnon had decided to send a message to her, via her husband, and she had joined me in a moment of evasiveness or obfuscation. We were not exactly lying, but almost. The man Duncan Matheson had said that MacKinnon did not lie, and MacKinnon had confirmed this in his statement that poets must not lie. Did I have such integrity? I hoped so. Lucy could not lie. We never lied to each other, our love was based on a foundation of truth. But in the accounts of Harris, of Mr and Mrs Aucoin, and now of Honoré Gallant, I had sensed evasiveness, obfuscation, bluster. Perhaps occasionally a person who is usually committed to the truth – Madame Gallant, I thought, and myself – will slip into a lie or half-lie. But are there some people in the world who are so used to lying that they lie all the time, without remorse, without even noticing it, to the point that they believe their own lies?

Again McNulty and I dined together. As was now our custom, we ate fish and potatoes and drank chilled white wine. The fish was baked mackerel. I did not even ask what kind of wine we were drinking this time. There was too much to discuss. We had a table outside again, looking across a lawn to a line of trees and a creek. I summed up the conversation at the Gallants' house. We decided, once more, to 'take stock'.

One: the purple spot on the baby's back. McNulty had heard of this, and that it was associated with native Indians, and with Chinese people. He said he had heard it called 'the Mongolian spot'. He had not heard of it occurring in Europeans. But he said he admired Madame Gallant's ingenious reasoning that since the Acadians had intermarried with the Mic Mac the spot was at least a possibility in a child of Marie. We had a tangential discussion about eye colour and heredity. I had read some essays by Darwin's cousin Galton about heredity, and I knew Darwin's theory of 'gemmules,' tiny particles transmitted across generations of plants and animals and somehow carrying traits – such as colour and shape – with them. But Galton worked with abstract statistics, and Darwin's gemmules could not be consistently identified under the microscope, although a man called Brown had claimed to identify something like them. If there were laws of heredity, they were not clear. Even the laws of eye colour were in dispute. It was generally agreed that two blue eyed parents could not have a brown eyed child, but there had eventually turned out to be exceptions to most of the rules that investigators, now called 'scientists', proposed. Even in our supposedly Christian society there might turn out to be, as they say, a cuckoo in the nest – a real father who is not the woman's husband. What colour were the baby's eyes, given that the dead girl Marie and her husband Harris both had blue eyes? But babies' eyes remained bluish for months after birth. Anyway, the purple spot on the lower back strongly suggested that the baby's father might be an Indian – on this island a Mic Mac. Where did the Mic Mac live? According to McNulty, mainly to the north west of the island, on a smaller island not too far from Malpeque where they sometimes came by boat to sell their wares. Some had drifted into Charlottetown where they lived on the streets begging for drink money, or in shacks along the harbour. Probably the baby was not Harris's. But who on earth could be the father? And if he was a Mic Mac, how could that be?

Two: Harris must have been distressed, to put it kindly, at thinking the child was not his. This might provide a motive for a murderous rage or for a more calculated sort of murder. How could we find out more about his movements on the day Marie was murdered? The people around him were either loyal to him or afraid of him. They were certainly paid by him. Who could tell us more about that day? Nevertheless, Harris had definitely dined in Charlottetown on the evening of the 30th of June.

Three: Harris and Gallant were thick as thieves. Or at least they propped each other up in politics. Each needed the other. Who was the dominant partner? We did not know enough about either of them. What had their early lives been like? What drove their partnership? McNulty said he would ask his colleagues in Charlottetown to investigate their histories, but he was not hopeful, given that the official histories, as it were, were already public, and people would be reluctant to report any secrets. We debated how much we needed help from our police colleagues, constables whom McNulty described as having varied abilities. I decided to ask McNulty to select two of the best constables from Charlottetown and send them to Rustico for the next day. They could keep a protective eye on the Gallants and at the same time on Lucy and her new friend Olivia Robinson.

Four: although Harris and Gallant propped each other up politically, I had felt a sense of unease at one moment in my questioning of Gallant when he discussed Harris's possible concern about the purple spot and what it implied. It had seemed to me that Gallant was at least hinting that Harris had reason to be very angry with Marie. How far was it from this anger to acting on it with violence towards her?

Five: whether the baby lived or died probably made no difference in our investigation of the murder. But it might determine how people behaved, and whether they would lose control of their emotions. Above all we had a moral duty to stand up for the baby's interests – Harris's child, or half Mic Mac or not.

Six: we must find the baby's father, if it was not Harris. Starting with another trip to Stanley Bridge and the Malpeque area, to ask questions about Mic Mac Indians in those areas, before going further. McNulty said there were only three or four hundred Mic Mac left. They were quite respected, but they kept to their own settlements – part camps, part villages. As a rule, they did not intermarry with English speaking Islanders, but occasionally they did with French. As Madame Gallant had said, they certainly had done so in the past when most of them were converted to Catholicism by French priests. In all early European colonies there had been a surplus of men, and many of them had married native women – to the displeasure of the native men, of course. McNulty said that in all Acadian areas – on Prince Edward Island, in Nova Scotia, and in New Brunswick – part of the Mic Mac population had been absorbed into the Acadian population. But in spite of this relative acceptance of the Mic Mac among the French, for a French girl of high standing like Marie to marry a Mic Mac man would be scandalous. The parents would prevent it.

Seven: what had gone on between Madame Gallant and Calum MacKinnon? If Lucy came to know Madame Gallant, would the truth begin to emerge? But I knew that if Madame Gallant confided in Lucy, Lucy would not break the confidence, even to me – unless, I supposed, if Madame Gallant's life was in danger.

We made decisions – to be confirmed in the light of day, with next morning's breakfast and coffee.

Much as I hated to leave Lucy and Will again, I would head

on my own to the north west. I would go first to MacKinnon. He might know something about Marie's acquaintances among the Mic Mac. Perhaps he would reveal more, now that he knew I had spoken with Madame Gallant. I would find out in Malpeque, either from MacKinnon or other people, more about the history of the Gallants when they lived there some twenty years ago. I would also go further around Malpeque Bay to Lennox Island, the main Mic Mac settlement, and learn more about them. And while I was away from North Rustico for a few days, Lucy would have time to establish a relationship with Madame Gallant and to help the baby survive, or so I hoped.

McNulty would go to Charlottetown and find out more about the Aucoins from acquaintances who had known them well since their arrival on the island. He would also get two constables to come to North Rustico and settle them on guard. Perhaps the Aucoins would return to Stanley Bridge. In any event McNulty would go back to there and question more people about any observations they might have made around the time of Marie's death.

The next morning, a Friday, we confirmed the decisions. I wrote a note to Lucy and sent it to the hotel. Then I rode west along the North Shore again. I enjoyed riding on my own across the lovely island landscape with occasional rising stretches where the sea of the Gulf could be seen over the sand dunes. I stopped from time to time to admire the views. It was sunny at intervals but every now and then there was a heavy shower. I kept going, got drenched, and dried out again. It took most of the day, with a stop at New London for an early lunch, before I arrived at MacKinnon's croft at Darnley in the mid afternoon. I found him in the goat field, mucking it out. He was shovelling patches of black dung pellets into a wheelbarrow.

'Shovelling shite,' he said to me cheerfully, as I tied the horse to the railing. 'You'll find a bucket near the well to water your poor old horse.'

I found the bucket, pumped the handle of the well pump, iron neatly painted green, brought the bucket over to the horse, a grey mare, and held it under her neck so that she could drink.

MacKinnon literally vaulted over the snake fence – what a fit man he was for his age! – and came to meet me, holding out his hand.

'Not with your Gaelic speaker this time,' he said. 'Have you been to North Rustico?' His eyes looked keen. He really did want to know. About what? I could guess.

The sun was still warm and he gestured to two white wooden chairs in the shade of the house. Each had a folding footrest. We settled ourselves, both with our feet extended. He waited for me to speak.

'I'll tell you about North Rustico.' And so I did. The whole story of the visit, from the time we arrived at Gallant's office, to my conversation with Lucy and her planned visit. But I omitted the item by item discussion with McNulty.

MacKinnon listened attentively, without comment. We sat silently for a minute.

'You'll be wanting to know about my relation with Madeleine,' he said.

'Yes, that was a slip of yours last time I was here. We had been talking about her as Madame Gallant.'

'Very gallant of you. Sorry – poor joke. But isn't it typical that in this society that we live in, a woman's name gets sucked into that of her husband?'

'Is it different anywhere – I mean anywhere European? My own wife is a Tsimshian from British Columbia and she has always had her own name, nothing to do with her family, although of course now people call her Mrs Hobbes.'

'You have talked about her as Lucy. What is her original name?'

'Lukswaas. It means a sudden shower of rain.'

'Lovely! And Lucy from Lukswaas makes sense. Ah well, Madeleine would have been Magdalen once. Just as Marie would have been Mary or whatever it was in Aramaic. Actually Madeleine is Marie Madeleine. The Acadians always have the first name Marie if they are women, and Joseph if they are men. Honoré Gallant is really Joseph Honoré, for example. Hobbes! I can drop the Mr, can't I? Hobbes. What you say about Madeleine distresses me. I love her dearly. You have guessed that. She loves me too. Have you guessed that?'

'Half-guessed. It's clear enough that she doesn't love her husband.'

'She never has. Do you want a long account or a short one?'

'A long one please. There is less chance of your censoring it.'

'But I *should* censor it. A gentleman does not reveal that he has a relation with a married woman. And certainly not to a Peeler! But I am not exactly a gentleman. Nor are you exactly a Peeler. Although you are clearly a gentleman. *Duine uasal* as we say in Gaelic. It means a noble person. But *uasal* comes from the French word *vassal*. What I find difficult about gentlemen is that they are vassals, servants, of other gentlemen. They are in a pecking order. They report up the line, but not down. Who do you report to?'

I described to him briefly my mission, and my exchanges with Brecken and Robinson.

'So what *they* are interested in is the politics. What does it mean for the island if Harris and Gallant fall? I can tell you straight away what no one has bothered to tell you, least of all the two gentlemen you mention, Brecken and Robinson, because they are not admitting they know it. But they will have heard rumours. That couple, Harris and Gallant, that almost married couple – not in the flesh perhaps, but who knows? – will turn! They are in favour of Confederation, and were elected as Liberals on that account. You described them just now in the cliché 'as thick as thieves'. They are indeed thieves. Most of their funding comes from smugglers. Why? Because at a given moment they will turn. They will regretfully vote against Confederation. In a sudden surge of attachment to Old England, perhaps, although Old England cannot wait to get rid of this island. Or a sudden realisation that Canada will make Islanders poorer because this island will have no clout in Canada, as it will provide less than five percent of the population. Harris and Gallant are powerful men. If two out of thirteen Councilmen "turn" in a close vote, it can decide the outcome. But they are bought men. Most people are. Everywhere. Bought and sold.'

He paused, and although what he said struck me as an important part of the story, and perhaps even of the murder, I was not very interested in politics.

'So you are not most people.'

'No. But I was. As I told you the other day, I came over here on an immigrant ship. That was most people. A human mass. Or an animal mass. I was born in the Isle of Mull. You know where it is?'

'One of the islands of the Hebrides.'

'Indeed. A large island. Over a hundred years ago, in 1740 or so, it consisted of crofts – families farming plots of land owned by clan Chiefs who were their kin. You know what the word "clan" means in Gaelic? It means "children"! But after the 1745 rebellion many of the Chiefs were exiled, and those who were not exiled had lost their power. They were no longer Chiefs, they were landlords. And their people, even of the same name, were no longer their children. The Chiefs no longer lived to accept respect and service from their people and in return to protect them. They lived to make money from them. Alongside Lowland landlords who had bought the lands of those chiefs who had gone into exile – bought it cheap. You have heard of the Highland Clearances?'

'A little. Thousands of people displaced by sheep.'

'Hundreds of thousands. Sheep made more money than people. So

121

the people were cleared off their lands. Their cottages were torn down or burned down. Sometimes with the people still inside! They had to burn alive or run out like rats. Then the moors were partitioned for hundreds of miles by stone walls – built by the labour of the evicted people. They were paid a pittance, just enough to keep off famine, to slave away for months building stone walls to keep themselves off their own land! And to keep the sheep in. And there were famines where the potatoes were diseased, and people ate grass and died on the ground. And being Presbyterian they had been taught they were doomed to everlasting Hell! – unless they were among the Elect who were to be saved. Some decided they might be able to resist eternal damnation, and instead of accepting their fate on the off chance that they were among the Elect, they emigrated.

'That's why I call myself a Gael, not a Scot. It was the Lowlanders, the Scots, and their English masters who carried out the Clearances. And since the days of the Pretender, Prince Charles, the English and Scots wanted to extirpate not only the Gaels themselves but what they called the Irish language. It wasn't Irish, it was shared among the Gaels of Ireland and of the so-called Scottish Highlands.

'So we left. I'm saying "we" now because I was one of them. I was born in 1808. I am now sixty-three. My family had been warriors, crofters, fishermen, story-tellers, and some of them poets. I was a poet. The old Gaelic poets were supported by Chiefs, in exchange for praise poems. I would never have been up to making praise poems. But everyone in my family had been up to farming a croft and sailing boats out to the fish! And some of us, being interested in learning and in words, taught in village schools. We taught writing in our language, we taught our history, and practical arithmetic. And we had poetry.' Again he pronounced it 'poyetry'.

'I notice you pronounce the word poetry in a Greek way. Have you studied Greek?'

'When I could, but I never went to university. We were too poor, and I wasn't going to be a minister – what you would call a parson. As it seems you know, "poetry" is from *poien* in Greek, meaning to "make". The Lowland Scots call a poet a *makar*. But we Gaels, in Scotland or Ireland, call the poet either a *file* – a *seer* – or a *bard* which is a "singer". There is music in our poetry and much of it is sung. And we see clearly. At its best, ours is a hard, clear, down-to-earth poetry. At its worst, which is probably now in our great nineteenth century, poetry has become mush. It is uplift, sentiment, high ideals. In English it is "The boy stood on the burning deck" written by someone who was never on a burning deck, or "Come into the garden, Maude" written by someone who doesn't know whether or not Maude has legs underneath her dress. It is the Irish versifier Ferguson's *Lays of the Western Gael* – by a man who knew no Gaelic. It's what the literary people are beginning to call "the Celtic Twilight" – a haze of romance. There is no haze in the real Gaelic poetry. It is clear as day or black as night. No twilight.'

'I grew up in Wiltshire, and some of the songs I would hear from the country people there were down to earth in the extreme – although certainly not poetry. There is one about a fly:

The floi, the floi, the floi be on the turnup,
Bugger Oi if Oi do troi
To keep floi off moi turnup.'

'That's good!' Calum said. 'Even if it's doggerel, it's human. Too much of the formal English of this century is like the horrible architecture we have – so-called Gothic, but it's a flowery imitation of the real medieval Gothic. Modern poetry in English is artificial like the pseudo-Gothic architecture we live with, or the romantic novels of Walter Scott. I've seen engravings of Gothic cathedrals in France and England. They are like our Gaelic poetry. They have *line*. Like one of the few English poets in my library, William Blake. His drawings have line. His poems have line. I send to London and Edinburgh for books. It takes half a year to get them, and then I pay twenty percent duty. I wish I could have brought more with me.'

'I must ask you again about that text in the ring. Is it a poem?'

'I know you must come to it, Hobbes, and I am playing for time to an extent, since these are questions which will cause me difficulty and pain. But let me say first how I came to know Madeleine Gallant – or Madeleine Poirier, as I prefer – her name before she was married to that swine. I have said I arrived in Charlottetown with my two boys. They are called Sorley and Hamish. We were weak from the voyage and the loss of my wife, their mother – Síle. As soon as I had the money I put up a stone to her in the graveyard here. But that was not yet. The boys and I came to Malpeque where there were Gaels who needed a school. There was only a French school. So I set up the Gaelic school. There are some who say Gaelic is a dying tongue. It's true we can't live in the wide world without English. I am now having to teach in English as much as in Gaelic, or no one would send their children to the school. English is the language to get ahead. But Gaelic is not yet dying where I am.

'I rented land for this croft. I now own it. I became a lobster fisherman too. People were welcoming to us. Not only our fellow Gaels, but the Acadians. They sympathised with our persecution, having been persecuted themselves. In 1758, as you may know, there were almost 5,000 Acadians on this island – Île Saint-Jean as it was then. The British deported about three thousand of them, many of them to die on ships, the survivors to settle in the swamps of Louisiana, in the English colonies along the Atlantic, or in France. They were part of many more thousands from New Brunswick and Nova Scotia. Thousands of dead bodies pitched into the sea. The Acadians would understand dead bodies of Highlanders on the moors. They knew little about us, but they knew we had been forced from our homes. They knew from their grand-parents what it was like to eat grass. They are the descendants of the ones who hid in the woods and stayed here, eventually to emerge, and of those who managed to come back. In this atrocious deportation, there was the miracle that Malpeque village was forgotten by some incompetent English officers, and about a hundred Acadians stayed, hiding around there. In 1850 when my sons and I arrived, the main shop in Malpeque was Poirier's *Magasin Général* – the General Store. It sold everything from food to pots and pans and fishing gear. Poirier is dead now, but he was only ten years older than I. His daughter, Madeleine, was aged twenty-one or so and she worked in the family store and was the wife of Honoré Gallant. He was the son of a fisherman who had managed to buy up a number of boats and had other fishermen working for him. The sea is not like the land. Everyone can take from it, and nobody owns it. But the old Gallant owned a lot of the boats. This is what some call commerce. I would call it human sharks taking over the sea.

'But young Honoré had his mind on higher things than boats. He had been well educated at the French school here, until the age of sixteen. The priests who ran the school encouraged him to go away to seminary, to become a priest himself. He went "over across" to Quebec. But after a year or so there he gave up on it. A sulky young man with ambition. Too greedy to be a priest. And not inclined to all that penitence! And later on he came back as a notary. There were no notaries in Malpeque. The nearest were in Summerside, fifteen miles away. He set up on his own. Mr Poirier and Mr Gallant the older talked together. It was decided that Honoré would marry Madeleine. He's a cold fish, and there was not much courting. At any rate this arranged marriage, for that is what it was, was underway when I arrived in Malpeque with my boys. I was a man broken with grief and breaking again with worry. And I was aged forty-two – twice her age. But there was a spark between us. It made no sense at all, but when we looked at each other there was a spark.'

MacKinnon paused. There was sadness in his eyes. 'I think you'll understand,' he went on, 'that I cannot tell you more about my relationship with a married woman. As I told you the other day, there is a reputation to protect.' He sighed, and looked at me.

'For now,' I said, 'it's enough for me to know there was a relationship. At least partly a secret one. A "rune", as I think the paper in the ring says. A secret inscription.'

'No doubt Sergeant McNulty will have explained that. What is a man like that doing in the police?'

'It must be a long story, but I don't know it.'

'Coming from Donegal his Gaelic is close to ours, so he got it right, although the spelling is different.'

'So the poem is to Madame Gallant – Madeleine. And Mairi – Marie Évangéline – was your daughter.'

'If you say so. I won't.'

'And this is why you were copying out the poem about the *nighean donn*.'

'Well, I could have been copying it down on account of hearing about her death.'

'Why was the ring on *her* finger?'

'I suppose her mother gave it to her.'

'And you gave it to her mother.'

'I did. As you pointed out, the inscription is in my handwriting. But as I know you understand, Hobbes, you are not going to hear from my own mouth what my relation with Madeleine was.'

'Or is.'

'Or is.'

'But we can still discuss what happened. You listened carefully to what I've said about my visit to North Rustico. What do you make of it?'

'About the baby with the birthmark? Or not strictly speaking a birthmark, since that purple spot fades away. I know about the purple

126

spot. Some Indians have it. Some Mic Mac children, I believe, although I've never seen it until I saw the baby. I noticed it, that day when Madeleine came to get her.'

He paused and thought for a while. The sun was lower, and there was a robin strutting around on the grass not far from us, stopping from time to time to pull a worm out. The worms were bloody and long, and the robin shook each one for a moment before gobbling it down. Another robin was singing from a tree somewhere. They were like English robins with their red breasts, but five or six times the size, and their song was as piercing as that of a blackbird, although limited and repetitive.

'There's a lot I must tell you,' said MacKinnon finally. 'Will you stay the night here? You are welcome, and there are too many bedrooms in this house for me now.'

'It wouldn't be right, unfortunately,' I said, 'You might be a suspect in the murder.'

'To hell with that!' said MacKinnon, standing up. 'My God, if you don't mind my saying so, you Englishmen can be prim and proper. You know I didn't murder my daughter. Yes, my daughter! Is that enough for you?'

'Yes.' I stood up too.

'It's becoming cool. We'll eat in the house. Lobster and potatoes. Fresh lobster from my traps this morning. Is that all right?'

9

MacKinnon lit some logs in the wood stove and started preparing dinner. He invited me to take a look at his library. Books in French, in English – mainly histories and reference books, a collected Shakespeare, the poems of Blake. No novels. Latin poetry – Catullus – and an anthology of Greek poetry. But most of the books were in Gaelic, some in Irish Gaelic which was recognisable by its different script. Many were of songs or poetry, as I could tell by the shape of the texts on the page. One or two had English translations on facing pages. There were English and Gaelic bibles. And there were two books of poems by MacKinnon himself – or so I realised in reading the name 'Calum Mac Fhionghuin' – both bound in top quality leather with gold leaf titles and what looked like expensive paper. One was called *Orán* and the other *Orán Eile*. Poems and More Poems? They had been published in 1865 and 1870 in Summerside, PEI, by MacKinnon and MacKinnon, his sons.

We sat down at the dinner table. No table-cloth. A jug of water. And, interestingly, a jug of red wine – claret.

'I drink it even with fish,' said MacKinnon. 'I buy it by the barrel from an importer in Charlottetown.'

We had two boiled lobsters each, boiled potatoes, and asparagus – fresh from the garden. The wine went down well. MacKinnon asked questions about Vancouver Island, and showed interest in all aspects of the place, and especially the Indians. We talked again about poetry. He never seemed to be able to keep away from the subject for long. But he said he very seldom wrote it. Only when he felt compelled to. 'It's a rare phenomenon,' he said. 'It comes when it wants to. Often *at* quiet times, but often *about* hard times. And I'm often addressing a woman in it – perhaps what Irish poets call an *aisling* or muse. Many of my poems are about Síle whom I haven't seen alive for twenty-one years. Suddenly something she said or did rushes into my mind in the form of a poem. You know, I have not *lived* with a woman in those twenty-one years. I have had housemaids here, but not living in. And as I said before, I have had women in my life. What can a man do without women? I mean I've had physical relations with a number of widows and young women. I don't feel able to have relations with married women though. I don't want to sleep with another man's wife if he's still sleeping with her. The one woman we have been talking about, Madeleine – she is another one I have been listening to and talking to in my poems. Sometimes when I think of her, I feel like the Gaelic poet William Ross who wrote about a maggot within his body, falling to pieces inside him. He died young of tuberculosis. But I don't think the maggot was tuberculosis. It was a hidden love.

'Thinking of which,' he went on. 'When I saw Madeleine the other day after a long absence, she was looking years older than she is. The horror and the grief! I don't know how we are both going to survive it, but I want us to survive or not survive together, not apart.'

He paused. 'I often wonder what Síle would be like if she were living now – a lady in her mid-fifties. I think of White Duncan MacIntyre, a Gaelic poet before my time, who wrote poems when he was young to the woman he married. Her name was Mairi, in fact. When he and Mairi were about eighty years old, some idiot said to him, "Duncan, your wife Mairi is not as beautiful as the Mairi in your poems." Duncan replied, "She is indeed as beautiful. You are not seeing her through my eyes."'

He got up abruptly and we began clearing the table. 'The wine has been talking,' he said. 'Let's go outside for a stroll.'

The sun was setting. Walking up a laneway across a field to the top of a small hill we could look westwards at the wide expanse of Malpeque Bay and more fields on the other side.

'You see, the Shore is lower as you go west,' MacKinnon said. 'It's flat over there.'

We stood silently for a while as the sun went down. Then in the twilight we descended the hill again. MacKinnon showed me the stable where I could lead my horse which had been grazing contentedly, on its tether, in the grass. In the stable there was a trough of hay, and a number of other horses who snorted in greeting from their stalls. MacKinnon replenished their water, and pitched in some hay from a stack along the wall.

We went back into the house. MacKinnon showed me a small neat bedroom with a bed already made, at the end of the hallway, and I brought in my bag. In the main room MacKinnon had lit some lanterns, and we settled into our armchairs in front of the fireplace. No need for a fire. But MacKinnon went into a larder and came out with two glasses and a bottle which he uncorked. 'Whisky,' he said. 'I distill it myself. There is even peat on this island, up Tignish way. The Irish up there use it in distilling their whisky – which they spell with an "e". *Uisce* just means water, but "Whisky Baugh" is the water of life – Eau de Vie. Your Health!' He stood up, and so did I. We clinked glasses, drank, and sat down. The whiskey was fiery but smooth and smoky.

'What do I think of your story from North Rustico?' he said, anticipating my question.

I suddenly realised that one of his main qualities was politeness.

'I'll start with the purple spot,' he said. 'It suggests who the father of that child is. Can I ask you one thing before I go on?'

'Go ahead.'

'I know I cannot dictate what you do, but I would like to be sure you will think before you act in any of this business. What I'll tell you is quite dangerous.'

'I'm not surprised, having met Harris's men.'

'They are only the half of it.' He laughed. 'In more ways than one. The man you call I-Guess – Cormier – has a twin brother. They can be quite dangerous. I'll get to them later. Anyway, the father of Mairi's child must be a young man called Noel. He's a Mic Mac. "Noel" is apparently a Mic Mac word for ice breaking up on the river. He was born in April, the month of the first thaw. And of course there is a name Noel in French. We call him Lachlan in this family. He must be the only Mic Mac in the world who speaks Gaelic.'

He paused. 'I didn't know he and Mairi had gone that far. I'm trying to remember when they first met. I hardly met Mairi myself. Only when she came back here from time to time with her mother, Madeleine, to visit her grandmother Poirier, Madeleine's ageing mother. Madame Poirier is still alive, just about. Madeleine and Mairi would come without Honoré Gallant. He was too busy and he had risen above the level of Malpeque. He was all over the island and in Nova Scotia making money. Madeleine and Mairi would pay a polite visit to me – an old acquaintance. Or Madeleine would come on her own. Do you know what it's like, Hobbes, to see a woman you haven't seen for months and before you even speak a word you are tearing each other's clothes off and... Do you know?'

'I know. In my case – in Lucy's and my case – it's still a matter of hours of absence, not months.'

'I don't understand how a man can live without a woman, can you? It's the knowledge of that place in her – where you lose yourself in her body and die. But what do men do who don't want that place? They exist. What did Honoré Gallant do? I had it from Madeleine's lips that he was impotent. She had managed to seduce him from time to time at the beginning, and he even thought Mairi was his daughter. But what was he doing when he was not making love with his wife, and didn't even want to? An ascetic? A celibate? I don't think so. But I'm leaping ahead of myself. No, I'll drop a clue. If a twisted self-centred man like Honoré

132

doesn't want that place – the vagina as we may politely call it – the "pit" in Gaelic, but it's not related to the English "pit" – where does he insert himself? In the hairless little girl, and in the rear-end or between the thighs of the little boy, that's where!'

I must have looked startled. He went on:

'He doesn't want to melt into a woman, he wants to keep his power. He doesn't give himself to the other, he takes. He doesn't harbour a secret love, he hides a secret hate. He doesn't enjoy, he destroys. He is crazy for power yet he has no courage. Where can he exercise power without courage? Over children!'

'You have power over children. You run a school. My school masters would say "This is for your own good, my boy", while they gave boys a thrashing.'

'I don't thrash children – ever. I explain things to them. I encourage them to help each other. I *give* them power, I don't take it away. I don't need it for myself. If I have power it comes from poetry working through me. In the school I teach the boys and the girls together in the same classes. They learn from each other.'

He calmed down. 'Do you think I'm drunk? Not at all. You have been watching me, and you have been matching me glass for glass. But the whisky does loosen the tongue. Have some more.'

He poured a glass for each of us. I took another glowing sip of mine.

MacKinnon continued. 'For now we'll forget what Gallant and Harris, those two potential fathers of Confederation if nothing else, do with their semi-sexual organs. Let me get back to Lachlan. He is aged twenty – almost the same age as Mairi. I mean as Mairi was. I still can't believe this… How is Madeleine? I know you told me. Tell me again.'

'She was indeed at breaking point. She was afraid the little girl would die. She was being "protected" by those people the Aucoins.

But she did feel free to speak. Her main fear was for the child, not herself. I have sent Lucy to her and I know Lucy can help. Fingers crossed.' I crossed my fingers, and so did MacKinnon.

'Lachlan. He was in the orphanage in Summerside. Nobody knew where he had come from, he was simply there. I suppose he had been dropped off by one or another of his parents. He himself couldn't remember more than that he had a caring mother and he missed her. And at first he had one language – Mic Mac. It's one of the Algonquian languages that all native Indians in eastern Canada speak. The Orphelinat, as it was called, was run by Acadian priests and nuns, but there were children there from various backgrounds – one might say various tribes. A few Mic Mac. Many French. Many Irish. All Catholics at that time. Or made so. When Lachlan was aged eleven or twelve (he doesn't know his exact birthday) he ran away from the Orphelinat. He headed north from Summerside, and arrived in Malpeque where he begged for food on the main street. I took him in. He lived here with me and my sons who were around ten years older. He attended my Gaelic school. He speaks Mic Mac – which he has brought up to date by talking with various passing Indians – and French from the Orphelinat. Of course English. And Gaelic. Four languages! But he was never a scholar. In fact he is still illiterate. He shows no aptitude at all for writing or for arithmetic. But he can trap and skin a racoon for the fur, he can fish and he can hunt, he can build a fence, he can assist at the difficult birth of a calf. He can do anything! Do you know about Francis Galton?'

This was a surprise. I imagined I might be the only person on the island who knew about this cousin of the dreaded Darwin.

'I've read his book *The Inheritance of Genius*', I said.

'I haven't read it but I've read about it in a journal. He believes that only clever people should have children, and that stupid people should not. Only people of his own class should have children. Superior people.'

134

'I know. But even his cousin Darwin cannot show how heredity actually works.'

'Just as well. What a cruel doctrine. What Darwin calls evolution states that characteristics are passed on from generation to generation only insofar as they ensure survival. It's a tautology, isn't it? "What survives, survives".'

I had to smile. This Gaelic poet had punctured a balloon that had been floating around my head for years. I said, 'I think that's a fair statement.'

'What survives among the Mic Mac are purely practical things. They had a way of writing, in pictographs. But it seems to have been no more complex than road signs. Yet they were survivors. They hunted and they fished. And that was all they needed to do. They had no invasions by outsiders with a written history until we Europeans turned up. I doubt if the Mic Mac women across the centuries (which they didn't bother to count anyway), would want to take up with the man who sat around the fire in the evening reciting poetry or discussing the meaning of life, or the latest splits in religious doctrine, or the distinction between the real and the ideal – the local Aristotle or Plato. No, the women would take up with the man who could hunt, and fish, and do things with his hands, and fight off intruders. The man like Lachlan! Do you agree?'

'Yes. And even Galton would agree. He is interested in the inheritance of so-called genius. But as you say, genius in the Mic Mac is not in reading or writing. It's in action, I suppose.'

'With a few exceptions. I suppose evolution is possible because there are exceptions. The present Chief of the Mic Mac on Lennox Island, Joseph Snake, is highly literate.'

'But the man Lachlan is a genius in another way?'

'Exactly. He speaks four languages but he cannot write much more than his own name. He has no idea what my sons are printing in those lovely books of theirs, but since last November he works with them.

135

MacKinnon and MacKinnon of Summerside would not get very far without Lachlan to transport deliveries in his cart, to cure the horses of illness or injury without the need of a horse doctor, and to mend anything that breaks – including the printing machinery which he understands in intricate detail. And he is a good-looking lad.

'As I say, from time to time Mairi came to Malpeque with her mother, and from time to time they came here to the croft. I don't remember when Mairi met Lachlan. I never noticed anything between them. They played together when they were twelve or thirteen. I believe Lachlan took Mairi out in the boat to collect lobster traps once or twice – when they were fifteen or sixteen or so. I doubt if they met more than twice a year.'

MacKinnon stood up. 'Let's take a breath of fresh air. Then I'll finish the story, as far as I can.'

I followed him outside. There was a waning crescent moon in a clear black sky to the west. MacKinnon faced it and bowed – nine times. Politely I bowed too, once. 'Always bow to the moon,' he said.

We walked down the road for a hundred yards or so. MacKinnon stopped and turned his back to me. He was taking a long piss into the roadside grass. I turned to one side and did the same. We walked back to the house.

10

'Lachlan had a story to tell,' said MacKinnon.

We were sitting in the armchairs again, facing the empty fireplace. We each had a glass of whisky and a taller glass of water, cold from the well.

'I heard the story piece by piece over a few years. I never brought up the subject, but we would be sitting down together for a rest after working on the lobster traps or in the fields, and he would talk about the Orphelinat. He always used the French term for it. We would be talking Gaelic. The Orphelinat had two separate buildings, one for the boys, run by priests, and one for the girls, run by nuns. There were perhaps twenty children in each. Classes were separate. Miserable classes too. Reading and copying, always using so called sacred texts – not even from the bible, which the Catholics don't read much, but from prayers and stories of the saints. Elementary arithmetic. No history. Of course Lachlan would have no interest in anything written. He preferred to look out of the window or – as he once told me – to imagine being by the sea running along the shore, or digging clams, or making lobster traps. So he was dismissed as stupid. "*Le petit ignorant*", they called him. Or "*le petit sauvage*" – the little savage.

'Every so often the Orphelinat would be visited by its patrons. Benevolent people who had money and gave it to the Orphelinat. At Mass in the local church, the children would light candles to these patrons and pray for them. And the patrons would sometimes attend classes, sitting in the front beside the teaching priest, listening to the children reciting their lessons. Some of the patrons were man and wife, but the man would come to the boys' school, the wife to the girls' school. And the children had "spiritual instruction". This was in addition to confession with the priests in the church – not exactly anonymous, since the priests and the children knew each other's voices. Some of the patrons were known as "lay brothers", and when they visited the school they would have "conferences" with the children, one by one. These were orphans, remember, and it was decided that since they lacked parents, it would be good for their spiritual development if they had a chance to talk privately with adults – often the parents of other children who were not in the Orphelinat of course. They would discuss the spiritual texts they had been reading. Something like what Presbyterians would call Sunday School. But one at a time.

'Lachlan's "patron" when he was aged eleven or twelve was Mr John Harris. As a lawyer of increasing wealth and eminence he gave money to the Orphelinat, and I'm sure many candles were lit for him and many years of Purgatory would be deducted – although Harris was an Anglican. I suppose you could call him an Anglo-Catholic. "High Church". Sympathetic to the Roman church, but not quite ready to come across to it. I suspect the priests welcomed him as a "patron" because they were hoping he would "turn". Anyway, when Lachlan had "conferences" with Harris, he would be asked about his secret thoughts. Did he have lustful desires for girls yet? Did he ever commit the mortal sin of "self-abuse"? There was a great emphasis on self-abuse from the priests. I dare say they were experts in the subject. But you'll see where I'm coming to. Harris asked to see Lachlan's sexual organ, and he undid Lachlan's fly buttons and fondled it to see if it could stick up straight and if Lachlan would thus be tempted to self-abuse. And when it stuck up straight, Harris would give him a few smacks on his bottom – not too hard. He would then – of course – ask Lachlan not to discuss this with the priests. It was a "secret treatment".

'Then on one occasion Harris, after the smacking, went back to Lachlan's member again and pulled at it until it ejaculated. Harris explained that this was a juice Lachlan had in him, and now he had got rid of it, his member would not stick up straight for a while. This embarrassed Lachlan, because it felt nice, and all of a sudden, as it happened, he thought of a little girl he had seen in the street. The feeling reminded him of when he had looked at the girl. He didn't want to tell Harris about this. And the next time Harris came for a conference he told Harris he would not allow anyone to touch him again. So Harris unbuttoned his trousers and showed Lachlan his member sticking up straight and said there was no harm in it, every man was the same. And Lachlan got up and turned away and said that if Harris ever tried to touch him again, he would lose his temper and punch him or perhaps even kill him by banging his head against the wall. Harris told him he was an ungrateful boy who did not know when a friend was there to help. He told Lachlan to say his prayers and think about how Jesus wanted us all to "love one another". But he left the room. That night Lachlan ran away from the Orphelinat.

'I should mention that Harris was then visiting the Orphelinat in Summerside from Charlottetown, forty miles away. The visits, being from far away, were "special". I suppose there is safety in distance, in case something like this were ever to get out. At any rate, Lachlan set off northwards thinking this would lead him to Lennox Island because he had heard there were Mic Mac there, but he took a wrong turn and ended up in Malpeque. Since he was alone and hungry the woman in the General Store – who happened to be Madeleine's mother, Madame Poirier – sent a message to me. As I've told you, I took him in and fed him, and he got along well with my boys – who were much older than he was and about to leave home – and here he stayed. He attended my school. He mended any broken thing or hanging plank he found. He helped me with the fishing. And when my boys had left for Summerside

139

he stayed on. He left the school because he was not learning much, once he had mastered the Gaelic. He speaks it like a native of the Isle of Mull. He worked with me on the croft and in fishing lobster for a while, and as I said earlier, last autumn he went to join my sons in Summerside. One of them is now married and the other soon will be. Lachlan lives with the youngest and comes to see me from time to time. He delivers consignments of books and stationery all through this area, known as East Prince County. And two weeks ago, he disappeared. He didn't tell my sons where he was going. Lennox Island is my guess. He is lying low.'

We were silent for a while.

'Another thing Lachlan told me when he came here was that there was another rich man who helped the Orphelinat. This other rich man was Mr Honoré Gallant, and of course a Catholic, but he preferred the girls' side. The boys from one building would get together with the girls from the other building – under strict supervision of course – for religious instruction and some school classes. So Lachlan was able to talk with the girls. He was a very open and friendly boy, and very decent. He never teased the girls or flirted with them. He took them seriously. Some of them told him they were mightily afraid of Mr Gallant because he would ask them about their secret thoughts about boys, and he would then "correct" them by making them lift up their skirts and bend over a chair and pull down their drawers, and he would take off his belt and he would lash them until they were burning red with stripes.

'Then, not to be out-done by the Roman Catholics, the Presbyterians in Summerside opened an orphanage of their own. It was on the same model as the Orphelinat, with two houses, one for girls and one for boys, but smaller. There were only a dozen children in each house, and they attended the local Presbyterian school with other children who were not orphans. Each house had a married couple to manage it. I hope it was a more human place than the Orphelinat, but perhaps not. The Presbyterian Minister who ran it, Hector MacNicholl, was a hard man. And would you believe it, he set up a model of patrons and "conferences" just as in the Orphelinat. And one of the patrons was Gallant! I suppose doing his bit for good relations between the French and Scottish communities. So just as the Anglican Harris visited the Catholic Orphelinat, so the Catholic Gallant visited the Presbyterian orphanage. Both with charity in their hearts, don't you think? So it's quite possible that Gallant got up to the same tricks there.'

Another silence as I absorbed this information. I might have felt anger, but I found I was feeling a sort of dread. Finally I asked, 'Did you tell Madeleine about what Lachlan had said about Gallant?'

'No. I didn't see her very often, and when I did – well, we enjoyed each other body and soul. I had time when I was not seeing her to ponder about whether to tell her or not. She would not stay with Honoré if she knew the story. Mind you, for an Acadian lady to leave her husband is unheard of – a disgrace – even worse than for an English-speaking lady. But she would not have stayed if she had known. It would have made a nonsense of her self-sacrifice in staying with him. So what if I told her? And she left her husband. Then what? Would she come to me? No. She might hate me for causing this pain. Or even if she thanked me for telling her the truth, would there not be a little worm in her heart twisting and turning, a secret worm of doubt like poor Ross's maggot, and she wondering if I only told her this story – true or not – to get her to myself?'

'I understand.'

'It did change one thing though. I mentioned to you that I did not have relations with married women. I could not make love to a woman knowing another man was making love to her. She had said to me that Gallant was "impotent". But even so, I think they got close physically from time to time. In fact I think I know that for the first few years of their marriage, they did occasionally, then after those few years it stopped. Since Mairi arrived early in the marriage, Gallant assumed she was his.

Madeleine hardly ever talked about Gallant, but she did tell me that.'

'But she told you he was impotent, and since you think they stopped having physical relations after a few years she must have at least hinted at that.'

'She didn't have to. I deduced it from an intimate fact. For the first years of the marriage she shaved off her pubic hair. When we first got together, she was like that. It startled me, because she looked like a girl down there, not a grown woman, although of course her whole body was that of a grown woman, and she was beautiful. We didn't see much of each other for about two years. Then she found excuses for visiting her mother in Malpeque more often. And she came to see me one day on her own and she wrapped her arms around me and wouldn't let go. And I found that her natural hair down there had grown back. She was now a fully beautiful woman – not a girl mother. I didn't know, at that time, about her husband's interest in little girls at the Orphelinat. But it was a notable change, and I deduced that they had stopped having physical relations. I felt free from that time on to be as close to Madeleine as I wanted. And so I was close – whenever we saw each other alone. In the same room – or the same field! Being alone together was enough, as I said to you earlier. The rest followed.'

'How recently have you been together?'

'About six months ago.'

'And did you see Marie then?'

'No.'

'When you did see her, before her marriage, or when she was a young girl, did she ever mention Harris to you?'

'No. But when I saw Madeleine about six months ago, she told me that Mairi was not really happy with Harris. It made us sad and we talked about it. Another pause. 'I'll have to finish the story of Lachlan,' he went on. 'Two weeks ago, he disappeared from Summerside. But he appeared here on the morning after Mairi's death. Or rather he appeared at the fishermen's huts in Darnley Basin which are a walking distance from Thunder Cove. He had the baby with him at Duncan Matheson's hut – it was just after dawn – and Duncan was coming there to start his day. Lachlan left the baby with Duncan, not me. "I found her floating on the pond!" he said. "Take her to Calum!" And he ran off – heading towards Malpeque. Duncan brought her here. I then asked him to go to Harris's house and deliver a letter for me. My housemaid came in shortly. She cleaned the baby and I could see it was a baby girl with a mark in the small of her back – what they call here the purple spot. It's said to be a sign of Indian blood. The housemaid rocked and walked with the baby and tried to get her to drink some goat's milk. I went out to Malpeque and sent a telegram to Mr Gallant. The rest you know.'

'Duncan told us – McNulty and me – that he had been strolling down to Thunder Cove to dig for clams when he noticed the cradle among the reeds at the edge of the pond.'

'He was covering the truth about Lachlan. As we agreed when he brought the baby. I make a thing of not lying. But I'm afraid I have it on my conscience – my bloody Calvinistic Presbyterian conscience! – that I persuaded Duncan to lie. I don't want those vicious people to know about Lachlan.'

'And Lachlan?'

'As I say, I think he has gone to Lennox Island, to hide among his people.'

'Tomorrow I'll go to Lennox Island then. How far is it?'

'Forty miles or so. A good idea. Or do you have to send for another policeman?'

'I don't want to lose time. From what you say, I don't feel in danger from Lachlan – or I suppose he is called Noel by others than you and your family. Could you be wrong about him? Has he deceived you? After all, he seems to have seen your daughter without your knowing.'

'But she is not my daughter in his eyes. Unless she told him she thought she was. But so far as I know she herself has no idea she is my daughter. Had no idea…' His eyes filled with tears. 'I'm tired, and you're tired. I could cry, Hobbes, and I could get angry. But I don't know enough. I'll let you know anything I find out.'

'But what do you think?' I said. 'Assuming Lachlan doesn't know Marie was your daughter, what he does know is that she was married to Harris and that Harris or his men may have killed her. How did he find the baby? Did Marie manage to give the baby to him before being caught up with? Was she running away? And when did all this happen?'

'You do have to talk to Lachlan,' MacKinnon said.

I paused. I was not going to share this part of my reasoning with MacKinnon. It was police business. The timing of events was important. Harris had been innocently enjoying a political meeting in Charlottetown in the evening when Marie was killed. But was she killed in the evening? Did she leave the baby at Thunder Cove that night and then return to Stanley Bridge, only to be killed in the morning when Harris could have returned from Charlottetown if he had ridden home overnight? His housekeepers might simply have thought he had gone out early on the Saturday norming. But why on earth would Marie leave the baby at the pond and go home? Or was Marie killed the day before and somebody else left the baby at Thunder Cove Pond? Was Lachlan expecting this? Where was he that night?

'When Madeleine Gallant came to fetch the baby, what did she say?' I asked. 'Did she mention your message?'

'The Aucoins were here too. They arrived before Madeleine. Mrs Aucoin was calm and expressionless – cold, I thought. I had never met her before. Mind you I could see from her face that she is a much more intelligent woman than her position in life suggests. It was she who told me that Mairi had been murdered. I almost fainted. Shortly after that, when Madeleine arrived, it was also her who told the same thing to Madeleine.

I had eyes only for Madeleine. She was frantic. She clutched the baby and held it and rocked it. It had been crying weakly on and off and it started again. Madeleine hardly looked at me. She was always under the eyes of Mrs Aucoin of course. They went together into one of my bedrooms – the one you'll be in – to check how the baby was. I could hear raised voices – Madeleine crying out. I almost ran in to rescue her but I realised it might be that Mrs Aucoin must have been giving her some details about Mairi's death. To my shame, I went quietly and listened by the door, just in case Madeleine was in some kind of danger. That's how I know some of the details about what they – whoever they were – had done to Mairi. Madeleine was insisting that Mrs Aucoin must tell her everything. When there was a pause, I came back into this room. They came out of the bedroom with the baby. They had both obviously been crying. They had a covered wagon outside, with Edgar Aucoin standing waiting. And Madeleine had not sent away the buggy from North Rustico. She put the baby back in the cradle and picked it up. She and Mrs Aucoin went with the baby in the buggy. Aucoin followed separately, I suppose going back to Stanley Bridge. Madeleine really rushed away. I wonder if she wanted to escape talking to me, for fear Mrs Aucoin would notice that we were more than friends.'

'Has anyone else noticed that?'

'Not that I know. By the way, as for your visit to Lennox Island tomorrow, I'm still not sure you are safe. I wasn't joking about the two Cormiers. I know it seems incredible, but yes there are two. Twins. Identical, I think, but one's hair is a bit lighter than the other's. They are never seen together. Apparently they hate each other so much that when they meet they try to murder each other. They have to be torn apart. One is called "I-Guess," and the other is called "Dunno" – for similar reasons.'

'This is almost too grotesque to be true.'

'You don't know the island. "Inbreeding" is a sensitive subject here, particularly on the north west side of the island where small groups of pioneers lived in the forests, and families of relations intermarried. There are rare diseases – I'm thinking of a kind of progressive paralysis and loss of physical sensation which has not yet been named – which occurs in certain families. And rare vices. Cormier is a common name "up west", some of them prosperous farmers, but this one branch of them is a bad lot. The father of the twins was jailed for buggering farm animals – including geese. I see you look startled, but it's true. "Bestiality". No doubt all sorts of people do it in secret – I hope not too many! – but he would do it so carelessly that the neighbours saw him quite often and at last reported him to a constable. Bestiality is buggery, in law. It used to be a felony, a capital offence, but a judge took pity on the family, on account of the little boys, and sent him off to jail in the Brig instead of hanging him. But the other inmates of the Brig, at least the few who were there long term, didn't want him among them, so they gave him a choice: either you hang yourself, or we hang you. He is said to have chosen to hang himself, and the coroner's inquest ruled it was suicide, but you never know. In the Brig it would be hard to find any private space to hang yourself in. I believe he was hanged by his own bootlaces from the top of a barred window. There must have been other people around.

'At any rate the twins grew up with their mother in a shack on the outskirts of Summerside, and eventually they were removed by the police because the mother was covered with bruises and cuts from trying to separate them when they fought, and the walls of the shack, being made of thin boards, were punched full of holes from the boys' fists. They were then put in the Orphelinat, housed at opposite ends of the building, but this didn't work. They began to wreck the building in order to get at each other. One of them, Dunno, was sent to a small home – a foster parent really – in the far east of the island, at George-town. I-Guess stayed in Summerside. Without Dunno in sight he is calm enough. He ended up working for Harris, under the supervision of Edgar Wedge, né Edgar Aucoin. The last I heard of Dunno, he was doing odd jobs for Honoré Gallant. When you think of it, they are like Romulus and Remus, the twins suckled by a Roman wolf mother, who fought each other all their lives until Romulus finally won,'

MacKinnon got up. 'Enough of our island story,' he said. 'But I'm going to accompany you to Lennox Island. If you say it's not "proper", I'll follow you at a distance all the same. For two reasons. First, you are not safe. I suggest you send to your friend McNulty for a constable – perhaps out of St Eleanors – to guard you wherever you go. Meanwhile, the two of us are harder to attack than you alone. And second, take it from me that if you arrive at Lennox Island and ask for Lachlan, or Noel, you will be met with great politeness and hospitality by Chief Joseph Snake, but he will not tell you a word of where Lachlan is. But they know me as his adoptive father and they will respect my right to see him. And so to bed!'

'One final question. Who do you think killed Marie?'

'It was either Gallant or Harris – both monsters, each in his own way – or people working for them. Not both of them together. They wouldn't trust each other that much. But…'

His voice trailed off. He looked at me, and I thought I saw sadness in his eyes.

'You know the story, Hobbes. Mairi was my daughter. Not that swine Gallant's! There was no physical resemblance whatsoever. And Gallant is no fool. He must have either thought or known that Mairi was not his daughter. He could have killed her. In fact he would have enjoyed it.'

The room was cool and pleasant, with a gentle breeze from the half open window, and a neatly made bed with a hard mattress of the kind I liked. But I did not sleep well.

11

I was reconciled to having Calum with me on my search for Lachlan, otherwise known as Noel. I had never met anyone as candid. And over the whisky we had agreed to use each other's Christian names. I thought of Lucy. Would she approve of this friendship? She would.

He knocked at my door after dawn – half past four or so. I was already awake. I helped him with his "chores", as he called them, making sure the hens' eggs were collected and that the goats and horses would have enough water in their troughs. He also set out food and water for the dog. We ate a huge breakfast of sausages and scrambled eggs and black coffee. I had half expected porridge but Calum said it was a Lowland thing.

We set off on horseback southwards about four miles to Malpeque, where McNulty and I had stayed overnight at the hotel. The village was at a cross-road with two or three side streets and two churches – pretty, like all villages I had seen on the island so far, with the houses widely separated by gardens of flowers and vegetables or paddocks for horses. We rode south across flat farmland with occasional glimpses of Malpeque Bay to the west. After an hour the road headed west along the south side of the Bay and after another hour we could see across the fields to the north of us the church spire of the village of St Eleanors. Calum said it was the administrative centre of Prince County for historical reasons, but it had been far out-stripped in size by Summerside, the second biggest town on the island, and was now in effect a suburb of Summerside. The Prince County courthouse building, which included the jail and police station, was in St Eleanors.

We were crossing the narrowest part of the island, in effect an isthmus. We passed through a village called Miscouche and eventually we turned north along the west side of Malpeque Bay through dreary flat fields, occasional farms, and scrubby woods. The road of packed mud was quite wide and straight and we made a good pace, trotting for long stretches. After two and a half hours or so, towards one o'clock, we approached the shore again at Lennox Island. There was a rickety wooden bridge. We walked our horses slowly across. Immediately we were in another sort of landscape. Calum had told me that Lennox Island had only recently been officially allocated to the Mic Mac, who had previously been scattered not only there but in small settlements across the island. Another piece of allocated land was Morell, in King's County. These were not called 'Reservations' in the American sense, and the Indians were free to move in and out of them, but in effect that is what they were.

On Lennox Island – an island off an island – there were canoes dragged up onto muddy beaches, and as we approached the settlement there were not only various shacks and low wooden one-storey houses, some of them still being constructed, there were occasional 'wigwams' – conical tents made of canvas stretched over poles. The people we saw along the road, by now a track, were dressed like any other Islanders, the men in trousers and jackets, the women in skirts and blouses and jackets. Most were bare-headed, although a few women had high conical straw hats of a style I had not seen before. The people looked like Indians, although I knew from British Columbia how many different sorts of 'Indians' there could be. I instinctively imagined Lucy among them. Yes, she would fit to a similar extent as she would fit among the Songhees in Victoria, Indians who lived close to Europeans and who had been exposed to the white people's diseases. The Tsimshian among whom she had grown up were another group altogether – tall, fit, and alert – at least at that time. During the last two years I had heard they were being ravaged by smallpox. These Mic Mac were more like white people – a mixture of healthy-looking and unhealthy. Lucy would have looked like a princess among them – taller, slimmer, with a commanding and direct gaze. But there was no denying that she would have fitted in, with her bronze-coloured skin and thick black hair, her high and wide cheekbones, her slanted eyes. Not that they would have understood each other except in English. The Algonquian languages extended all the way from the Atlantic to the Sioux on the Western Prairies, but not to British Columbia.

In the centre of the settlement were several more prosperous-looking new houses with gardens and flower beds. We stopped in an open area overlooking a bay with a dock where small boats were moored. Some men came forward and took the horses, tethered them and went for buckets of water. Calum announced loudly that we were here to see the Sagwa Joseph. Sagwa meant Chief or Leader.

A tall man in a grey cotton suit came out of a house to meet us. He greeted Calum and they shook hands. Calum introduced me. 'This is Mr Hobbes who is the new Police Superintendent. This is his Honour Chief Joseph Snake.' We shook hands and the chief asked polite questions about our journey, speaking the usual Island English perfectly fluently. Calum had told me that they only spoke Mic Mac among themselves, and that because of their old alliance with the Acadians they spoke French as well as English. I found myself thinking that I had never been in a place where so many people were bilingual or multi-lingual as on Prince Edward Island.

Calum had taken a cloth bag from the saddle-bag of his horse, and he held it out to the chief who opened it and pulled out a bottle of Calum's home-made whisky. He thanked Calum warmly, and invited us to follow him. He led the way along a path between his own house and another one and into a clearing where there was a wigwam. It was much larger inside than I would have expected, with logs burning in a fireplace in the middle, the smoke spiralling out through a hole in the peak of the wigwam where the poles of the structure converged. Around the edges were beds, neatly made up with patchwork quilts, and near the fire were tables and wooden chairs, and several quite elegant wooden armchairs with green chintz covers. We sat down in a circle around the fire.

'This is my usual house,' said the Chief. 'I have a new house, but I prefer this one to welcome friends.'

A polite conversation ensued in which Chief Joseph asked Calum about his school, and Calum asked about the well-being of the settlement, there were exchanges about the weather, the imminent run of herring, and how lobsters were more abundant than usual this year. Chief Joseph asked politely where I was from and I explained that I had come from the West Coast, and I was originally English, and that I was investigating a murder in Stanley Bridge and I would like to meet Noel, MacKinnon's adopted son, if he were available to talk to.

'You mean you think Noel committed a murder?' said the Chief, as evenly as if he were discussing a point about the year's weather.

'Not for a moment,' I said. 'But I think he may know some things about it that will help me find the man or men who committed the murder.'

'I'll send for him. And you can talk. But unless you can give me evidence that he has committed a crime, he will not leave Lennox Island without my permission.'

'I find that reasonable,' I said.

'Since you are with Calum, who has always been our friend, I trust you,' said Chief Joseph simply. He spoke in his own language to a man who was nearby and who then left the wigwam. 'You will stay for lunch with us,' the Chief said, addressing us both. Then to me: 'Mr Hobbes, what is your first name?'

'Chad.'

'Chad. Unusual name. You call me Joseph, I call you Chad. We are both Christians, are we not? So we use our Christian names.'

'Of course.'

'I like the way you speak. It reminds me of Governor Robinson. He visited us just over a week ago. By the end of our conversation he was calling me Joseph and I was calling him William. I was very touched by his warmth towards us. And you may have seen in this week's *Islander* an open letter of thanks to us for receiving him in which he concludes: "You may count on me as your protector and your friend."'

'Good for him' I said. 'As you no doubt realise, that's his guarantee – in a public letter so that others as well as you will read it – that he won't allow any Government here to curtail your rights. At least the Colonial Office in London is behind you.'

'I do know, and, believe me, I appreciate it. And now we shall eat lunch outside.'

Chief Joseph stood up and led the way out of the wigwam into the dusty area between the houses, then along a path which led into the woods, cool with fir trees and maples mingled together. We came to a clearing with a log fire in the middle. A stout but good-looking woman of about thirty was waiting for us and we were introduced. Joseph's wife, Sarah. We sat around the fire on low wooden stools. Calum's whisky bottle was opened, glasses were poured, and to my surprise Joseph stood up and Sarah and we did too, and he raised his glass and said 'The Queen, God Bless Her!'

We drank the toast solemnly. We could have been in an Oxford College! We settled back onto our stools. Women in skirts and blouses – it was getting warm – and without their hats, with thick black hair like Lucy's, brought us wooden platters with skewers of mussels and clams grilled over a separate small fire on one side of the clearing. They also brought to each of us wooden bowls of salad – leaves I recognised such as lettuce and spinach, but also small curled tips of ferns that tasted like asparagus. 'Fiddleheads,' Calum exclaimed. 'Delicious. And these clams are cherrystone clams, meaning small "quahogs" – a Mic Mac word used all over the island for clams. Large quahogs are tough. These are a delicacy.'

This lunch did remind me sharply of the Tsimshian of the Pacific. They too ate clams and mussels and shrimps from skewers, along with salads of raw vegetables. Lucy and I ate like this at home. Washed down with whisky and water the lunch was certainly good. I began to feel slightly dizzy. But as we finished a young man appeared with a tray on which were cups and saucers with black coffee. Just right.

Calum and Joseph were embarking on a conversation about pictographs, the symbols the Mic Mac still used. Were they or were they not an alphabet? Joseph did not think so. But there had been a scholar visiting from America – Harvard University in Boston – who had said he thought the pictographs were like runes, the alphabet of the Vikings, and the Vikings had possibly visited the Atlantic coast of America.

'I wouldn't put it past them,' said Calum. 'They visited the Highlands of Scotland as well, and they travelled between their own lands and Iceland and Ireland, so why would they not have come here?'

This seemed to please Joseph. He seemed to know the geography involved. He must have been to school in French or English. 'So maybe we are all cousins!' he said, as if this were a great joke, 'That is, if the Vikings got together with your women and ours!'

'I agree,' said Calum. 'Why not?' Then he looked at Joseph seriously. 'And how is Lachlan coming along?'

'He was very frightened at first. He told me he had come here to escape a danger. He had never been among us before, but he knew he was one of us. True. He is one of us – as we would say, one of the *L'nuk*. The *L'nuk* means something like "the People", in English. And Mic Mac means something like "the Family". He speaks our language. He was always a *L'nu*. Now he is with us he is Mic Mac. We have welcomed him into our big family. And we shall protect him against any danger.'

'Can you do that?' said Calum. 'What if evil people come here looking for him?'

'We can. We're all armed here. But since our friend Chad is with us, I can ask him.' He looked me in the eye. 'If bad people come here looking for Noel and we have to use force to stop them, what will the authorities do? What will the police do?'

I thought of my conversations with Brecken and with Robinson. 'This is an important investigation,' I said. 'I'm new to the island, but I can tell you – on my honour – that if anyone comes here and offers violence to Noel or to any of you, you are free to defend yourselves as necessary.'

'The way things come to pass here on the island,' said Joseph, almost gently, 'I don't think you can be completely sure that what you say is as you wish. But you say it on your honour, and I accept that. And I am strengthened by what the Governor wrote in that open letter.'

'Can I ask you a question, since I am interested in languages? The word translated as "Cradled on the Waves". Is that correct?'

'Yes. "Cradled on the Waves", or "Resting on the Waves". Only we say *Epekwitk*.'

'Do you use cradles for your babies?'

'Yes of course. We make them out of willow branches tightly woven together. Or we may carve them out of wood.'

A man came up and spoke to Joseph in Mic Mac.

'Noel is here,' Joseph said, getting up from his stool. He led the way back along the path to the central area of the village.

A young Indian man was standing there with a bow slung over his back, and a quiver of arrows hung on his belt. He was wearing canvas trousers with brown leather boots, and a checked red shirt. He was tall and sturdy with thick black hair and jet-black eyes. At his feet on the ground was a canvas bag.

'Dad!' he exclaimed, stepping towards Calum and giving him a hug. '*Fayuch!*' he said excitedly, '*Duh voola mee bradawn lesh an woegan is sagta!*' Or so I transcribe it. It was Gaelic of course.

'*Mah hoo a vic!*' said Calum. 'But we have to speak English here.'

He turned to us. 'Lachlan is saying "Look! I shot a salmon with a bow and arrow!" And I'm saying "Well done, my son."' He turned back to Lachlan. 'Let's have a look.'

Lachlan bent down and opened the canvas bag and revealed a huge salmon lying on a bed of reeds. He lifted it out by its gills. It had a gash in its side. He set it down again. 'You would never believe it, but there's a kind of arrow that goes through the water. Look!' He turned and pulled an arrow out of his quiver. It had a vicious-looking tanged iron head, but it was unusual in that the arrow shaft had been planed flat and narrow. 'And the bow has great power' he said. He took the bow off his shoulder and held it out for us to see.

I had never seen anything like it. It was shaped like an ordinary long-bow, but shorter, and with a straight bar attached to the outside of the curve and parallel to it. The string was tied at each end both to the end of the bow and to the end of the bar to which it was attached. A sort of double bow.

Lachlan suddenly became serious. 'How is Mairi?' he asked.

'Let's go and sit down somewhere quiet,' MacKinnon said.

'Is she not all right?'

'No she's not. I'll tell you more in a moment.'

'There's a bench down beside the creek.'

Lachlan led us, walking fast, to where a small river ran into the sea. The tide was out, and the river was fanning out in rivulets across pink sand. Overlooking this was a wooden bench on the raised land behind the beach. We sat down on the bench, with Lachlan between us.

'Is she dead?' he said sharply.

'Yes, she is.'

Lachlan let out a howl and sank his face into his hands and began sobbing loudly. MacKinnon put his hand between Lachlan's shoulders and kept it there. Lachlan cried for a long time. Eventually he raised his head, wiping his eyes with the back of one hand. I noticed that he was right-handed, thinking of what Dr Reid had said about the blows to Marie's face being possibly struck by a left-handed man.

'Did that man Harris kill her?' Lachlan asked me, his eyes glaring.

'She was killed in Harris's house. But he was not there at the time – or so it seems, as other people saw him in Charlottetown.'

'Then his men killed her. What did they do?'

'Whoever it was, they beat her. I think she may have died quickly from a blow to her head.'

'I will strike them down!' Lachlan said. He stood up abruptly.

'No!' said Calum. 'I forbid you! If anyone strikes down whoever killed her it will be Chad here. He has the right to do so. You and I don't.'

I was not sure about having the right, but I let it pass. 'Please tell me,' I said, 'It's very important. Did you meet her when you found the baby? What happened?'

'No I didn't meet her. She wasn't there! There was just the baby, floating on the pond in its cradle, sheltered by the reeds. I knew the cradle! I sent it to her. I bought it in Summerside, from a Mic Mac who made these cradles – wicker-work, of willow branches, so tight that this one floated! I sent it to her, by the mail, a few months ago. There was no letter attached. I can't write! But she would know it was from me.'

'When did you last see her?'

'When the baby was made! She had been married only a couple of months and she was visiting her grand-mother in Malpeque, and we made the baby. Then she went back to Stanley Bridge.'

'There's a repetition here,' I said, turning to MacKinnon. 'A young woman marries a man whom perhaps she dislikes, and she then goes to another man she loves and becomes pregnant.'

'Yes,' he said. 'But in the second case, the woman has an example before her. It makes me think that after all she does know about her mother and her real father. She decides to do what happened in the first case. It's not just a coincidence.'

'I don't understand what you're saying,' Lachlan said, looking back and forth between us.

'Can you tell me about finding the baby?' I asked.

'I went to the pond at six o'clock. It was a Friday. That was our agreement. We used to meet at the pond last fall. A couple of months after Mairi got married she came to see her grandmother in Malpeque and she sent a maid to find me at Calum's croft and to tell me that we could meet at three o'clock in the afternoon at the pond behind Thunder Cove. It's a quiet place, out of sight of the shore and the beach, and it's out of sight of the fishermen's huts at Darnley Basin because of the hill. That's where we made the baby. We met every day for a few days. There's a hidden place in a small wood just above the pond.'

'Did she want to make the baby? Was it her idea?'

'Yes, but I wanted it too. It made me so happy to be with her again, and I knew it made her happy too. Before she met Harris, when we were together I wanted to be with her all the time.

'She said to me, "From mid-May, I want you to go there every Friday – rain or shine – around six o'clock, and wait there for me until it's dark. I won't be there most times, but I might be. I need you to do this for me because if I need to see you, it will have to be in secret, and since you can't read very well I can't send you letters. Can you do this?"

'Of course I agreed. So from around mid-May, I went there every week on the Friday, as she had asked. It was easy enough, although I had to travel from Summerside, but my work there doesn't take all my time, and I would often go up to the Basin to work with Duncan or Calum. I got a ride with a friend who came to Malpeque Bay by horse trap to harvest oysters. He and I would sleep overnight at a friend's place and return to Summerside the following day. But Mairi never came. Then that Friday evening two weeks ago, I went to the pond around six o'clock. I don't bother with reading, but I have a watch. These are the longest days of the year, and the sun sets around nine o'clock. I had stopped off in Darnley

Basin and I saw Duncan and he gave me a bowl of some clam chowder he had been cooking, then I went to the pond. I sat in the little woods above the water and I waited for Mairi. I could see down to the end of the pond and then over the sandhills to the sea in the distance. As usual Mairi didn't come. I felt very sad sitting there waiting for her and wishing she would come. I waited longer than usual after the sun set and it became almost dark but the moon came up and it was almost full. Then I heard a sound. It was a distant sound of a baby crying. I followed the sound and pushed through the reeds. I couldn't see very clearly, but there was the baby, floating on the pond in its cradle in the moonlight, snug in the reeds at the shore end. I picked up the cradle and I walked around the pond towards Darnley Basin. The baby was still crying at first, but I tucked its blanket around it and I held the cradle in my arms and I rocked it and the baby became quiet. And once I was walking, perhaps this rocked the cradle too, so the baby went to sleep. I followed the path by moonlight to the basin shore and the fishing sheds. I recognised Duncan's shed where I had been earlier, and I walked in. Nobody locks the doors to those sheds. I put the cradle on the table. I knew where Duncan kept his candles and matches, so I found a candle and lit it. The baby began to cry again, and I rocked it. Its clothes were wet and there was a smell. The baby was wearing a nightdress and underneath it was a cloth wrapped around it and pinned. So I pulled out the pins and took the cloth off and I saw I needed to wipe the baby and I found a dish towel and I took some water from Duncan's bucket and I cleaned the baby. I could see she was a girl. And she was dark and I knew she was mine! – as well as Mairi's. And I took another dish towel and wrapped the baby up. She was crying again. And I found the left overs of the chowder in a saucepan, and I dipped my little finger in it and gave it to the baby to suck, and I managed to feed her a little, but she spat out the chowder. It helped to have her suck on my little finger. But she needed the tit! I knew I couldn't walk all the way in the dark to Calum's croft. Even though the moon was out. It was chilly and I was worried about the baby getting cold. And I was tired. In Duncan's shed there's a bunk with some blankets. So I walked back and forwards with the baby, rocking her in my arms, and she went to sleep. So I lay down with her on Duncan's bunk and I pulled the blankets over us, and eventually the baby and I went to sleep. And in the night she woke up and I got up and walked and rocked her some more, and she didn't cry so much, maybe she was very tired, then we went back to bed again. I was afraid of rolling on her, so I lay on my back and put her on her tummy next to my heart and I sang to her a bit and she became quiet. Then I must have fallen asleep.

'When I woke up the baby was crying again and the light was coming in through the windows. I got up and I cleaned the baby again, and pinned a clean wash-cloth of Duncan's around her, and wrapped her in her blanket. And then Duncan arrived. He lives not far away and he comes to his shed soon after dawn to get his boat and go out to collect his traps. So I asked him to take the baby in the cradle to Calum's croft as fast as he could. I told Duncan where I had found the baby, but nothing about waiting there for Mairi. I was afraid. Something terrible must have happened to Mairi. What if bad people were searching for her or for the baby? Her husband is a very powerful man in Charlottetown. And the baby was obviously a Mic Mac baby. What if they wanted to kill me, and kill the baby too? So I decided to go to Lennox Island. I would ride back to Summerside with my friend and then make my way north to Lennox Island. I knew it was the best thing to do. Dad, Calum, I didn't want to get you into danger if I was seen with you and people were looking for me. And I've always known that my own people, the Mic Mac, would protect me if I needed them. And it was the right time, that's all.'

'It was indeed,' said Calum. 'You did well. I'm proud of you, son.'

'I knew she was safe once she was with you.'

'I think you did well too,' I said. 'You'll be a good father to that baby and I hope you see her again soon. But I have to ask you: how do you think the baby got to the pond?'

'Mairi must have brought the baby with her and then had to leave. Perhaps she ran away. Perhaps she was taken by her husband or other bad people. They must not have seen the baby. She must have left it there for me, then run away. If so they must have caught her.'

'Did you ever meet her husband, John Harris?'

Lachlan looked at Calum who simply looked back at him, then he turned to me. 'I knew him when I was at the Orphelinat. He was a bad man then. I don't know why Mairi married him. When I saw her and we made the baby, she said she had found she could never love him. She liked him but she couldn't love him. She had felt sorry for him, and he seemed to want her so much, and her father told her she should marry him.'

'Did she say what her mother thought about that?'

I was perhaps being cruel here, with Calum sitting beside me, but I wanted to know.

'She said her mother was against the marriage. Her mother said she, Mairi, should marry only a man she truly loved. Later on, when Mairi came back from her trip to Quebec with Harris, after the wedding, her mother told Mairi how the man she herself truly loved was not her husband, but Calum, and that Calum was Mairi's Papa, but that no one in the world should ever know.'

'Did you tell Marie that you had known Harris at the Orphelinat?'

'No. When we were younger, Mairi and I knew each other, and she was not with Harris then. And later on when I knew she was with Harris and she was going to marry him, I couldn't believe it. If I had told her what I knew of Harris perhaps she wouldn't have married him after all. But she would have hated me for telling her.'

I looked at Calum and said – I could not help it – 'I've heard something like that story before.'

Calum looked back at me sadly. 'It seems that truth doesn't pay. Or does it, after all?'

'When you saw Marie,' I said to Lachlan, 'Did she talk about Harris harming her in any way? For example, did he hit her?'

'No. Actually she said he was very nice most of the time, although sometimes he was very quiet and what she called "far away, even in the same room". She even said that he was not a bad man. Well, I knew he was a bad man, but I didn't say.'

'Did she talk to you about leaving him?'

'Yes, she did. She said she had mixed up "liking" and "love". She said she was capable of liking John but not of loving him – not what we were doing in making the baby. She said that at the beginning of the marriage they had "made love" a few times but it had been very sad and it had not worked. I didn't understand this. But she said it had worked just enough to make her know what she needed. She said she needed love – she needed to do what we were doing, and she couldn't do it with him.'

'You call it "making the baby". Did she call it that?'

'She said something like it. She said she knew what we were doing would make a baby, and she wanted that. She said other things that were private between us.'

'I'm sorry, but I have to ask you about them. What did she say?'

Lachlan looked at Calum and said: 'They were private things. And she said I mustn't tell other people about *anything* we said to each other, or even that we were meeting.'

'I know, son, but you do have to tell Chad about them. I think that now Mairi is gone, and since Chad is doing his best to find out everything about what happened to her, it will be all right to tell him.'

'I can't believe she's gone!' Lachlan wailed, and put his face in his hands again for a moment. But he straightened up and looked at me.

'She said she loved me and of course I had already said I loved her. When we were making the baby we would both call out that we loved each other. She said that one day she would come and live with me. But she said this would be very difficult and it would cause a lot of trouble, and it would hurt John very much, and it would hurt her parents, and her father – meaning Mr Gallant – would be very angry. If she just got up and left her new life with John who had all that money and two big houses, and then came to live with me, then people would think she was crazy. And what's more, they might do us harm. They could lock her up and say she was a lunatic. Or they could take her away from me and hurt me or even kill me.'

'Who did she mean by "they"?

'Her father and John, and the people who worked for them, I suppose. But I said I could fight for myself, and I knew Calum would help us, and we would not be all alone. And she said that one reason she wanted us to make a baby was that it would make it easier for her to leave. Because the baby would look like me and her. We are both dark haired, although Mairi had blue eyes, and I am dark skinned. But John is very fair, with light hair and white skin – whiter even than Mairi's. So she said that when she was ready to have the baby she would come to be with me. Then she would have the baby, and we would say, "Look, this is our baby!" and John would have to accept it, and so would everybody else. In fact, if she had the baby by another man, that is by me, then John would definitely want nothing more to do with her! He would make her leave his house. And even if her father was angry, her mother would want to help. She said she hoped her mother would at last have the courage to leave Honoré Gallant. She said that if she had a baby there wouldn't be the same risk to her or me. They wouldn't lock her up or do any harm to me. They would have to accept the truth. They would make life hard for us but they wouldn't dare harm us, because everything would be out in the open. And I agreed!'

'Again, you did right, Lachlan' said Calum. 'And Mairi too. She was finding the only way to get out of the mess she was in. So when she arranged for you to come to the pond every Friday at six o'clock, you expected her to be ready to give birth to the baby? And you would come together to my croft and she would have the baby there?'

'Yes! She said it would be summer, and the weather would be good, and even if she was expecting the baby in two or three weeks, she could sail the boat along to Thunder Cove.'

'My God!' Calum interrupted. 'When did you make the baby?'

'It was in the middle of October – what we call Indian Summer – when there had been some frosts but the days were still warm.'

'But…' Calum looked at me.

'Yes, my God!' I said. 'A baby conceived in the middle of October would be due towards the middle of July – not the end of June! It must have come early! But no one has said it was premature.'

'I saw no signs of that,' said Calum, 'although she's a small baby, right enough. A couple of weeks early is not exactly premature. One of our boys came early like that, and the other late. But Mairi must have been caught by surprise. It was a reckless idea. I'm not saying she was wrong in choosing to do what she did, but she was cutting it fine. And when did she call for Madeleine and the midwife? I suppose when she felt the pangs coming on and she knew it was too late to make her escape. The midwife was this woman Modeste, just next door. Madeleine could be there with a hired buggy from North Rustico within a few hours if Aucoin came to Rustico, with Madeleine then going to Stanley Bridge with her driver.'

'This explains a lot,' I said. 'Instead of coming to meet Lachlan and to give birth at your croft, she had to give birth at Stanley Bridge then decided to escape to you after a few days.'

I turned to Lachlan again. 'You said she could sail the boat along to Thunder Cove. That was the plan?'

'Yes. She had a skiff with a centreboard and a small sail. She always liked sailing.'

'But that's a long way,' I said, looking at Calum.

'Not impossible' he said. 'It's only about twelve miles by water. It would be a very hard row. But by sail, she could either catch a wind from the east to blow her along and make the trip in an hour and a half or so, or if the wind was from the west she could tack into it and it would take about two hours. The dangerous part would be getting out of New London Bay past the Spit where there can be strong tidal currents, and then making a safe landing at Thunder Cove. But on a relatively calm day she could coast in on the waves.

'Towards the end of the shore in front of the pond, there's calmer water in the shelter of the headland and the red arch – especially if the wind is from the west as usual,' Lachlan said. 'So I thought that even if she was nearly ready to have the baby, she could sail all right. She could even row a little. There are lots of women who are going to have babies who go on working right up to the day the baby arrives. Of course if Mairi sailed to Thunder Cove and beached the boat, she would never be able to get it out again against the waves. But she wasn't planning to go back! She would come with me. We would go to Dad's house.'

Lachlan looked at Calum. 'I'm sorry,' he said, 'but we couldn't tell you. It was a secret.'

'I would have taken you all in,' said Calum. 'You were right to think that.'

He turned to me.

'So having had the baby unexpectedly early, Mairi took off with her when she could. She must have told Madeleine she no longer needed her, and encouraged Harris to go to Charlottetown. And on the Friday she knew Lachlan would be there, she took the baby in its cradle and sailed the boat to Thunder Cove. She was seen, she was followed, then she was seized and taken back by force.'

'I saw the skiff, at the little wharf behind Harris's house,' I said. 'It's back there now. But if she was followed by other people in a boat,

165

wouldn't they have seen her arrive at Thunder Cove and then taken the baby as well?'

'Unless they rode along the roads and didn't get there in time, and they just found her on the shore. Or even if they were behind her on the water. If she saw them coming she could have beached the boat, run and hid the baby and ran away in another direction before they caught up on her. Then they would have taken both boats back.'

'She was bound and gagged,' I said.

'I didn't know that,' Calum said. He and Lachlan sat silently for a moment.

'There's one more thing,' Lachlan said. He hung his head as if embarrassed. 'I found a letter stuffed between the cracks of the basket, behind the baby's head. The paper was wet. When I picked up the basket I took the letter and put it in my pocket, and when I gave the baby in the basket to Duncan I forgot about it. I had been so busy with the baby! I only remembered the letter when I was on my way here to Lennox Island. It was still in my pocket. I decided to wait to give it to Calum, but then, Calum, I haven't seen you until now, and I didn't want to leave here, and I don't know anyone I could have sent it with. I dried it out and I put it back in my pocket.'

He reached to the pocket of his red checked shirt − over his heart, I found myself thinking − unbuttoned it and took out a small piece of folded paper. He gave it to Calum.

'Thank you,' said Calum, 'You did well.' He handed the paper to me.

I gave it back to him. 'It may be to you. You read it first.'

Calum unfolded the paper carefully. There seemed to be only a few lines written on it. He read it. He gave it back to me, then wiped his eyes with the back of his hand.

The letter was in French, in damp-smeared pencil.

Chère Maman, Cher Papa Calum,

J'ai peur. Quelqu'un me poursuit. Je ne sais pas qui c'est. Prenez soin de mon bébé chéri. Je l'appelle Aline. Je vous aime. Soyez heureux ensembles.

Marie

I handed it back to Calum. He read it out in translation:

Dear Mummy, Dear Papa Calum,

I'm afraid. Someone is following me, I don't know who it is. Take care of my darling baby. I call her Aline. I love you. Be happy together.

Marie

Calum gave the paper to me, and I put it in my own pocket.

Calum turned to Lachlan. 'She was telling us in the letter that the baby was called Aline. And she calls me Papa. I am her Papa.'

'Yes, she told me that when we met to make the baby. It made me happy. It makes me happy now. But why did they do this to her? Why did they kill her?'

'They saw the baby,' Calum said gently, 'and they knew it was not Harris's baby.'

'That's why I came here to Lennox Island. When I saw the baby myself, I knew for sure it was mine. So they killed her because they knew that!'

'It's not so simple,' Calum said. 'They don't know who you are. And listen! I'll go on speaking in English because I want Chad to hear, and I know you understand. But listen! I don't want you to think these bad people killed Mairi because of you. Do you know something? They would have killed her in one way or another, whether right away, as they did, or across dozens of years. They would have killed her because they are bad and she was good, because they are full of hate and she was full of love. She made a mistake in going to those people – in marrying Harris in the first place. I don't know why she did it. We can talk about it many

167

times and I don't think we shall ever know why. But it was her mistake, not yours. One of the best things she ever did was to love you and give herself to you once she knew she could never love Harris. And some day soon you will see that baby of yours and hers again. Now I want you to be brave and upright and be ready to be a father to that baby – Aline. You were the first person to take care of Aline so long after her mother. You won't have to look after her all the time. Mairi's mother and I will do that. I know that sounds strange, and perhaps even Chad here doesn't believe it will happen, but I swear it to you, because I know it in my heart, that Mairi's mother and I will look after that baby. And you will come and see us and the baby will grow up knowing you are her father.'

'Dad,' Lachlan said. He pronounced it something like 'Die-dge,' and by now I recognised it was the Gaelic version. 'Thank you and I trust you. I'll look after myself and I'll stay here for now. But the moment you need anything, you must call for me.'

'I will.'

We got up from the bench and walked back to thank Sagwa Joseph and say goodbye to him and to Lachlan whom MacKinnon held in a hug for a moment. Then MacKinnon and I mounted our horses and rode over the bridge and off Lennox Island.

On a wide stretch of the road we were able to walk our horses side by side, and we talked a little.

'I still don't understand,' I said, 'why they – meaning, as you said, either Harris or Gallant or their people – why they killed Marie. Just to get rid of her? It doesn't seem they knew about Lachlan. They would have known nothing about how the baby was conceived. But the story of the baby being a Mic Mac was out, since Dr Kelly had seen her. Now that Marie has been murdered it has caused another scandal for Harris on top of the potential scandal about the baby. I can't imagine the murder being for political reasons, or because of some conflict over smuggling. Marie was involved in none of that.'

'It's nothing public,' Calum said. 'This is personal. Someone wanted her dead – not only that, he wanted to kill her. I say "he" because I can't imagine it being a woman, and because as you described she was… Jesus Christ!' he burst out. 'Whoever did it was a monster! As I said to Lachlan, the deed was done from hate. There was no *reason* for it. How could there be? Once the truth came out – through the birth of that innocent baby with its Indian mark – then someone wanted to kill both the baby and Mairi. Maybe they would have tried to find out who the father was and gone and tracked Lachlan down and killed him too! It could only have been either Harris or Gallant – plus perhaps Edgar Aucoin who works for them both. Or both of them together, with Aucoin? But I don't think Harris and Gallant trust each other enough for that. They are both skunks. It would be one or the other of them. Yet, skunks though they are, it's hard to believe. From what I know of them, their first instinct would be to cover things up. They have money – more than is good for anyone. They could send Mairi and the baby off island – away for a health cure or some such fiction. They could bribe Kelly with a few cases of brandy to shut up. They could intimidate the others who knew – the Aucoins and Madeleine. By "they" I mean either of them. Harris or Gallant. It always comes back to them. But I still don't understand how either of them could have actually killed her – and so brutally.'

12

Calum was riding his own horse, a brown mare, and I was riding a speckled grey gelding that was part of the horse hiring relay of the island. At one point the road, which was the usual hard red earth, cut through some woods. The terrain was flat and the road was raised above water-logged drainage ditches on each side. Suddenly I heard a bang and my horse reared backwards and threw me. I landed with a thump on the road and lay there shocked and winded. Immediately there was another bang and I saw Calum's mare, just in front of me, collapsing sideways to the ground so that Calum was able quickly to disengage one leg and slide off. I was dazed. My horse was lying on the ground making a shrieking whinnying sound with blood pouring from his head and foam from his mouth. I staggered onto all fours and crawled into the ditch beside me with a squelch. It was boggy and muddy. Calum threw himself down next to me, reaching into his pocket for his revolver, and I reached for mine. The mare was not moving and not making a sound. My horse was now making a moaning sound and its body was convulsing. It stopped.

There was silence. Calum tapped me on the shoulder and made a gesture that he would look in front, and I should look behind. I swivelled around in the mud and water and looked behind me in the woods. No movement. All was quiet. Neither of us moved.

The horses had each been shot in the head. I could see the poor speckled grey gelding over the edge of the ditch, a mass of blood spreading from his head onto the road.

We lay for a long while, waiting. Nothing happened. Nobody else on the road. We looked at each other. Our clothes, faces and hair were wet and muddy. 'That was a warning,' Calum said. 'Whoever did this could have shot either of us.'

We waited for a while longer. Twenty minutes or so. There was no sound except the occasional cry of a bird. I stood up. Nothing happened. Calum stood up beside me. Each holding a revolver and pointing it from side to side, we inspected the horses. Each had been shot in the same place, exactly between the eye and the ear on the left. In each case the bullet had gone through the head leaving a wide and messy exit wound on the other side. We looked at the road surface behind their heads and around their bodies. Both had voided dung. The blood was profuse, covering the road around their heads, and with a butcher's shop smell that reminded me of the post-mortem in Charlottetown.

'I can't see any bullets,' I said.

'Nor can I. They'll be miles away. So far as I know there are two kinds of rifles that could do this – the Enfield and the Springfield. A lot of them came up here after the American Civil War. People use them for long-range shooting of moose or deer. No problem at all for an experienced hunter to hit the horses in the head accurately from eighty yards or so.'

'I had an Enfield 1853 in Victoria. I agree they are accurate. But they take at least ten seconds to reload. These shots were only a few seconds apart. There must have been two marksmen.'

It is impossible to move a dead horse. They were blocking the road. We decided to walk ahead, towards the next village, Miscouche. We detached our bags from the horse harnesses and carried them. We were soon out of the woods into more flat land, now with fields on each side. Towards us came a one-horse wagon with a man and woman sitting in front. The man reined in and stopped. He knew Calum by sight. Calum explained that our horses had been shot from under us and we needed to get urgently to St Eleanors to report the incident and send messages.

We helped the man turn the cart, and then with us sitting on the back of it side by side with our legs dangling, he headed along the road and after fifteen minutes or so we entered a long straggling village of wooden houses. The farmer called out and people came out of their houses. 'Two dead horses back on the road!' There was a brief conference of neighbours and it was decided that one farmer would take out a pair of horses with ropes to drag the dead horses into the ditch. Someone ran off to find the village blacksmith who might want to scavenge the corpses. It was as if the two dead horses represented a treasure fallen from heaven.

Calum and I stood outside in the sun and took stock – again.

He said he wanted to go back to the croft. It would only take him a few hours to walk to a friend's house in Kensington and stay the night there. He was adamant that this would not be dangerous. For one thing, he would walk through fields and woods, not along the road. For another, he thought that if we were being observed, it would appear that he was no longer involved in my investigation, which was perhaps less threatening to whoever had shot at us. The next day he would find a ride to Malpeque. And when he got back to the croft, he would ask Duncan to stay with him. As for myself, I decided to go to St Eleanors. I could get a Miscouche villager to take me in a wagon, and I could send a telegram from Summerside to McNulty.

'I want to question people who had to do with those orphanages in Summerside. I'll make sure not to meet anyone alone. McNulty will have been doing his own investigations about the orphanages and who was involved with them. I have a sense that there must be more of what we have called Harris's and Gallant's people than just the Aucoins and Cormier – the one Cormier we know about at least. Let's say that it might have been Aucoin who shot at us. From what we know about Cormier he would not have been capable of it. I doubt if Aucoin could have followed us and shot at us without help from others. And I don't

173

understand the short interval between the shots unless there were two marksmen'

'In any case they are warning shots. What's the warning? Something like: "We are watching you. We are following you. We can kill you any time." Although admittedly this ignores the consequences of killing us. There are not such consequences from shooting a couple of horses. There would be great consequences from killing you with your mission from on high in Charlottetown. If they have been following us they must wonder why we have been together, why we went to see Lachlan, and what Lachlan might have had to do with the finding of the baby. I presume they already think Lachlan is the baby's father, and that I will know. So they may think it's a good idea to scare me off, no matter what I have told you. They are also showing us they have power and numbers. As in fact we are concluding now.'

'Yes. But there are two of us. I can understand they are warning *you* off. They are sending a message to you via a bullet in your horse's head: "MacKinnon, clear off! Don't get involved in this murder investigation!" Or is it more personal? "Stay away from Madeleine Gallant." Or "Make sure your adopted son stays on Lennox Island!" But as for me it must be more general. I am simply doing my job for Mr Brecken. Yes, the warning is "Keep off!" But that won't work. I cannot keep off unless I resign from my engagement. I may be more cautious from now on. But as I say, although whoever it was shot both our horses, I do think the most urgent warning was for you. They are frightened of you for some reason. What can that be? You know too much. All right. But what about your involvement with Madeleine? Is there a "Keep off" message there too? If so, I wonder if Honoré Gallant is behind this.'

'But Honoré doesn't know!' said Calum. 'I mean about me and Madeleine.'

'Don't be so sure. You must be careful.'

I was wondering rather anxiously what Calum might do next. I doubted if he would lie low in his croft for very long.

'I've got to get Madeleine out of there,' he said. 'I must go to North Rustico.'

'Look before you leap,' I said. 'I hope my wife and her friend are helping Madeleine. If they are being prevented from doing so, I'll want to know. McNulty will know if she's safe – if they're all safe.'

Suddenly the giddying thought of Lucy and our own baby Will perhaps being in danger made me feel sick and anxious. But I reminded myself that she was at Ocean House in the company of the Governor's wife, and if McNulty had sent policemen there as planned, she should be safe. All the same…

'I won't stay in St Eleanors for long,' I said. 'I'll go to North Rustico the day after tomorrow.'

'Then so shall I. Where do you stay there?'

'The Seagull Tavern.'

We shook hands, and I went back to the General Store to arrange transport to St Eleanors. I borrowed a brush from an assistant and managed to clean patches of drying earth from my blue police coat and grey trousers.

I ended up riding a hired horse, with the man who had hired it to me riding another horse to keep me company. He was a talkative Acadian but I said I could not answer his questions and I needed to think. He said he would leave me at the courthouse building in St Eleanors.

This was another square wooden building, as in Charlottetown, but smaller and prettier, with a lawn and flowerbeds and a low fence of iron railings.

I dismounted, paid my guide, and walked up to the door. It opened. A red-haired policeman in uniform looked at me curiously.

'I'm Hobbes,' I said, as usual not sure what title to use. 'I would like you to telegram Sergeant McNulty in Charlottetown, immediately.'

He broke into a smile which he tried to suppress. 'Oh there's no point in that, Sir,' he said, 'The Sergeant has arrived just now.' He let me into an office where McNulty had just stood up from a desk.

We sat in a large back room of the building which was used as the police station, with its two windows open to let in a breeze in which I could see the green branches of elm trees gently waving. It had been a hot day. At least the building, although smaller, was roomier than the Brig in Charlottetown. Part of the ground floor was used as a lock-up for people arrested in brawls or other disturbances of the peace, but the building was quiet. There was a court room on the upper floor.

The first thing I wanted to know was how things were at North Rustico.

'They have sent Mr and Mrs Aucoin packing. Gallant is out of town, in Georgetown or somewhere down east doing notary work – supposedly. By the time I had got there, Madame Gallant had asked the Aucoins to leave. I'm not sure of the details. Mrs Hobbes and Mrs Robinson had been visiting, and it was decided that Madame Gallant and the baby would stay with them at the Ocean House.'

'Did you see my wife?'

'Yes, I paid a courteous visit to Ocean House and was welcomed into the lobby where I had a talk with all three ladies, and an opportunity to see I think five children, including the baby who is apparently in better health. Again, I suspect the details are family matters that Mrs Hobbes will tell you about. She pressed me to describe where you were and what you were doing, which of course I could not. I reassured her that I had asked for one policeman to be sent from St Eleanors to assist you. I didn't mention that I had no idea whether he had caught up with you or not. But now that you are here in St Eleanors, this can be done. She's a lovely lady, Sir, if I may say so, and apart from her concern about yourself, I would say she looked happy. And your little boy was running around with

176

the other children. They are livening up the Ocean House, I dare say, but as a new hotel it's not yet full, and I imagine having Mrs Robinson there gives the owners pleasure. Otherwise the guests seem mainly Americans.'

'I'm relieved to hear all this. Now to catch up… But first, if we could call a local constable in, I have to ask him to follow up events in Miscouche.'

McNulty called in the red-haired young constable who had opened the door to me. His name was Armstrong. I recounted to McNulty and him what had happened following my meeting with MacKinnon and the Mic Mac on Lennox Island. McNulty listened thoughtfully. Armstrong took a few notes on a pad, then leaped up.

'Excuse me now Sir, with your authority I'll send a man out to Miscouche now to see what's going on and take any information he can find out.'

'I'm puzzled by the shooting of your horses,' said McNulty. 'It doesn't make any sense.'

'We thought it was a warning. "Keep off!"'

'But keep off what? You are not going to stop your investigation. Even if you wanted to stop, the police would have to continue somehow. I presume the warning was more for MacKinnon than for you, although whoever it was must have wanted to unsettle you, put the wind up in you. Whoever did it was a good shot. I think of myself as a good shot, but I'm not sure I could have achieved something like that, with the horses moving. How far away do you think the person was?'

'Something over eighty yards, which is where the patch of woods began.'

'Anyway, they'll be long gone now. But you'll have to be cautious, Sir, when you travel.'

'I will be.'

I gave McNulty an account of my visit to Darnley and Lennox Island, which took the best part of an hour. I left out Calum's intimate relationship with

177

Madeleine, and focused on Lachlan's story of the Orphelinat. I also included what Lachlan had told Calum and me about his relationship with Marie, leaving out the emotional parts. McNulty listened with only occasional questions. I already respected his sharpness of mind. No need for him to take notes.

When I had finished he said, 'The story of this young man Lachlan explains many things about why Marie did what she did. So it resolves that puzzle. But it doesn't add anything to our understanding of Harris and Gallant. After all, once Dr Kelly had made his statement about the baby being an Indian, there was the possibility that the father would be a Mic Mac. And the facts that MacKinnon knew Marie and Madame Gallant, on the one hand, and that he had brought up that Mic Mac boy on the other, are well known. So Gallant and Harris will have put two and two together already. Given the warning shots I suspect there are many more villains involved in this affair than we knew last time we met. I suggest we go outside into the garden for a change of scene and some fresh air, and I can bring you up to date from my end.'

Outside under the elms there were white wooden chaises longues on the grass. We each took one.

'I've seen Mr Frederick Brecken,' said McNulty. He took a folded piece of paper out of his inside jacket pocket and handed it to me.

> *Charlottetown*
> *14 July 1871*
>
> *Dear Superintendent Hobbes,*
>
> *This will confirm that I asked Sergeant McNulty to see me to receive some information he will divulge to you. All good fortune to you in your continued investigation in which you and Inspector McNulty have my support.*
>
> *Frederick de St Croix Brecken*
> *Attorney General*

This was written in black ink. 'What is this slip in which he calls you first Sergeant and then Inspector?' I asked.

'He does have a sense of humour, Mr Brecken. Indeed I entered as Sergeant McNulty and left as Inspector McNulty. He promoted me.'

'Congratulations! That will make things easier for us I hope.'

Yet for a moment I felt a sense of chagrin. The proper thing to do would have been for Mr Brecken to consult me about promoting McNulty before doing it. I obviously did not know enough yet about 'the island way'.

'I thought I should ask him for the note,' McNulty continued, 'so that you could be absolutely sure of the origins of what I'm going to say. When he sent for you, I went instead. I gave a brief summary of our investigations. Luckily he knew something about me – I mean something positive about my work. There are many less positive things about my history, as you know. He asked how the police constables in general and myself in particular had reacted to you being appointed Superintendent, as it were out of the blue. I said we all respected you and followed your orders. He also asked whether we missed the former Marshall, Mr Morris, and what rumours we might have heard about him. He explained to me that he didn't think it would be fair to Mr Morris to explain the facts to you or to the rest of us in the police before they were more fully established. The first fact is that Mr Morris was suspended for accepting bribes. An alert new bank manager – or perhaps he had other motivations than the public good, I don't know – had notified Mr Brecken's office that large sums of cash had been deposited in one of Mr Morris's accounts over a period of time until about three years ago. Mr Morris could not explain this, so he was asked to leave, and did so instantly. This was about three weeks ago, before the murder occurred, and Mr Brecken was left facing an emergency with no one commanding the police in Charlottetown who could have taken over the investigation of the murder of Marie Harris.

'At any rate in our interview Mr Brecken asked me to communicate to you that he had sent for Mr Morris the day before yesterday and questioned him about whether he knew of any prominent men on the island being involved with crime, or with smuggling, or with other scandals that might have been swept under the rug. The sweeping under the rug question inspired Mr Morris to say that over the years, from time to time, events had occurred involving boys and girls who had been in the orphanages in Summerside and Charlottetown, which closed about three years ago. These events were usually injuries found in the children by doctors, suggesting they had suffered severe punishment. Mr Morris had taken this up with the governors of the orphanages who had offered to donate money to him "for worthy causes of his choice", if he would refrain from pursuing these matters further. They had also assured him they would look into any such matters and make sure they would not occur again – if they had in fact occurred. Mr Morris had accepted these donations and now seemed to remember that he had indeed passed them on in cash to his church over a period of time. He said the governors of the orphanages had told him how difficult some of the orphan children could be, and about their delinquent behaviour, and how the over-worked attendants in the orphanages would inevitably lose their temper at times. Mr Morris repeated all this to Mr Brecken, but he did not name names. He reminded Mr Brecken that the governors and Board members of the orphanages were changed every year or two. Nevertheless Mr Brecken knows that both Mr Gallant and Mr Harris were involved with charitable contributions to the orphanages.

'I am of course investigating this – quietly. But I'm not optimistic. Hearsay evidence is useless, and rich people can in theory hire lawyers to sue us for slander and or libel. I say in theory, because such suits simply never occur on the island. As in other legal matters the threat is what counts. Messrs Harris and Gallant were, as it turns out, occasionally on the governing boards of both orphanages – as were many prominent citizens. It's their provision of "conferences" with the children that interests us. But the more I think of it the more I doubt we shall ever be able to bring these men or others to justice. Let's suppose the most extreme case, that they tortured or even raped children. We would never be able to get enough evidence for a jury to convict them – no matter what hearsay was brought into court. You're a lawyer, Sir. Do you agree?'

'I'm not a practising lawyer, I'm pleased to say. I only studied jurisprudence at that totally impractical place, Oxford. But yes, I agree.'

'Now to my next point, Sir. It was not difficult to find out more about the Aucoins. Of course I did know already that Edgar was a bad hat. But no details, and he has no history of convictions for crime. And I am relatively new to the island, having come from "over across" in Nova Scotia. In fact the Aucoins also originated in Antigonish, but before my time there. A little digging revealed that Edgar Aucoin, otherwise known as Edgar Wedge, and his wife or supposed wife Modeste, used to run two drinking dens, or as the Irish call them *shebeens*, one in Charlottetown and then one in Summerside. Both were known as places to "pick up" women. Elsewhere they might be called brothels but those don't exist here. Both appear to have closed about three years ago. Note, they were not closed by the police. They closed. Again, I'm investigating. One thing I do persistently hear is that children were available in both establishments. Again this would be hard to prove. People don't use their real names if they are prostituting themselves, or reveal their true ages. But boys and girls coming from the orphanages were, as I say, available.'

'Not surprisingly. It has no doubt been the same everywhere across the ages. But we do live in especially hypocritical times. It's all invisible except to those who know how to look and find. But I see where you are tending: there's a possibility that boys and girls proceeded from the orphanages to those drinking dens of a particular kind – the *shebeens*.'

'Exactly. And legally this is "procuring", and if it can be proved, convictions for it occasionally occur. I mean out in the wide world "over across" they do. There have been none on our island "Cradled on the Waves" so far. But for the future, who knows? Pardon me, Sir, it's tactless to use the phrase "Cradled on the Waves", given our current investigation.'

'Between us – Inspector – you can be as ironical as you would like.'

'Thank you.'

'Since our current investigation is into a murder in this area, I think we are justified in finding out everything we can about Messrs Harris and Gallant, including their previous involvement with the orphanages, in particular the ones in Summerside. With the orphanages closed, how are orphans taken care of these days?'

'The buildings have become a boys' school and a girls' school. The orphans stay with families and attend the schools along with children from ordinary families. I think this happened because people are now more prosperous, and there are more doctors, so there are less deaths of young parents, and consequently there are less orphans. And the church now pays for families to take in orphan children.'

'What about the Presbyterian orphanage? It was smaller from the start, I believe.'

'It has closed down I think, and similarly orphans are sent to live in ordinary families.'

'I want to talk to the former religious supervisors of the former Orphelinat and the Presbyterian orphanage. Who are they?'

'Father Arsenault and the Reverend MacNicholl. I've already sent messages to them saying we might wish to visit them tomorrow. Perhaps being promoted to Inspector has given me confidence. I should have preferred to discuss the idea of visiting them with you first, but I thought it was reasonable.'

'Of course it is.'

'Dinner time, Sir? There is an excellent hotel here. I've already booked a room for you, and I am staying there myself.'

'Let's have a walk first. I want to stretch my legs, and I'm curious about Summerside. It's within walking distance, isn't it?'

'About half an hour.'

We set off, with Armstrong walking behind at a distance. I was surprised at how prosperous the Summerside area looked. The road led down a gentle slope and the town lay in front of us with the sea across the entire horizon to the south. We passed by farms, then a few clusters of shacks and small cottages, then we entered a grid of wide tree-lined roads with large wooden houses, painted in pastel colours, some of them ornate and 'ginger-bread,' some 'Gothic,' others more austere, all of them with outbuildings and large gardens and lawns. The place was busy with people, walking or in one-horse traps, who greeted us, raising their hats. I had no hat. I must have left it in the ditch. There were glimpses of a harbour at the bottom of the street we were on, with docks and the masts of ships, then we entered an area where all the houses and buildings – various stores, several banks – were made of red brick. It all looked sparkling new.

'It seems very different from Charlottetown,' I remarked.

'That's because it's not the capital, and the harbour, although it's excellent, is not deep enough for the big ships of the Navy without constant dredging. This is a commercial place. They build small ships, and they are the market town for the north west half of the island.'

We took a leisurely walk around the main streets. Other people, including whole families were doing the same. McNulty and I walked together, with Armstrong now following close behind.

Summerside was well named. Unlike Charlottetown which faced southeast and was somewhat hemmed in by low hills and many more buildings along the wharves where naval ships were moored, the town faced south, with a wider and more open expanse of sea, and flat promontories and shores on both sides where green fields glowed in the golden light of the setting sun.

As we were walking along the harbour I noticed an exceptionally elegant schooner – *The Fair Isle*, the one on which we had sailed to the island from Tatamagouche. I hailed a man on the deck and asked if Captain Munro was on board. The man said he was, went into the cabin, and emerged with Munro who gave a cheerful wave.

'Can I come aboard?' I called.

'You're welcome!'

I turned to McNulty and said, 'Why not wait for me back at St Eleanors? I'd like to have a chat with Captain Munro. Armstrong, do you mind waiting for me on the quay here?'

I crossed the gangplank and shook hands heartily with Munro. The sun was beating down on the varnished deck, so he invited me into the cabin where we sat on opposite sides of the table and drank glasses of rum and water. Munro was in Summerside to pick up a group of traders from Moncton, New Brunswick, who were visiting the island. He would run them back tomorrow to the mainland at Cape Tormentine – wonderful name!

'When I saw *The Fair Isle*,' I said, 'it struck me that you were just the man to ask about something I don't really understand: smuggling.'

'A particular case?' Munro said, in a suddenly guarded tone.

'No. But in my investigation – which I won't need to talk about – I come across people who speak darkly about the role of smuggling in island politics. They say certain members of the Assembly and Council are in the pay of smugglers and are influenced by them. Since you travel the seas around here, you must know a lot about it.'

'Indeed I do. But can I speak to you without what I say being quoted to others?'

'Absolutely. And you don't need to name names. I just want to know how important smuggling and smugglers are to the economy and life of the island.'

Munro seemed to relax. 'Very important,' he said. 'By definition what evades the Customs is not counted, so there are no exact figures for the trade involved. But look at the extent of it! This rum we are drinking, for example, comes direct to the island, in fast schooners only a little heavier than this one, from Jamaica. It is unloaded at night in any one of the bays or estuaries along the east parts of the island. And I'm sure you have found there is excellent French wine on the island, in any hotel or tavern. It's from Saint Pierre and Miquelon, which are French islands just south of Newfoundland, only a few days' sail from here. Hundreds of times more wine comes from France into those islands, which are legally part of France itself, than the few thousand inhabitants can consume. It then goes to the States or to Nova Scotia or to here. The Americans are more efficient at catching smugglers than we are. Even the Nova Scotians are more efficient. As I said when we first met, our Customs service is large – and the officers are well paid, so as in theory to remove the temptation of turning a blind eye to smuggling and charging their own private tariff, as it were. They are usually a lot better off even than their official pay would support. Because, you see, Mr Hobbes, we are all smugglers. Whether it's a farmer bringing in the thorough-bred horses from the States and Canada which have enabled our local breeds, which used to be so small as to be almost dwarves, to be bred up to the normal size you now see... Or whether it's you as a private citizen buying a few barrels of claret from the likes of me... I'm a smuggler myself, Mr Hobbes – not in a big way, but I've been an active trader with the French islands. I bring back cases of bottled wine as well as casks for those nice provision stores in Charlottetown, and some of the cases go through Customs in Charlottetown Harbour – enough for everyone to be satisfied – and some of them will already have found their way ashore in, let us say, Brudenell Bay, as we have made our voyage around the island coast. And thinking of the stores in Charlottetown, have you seen the fine fabrics and ornaments from all over Europe? A good smuggler will "play the tariffs" on such things. If the tariff on an item is lower in Canada than here, the item will come into Nova Scotia, pay the tariff and be transported by small boats across to here. Or it can be vice versa. Mainly our tariffs are lower than in Canada. As agreed, of course, by the Assembly. In a certain sense they too support smuggling.'

'Then, as someone said to me, there is smuggling *in* and smuggling *on*.'

Munro smiled. 'Well put! And in terms of the politics, there is what I call the smugglers' paradox. Namely, that smugglers have a large interest in keeping the island independent and outside the Canadian Confederation, but their activity undermines the island's independence! Naturally: if taxes and tariffs are not collected, the island cannot balance its books. It goes into debt. It is in debt now and the situation is worsening almost as we speak – especially with this ridiculous railway costing more than expected. Or more than officially expected, as everyone knew it would cost more. I fear that as a result we shall be forced into Canada. And although some of our politicians run around spouting about the benefits of joining Canada, there is a deep resistance to it in the population. I don't want to think of myself as a Canadian any more than as an American. I'm a Prince Edward Island Scot.'

Munro seemed to have enjoyed this discourse. 'So that is the general picture,' he concluded.

'So from what you are saying, smuggling is a sort of communal activity. Then why do I hear talk about malign influences being brought to bear on certain people, or of huge vested interests? Are there important figures in the world of smuggling who can, for example, blackmail others or be blackmailed by them?'

'I don't know of any. Blackmail would be a question of the kettle calling the pot black – no pun intended. Certainly, the more active smugglers who make most of their income from smuggling will tend to support Assemblymen or Councilmen who are against Confederation, because it would do them out of business. But as I say, they don't seem to be aware of the smugglers' paradox – that their smuggling will eventually force us into Canada! Occasionally there are fights between smugglers over who lands goods in some favoured creek mouth. Let's say I set up a floating dock in some out of the way inlet and I unload casks of wine, and I find someone else is using the dock, I'll warn them off. But another paradox is that smugglers must behave well and not disturb the peace, otherwise they risk spoiling their own business. And it's a business like any other.'

'Thank you. You have really enlightened me.'

We tossed down the remains of rum in our glasses, and said goodbye in the warm hope we would meet again.

Armstrong was waiting on the wharf and we walked back to St Eleanors. Munro had confirmed a doubt I already had about the role of sinister smugglers in the crime I had to solve. But then why did McNulty always make so much of it?

The hotel was indeed excellent, and McNulty and I enjoyed one of our usual meals of fish – here not only fresh sole, but shrimps and prawns. With two jugs of chilled Chablis. And of course potatoes. McNulty ordered the same dishes for Armstrong who was sitting over in a corner and drinking water.

13

The next afternoon at two o'clock, McNulty, and I went to see Father Arsenault, in Summerside. We agreed that we did not need Armstrong to follow us on these visits. It was a Sunday, and the two prelates we wanted to interview would obviously be at church in the morning. I had walked into Summerside again, to look out over the harbour, and then back to St Eleanors. McNulty's messages of the previous day to Father Arsenault and to the Presbyterian Minister had apologised to each of them for us having to visit on a Sunday afternoon.

Father Arsenault lived at the local presbytery, a plain house of white clapboard near the Catholic church. There were beds of colourful dahlias along the front of the house. He was now retired, helping the local priest with some of his duties. A maid showed us into his sitting room. He was a robust-looking old man in a black cassock, with thick white hair for his age, who stood up to greet us. '*Soyez les bienvenus, Messieurs.*'

We apologised for not speaking French and he turned to a clear and accurate English.

'Do sit down. How can I help you?'

'We are here to ask about the Orphelinat' I said.

'Why? It's no longer in existence. Are you investigating a crime? There were no crimes in the Orphelinat.'

'We are investigating a crime, yes, but it has nothing to do with the Orphelinat. It's the violent death of Marie Évangéline Harris, daughter of Mr Honoré Gallant.'

'How did she die? I know nothing about that. In fact I did not even know this Marie Évangéline existed.'

'She was beaten to death, we don't know by whom. Mr Gallant is not available for questioning at the moment, although we shall see him shortly.'

'That's a horrible story. But why do you want to talk to me?'

'Because his family seems to have enemies. Possibly Mr Gallant's enemies were also enemies of his daughter. Possibly he made enemies when he was a patron of the Orphelinat, and helping the children in "conferences," as I believe they were called. We wonder if perhaps a child developed a grudge against him and his family.'

This was pushing the truth a little. It did not work.

'How could you ever prove such a thing? What child? Have you any names? I can't help you with this.'

'Possibly some children left the Orphelinat with anger and resentment.'

'"Possibly, possibly". What do you mean?'

There was no alternative other than taking the risk – namely the risk of a suit for slander, eventually, if Father Arsenault discussed what we had said to him with Mr Gallant or Mr Harris.

'We have spoken to a young man', I said, 'who states that when he was in the Orphelinat he had weekly "conferences" with a patron who used to get him to lower his trousers and would examine his sexual organ, ask questions about whether he touched it, and smack him on his buttocks.'

'And why not? If the boy had been doing evil things, he deserved chastisement, did he not?'

'It's not evil for a boy to touch his own body.'

'Are you a theologian, Mr Hobbes? What do you know about such things? Are you a Catholic?'

'A former Anglican.'

'An atheist?'

'As I said, a former Anglican.'

'What about you?' Father Arsenault turned to McNulty.

'I'm a former Catholic.'

'Former this, former that. What are you doing coming to me and telling me that a practising Christian, whether Catholic or Protestant, should not rebuke a boy for defiling his body?'

'Father Arsenault,' I said, 'I am not referring to "rebukes", I am referring to a report that the patron touched the boy's genital organ. And then that the patron showed the boy his own organ.'

'And this is a report from a boy who has been defiling himself!'

'It doesn't matter.'

'It does matter, Mr Hobbes. The boy is a liar. We call these children orphans, and sometimes they are, but usually they have been abandoned by mothers who are leading vicious lives. When they arrived in the orphanage they had already been abused and mistreated. They expected that from adults. And do you know what? When they met a pure and upright Catholic, they could not understand the difference. We had all kinds of scurrilous accusations from children about teachers and patrons – even about priests! It's the world the children came from, Mr Hobbes. And the "conferences", as we called them, were to introduce the child to the life of the spirit – the child who until then had been living in the gross and material world of the flesh. Do you know what evil is, Mr Hobbes? It is to become so attached to the world of the flesh that you live in it like a pig in a stye. We have a phrase in French – *la nostalgie de la boue*. It means "nostalgia for the mud". These children had been mired in mud and they still longed to wallow in it. To enter into the spirit, we must often chastise the body. Think of the martyrs. Even as a "former Anglican" you must know about them. They rejoiced in their martyrdom – in having their flesh burnt or cut away from them.'

'But all of us, you, and I, and Inspector McNulty here, are constituted of the body. And the communion sacrament is the body of Christ. As you know, Protestants don't believe in transubstantiation – the actual embodiment of Christ in the Mass. But you do!'

'You *are* a theologian, Mr Hobbes! And if I may say so, of a very ignorant sort. As St Augustine said, *Inter faeces et urinam nascimur*. Shall I translate?'

'*Non necessit*,' I could not resist saying. ('It is not necessary').

'We are born between the shit and the piss,' McNulty said suddenly.

'How dare you use words like that in this house?' Father Arsenault said angrily. 'Please leave at once.'

'I apologise, Father,' said McNulty. And turning to me, 'I'm sorry Sir.' He looked at me, then back to the priest. 'All three of us here understand Latin.'

'I'm sorry Inspector McNulty got carried away,' I said.

It would have stuck in my craw to keep calling this priest 'Father'.

'But in pointing out that all three of us understand Latin', I went on, 'he was perhaps referring to your remark about my ignorance. Of course we shall leave. Thank you for seeing us.'

McNulty and I stood up. The priest remained seated, looking into the distance. Then he said, 'I may have been intemperate just now. What you report is distressing. But the orphanages were closed three years ago. It is all in the past – *if* it occurred. I cannot believe such a story. We had some very evil children in the Orphelinat, and their evil contaminated others – as rot spreads from a bad apple in a barrel. It sounds as if you have met one of the rotten apples from the barrel.'

We walked out into the sunlight.

'I do apologise again, Sir,' said McNulty. 'I over-reached myself. As a former priest…'

'Don't worry. As a former Anglican… I must have sounded rather silly myself.'

'When I was in the seminary, in Ireland, each seminarian had a cell to himself, along a corridor, with a bed and a table and a chair, and with a space above the door so that every sound from each cell could be heard. The priests used to pass by, listening. And on a hook on a wall in each cell hung a whip. Whenever we had a sinful thought, we were supposed to lift our cassocks and lash ourselves on our bare backs and buttocks. All night the corridor resounded with the smacking sounds of the whips and cries or groans of pain. I used to beat my leather satchel rather than myself, each time letting out a groan. The priests used often to quote St Augustine.'

At four o'clock we visited the Reverend Hector MacNicholl. He lived in a small, trim, grey clapboard house, on a pleasant street with elms and maples for shade, and with a particularly well-maintained lawn and beds full of vegetables, not flowers. Austere and practical. The door was opened by a middle-aged woman in black – possibly mourning – who said she was Mrs MacNicholl and led us into a book-lined study where we were greeted by a tall, lean man with an almost completely bald head and rather bulging grey eyes behind spectacles. He shook hands briskly, and we sat down in equidistant leather backed chairs. It reminded me of being called to the headmaster's study at school.

As with the priest, I explained our mission, to investigate allegations of harm to children in the past, when the Presbyterian orphanage existed.

'We do things differently now,' he said. 'It's more like home for the orphans to live in a family – provided the family is respectable and religious. There was always great immorality in the boys and in the girls. However the boys apply themselves more seriously to reading, once their animal impulses are controlled, than do the girls who are full of shallowness and gossip and vanity.'

There was no particular incident I could refer to on the girls' side – nothing to match the story of Harris. 'So you had no unexpected events among the girls,' I said, making a stab at a controversial subject.

'You mean did they get in the family way? Of course they did, from time to time, the wee hoors. Nothing would keep them away from the boys from the town. Not our own boys! After nightfall they were kept in under lock and key, I can tell you. So were the girls, but they were more devious. They would find ways of getting out of the girls' house and into the bushes even. We would go around the gardens of the neighbourhood at night with lanterns and flush them out – shameless they were, rolling half naked with boys in the soil beneath the bushes. And the boys would threaten us with their fists and tell us to go away – in the usual obscene language of this island. Now imagine!' – he said vehemently – 'imagine you are directing an institution of this sort. You cannot expel anyone! You cannot send the child back to where it has come from, or to its parents. There are no parents. All you can do is punish them.'

'How?'

'You can lay on the rod. But how does a man lay the rod on a girl without obscenity? No, we punished the girls through confinement and isolation. They hated their school classes, the little hussies, but they longed to be back in the classes when they were locked for day after day in a bare room with only bread and water, and of course the Bible to read. Then they would repent! They would go down on their knees and cry – whether the tears were true or false we could never know – and beg to come back to classes. In our ministry we don't have confession, a hypocritical act, a matter of babbling prayers in a Latin they don't understand. We want genuine repentance. If you are alone in a room for weeks, except for a knock on the door to say your plate of bread will be handed in, you will read the Bible. You will be reached by the Word! And we taught almost all of them, excepting of course the congenital idiots, to read. They will thank us for that! As old ladies suffering on the hard road of life, they will reach for the power of the Word! Alpha and Omega, the first and the last word, that is the Lord!'

McNulty spoke suddenly. 'I recall a church in the North of Ireland where there was not a single graven image, there were only chairs for the congregation and the Communion table without even a cloth on it, and the windows were all of clear glass, only for the main one in the east end that had two letters on in it in golden glass: the Greek Alpha and Omega.'

'And what was your church?'

'We were the First Wee Free Presbyterians of East Donegal. Our motto was "Freedom is Dissent".'

'I know that motto. A dangerous one. It leads to Unitarianism. There is no dissent among the Elect!'

'There was much dissent among Presbyterians where I lived,' said McNulty. 'In my town there were five different manses: the "First and the Second Presbyterians", the "First and the Second Free Presbyterians", and the "Wee Frees". All according to how the Bible was read.'

'And I dare say there was a Unitarian church too. And then a Reformed Unitarian. But these differences can happen among the common children of a father, each trying to understand his Will. Our church is a Father, not a Mother like the Roman church whose children cling in fear to her skirts and are afraid to speak their minds!'

I interrupted. The last thing I wanted was a ferocious discussion of theology. I was a little surprised that yet again McNulty had spoken out so bluntly. It was in character, of course, but was his promotion going to his head?

'What about "conferences"?' I asked. 'They were part of the care for both boys and girls, were they not?'

'Indeed. Our church Elders offered these to both boys and girls. To give them a chance to repent! To provide them with the words with which to talk to God!'

'Where? In the isolation rooms?'

'Of course. Where else! The Elder would kneel on the bare floorboards beside the girl and bow his head while reciting the words of "Our Father…"'

I interrupted again. I did not want to hear the whole prayer. 'And they would discuss the girl's predicament?'

'The exact word, Mr Hobbes. The "predicament" of the tormented soul before God!'

'And you never heard of anything improper occurring in these conferences.'

'What sort of a mind do you have, Mr Hobbes? Is the purpose of your visit to ask me about allegations of impropriety when the orphanage was still open? If so, my answer is simple. There were no allegations, and no impropriety. And when the orphanages all closed three years ago, they had the best of reputations.'

'But some of the older girls became pregnant. By whom?' I may have been over-reaching myself here.

'You mean, "in the family way"? Watch your language, Mr Hobbes. This is a manse you are in. And "by whom"? By whom else than the filthy boys who were after them, the dirty wee scuts.'

'Do you remember Honoré Gallant?'

'Of course. Mind you he was a Roman, not a Presbyterian, poor man. But he had an open mind. I thought he might at last abandon idolatry and let the Word in! He would journey from North Rustico to Summerside every two weeks to do his duty with the children – particularly in conferences with the girls. He was like a kind father to them.'

'And what about Mr Harris?'

'Like Mr Gallant with the girls, he would provide conferences with the boys. A rock, Mr Hobbes! A rock of Christian faith! I am happy to have him among my acquaintances. He still visits me whenever he is in Summerside. That poor wife of his! Now I see why you are here. Leaving no stone unturned. I forgive you for your previous rash words. It is something to become agitated about, when a man's wife is taken from him in such a violent way. Mind you, she was a Roman Catholic, and the marriage was doomed from the start.'

I could say nothing to this. 'Thank you for receiving us. It has been most helpful to hear about the orphanage – when it existed.'

We all stood up. We shook hands. McNulty said something to the Reverend MacNicholl in a language which I now recognised by its sound as Gaelic. The Reverend gave a sour smile and said, 'I'm a Lowlander, Mr McNulty, and we have long come out of the Tower of Babel.'

Mrs MacNicholl reappeared in the hallway and opened the door to let us out. She looked tired. 'Browbeaten' was the word that came to mind. But I had been influenced by my meeting with her thunderous husband.

McNulty and I walked from Summerside back up to St Eleanors.

'Again, I must apologise, Sir,' said McNulty. I find that meeting these men of God reminds me of my own religious travels, and I find it hard not to speak my mind.'

'Oh well, it's a Sunday, and I suppose it's easy to think of religion. I don't think you did any harm in either case. And I do appreciate having you with me in these questionings, and being able to count on your observations when we discuss them afterwards. But you had best leave the questioning to me, until I ask you if you have any further questions. I am usually following a direction.'

'Understood, Sir. If I ruffled any feathers, you smoothed them down again.'

14

Before we set off for North Rustico the next morning, on newly hired horses, McNulty and I had a discussion of fire-arms. I still had the Colt percussion revolver I had been given by the police in Victoria, McNulty had the more modern Colt cartridge revolver. Both were powerful weapons, with large .45 calibre bullets, although inaccurate at more than ten yards or so, and not quick to use, since the hammer had to be cocked by hand before each shot. I had heard that 'double action' revolvers that cocked themselves as the trigger was pulled were coming into military use, but I had never seen one. I had done a lot of practice with my own revolver however, and I could draw it with my right hand and cock it with my left in one movement just before I fired. Most police forces also used shotguns, with slugs for ammunition, since they could kill someone at close quarters but the slug did not travel as far as a bullet which would risk injuring by-standers. The police did not need marksmen. On the other hand, MacKinnon and I had been fired on from a distance.

'We have an Enfield 1853 here,' McNulty said. 'The Enfield would be the sort of rifle that was used to shoot your horses at Miscouche. It's a British rifle. Or they might have used an American Springfield. Each cartridge has to be loaded one at a time by hand, although a practised shooter can do this in around ten seconds. What was the gap between the shots at Miscouche?'

'Three or four seconds.'

'Then there must have been two shooters, both good marksmen.'

Armstrong turned up carrying an Enfield 1853. I had not had time to tell McNulty that I was used to rifles and shotguns, having used both for hunting deer when I lived on a farm on Vancouver Island. In fact I had owned an Enfield 1853. A skilled marksman would be able to reload a cartridge within five seconds. But I was not going to argue about this.

Armstrong had some difficulty fitting the Enfield into his usual shotgun holder – a leather tube that ran across the side of the saddle, almost from tail to neck of the horse – since the rifle was about a foot longer than a shotgun. I gave him a hand.

We rode out of St Eleanors for about an hour to a small village called Kensington, where there was a turn north to Stanley Bridge and New London, but we continued due east inland for another three hours or so, turning north again towards North Rustico at Hunter River, where we stopped for a lunch of coffee and sandwiches. It was another brilliant and sunny day and we had taken our coats off and slung them behind us off the back of our saddles. We reached North Rustico without incident in the early afternoon and went to the Seagull Tavern. I asked if a Mr MacKinnon had arrived yet, and was told he had not, although they were expecting him. I excused myself from McNulty and Armstrong and walked briskly to the Ocean House. I wanted to see Lucy with a sudden feeling of desperation and I must say, desire.

I was told in the hotel lobby that the Robinson party had just left for a picnic on the beach, with their police escort, but that Mrs Hobbes had stayed behind, to follow later. I mounted a broad staircase to the second floor and walked along a corridor with a light summer carpet to her door, number 203, and knocked.

The door opened at once. She was standing there in a light pink-and-white-striped muslin dress, her hair pinned back. 'Chad!'

'My Darling! Lucy!'

We clasped each other. She tilted her head back and looked at me.

'We were all about to go out when the constable said he had just heard that you had arrived in North Rustico. I looked at Olivia and she looked at me, and she offered to take care of Will if I stayed here to meet you, and off they went.'

We started pulling at each other's clothes and peeling them off each other while still embraced, until we were naked. Lucy detached herself for an instant and pulled the bed covers off and we plunged onto the bed. My lovely girl! Her belly was now softer and had some fine lines from carrying Will, and as I suckled instinctively on her breast, milk oozed out. I breathed her in. After a while we convulsed together as we had always done, as simply and innocently as in the pitch dark of the West Coast forests. We were one.

We lay on our backs. The ceiling was decorated with new plasterwork – very expensive. 'Tell me what has been happening in your search,' Lucy said.

'Do you have time? Your friends are waiting for you at the beach. What about Will?'

'He'll be all right. If he needs "num-num", the other women will cuddle him close and play with him. If we could, we would nurse each other's children if the mother was away, but children much prefer to nurse with their own mothers. I mean, if they have a mother. Olivia is nursing her youngest child. Madeleine is nursing little Alice at least partly. I think in another week or so she will be nursing her as fully as any mother can.'

'Alice? Where did she get that name?'

'She thought of it.'

'The baby's name is Aline – I heard recently that was what her mother wanted. And how can Madeleine nurse her granddaughter?'

'It happened often among the Tsimshian. A mother would die in childbirth or be ill and her own mother would take over. I showed Madeleine how to do it. At first the breasts are dry but with the sucking the milk begins to come. And she cares so much for the baby that I'm sure

201

it helps. And at first for the milk she would pass Alice to Olivia and to me.'

'I can understand you doing this. You come from a more natural world. But Olivia?'

'She is what you would call natural. She's more complicated than I am, of course. Or at least she knows many things I don't – and vice versa.'

One disadvantage of Lucy's having learned English from me was that she could sometimes sound bookish – 'Vice versa!'

'She reminds me of Aemilia,' Lucy went on. Here she was referring to our beloved friend on Vancouver Island, now dead with her husband and son. 'Mind you she is not quiet like Aemilia, she is rather noisy and boisterous. But she loves music like Aemilia. She sings. And her husband William plays the piano and composes songs for her to sing. She misses William. Madeleine misses a man called Calum. And I miss you.' She stroked the side of my foot with her foot. 'Now tell me what has been happening.'

I did, for about an hour.

'You are a Silly Billy,' she said. Sometimes she would come out with expressions in English that she had learned from me, but use them in an unexpected context. 'You are a Silly Billy because you trust people. You are open. They are closed. But they pretend to be open. Like McNulty. He meets us at the hotel soon after we arrive. Ever since you are here he is leading you to this thing or that thing. But you are his boss! You are the leader. It's time for you to lead him!'

I felt hurt. 'I know what you mean. As I told my story I didn't say that I have a growing feeling of mistrust in him. I have no evidence for it.'

'Your feeling is the evidence. How do you feel about this other man you have travelled with, the man Madeleine has mentioned, Calum?'

'I feel very fond of him. I warm to him. I like McNulty, I like his sharp mind, his ideas, his observations. But I don't warm to him as I do to Calum. There is something cold in him.'

'That's what I saw when we first met him. He has a jagged light around his head, like lightning.'

We had often talked about lights around people's heads. Lucy saw them. I did not. But I believed her.

'Another thing,' she said. 'Bad people are trying to stop you in your search. So much that you can now go nowhere without police to protect you.'

'McNulty has made sure of that.'

'Yes. But you and McNulty travel back and forth on this island and nobody shoots at you. You travel with the other man, Calum, and somebody shoots your horses from underneath you. Why?'

As so often, Lucy's mind brought forth things I had been hiding in mine.

'They want to scare Calum off,' I said, 'because he knows too much.' But I realised I was not satisfied with my own explanation.

'I suppose I should go now,' Lucy said. 'But first, hold me again.' She turned on her side, with her naked back to me, and pulled her knees up.

I held her from behind and caressed her breasts, allowing our lower bodies to find each other until I went into her. We moved for a long time until we shook in ecstasy on the bed. Again as one.

We got up and dressed. We went down the stairs to the lobby. Armstrong was sitting in an armchair, facing the stairs. He rose to his feet. I introduced him to Lucy.

'I must go to see my friends,' she said.

She turned her cheek to me for a kiss, and left the hotel. Another policeman who had been sitting in another chair jumped up and followed her.

'Thank you for being so efficient,' I said to Armstrong.

'Not at all, Sir. Inspector McNulty has had to go down east to George-town. He suggests we follow him there.'

Who was leading who?

'Why?'

'He had a report that Edgar Aucoin had been seen there, with one of the Cormier brothers. And Mr Gallant is apparently there too.'

'How far is Georgetown?'

'Fifty miles or so.'

'A lot too far for us to get there this evening. Did the Inspector mention any danger? Did he talk of needing extra arms or police? Or of threats to other people?'

'None of those, Sir.'

'We'll go tomorrow, first thing. The island roads are good. We should be there by mid afternoon. By the way, do you know if Mr MacKinnon, from Darnley, has arrived at the Seagull?'

'I believe he has, Sir. He came and asked us where you were.'

'"Us" meaning who?'

'Myself and the Inspector, Sir.'

'I need to talk with Mr MacKinnon. Ideally we should provide him with police protection but of course we don't have enough constables to do this. I'll warn him to be careful.'

'Yes Sir.'

MacKinnon had secured a room at the Seagull, but on the second floor. I asked Armstrong to arrange with the landlord that MacKinnon should move down to a room next to mine. Then I went to find him. He was pacing back and forth in the grassy area, almost a field, around the hotel. 'I want to go to Madeleine,' he said, 'but I've been waiting to hear from you first.'

'Let's go for a walk,' I said, 'then have dinner. I can see you're pretty restless, but I don't think you should see Madeleine until tomorrow morning. I'll explain.'

Armstrong had reappeared, and I asked him to follow us as we walked. It was still daylight and there were a lot of tourists from what

204

was known on the island as the Boston States. They were walking along the wharves where brightly painted fishermen's huts looked down on the traffic of people, and small sailing boats were tacking into the harbour and unloading boxes and tubs of gleaming blue and white fish. There was apparently an early 'run' of mackerel which were caught by long hand-lines with dozens of hooked lures attached, paid out behind the boats. Around a headland beyond the wharves was the shore – a curving beach of pink sand, with only a few people walking along it here and there. The party from the Ocean House would have returned. MacKinnon stopped on the sand and looked back over the dunes at the huge hotel on its hill, with the sun beginning to go down behind it.

'Did you see them all?' he asked.

'No. Just Lucy – my wife.'

We set off along the beach on the strip of hard sand where the waves were gently pounding as the tide went out. Occasionally we had to dodge around puddles and pools. Seagulls swooped down and shrieked noisily as they plucked at various objects stranded or unearthed by the tide – pieces of rubbish, shellfish, small jellyfish, tiny fish in puddles. Plovers scurried piping from puddle to puddle. Flocks of geese descended honking and splashed into the sea behind the waves.

I told Calum about my visits to Father Arsenault and the Reverend MacNicholl – leaving out McNulty's comments. These were police inter-views, but I wanted to report to Calum anything relevant to Lachlan's experience of the Orphelinat.

When I had finished, Calum said, 'Two coins out of the same purse! Can you see how alike they are? It goes back to St Augustine, or further to St Paul – or who knows, perhaps to Jesus Christ himself although I hope not. It's the terror of the flesh, its mortification, the hatred of what you fear. During the Highland Clearances our church ministers let us down. For one thing they were snobs, they sucked up to the chiefs who had sold their souls for money. For another they proclaimed that since everyone was damned to everlasting hellfire anyway, it was wrong for people to resist when they were turned off their lands and their cottages torn or burned down. As the flocks of sheep came into the land, flocks of Gaels, God's own sheep, left it for North America. They were all doomed! There was a tiny chance that they might be among the Elect who would escape damnation. But the slightest sin of the flesh meant they were not. The old songs that celebrated the joy of the flesh and mourned its death, and the language they were spoken and sung in, belonged in the eternal fires! And by God, this worship of Hell – that's what it is, after all – has followed us over here, to New Scotland and New Ireland, as Nova Scotia and Prince Edward Island were originally named. It's a beautiful place here! As you can see. But we are not allowed to live up to its beauty. Look at Madeleine – a prisoner in an arranged marriage with a rich and grasping man who has "got no courage in him", as the old English song says about impotence. And look at what happened to our daughter! My God!'

His voice had risen to a roar. But he looked around at the dazzling spray of the waves pulling back in the setting sunlight, and became more calm.

'Tell me about Madeleine,' he said. 'How is she?'

I told him more or less everything Lucy had told me. 'They're happy,' I said. 'I spent some time with my wife, but I would have felt like an intruder if I had gone to see the other ladies and all those children. They are women together – women and children. Men don't belong with them. Mind you, there are police at a distance, for protection. I imagine Madeleine must want to see you as much as you want to see her, but you'd be better not to intrude right away. Find the right moment. And pay court to her. I know that sounds old-fashioned, but they are in a way holding court.'

'A Court of Women!' Calum said. 'How wonderful! And it's indeed wonderful what you say about Madeleine nursing the baby.

What a miracle! What your wife and Mrs Robinson are doing to help Madeleine beggars belief. I'll not barge in. I'm happy for my granddaughter. Alice! Or Aline! A coincidence, one might say but perhaps it's a law of affinity or some such thing. When poems form, words seem to pair up from thin air. Perhaps this is happening with the names Alice and Aline. And you are describing something from the old days. Women in the Highlands would nurse each other's children. The great woman poet of the 17th century, Margaret Ni Lachlan, who lived to be over ninety and had many children of her own, is said to have suckled as a foster mother sixteen other children. All of the children she had herself and all the sixteen she fostered are said to have died before her, but I think that is hyperbole by way of tribute to her great age.

'I'm getting to be an old man, but I feel young. I would be honoured to have Madeleine as my wife. But since she cannot be in the Christian sense, I'll ask her to be my wife in the old pagan sense. We'll bring up our grandchild together, no matter what the world thinks! But yes, I'll take it slowly a while longer. God, Madeleine and I have been broken by what happened to Mairi! And here we are beginning to hope again. I'll wait. I have waited for years, but it's my own timidity that has stopped me – my fear of what the world would think, of having to close my school because the ministers – the various Hector MacNicholls – would be forbidding the parents to send their children to me. So be it! I'll pass the school to someone else, and I'll farm my croft, and I'll trap lobster and rake clams. And in the evenings Madeleine and I will read together – and cry together about Mairi – and go to bed together.'

We walked back along the beach in the dying golden light. Over our lobster dinner – with jugs of claret in defiance of the convention of white wine with fish – we discussed the ins and outs of Christianity as we both had experienced it. I was tactful in my reporting of McNulty's interventions. I did not know what to make of McNulty.

I went to bed and thought of Lucy. I could smell her on my body. Sometimes I thought we were like Babes in the Wood, innocents who had lived together for two years locked into each other's thoughts, talking almost entirely to each other, as Lucy learned more and more English, carefully and in fascination. We would stay up by the fire in winter discussing the meanings of words. I would tell her about English history, and discuss what I knew about the various countries on the globe we had in our sitting room. I knew so much more than she did about this world we now lived in. But as always she had the ability to catch me up short with the truth about myself. 'Silly Billy'. Yes. I had allowed myself to be led by McNulty. Why? Because he was at home on this island. Because he was already part of the police force. Because he was about twenty years older than I was. Because he was bright and well-informed.

Yet when I thought of Calum – who was almost forty years older than I, and who had been on the island much longer than McNulty, and was infinitely more a scholar, and was a poet, fisherman, farmer, and teacher – I realised that in my discourse with him I had felt no need to be led, and that I had in fact been very frank and blunt with him. I was not a 'Silly Billy' with Calum at all. I had liked Calum from our first meeting, and I still liked him. I had never been sure how much I liked McNulty. I respected him, yes, but when he spoke, I was sifting what he said. I did not instinctively accept it as I did with Calum. I suddenly realised that I did not even know McNulty's first name! I had never asked. How strange it was, that my ambivalence about McNulty left me open to following his lead – up to a point at least. How strange that instinctively not liking a person seemed to distort one's behaviour. Is it only with people one likes that one is oneself?

15

I woke up the next morning thinking about rifles. I went down to breakfast. Armstrong was already there in the lobby.

'How many shotguns and rifles do you have at St Eleanors police station?' I asked.

'Six Purdey shotguns, Sir, and four rifles – two Enfield 1853s, and two of the new Snider-Enfields.'

'How new are they? I've never seen one.'

'I think they have only been manufactured in the last five years or so. We only got ours recently. They're about six inches shorter than the 1853, and they are breech-loaded, so they can be shot much more quickly – ten or twelve rounds a minute. I brought the 1853 with me because I haven't had practice with the Sniders. They are apparently amazingly fast. I hear they were used in the Fenian raid in Canada, in Ontario, last year. Mind you D'Arcy McGee was shot with a revolver. But the Sniders are suited to something fast and surprising like the Fenian raids. And perhaps for some kinds of police work. Which I suppose is why Sergeant, I mean Inspector, McNulty ordered some in – two for each police force on the island: Charlottetown for Queens County, St Eleanors for Prince, and Georgetown for Kings.'

'And when you picked up your 1853 at the police station yesterday, the Snider-Enfields were there?'

'One of them was. I assumed Inspector McNulty had taken the other, after that incident where you were shot at. Now we are all on the defensive against sharpshooters. But I couldn't see that he had it

209

with him when he was here yesterday.'

'Before we traipse over to Georgetown, which I understand is more than half a day's ride, would you send a telegram to the Police there?'

'I can get it sent now. The telegraph station in Georgetown is just across the road from the police station, and they can deliver it and take a reply.'

'Please do that.'

I asked for a notepad and wrote:

> *Georgetown Police. Please confirm arrival of Inspector McNulty yesterday and that he is now in Georgetown. Hobbes*

Armstrong went out with the note, and I went in to breakfast. Calum was there, to my surprise extremely well dressed, in his usual grey suit but wearing a waistcoat and a neck-tie. It was not yet very warm although it was sunny outside. I sat down opposite him.

'In a few minutes I'm going to visit Madeleine,' he said. 'No, don't worry, I am not going to intrude on the Court of Women. But I'll ask to see her, and I'll talk to her in the lobby, and I'll tell her simply that when she is ready I am ready. That's why I came here. Then I must be off again. I received this note this morning, by the horse mail.

He reached into his jacket pocket and passed me an envelope with *UASAL CALUM MACKINNON* written in black ink in block letters. I pulled out a piece of folded lined note-paper with neat handwriting:

> *De Luain*
>
> *A Dhaid a chara, Tha mise i ndeacaireachd …*

'I assume this is Gaelic,' I said, passing it back to him.

'Of a mongrel sort. It says,
Monday'

Calum paused. 'You can see in the first word how the letter is written. In our Gaelic we would write *Di-luain*. *De Luain* is Irish. There are misspellings of this nature throughout. But the letter says,

Dear Dad,

I am in difficulty. I need your help. I am still at Lennox Island but white people have come looking for me, and Chief Joseph is worried. He will allow me to stay, but he wishes to talk to you urgently.

With love from your Lachlan

I am being helped by a Gael from Tyne Valley who apologises for his bad spelling.

'Lachlan could have dictated this. Tyne Valley is about ten miles from Lennox Island and there would be Irish Gaelic speakers there. I'll go to Lennox Island, once I've spoken to Madeleine. Now you'll say I'll need an armed escort!'

'Let me think about that. But first I'll say I am concerned this is some sort of a trap.'

'I've thought of that. But why would it be?'

'Any number of things. The least harmful, perhaps, is that someone may be trying to get you away from Madeleine. The most harmful is that someone wants to ambush you and kill you. Remember the warning shots!'

'Another possibility,' Calum said, 'is that they are trying to get me away from you, now they have seen us together again here in North Rustico. Or another is that they are trying to get you to come with me, so that they can execute on both of us what the warning threatened. I wish I knew who we're dealing with here! I don't think Aucoin, for example, would be capable of such complicated planning.'

'I suggest you go to Ocean House and meet Madeleine as you have to. Tell her you have to go back to your croft. Come back here, and I will have had time to think.'

'Good.' Calum got to his feet. Without looking back, he marched out of the door.

I sat with my stomach churning. I was too anxious to feel hungry, but I forced myself to eat sausages and bacon and eggs. I might need the energy. Two mugs of strong black coffee helped.

Armstrong was coming into the room towards me. I got up and he turned and we walked out into the hallway. I gestured to the garden door, and we went outside into a pleasant din of birdsong and the fresh green of the shade trees. We stood on the lawn half-facing each other. Armstrong held out a telegram:

No sign Inspector McNulty Georgetown yesterday or today so far.
Constable Mackie

'Armstrong, how long have you been in the police?'

'Two years Sir.'

'What is your education?'

'I finished school in Summerside with high marks. I was good in all subjects. I would have liked to be a lawyer, but my parents have little money, and I need to earn some so that I can eventually go away to College, "over across". I'm thinking of Windsor, Nova Scotia. But that won't be possible for a few years. I'm now a policeman to save up the money, and because it's one way of learning law.'

'Who is your superior in St Eleanors?'

'There is no supervisor as such, but in serious cases, which do not happen often, Marshall Morris from the Charlottetown Police would supervise us. Otherwise we divide the work amongst ourselves. So I have no boss except yourself – or Inspector McNulty I suppose, although he is part of the Charlottetown police.'

'Have you known Inspector McNulty very long?'

'Only by sight until the other day in St Eleanors.'

'You seem to be somewhat in charge of other constables in this case. Why?'

'Believe it or not, Sir, they are less experienced than I am with my two years.'

'All right. I am appointing you Acting Sergeant. You are directly responsible to me and me only. I'll send another telegram, this time to Mr Brecken.'

'Yes Sir. Thank you, Sir.' Armstrong produced his notepad again. I sat down on a garden bench and wrote while he stood waiting.

Frederick Brecken Attorney General Charlottetown. Newly promoted senior officer missing whereabouts and intent unknown. Am in North Rustico heading towards Lennox Island Tuesday with Constable Armstrong promoted Acting Sergeant. Missing officer possibly hostile. Please issue instruction for detention if found. Apologies if wrong but necessary precaution. Hobbes

I handed it to Armstrong. 'Just a moment, here is another one.' I wrote

St Eleanors Police. Please send two constables Stanley Bridge Tavern to join Acting Sergeant Armstrong and undersigned. Arm themselves rifles extreme vigilance. Hobbes

'Read them both and send them,' I said, 'then come back here and we'll discuss the day.'

I sat on the bench listening to the birds. Had I been overreacting? No. One thing was certain: McNulty had wanted me to go to Georgetown on a wild goose chase – to meet him, supposedly, but he would not be there. If I had arrived in Georgetown quite late in the evening yesterday, I would have been stuck there until today. I would not be back in North Rustico until this afternoon. By which time… what?

Another thing was also certain. McNulty had lied to me about the armoury in St Eleanors having only the Enfield 1853. He had not mentioned the fast-shooting Snider-Enfield rifle – the only weapon in existence which could have fired two shots at such a short interval as to convince me and MacKinnon that there were two marksmen shooting at the horses – something McNulty had wanted me to believe. And McNulty must now have one of these rifles in his possession. Indeed he had probably shot the horses out from under Calum and me – all on his own.

Thirdly, MacKinnon was now about to embark on another possible wild goose chase back to Lennox Island – provoked by a letter in Gaelic, supposedly dictated by Lachlan to an Irish speaker of the language. McNulty was such a speaker.

What was McNulty up to? He was taking huge risks. If he were to walk into the Seagull this very minute, he might have some excuse that he had indeed gone to Georgetown urgently to see Gallant and he had not had time to meet the police there. Or if he turned out to have a Snider-Enfield near at hand, he could always say it was for his and my protection and he had forgotten to tell me so.

There were these margins for escape for McNulty if I arrested him. And he was a very clever man. I supposed he could, at a pinch, get away with it. Nothing to convict in a court of law. Convict of what?

I was disturbed in this reverie by the arrival of Calum. He stood in front of me on the grass and looked at me seriously. 'I did it,' he said. 'I said I was ready.'

I could not tell from his expression what the outcome might have been. 'And...?'

'She said that when she was ready she would come to me. And she would be ready when the crime was solved. Although she would still be in pain she wanted to share the pain with me, and me alone.

And she said she was not only the *grandmother* of Aline, she was now the *mother* of Aline. I would have to accept that. I said I would. And finally I told her about Lachlan being the father of Mairi's child. She was not surprised. Then she said she loved me. And I said I loved her. And we said goodbye and gave each other a quick kiss, like two lovers parting. Which we are. And my God she is half broken by grief but she is so beautiful!'

I could not help smiling. 'I agree,' I said.

'Now we have to solve the crime,' he said.

'And we have to make sure you survive,' I added.

I told Calum about my conversation with Armstrong, my telegrams, and my tentative conclusions about McNulty.

'A Fenian!' said Calum. 'Now there's the beginning of an explanation of what may be going on. McNulty has already been a Presbyterian, then a Roman Catholic. Why not a Fenian next? They are all at extremes. They give people an excuse to stop at nothing. So imagine he is a Fenian. He comes to the island to try and keep it out of Canada. It's not in the Fenians' interest to have a unified country spanning half the continent of North America. He joins the police. What better way to discover the secrets of a place? For one thing he can find recruits among the Irish here. He doesn't find it easy though, since as in Canada itself, the Irish are all ardent supporters of Confederation – unlike the rest of the Islanders! How about the politicians themselves? As I mentioned back at the croft, our friends Gallant and Harris will turn. Two Councilmen out of thirteen, holding the balance between opposing camps and currently both in favour of Confederation, change their minds, and vote against it! If I were a Fenian I would seek out such people and put pressure on them to do this. How? Blackmail? Threat of scandal? But there I must stop. I cannot see how all this ties in with the hollow marriages of Harris and Gallant, and the murder of Mairi.'

'Nor can I. What you say adds another dimension to my enquiry. But it seems that those people want to lure you out of North Rustico and perhaps to harm you. We'll have to forget all the *whys* and come back to the *hows*. *How* can they harm you today? I want to get Armstrong here.'

I went briefly back into the Seagull Tavern. Armstrong was sitting in an uncomfortable chair in the hallway. I asked him to join us. In the garden we pulled up another bench for him to sit on, and had an L-shaped meeting.

Calum would leave shortly to ride to Lennox Island. He would take the road along the North Shore through Cavendish to Stanley Bridge and New London, about fifteen miles, then turning southwest eight miles or so to Kensington, then heading west via Miscouche to turn up to Lennox Island – another twenty miles or so. At what points would he be most vulnerable to attack? Any lonely point on the stretch to Stanley Bridge. There would be summer travellers on the North Shore road, but not as many people as on any of the roads after New London where the farms were more densely placed and there would be wagons going to Charlottetown full of fresh fish, canned lobster, and other goods. Supposing an involvement of McNulty with either Harris or Aucoin, then points close to Stanley Bridge might be suitable. But unless some informant from here was already on his way to tell the attackers that I was in North Rustico, they would presume that I was at the very closest three or four hours away on my way back from Georgetown. Calum would not have police protection. He would be travelling on his own account, alone. Into a trap.

So Armstrong and I would have to follow Calum at a distance. Armstrong had a pair of strong field glasses and we would watch. If Calum encountered trouble he would turn back to escape and presumably be pursued, but we would be thundering towards them from the other direction. Then what? A battle with revolvers and rifles? We only had one rifle – the slow-shooting 1853. Revolvers could shoot a round every two or three seconds but were only useful at short range.

On the other hand, think of the risk of a few armed men attacking another man on a public road. Shots would be heard. People would arrive. The attackers would be seen. On balance the three of us thought it most likely there would be a trick – something to make Calum stop, perhaps. A wagon with a broken wheel. A horse with a broken leg. And a lonely and remote stretch of the road. We could imagine too much…

The most deadly thing we could imagine was a single shot from that Snider-Enfield – through Calum's head – not a horse's. Calum dead on the road with a note in his pocket warning him of danger to his adopted son. Certainly a diversion of interest away from such as Harris and Gallant. Would the power of the law come down on the perpetrator? The power of the law on the island was currently a shambles. And if Calum were killed then my own position would be weakened. The well-paid new superintendent unable to protect him!

On the other hand, shooting a traveller from a distance with a rifle – as a follow-up to the episode of shooting the horses from under Calum and me – could cause quite a panic on the island. But it might be more likely that an attack on Calum could be disguised as a highway robbery – although these rarely happened on the island. For one thing, many travellers carried a pistol, just in case. Calum would be carrying his Colt pistol, but it would be hard for a man on horseback to shoot back quickly in the event of a sudden attack by several men.

The best we could do in the event a distant marksman was waiting would be for Calum to pause every mile or so for a rest, or to fuss over his horse, or to relieve his bladder. At those times, Armstrong or I, two distant horsemen back on the road, would sweep the land around Calum with the field glasses. And since I was a good shot with a rifle, I would keep the Enfield 1853 loose beside me, not in its case but loosely wedged between my saddle straps, with a chewed off cartridge already in it. If I leapt off my horse, grabbed the rifle holding its barrel upwards to keep the cartridge in, raised it and fired – this would only take from five to ten seconds. I would shoot – or shoot a warning shot at – anyone we saw with a gun within range of Calum.

'Are you sure you want to do this?' I asked him.

'I'm sure.'

We set off.

It was now about ten o'clock and the road along the North Shore once we got out of North Rustico was empty – long strip fields sloping up to our left, and the Gulf glittering blue to our right as we looked over low grassy headlands and dunes. There were no trees, no cover. It was tedious when Calum stopped every mile or so, and Armstrong and I took turns to examine the landscape through the field glasses from half a mile or so away. But as it turned out, the attempt came about half way as the road began to descend gradually towards Stanley Bridge. To our right now was a stretch of grass then sand dunes and the sea behind them. There were frequent sandy paths through the dunes down to the sea. There was a slight rise in the road and I realised that Calum would be lost from sight as he went over it. I gestured to Armstrong and we cantered up to the rise. As we came over we looked down the road a few hundred yards to where a group of men emerged from a path in the dunes, and one of them ran up to Calum's horse which reared up throwing Calum onto the ground.

I went into a full gallop and charged down the road, pulled my horse up and leaped off into a scene of chaos. Calum was grappling with Aucoin who was brandishing a club over his head and who suddenly let out a shout and fell backwards. McNulty, carrying a rifle – the Snider-Enfield – swung around to face me and was raising the rifle to his shoulder. I pulled out my revolver with my right hand, cocking it briskly with the left, and shot him. He fell backwards onto the road, the rifle dropping out of his hands. I rushed over to him and pointed down with my revolver which I cocked again. He was sitting on the ground, and his left shoulder was bleeding through his coat and set at an odd angle, obviously broken. I bent down and grabbed the rifle with my left hand and threw it to one side. I turned back to Calum. He was sitting in the road holding a long narrow dagger in his right hand pointing it towards Aucoin who was also sitting in the road and was clutching his side. Armstrong was running along a path chasing another man down into the sand dunes. Two of the horses milled around, their reins dangling. Another lay on the ground, struggling to get up but not succeeding and making whinnying sounds.

Calum was back on his feet. We looked down at Aucoin and McNulty.

'Christ!' said Aucoin, 'Get some help! I'll bleed to death!'

He lay backward, clasping both hands over his side, trying to stop the blood. McNulty said nothing. His face was very pale. His right hand moved away from his shoulder.

'Stop!' I shouted. 'If you touch your revolver, I'll shoot you again!'

His hand froze. Calum stepped over, reached down and took McNulty's revolver out of his coat pocket.

Armstrong came running back, panting heavily. 'He's too fast for me,' he gasped.

'Who is it?' I asked him.

'It's I-Guess,' said Aucoin with a groan. 'On the loose. God help the world!'

I ordered Armstrong:

'Gallop down into Stanley Bridge. There's a doctor there called Kelly. Get him out here as quick as you can!'

Our two horses had calmed down now and were munching grass along the road. Armstrong grabbed the reins of his horse, mounted it and rode off at a gallop.

MacKinnon's horse was still struggling on the ground. It must have broken a leg.

I went to my horse. There was a first aid pack in the saddle bag. MacKinnon took care of Aucoin, I took care of McNulty. He avoided my eyes but allowed me to cut part of his coat away with my knife and to put a pad and bandages over his shirt on his shoulder. Then he fainted and slumped from his sitting position, sprawling on the ground. I pulled him onto one side, with the wounded shoulder upward. He came out of his faint, and his eyes flickered around the scene.

Aucoin was sitting sullenly as MacKinnon bandaged his side. There was pool of blood on the hard ground beside him. The road had been of packed earth all the way, but occasionally there were patches of red sandstone shale.

'You'll be all right, God damn you!' said MacKinnon. 'It's a shallow wound. I missed your guts, it's just a slash. But if you try and move out of here I'll blow your brains out.'

He stood up and took a few steps back, turned and picked up a short club with a handle of smoothly polished pale wood and a head made of iron. He brandished the club and said,

'You know what they call this? A priest! Because it performs the last rites! It's used for killing big fish in nets or after they've been reeled in. It will crush a man's skull. And you know what they call this?'

He reached down and picked up the dagger he had left on the ground. He waved it in front of Aucoin's eyes. The blade was about a foot long.

'It's a dirk! I had it in a sheath on my leg. You think twice before you attack a Gael!'

He turned to face me.

'The man I-Guess ran up and dragged me off the horse, then Aucoin came at me with the priest.'

'We weren't going to kill you,' said Aucoin to MacKinnon. 'Just rough you up.'

'Shut up Aucoin,' said McNulty sharply – still lying on his back.

'Whisky,' said Aucoin. 'Give me some of the whisky.'

There was a leather flask on his belt. I un-hitched it and unscrewed the top. It was half full. I held it to Aucoin's mouth and he took a glug. He said nothing more.

MacKinnon was standing looking at his horse which was thrashing around and making sounds of pain.

'She's broken a leg,' he said. 'Just give me your revolver and I'll deal with this.' He turned and shouted back at Aucoin and McNulty, 'You bloody bastards! I'm going to have to shoot this horse!'

I gave him my revolver and turned my back. There was a crash from the revolver and the horse's noises stopped. MacKinnon gave me back my revolver, its barrel hot. The wounded men sat on the ground. MacKinnon and I stood to one side. With the midday sun beating down on us we waited.

16

Armstrong returned with a procession of people. We could see them coming in a cloud of dust up the road from Stanley Bridge. Armstrong and another policeman on horseback – presumably one of those I had sent for, who had been waiting at Stanley Bridge. A wagon with a driver and Dr Kelly sitting in the front seat. A horse and trap driven by Mrs Aucoin, with a woman beside her who turned out to be Dr Kelly's nurse.

'*Chéri!*'

Mrs Modeste Aucoin, that austere-looking woman, jumped off the trap as soon as it came to a halt, and ran to kneel in the sand and embrace her husband.

Dr Kelly and the nurse examined McNulty first. He said nothing but was in pain, as indicated by the drops of sweat on his forehead, a greyish pallor, and shortage of breath,

'That's a nasty one,' Dr Kelly said with relish as he tested the movement of McNulty's shoulder, and examined it from in front and behind. He clearly enjoyed coming back to the sort of work he must have done as a military surgeon. 'You'll live, but you'll never move that arm well again. Right-handed, I assume?'

'Yes.'

'Then you're in luck. I'll strap it for you. This will hurt.'

If it did, McNulty did not show it. He sat stoically as Dr Kelly bound his shoulder.

The nurse had been attending to Aucoin, as his wife Modeste sat in the sand to one side of him, her legs stretched out, rocking his head gently on her lap and crooning, 'It will be all right, my love, it will be all right.' The nurse had cut Aucoin's shirt off, revealing a chest with thick iron-grey hair, and she unwound the bandage MacKinnon had placed, revealing a fearsome but probably shallow gash just below his ribs on the left. The bleeding had already almost stopped and the nurse stopped it further.

Soon we were underway, back to Stanley Bridge. A farmer had turned up and offered to haul away the dead horse, for use as feed for his dogs. I acceded.

Aucoin and McNulty would proceed from Stanley Bridge under armed guard and with Dr Kelly's nurse to Charlottetown. In theory they should be confined in the Brig – that hell-hole of a jail. But they were both injured. At Stanley Bridge I discussed this with Armstrong – now for sure my right-hand man. I wanted to keep them out of the Brig – not only for medical attention, but because it was no place to interrogate anyone in peace. Armstrong said he had heard that Dr Reid would offer secure rooms in his sanatorium to prisoners who were ill – that is, of course, if they had the money to pay for it.

I instructed the two policemen who had come to Stanley Bridge to take McNulty and Aucoin to Charlottetown to Dr Reid's house, and to send a man ahead as soon as they could with a note from me. I wrote the note on a paper from Armstrong's notebook, asking Dr Reid if he would kindly admit McNulty and Aucoin to his sanatorium under his medical care. I would make sure they were under guard day and night, and that their bills were paid.

MacKinnon said he would go back to Darnley and his croft. He would walk to New London, then hire a waggoner to take him home. I agreed with him that he was probably safe, but warned him to be on the lookout. We parted at Stanley Bridge, looking each other in the eyes and giving each other a hug. '*Mar sin leat!*' he said. 'It means all the best to you on your way.'

I had decided to take advantage of the fact that I was at Stanley Bridge to go and see John Harris, if he was at home. Armstrong and I left our horses at the General Store and walked the few hundred yards to Harris's house. We had not wanted to leave our fire-arms on the horses, so each of us was carrying a rifle – Armstrong the Enfield 1853, and myself the Snider-Enfield I had retrieved from McNulty.

The servant who opened the door of Harris's house looked startled when he saw us. I stated who we were and asked to speak to Mr Harris. The servant, a young man I had not seen before, left us standing in the hallway and walked up the staircase. After a few minutes he came down again.

'Mr Harris will see you, Superintendent Hobbes, in the library.'

'Please make sure Sergeant Armstrong is made welcome,' I said. I left my rifle with Armstrong, and marched up the stairs.

Harris was standing in the hallway, informally dressed in shirt and trousers with indoor shoes. As before, he looked simultaneously elegant, awkward and aggressive. We shook hands stiffly and he showed me into the library. It had been completely cleaned. The leather-backed books were tidily packed along the shelves, and there were new carpets and armchairs. There was also a new desk. New curtains hung in the tall windows overlooking the bay and the spit.

We sat down in facing armchairs.

'This is a surprise,' said Harris. 'It would have been better to forewarn me. You are welcome of course, but we are only beginning to recover from chaos here.'

'I happened to be here in Stanley Bridge after a chaotic event on the road. Please excuse my looking so rough. I have in fact been in a fight.'

'A fight?' Harris's look was quizzical, as if I were reporting a tavern brawl or some such.

'Yes, in making two arrests. At least one of them concerns you. Your factotum, Mr Aucoin.'

'Yes, that does concern me,' Harris said calmly. 'Although Mr and Mrs Aucoin are no longer working for me, I'm allowing them to stay for a while in the house nearby, but I am reorganising my staff. As for me, I am reorganising my entire life – or you might say constructing a new life.' He went on, with a sweep of his hand: 'This library for example. The scene of a horror, a scene from Hell in a painting by Hieronymus Bosch – a Dutch painter.'

'I know.'

'A scene from Hell!' he repeated. 'I thought of leaving this house. But no. It's a family house, it's my house, and I have a duty towards it, in a way, as I do to my constituents in this part of Queens County, to my family tradition, and to myself.'

With that fine flourish, he looked quizzically at me again. 'And why did you arrest Mr Aucoin?'

'Because he was attempting to kill or injure Mr MacKinnon – the Gaelic schoolmaster in Malpeque.'

'The man who sent his friend to my house to tell me about the baby being found? I've never met him. Malpeque is in Prince County, not in my electoral district. Where did this attempt occur?'

'A couple of miles from here, where the road from North Rustico comes over the hill.'

'Is this Mr MacKinnon injured?'

'No. But Mr Aucoin was injured in the general fracas. He is being brought to Charlottetown, along with Inspector McNulty who is also injured and under arrest.'

'That's a surprise!' Harris looked shocked and questioning. 'What on earth happened?'

'It would seem that Mr McNulty was involved in a conspiracy to injure Mr MacKinnon. Of course this will be established or not, in due legal process.'

I hated spouting clichés like 'due legal process,' but it was my job.

'He must be very important, this Mr MacKinnon, to attract so much hostility.'

I felt stumped. Did Harris really know nothing about Calum knowing his dead wife and his mother-in-law? I decided to take Harris as he presented himself – for now.

'Do you know Mr McNulty?' I asked.

'Goodness no – I mean not apart from your investigation of my poor wife's death.'

I decided to take the plunge. 'Have you seen your baby daughter lately?'

'Only once when I went to North Rustico for Évangéline's funeral. The baby is with her grandmother. I receive regular bulletins reporting that she is in good health.'

'Bulletins from whom?'

'From my friend Mr Gallant. Madame Gallant is, I understand, very busy with the child, and she cannot herself communicate. I imagine I shall visit my daughter soon again. I'm not used to infants, I must say! But what counts is that she is well.'

'Are you sure she is your daughter?'

'How dare you ask that? You asked something similar when you were here before. It's extremely offensive. What evidence have you got to spur a question like that?'

'Mr Harris, I'm here because I want to find out the truth about what happened to your wife. I'm assuming that you want to find it out too, and that you don't already know it. I'm alone, and I'm not taking notes. Anything I may report in future about this interview is merely hearsay. For that reason, there is nothing you can say that will incriminate you in a court of law or even elsewhere. Furthermore, I can tell you I have only one axe to grind: I want to find out who killed your wife and how. I am not interested in grinding other axes. Certainly not political ones. I'm a visitor to this beautiful island, and I have no investment in its future beyond a human feeling of wishing it well. But I know there is a nexus of relationships around your wife, and you must know this too. Please be frank with me – or say nothing. But let us not pretend that everything is as it should be. It is not. Some person or persons murdered your wife in this room. Why?'

'I don't know why, and I don't know who,' he said. 'And as for incrimination and the law, leave that to me. You're not the lawyer, I am.'

'I *am* a lawyer,' I said. A white lie.

'All right, forgive me, I didn't know. I forgot for a moment that you had been engaged at a high level – by Mr Brecken.'

'So please let's return to my question. Are you sure the baby is your daughter?'

'I want to think so, Mr Hobbes. But yes, there is a question. She has, as you may know, a dark complexion, and I certainly do not. Even my wife, although an *Acadienne*, had blue eyes, as do I. I understand that babies' eyes are usually blue. This baby's eyes are very dark. It does worry me.'

'I believe babies' eyes, even if dark, are always blue. They only find their true colour after six months or more.'

I was thinking of my own baby here: Will's eyes had started as very dark blue, then turned gradually after nine months to something like mine – blue-green. Lucy's eyes are almost black.

'Some people think that two blue-eyed parents cannot have a brown-eyed child,' I said, 'so I imagine if you are going by eye colour alone, if you were *not* the father, this would be clear within a year or so. Of course the question would not be resolved without a doubt.'

I was hoping to soothe Harris with science here – or pseudo-science, for all I knew – and it worked, since he replied calmly enough, 'I've thought of this angle. And as you imply there is more than eye colour to be considered.'

There had been no mention so far of the dreaded purple spot as evidence of native Indian blood. Did he perhaps not know of it?

'Where there any other physical signs that make you think the child was not yours?'

'What do you mean? Nothing apart from what I've said – complexion and perhaps eye colour.'

'But Mr Harris, if you have doubts, as you admit, this implies doubts about your wife – please!' I held up my hand. 'Please remember what I said about this interview. I am not out to incriminate you or to impugn your wife's behaviour. But I want to know the truth.' Which, at least in this respect, I already knew...

'All right, Mr Hobbes, I'll come clean about my doubts. I loved my wife. But our physical relationship was not a strong one. Would you believe it, our relationship was largely an intellectual one? She was twenty years younger than I, and her first language was French. But she is – she was – an only child, and she grew up discussing history and philosophy and politics with her very articulate and well-read parents. I saw her on and off throughout her life, on occasional visits to her parents, and I simply knew her as a polite and lively young girl. I occasionally saw her wearing overalls, like a boy, which amused me. But a couple of years ago I was there for dinner, and so was she, now a mature young lady, and we had a terrific argument about the philosophy of liberalism, John Stuart Mill, the American writers Thoreau and Emerson. And out of that argument, and over subsequent visits which I made sure were more frequent, came a friendship. Her parents noticed and encouraged this, of course. You will have heard it said, no doubt, that this marriage was an "alliance" between Mr Gallant and me. I don't deny it. For that reason Mr Gallant was not concerned about the age difference between us. I might have expected Madame Gallant to be concerned, but she was not. She even said once that "between a man and a woman a difference of twenty years means nothing. Some women

229

like older men for their quality of mind, and many men in middle age are as fit and strong as any young man."'

I could not help thinking of Madeleine's love for Calum. What an irony that this had affected what she said about her daughter and Harris.

'So both parents approved,' I remarked politely.

'No. To my surprise, given Madame Gallant's positive remarks about age differences, she was implacably opposed. But she was over-ruled by her husband – and her daughter who wanted to marry me. We could talk about anything! We also had a shared aesthetic sense. We both liked the wallpapers and furniture designed by William Morris, we both read the novels of George Eliot – a woman, you know.'

'Yes. But you say that physically…?'

'I found her beautiful, to be sure, a pre-Raphaelite beauty, if you know what I mean – tall, slim, a long face, with blue eyes and long brown hair. But… Mr Hobbes I cannot talk about such things. I refuse.'

'All right. But obviously the marriage was consummated.'

'Yes. But… I'm a gentleman, Mr Hobbes, and so I realise are you.'

'So we cannot talk about such things? On the contrary, you must know that gentlemen *do* talk about such things to their friends.'

'We are not friends.'

'But you see my position here, Mr Harris. How can I not wonder about this question? You yourself have had moments of doubt about the paternity of your supposed daughter. And your wife has been murdered. What can have happened? You can imagine what I must consider. Was she killed by a jealous lover? Did her husband – you! – kill her or have her killed, out of jealousy? Or out of rage at finding you had a daughter who was not easily recognisable as yours?'

'I swear not the last two. I swear it to you and I would swear it anywhere. I neither killed poor Évangéline, nor had her killed.

All right. I admit that I have been assuming that you and Sergeant McNulty would eventually track down the murderer, and that this might be her lover and even the father of my "supposed", as you put it, daughter.'

'So let us put our heads together Mr Harris. Who could this lover be?'

'The baby is dark, as I said. I assume an Acadian, perhaps a friend of hers. You will have to make those investigations. I cannot.'

'But why would a lover have killed her?'

'In revenge for her having married me.'

'But if the baby is not yours, this means your wife went to this supposed lover after you were married.'

'That has tormented me. I cannot understand it.'

'Forgive me getting back to this, and I'll remind you again that anything you may say to me can only be considered hearsay and can easily be discounted: your marriage was consummated. When?'

'A few days after the event.'

'You mention a possible lover. Did you find your wife was not a virgin?'

'I see where you are going, Hobbes, you are in the police after all!' Harris said, his voice becoming angry again. 'I find my wife is not a virgin and I brood on this for almost a year, and then I kill her.'

'No. It's a question of whether this lover was already in her life or whether he entered it after the marriage. And, most important, whether you knew about it.'

'I have no idea. I have no idea even if she was a virgin or not. I know nothing about women!'

'At the age of what – about forty?'

'Yes! *I* was the virgin! I had never been with a woman. You know nothing about me, Hobbes. I was a lay brother in the

Anglican church, and of course I could have married, but I took it very seriously. "Better to marry than to burn": I chose to burn!'

'I know you worked as a lay brother in the Orphelinat in Summerside. I have talked to boys who knew you.' Another white lie, to say boys in the plural.

'Have you indeed? And what did they say?'

'That you encouraged them to confess to sinful thoughts about girls, and to self-abuse, and that you chastised them for these sins by smacking them on their bare buttocks.'

Harris was now suddenly pale. 'What?'

'What I said.'

'And is it a sin for me to chastise these sins? Are you accusing me of ill treatment of those children? They had no parents, remember. I was *in loco parentis*. Spare the rod, spoil the child! Were you never smacked by your father?'

'No, I wasn't. He preferred to correct with kindness. He was, by the way, an Anglican country vicar.'

'I would have been failing in my duty if I had not punished those boys. But I admit I was an over-zealous young man. This was many years ago. I would not now be so harsh – not after my discussions with Évangéline!'

'There was another thing. At least one boy reported that you had asked to see his sexual organ and that you had touched it. And you had shown him your own organ.'

Harris had gone pale, and for a moment he seemed to gasp for breath.

'Mr Hobbes. This is absolutely mortifying. I was a young man of very little experience, as I have said. My experience came more from books than from life. I had, however, been at a boys' boarding school where it was commonplace for boys to look at each other's organs and compare them, and even to touch them – you might say experimentally. Most of us had been told nothing about what are called "the facts of life". I assume you yourself went to a boys' school?'

'Yes I did. And I know what you are referring to. There is a lot of horseplay among boys which satisfies curiosity, and I suppose assures them that they are not different from other boys. But as a "patron" in an orphanage, and a grown-up man, you were in a different situation.'

'But I wasn't grown-up, you see!' Harris said in a kind of anguish. 'I had never been with girls or women. I felt affection for the boys in the Orphelinat. Yes, I was even drawn to them. I wanted to be their brother! By the way I was an only child, I never had brothers. And I was curious in the way you mention. And do you know, I loved my boys' school? It was Prince of Wales College, in Charlottetown. I was happy there for the first time in my life! I'm horrified that some boy from the Orphelinat – a grown-up now, I assume a man of twenty or more – told you about an incident of that sort. There were only a few such incidents. I feel horrified when you remind me of them. As I feel horrified when you remind me that I used to smack these boys from time to time. But we all did that – I mean all the teachers or patrons. "Spare the rod, spoil the child". That's what we all believed. But as I said, I would not do this to a child of my own now. I would no more smack him or her than your father smacked you! And I'll tell you another thing. I am horrified at your questioning because I wonder if you are assuming I am a pathic! Some kind of degenerate pervert! After all, I have not denied that I found it difficult, to establish the usual relations between a man and a woman with my wife. Although I loved her! But I can tell you, Mr Hobbes, that I am not a degenerate man. I admitted to you that I was a virgin when I was married, and I meant that in all senses of the word. Now that my beloved Évangéline is no more, I find myself wondering if I should take my life in my own hands and put an end, even, to my career in government. I am more suited to the life of the cloister, you might say. I sometimes wish I were a Benedictine monk with access to one of their glorious libraries! But I never could be, because I'm an Anglican and will remain so. You see, I do have principles!'

'Thank you,' I said. 'I greatly appreciate your telling me all this. And I'm beginning to understand your predicament. But let me ask you the most urgent question I can: Do you know who killed your wife?'

'No. As I said when we first met, I simply cannot understand it. If anyone might have a motive for killing her, it would be me – on account of her perhaps having a child by another man. And so you are questioning me ruthlessly about it. What a humiliation! But as I hope you realise, I just don't have such an impulse in me. I feel hurt and pained, that's all. And terribly sad for Évangéline. She didn't deserve what was inflicted on her!'

'Who else would be so angry with her?'

'Nobody that I know. Now, what is needed is that the baby is taken care of. I am grateful that Honoré and Madeleine Gallant as Évangéline's parents are taking care of her child.'

'You say her child. So you do think she is only Marie's child, and not yours?'

It seemed from Harris's account that he had not succeeded in consummating his marriage, but that he supposed a child might have been conceived in some abortive attempt at coitus.

'I hope against hope,' Mr Hobbes, 'but I also fear it cannot be. Madeleine Gallant assured me such a dark appearance – and other signs – do occur among the Acadians. But in my heart of hearts I sometimes fear the child is not mine. And how can it be proved either way? Unless in your investigations you come up with the father. That's another reason I think, after all, the child might not be mine. If the father is here on the island – perhaps a Mic Mac Indian or an Acadian – perhaps it was he who murdered Évangéline!'

'But – again – why?'

'Out of rage and frustration that she was married to me and I would be bringing up her child? I can only speculate. I'm grasping at straws.'

'So are we, Mr Harris, I'm afraid to say. Thank you again for your candour. None of what you have said about your private life will go any further. Please let me know if you learn anything whatsoever that might help us find out who killed your wife.'

'I shall.'

Armstrong was waiting below. We walked the few hundred yards back to Stanley Bridge in silence. I was thinking. As at my first meeting with Harris, he had shown candour at times – or what looked like it. A tormented man. But as McNulty had pointed out, he had lied or half-lied about a number of things. McNulty! Harris had shown no sign of recognising McNulty at our first visit, and he had now denied knowing him previously. Was this a lie? And he had denied considering any signs of the baby possibly not being his, other than dark complexion and eye colour. Then at the end he had mentioned 'other signs' – meaning the purple spot that Dr Kelly had so brutally drawn attention to? I did not think Harris had been lying in our conversation just now. When I thanked him for his candour I meant it. And I understood better how Marie had come to marry him – and what had gone wrong. His account in both interviews of the intellectual friendship between him and Marie made sense. It explained why this girl took up with a man who – however one explained it – was not attracted to women. And then there was the tomboy aspect – seeing her in boy's clothes. And he was, to put it kindly, interested in boys. And he had definitely gone wrong with boys when being a 'patron' at the Orphelinat. But I believed, and even respected, his assertions that he felt more like a monk than an ordinary man.

Governor Robinson had described Harris as 'slippery'. I knew what he meant. Harris was certainly not straightforward, as perhaps he had something horrible to hide in his inner thoughts. I hoped whatever he had done with the orphan boys was no more horrible than what Lachlan had described. Lachlan had not been warped for life on account of the incident – but then he seemed to be naturally resilient. And Harris seemed to be fighting hard within himself to stay decent. All the same,

I doubted if anyone was ever fully honest about their sexual behaviour. Perhaps Harris's true story was worse than I – or even he – wanted to think. Marie had made the wrong decision in marrying him. But she was obviously no fool. If she had seen something good in him, it must have been there.

I also realised that after our initial interview with Harris, McNulty had been finding ways to cast doubt on Harris's version of events and on his integrity, providing evidence – in retrospect spurious evidence – of Harris's various 'lies'. Now I suspected this had been a tactic to divert my attention towards Harris as a suspect. Of course there were reasons for considering Harris as a suspect, but McNulty had been adding more. And if he was directing my attention towards Harris, in effect he was diverting my attention away from Gallant.

17

We were almost at Stanley Bridge. 'Wait!' I stopped. 'Sorry, Armstrong, before we leave I want to go back to the Aucoins' house. Just in case there is something of interest.'

'Yes Sir.'

We walked back the way we had come. No sign of life at Harris's house. At the Aucoins' house a large dog on a chain lunged and barked at us. We would have to pass within his range to go and knock on the door. But it opened. Mrs Aucoin stood there. '*Tais-toi!*' she yelled at the dog. Even I knew this meant 'Shut up!' – and even though she pronounced it *Tais-toé!* She stepped down past the dog and stood glowering at us with her arms crossed. 'What do you want?'

'Aren't you following your husband to Charlottetown?'

'I wasn't arrested, was I? Here's an idea. Why don't you arrest me and send me there, so at least I can see him?'

'For one thing, if you were arrested you wouldn't see him, you'd be kept separately. For another, we have no reason to arrest you. Can you think of a reason?'

'Not that I'd tell you.'

I thought of her surprising tenderness to Aucoin back on the road. I almost wished I could cheer her up. But she was herself a criminal. She had owned what was in effect a brothel. According to McNulty…

'I suppose you've paid your dues,' I said. 'I was told that you and Mr Aucoin ran houses of ill repute in Charlottetown and Summerside.'

'Who told you that?'

'I can't say.'

'Were those the words used – "houses of ill repute"?'

'They were described as drinking dens where prostitution was practised.'

'You mean a whorehouse?'

'Of a sort.'

'That's illegal. We would have been done for it – arrested. We were never arrested. So what were these places?'

'I'm asking the questions.'

'Mine was what I believe is called a "rhetorical question" – meaning that when I ask it I know the answer.'

I waited.

'They were what we call "dance-nights", she said. 'Not drinking dens. We did sell drinks. But so does any guesthouse. Not whorehouses – meaning, I believe, a place where a man goes in and eyes up a bunch of women and chooses one and pays – and that's all that's on offer. Edgar and I invited musicians into one of our own houses, we paid them to provide music, and we provided drinks – and food too! And we rented rooms. If people got together in a dance and they wanted to rent a room, then we rented them a room. So what's illegal?'

I waited again.

'I'm not telling you anything more! If you want to know more, I'll need something in return. The release of Edgar.' She stood, arms folded, glaring at me.

'That's not possible. He may be charged with attempted murder. If he's found guilty of that, I'm afraid no amount of information will get him off.'

'You'd be surprised,' she said. 'There will be a number of people in Charlottetown who'll be sleeping badly tonight. They'll be lying awake worrying about what Edgar and I could say about them. And tomorrow they'll be talking to this powerful man and that – whoops! I forgot. Some

238

of them actually *are* this powerful man and that. And then the message will come to you from above, "Take it easy, Hobbes…"'

'Mrs Aucoin,' I said. 'Your wish will be granted. I am arresting you on suspicion of being an accomplice to an attempted murder, and for making an attempt to suborn a police officer. "Suborn" means to use bribery or other means to influence the officer in his pursuit of justice. You are warning me that if I want to do my job I shall be prevented by my superiors.'

'I know what "suborn" means. Give me a minute and I'll pack a bag.'

She went back into the house. Armstrong and I looked at each other.

'Who knows?' I said. 'She may even be safer in custody than out of it. I wonder who are "this powerful man and that". I suspect we already know one or two, but there will be others. In any case I would like to have her in Charlottetown, under our eyes. But how can we avoid putting her in the Brig?'

'We can't. But there's a ladies' lock-up out the back. It's quieter, and it's often empty.'

'That will be all right then.'

Mrs Aucoin came out onto the porch clutching a small leather suitcase. She paused to pat the dog who was now lying at the foot of the steps, and said something quite lengthy to him in French. Then to us:

'In case you think I'm giving Bo-Bo here secret instructions, I'll translate: I said to him "Don't worry, Bo-Bo, I'll stop in the village and ask someone to come out and feed you, so be sure you don't bite them." And in case you're wondering what his name means, *Bo-Bo* is a word we use to mean an injury or hurt. "*N'est-ce pas*, Bo-Bo?" she called back at the dog.

'Bo-Bo bites people,' she said, as we walked along the road. 'Thinking of which, did you manage to catch I-Guess?'

'You mean I-Guess bites people?'

'It has been known to happen. I asked, did you catch him?'

'I don't know yet whether my colleagues have found him.'

'The sooner the better,' she said. 'I'm almost glad I'm going to jail, with him running around without Edgar to control him.'

'What do you mean?' I asked. But she would not reply.

Armstrong and I travelled in a two-horse trap to Charlottetown – bone-shattering and fast. Mrs Aucoin was in a slower wagon behind with a driver. We arrived at the Brig at around eight o'clock. There were two constables there, one of them a giant of a chap called Higgins. When I introduced Armstrong as a newly promoted sergeant, Higgins went to a drawer and fished out a piece of cloth with sergeant's stripes and attached it to Armstrong's coat with a safety pin.

We had a quick discussion about what to do with Mrs Aucoin when she arrived. The women's lock-up was empty, and would remain so unless some other woman was brought in because of a fracas or assault, or drunk and disorderly. There would be a constable guarding Mrs Aucoin. One of the Charlottetown constables would be assigned to me for my protection when Armstrong was not accompanying me.

Armstrong and I walked over to Dr Reid's. He welcomed us in his usual jaunty way and said he was more than happy to look after the 'two gentlemen' we had sent him, and they were safely installed, under guard, in separate rooms in the sanatorium. They would be secure, he said, as a few rooms in the sanatorium had bars on the windows for just such guests as these. There were two nurses in residence in the sanatorium, and he would also take a look in every so often. He said he had already 'set' McNulty's shoulder.

I was allowed in to see McNulty, lying on his back with his eyes shut on a bed in a fairly spacious room with a large barred window. A constable was sitting in the room on a wooden chair reading a penny-novel. McNulty's shoulder had been set in plaster of Paris and he had been given opium. He was either asleep or pretending to be. I told him loudly that I would be back to see him in the morning.

I then went with Armstrong to see Aucoin. He was sitting up in bed in a similar room, in a nightdress, having just finished his supper, which Armstrong had discovered consisted of shepherd's pie. A tall man, even sitting up, Aucoin maintained some dignity. I had been told his wound was not life-threatening, and no organs had been pierced, but he had lost blood and would without doubt be in pain. His eyes were glassy as he looked expressionlessly at me. I pulled up a chair, and asked for Armstrong to take notes.

'I'll have a proper talk with you tomorrow,' I said. 'But I should let you know that we have arrested your wife Modeste, and she will be held at the Brig. No, don't worry!' I held up my hand. 'She will be in the ladies' lock-up, not in the general jail. You won't be allowed to see each other for a while. It may depend on how open you are with us about what has happened.'

'You can't blackmail me like that,' he said. 'Or Modeste. But I'm glad she's behind bars.'

'Why?'

'I-Guess.'

'That was the first thing I was going to ask you about. This man I-Guess used to live with you and Mrs Aucoin. He worked for you, I gather. Why would he do you harm?'

'He wouldn't do me harm. He calls me "Pop". But he would do anyone else harm, including Modeste, if he were left to himself and he wanted something from them. I can just see him turning up at the house asking for Pop, and Modeste saying Pop is in jail, and I-Guess beginning to smash things and then turning his attention to her. On the other hand he may be out looking for Dunno. You know who Dunno is?'

'Tell me.'

'I-Guess's twin brother. They seem to be identical twins. I say "seem" because they are slightly different. Dunno is similar to look at, same build, but darker. Brown hair. If they meet each other they fight. They have to be kept apart. Like one of those combustible mixtures, I don't know, nitro and glycerine – whatever you make explosives with. If they get together there will be an explosion. Anyone nearby will get hurt.'

'Where is Dunno?'

'I dunno… I guess…' Aucoin laughed harshly, then grimaced with pain and clutched his side.

'But if he is like I-Guess he must need someone to look after him. Who is the Edgar Aucoin of Dunno?'

'Sometimes it's me, the same Edgar Aucoin. And sometimes it's someone else. I won't tell you. And don't go thinking that if you release Modeste I'll tell you about Dunno so as to keep her out of danger. If you release her she'll make a run for it. She'll go off island.'

'Mr Aucoin, you're just trying to make sure I keep her locked up and safe. You're going to have to tell me a lot of things. Not tonight, perhaps. But soon. If you go before a court you'll probably be charged with attempted murder – a felony. Since Mr MacKinnon was not wounded in the attempt, and since it's possible that another person or persons launched the attempt, you have some chance of a relatively short jail sentence in this lovely Brig we have. Otherwise it's the rope. So it's in your interest to be helpful. And what is *not* in your interest is a new crime by someone else who has been involved in this one. Because then we can conclude that if you had helped us, then the next crime might not have occurred.

'For tonight I want you to reconsider your position about this man Dunno. From what you have said, you are worried about the combustion that may occur when I-Guess and Dunno meet. As you say, other people may be hurt. And in not telling me where Dunno might be, and who is in control of him, if someone is hurt it will be in part *your* responsibility.'

'I get the point. All right. He usually takes orders from Honoré Gallant. But Gallant needs help from *me* in controlling Dunno if he gets out of hand. But I'm out of action. I don't know how Gallant is going to manage. Especially with I-Guess on the loose and looking for Dunno. Or if Dunno has heard that I-Guess is on the loose and goes looking for *him*.'

'Actually looking for him?'

'Oh yes. They both need to be kept busy. On a job. They both have to be told what to do. You understand? Otherwise it's "Was it you who did that, I-Guess?" I mean something like going and killing a goose or smashing a chair. Answer: "I-Guess." Or "Why did you do that, Dunno?" Answer: "Dunno." 'And by the way in French they are known as *Shpanss ben* and *Shpaw*.'

'What?'

'All right, listen. "I guess" in French is *Je pense bien que oui* – "I think so." But we pronounce that, in our old Norman French as *Shpanss ben*. In fact Modeste told you that the first time we met. And "I don't know" is *Je ne sais pas*. But we pronounce that *Shpaw*. So they are *Shpanss ben* and *Shpaw* – or I-Guess and Dunno. But it sometimes helps to use their real birth-names. Maybe it reminds them of their mother or something. I-Guess was originally called Zénon and Dunno was called Zotique.'

'I've heard before that I-Guess is Zénon.'

'I know they're odd names. Acadian priests when they baptise kids like to keep the old saints' names going. But you have to pronounce the names the way their mother would.' He raised his voice: 'Zén*an!*' 'Zat*ick!*'

'Zén*an!* Zat*ick!* Thank you.' My mind was reeling from this language lesson.

'I've had enough for today,' said Aucoin. 'That old bastard MacKinnon and his knife in his sock.'

'You mean my friend Mr MacKinnon.'

'Your friend Mr MacKinnon. Shit!'

'What?'

'Shit! I've just had a thought. Dunno will be waiting somewhere for orders from Honoré Gallant. After a day or so he may go looking for Gallant. And I-Guess may be looking for Gallant too. You see what I mean? I'm in here. Where is Gallant?'

'I have no idea where he is. But he comes to Charlottetown pretty often, doesn't he?'

'You'd better check it out. Sorry, Superintendent, I don't mean to order you about. It's just a suggestion.'

'Thanks.'

Armstrong and I went back to the Brig. They were having a noisy evening there, and our police room was cramped. I apologised to Armstrong for keeping him busy so late, and asked him to send telegrams to Honoré Gallant at his houses in both North Rustico and Charlottetown, and at his offices in Georgetown and Summerside. I wrote down a text:

Please be aware that I-Guess may be looking for Dunno where you are. Highly dangerous if they meet. Send immediate telegram or message to police if I-Guess seen and keep Dunno close at hand. Hobbes

The sun was going down. I was tired and hungry. First I would eat, then I would have to pen a report for Mr Brecken. Higgins had booked me in at the St Lawrence Hotel. I ate alone, then went to my room. Higgins stayed on guard in the hallway. I missed Lucy and Will who had been with me the last time I was here. I sent for a bottle of brandy, meaning Cognac. They sent me up a bottle of Nova Scotian apple brandy. I rather liked it, and drank several glasses.

Next morning I had breakfast, took a walk along the harbour – with the giant Constable Higgins in tow – and returned to the Brig. My report to Mr Brecken was dispatched. I sat down in a room with Armstrong for a discussion of plans. Armstrong confirmed he had sent the telegrams to Gallant the previous evening.

'When I arrived here,' I began, 'Mr Brecken told me there were six policemen in Queens – including McNulty – four in Prince and three in Kings. So am I right in thinking there are only twelve policemen left?'

'Yes, twelve. Plus yourself, Sir. Number thirteen! As you know we just call them all constables. Mr McNulty became a sergeant, and then an inspector, and you – well, we call you superintendent – and now you've made me a sergeant. I don't know how it works out in terms of pay. I guess I'll receive something extra. It's all up to Mr Brecken.'

'So when I have been merrily calling up constables from here and there over the last few days, this is taking them off their normal duties.'

'Yes Sir, but in fact they are not very busy. A murder's a rare event on the island – maybe one every couple of years, and even then it's usually an accident, from a fight. An Acadian woman was raped and murdered some years ago, but we never got the man who did it. And the last murder we had – I mean before the ones we are facing now – was in 1869 when that poor devil Dowie got hanged three times. The police go on patrol in the towns at night to stop disorder and drunkenness. And they investigate thefts, but they can't do much about them. And in most places people don't lock their doors. On farms and in most houses there are dogs to warn if other people are coming. Almost everybody has a shotgun in the house, and a lot have revolvers. And of course there are rifles for hunting. Crime against other people is already a risky business without the police getting involved.'

'So really, an investigation like this is up to one or two people. Until I was called here, Marshall Morris and, after his departure, McNulty would have been in charge of any investigation of a murder whether in Charlottetown or elsewhere on the island. And what about fraud, or prostitution, or swindling?'

'Nothing. People look after themselves. Sure there are swindlers and fraudsters around, but "Buyer Beware!" As for prostitution, how can you prove that? It's not illegal for a man to go with a woman and give her a present of money. If a woman is prostituting herself quietly, who cares? If she is drunk and disorderly on the street, that's another matter. A constable may take her to the lock-up in the Brig then let her go the next morning. You can see for yourself what this place the Brig is like. It's just a huge lock-up. Very few people stay here longer than a few days. There are only a few long-term customers.'

'Are there any brothels on the island?'

'There are a couple of houses where loose women live, usually with a landlord and landlady. I don't know if that's a brothel.'

'Dance halls?'

'In a sense. Two or three in Charlottetown, one or two in Summerside. But they keep changing, usually from the back room of one tavern to another. Or in some cases they are run in a private house which rents rooms to customers who have drunk too much – or who want to share a room. They are not exactly institutions, if you know what I mean – not like, say, a dance academy where you take dancing lessons. Though I dare say some dance academy lessons turn out to be more than that. The word "dance hall" is unusual. We call them "dance-nights."'

'Any dance-nights for men only?'

'I don't know what you mean, Sir.'

'I mean for men who don't like women.'

'I don't know of any.'

'Or dance-nights where the partners are under age?'

'Hard to say. There is no what you call 'age of consent' here on the island. "Over across" in Nova Scotia, and I think in the other Canadian provinces, it's twelve. As it is in Britain of course. We follow British law. But it's easy to make mistakes. People are whatever age they say they are. Rape is illegal of course.'

'And buggery?'

'Again we use British law. It was punishable by death until a few years ago I think.'

'Until 1861.'

'But I've never heard of an indictment for it, meaning somebody being charged for it. Mind you old Cormier, the father of I-Guess and Dunno was jailed for it over twenty years ago, instead of being hanged – but he got hanged anyway, by the other prisoners. If buggery exists, it's well out of sight – on farms most likely, with animals. Apart from the legend of Cormier, I've never heard of anyone being prosecuted for it.'

'So what are called "crimes against nature" are ignored. And a constable is not going to go into a dance-night and pick out little boys and girls and send them home.'

'Right. The constable would figure it was none of his business unless there was a fight or a commotion.'

'What if a respectable or eminent citizen – say, an Assemblyman – were seen going in or out of a dance-night?'

'If he were seen going in and out of a dance-night or into any house where girls "worked" in the sense we've been talking about, news would get around. But then news gets around about anything. I don't know what it's like in bigger places, but here if, let's say, the news gets around that Mr So-and-So is spending the night with Mrs This-or-That when Mr This-or-That is out of town, then everybody knows, but it doesn't make any difference. You may know that Mr So-and-So is running around on his wife, or even has a relation with your own wife, but you might be kneeling next to him at Communion on a Sunday and shaking hands with him afterwards. What he does is everybody's business and nobody's business.'

'You mean there are no secrets on the island?'

'Not exactly, but it's as I say, there are *open* secrets. Things are known but not mentioned. In a small place like this we all have to get along

247

together, and we do. And we all go to church and know our Bibles. "He who casts the first stone…" and so on. We don't cast stones at each other.'

'All right. What do you personally know about Edgar Aucoin?'

'He's also known as Wedge. He and his wife used to run dance-nights, and they used to own a boarding house here in Charlottetown where a number of young ladies lived, along with a number of kids who had been in orphanages and were beginning to work at cleaning jobs or cooking jobs. So landlords would rent a room to three or four of these kids, boys or girls, all bunged in tight. I went to school in Summerside, and it was known that there were dance-nights at a house there which was owned by the Aucoins. They are known as having a colourful past, but they've never been arrested for anything. And since they've been working for Mr Harris, they're seen as kind of respectable.'

'And Mr Harris. How is he seen?'

'Maybe he does have secrets. He never married until a year ago. I suppose he had lady friends, but his marriage was a bit of a surprise. He didn't seem like the marrying type. A confirmed bachelor. He travelled away several times a year – to Halifax or Montreal. Maybe he went to dance-nights there. Not here that I know of.'

'And Mr Gallant?'

'He's a very respectable notary who works in all three counties. I've heard that he makes things easy for people. If you want contracts to be drawn up without too much examination of the details, he'll do it. He spends a lot of time in Georgetown. Rumour has it that he does legal documents for smugglers out there. Georgetown is on the Brudenell River where it enters the sea opposite the Nova Scotia coast, and a lot of rum comes into this island directly from Jamaica and ends up in Nova Scotia, then the rest of Canada. There are cargo manifests, and documents that have to be notarised.'

'But if Gallant profits from smuggling, then his being in favour of Confederation works against him, since there will be no more differences in tariffs. Not to speak about what someone referred to as "the smugglers' paradox" – that the smugglers want the island to be independent, but their avoidance of tariffs deprives the island of the funds it needs to remain independent.'

I was also thinking about what Calum had said about a possible last-minute switch of Gallant and Harris from being pro-Canada to anti-Canada. Sure enough, Armstrong confirmed this.

'Maybe Gallant's allegiance is for sale. You never know with Councilmen and Assemblymen. They get elected promising one thing, then they do something else. Someone will have made it worth their while to change. As in the Railway Bill a few months ago. It was public knowledge, and even reported in the *Islander*, that some people changed their votes for money. The fee mentioned was high – £200. And no matter how often Councilmen in particular change their minds, there's not much people can do about it. They're elected for eight years at a time!'

'You know something, Armstrong? I'm beginning to realise that any ideas I have had of doing "detective work" on this island, that is by investigating evidence, and by interrogating people in order to find out various secrets, are completely unrealistic. All I need to do to find out secrets on this island is to ask you!'

'Or anyone else, Sir. But I suppose there may be a few really deep secrets that are buried out of everyone's sight.'

'I agree. Now, to change the subject, I'm worried about the Cormier brothers. I hope Mr Gallant took our telegram seriously, wherever he got it. And I want to talk to him again.'

'I'll find out where he is. With luck he's in Charlottetown, and we won't have to trek out to North Rustico, Summerside or Georgetown.'

Within an hour Armstrong had ascertained that Gallant was indeed in Charlottetown, and had sent a message to be delivered to his office saying we would see him that afternoon at four o'clock.

Gallant's office turned out be around the corner from the Brig, on a smaller and quieter square, in one of a row of brick buildings. The office was not large but it was well appointed, with a waiting room, although we were admitted immediately.

Gallant was sleek and well dressed, although still in black, and certainly less anxious than at our previous meeting. I introduced Sergeant Armstrong, and we sat in wooden chairs with leather padded seats while Gallant sat behind an impressive oak desk with the usual green leather surface. On the wall was a plaque with the Island crest of two large oak trees sheltering one small one with the Island motto, *Parva sub Ingenti* – literally 'The little one under the huge', but usually translated 'The small under the protection of the great', meaning the Island and Great Britain. A notary was not a government official but the plaque gave a sense of gravitas. And of course Gallant was *in* the government.

'This terrible attack on Mr MacKinnon!' he said. 'The report was in the *Examiner* this morning, and of course it mentioned your part in the rescue and in the arrest of the former Sergeant – or I should say the former Inspector – McNulty, and of Mr and Mrs Aucoin. What a shock! For us all, of course, but especially for you, having worked so closely with Mr McNulty. What on earth did he think he was doing?'

A good performance, I found myself thinking, but perhaps he thought he had not much reason to be disturbed. Did he think or know that McNulty was unlikely to talk much? Or had he simply not thought through the possibility of a link with his supposed daughter's murder? Had he no idea at all of MacKinnon's involvement with his wife?

Gallant was looking at me, waiting for a reply. 'We'll find out,' I said. 'The first reason we are here is to warn you about a man known as Dunno. Zotique Cormier, whom I understand you employ. I sent you a telegram about him last night.'

'Yes, I was rather puzzled by that. You overestimate my authority over him. I wouldn't even say I employ him. I send him on errands here and there. He can't read or write, you see, and it's very useful to have someone illiterate to deliver confidential documents. Curiously, he has a very good sense of direction. He could never read a map but he knows how to get to anywhere on the island.'

'Where is he now?'

'I think he's here in Charlottetown. He stays in boarding houses or with friends. He's always on the move.'

'Yes, I believe he moves approximately where you move. Clearly, he depends on you for employment – doing errands as you describe it. When you want him to do an errand for you, how do you get in touch with him?'

'He tends to come by every morning, soon after nine o'clock, and again after lunch, to see what I have for him to do. It's true that if I am moving on to one of my other offices the next day, he will be there the day after. And I do have one of my assistants let him know where I shall be. He wasn't here this morning though. That's unusual. I don't know even if he can tell the time, but he has an excellent memory, and follows instructions. I pay him a few shillings a week.'

He was still unruffled. I decided to ruffle him. 'And how is Madame Gallant?'

He smiled. 'I suspect you know as well as I do, Mr Hobbes, since she is spending most of her summer, it seems, at this new Ocean House hotel in the company of Mrs Hobbes and Mrs Robinson. I hope it will allow her to recover from this horrible shock, and I understand the baby is doing well at last. Of course the burial of our daughter was a dreadful occasion. It was private, so there were no onlookers at least, but it was very painful.'

'I'm pleased Madame Gallant is with other women who can provide emotional support,' I said.

251

My God, I was getting nowhere with this unflappable man. I decided to push on.

'Might I ask you about the charitable work you did some years ago, in the Summerside orphanages before they were closed? I understand you provided help as a sort of lay brother on the girls' side.'

'I did, and I hope I achieved something of good.'

'Have you seen any of those girls since?'

'Of course I have. It was a long time ago, Superintendent, and I occasionally see one or other of those girls in the streets of Summerside or Charlottetown. Young mothers of families now.'

'How well do you know Mr Aucoin?'

'Not very well. My friend Mr Harris knows him better, of course, having employed him more than I.'

'Do you know that some of the girls you met at the orphanages eventually ended up working at so-called dance-nights where they ended up having relations with much older men?'

'I wouldn't be surprised. Some of them were of very poor character. But they were over twelve years old. That's the legal age of adulthood here. They wouldn't have left the orphanages before that age, and some stayed longer. Those who did leave at the age of twelve usually went into service.'

'With regard to Zotique Cormier, or Dunno, I must ask you to be very careful. Please let the police know immediately, by messenger, if you see him. Edgar Aucoin has described the two brothers to me as like two elements of a volatile mixture. He compared them to nitro and glycerine. When they meet under unstable conditions there will be an explosion in which possibly other people will be hurt. It's important that they should not meet. If we find either one of them, we shall detain him for his own safety – and for public safety.'

'I understand. What a shocking business!'

I took my leave politely and walked out into the street. I could have banged my head on the nearest wall in frustration. 'The trouble is,' I said irritably to Armstrong, 'that so many people do horrible things, but these things are not illegal.'

'You have a point, Sir. But if we rounded up all the harmful people on the island, where would we put them? How would we even feed them? Best to leave them alone to make their own lives. It's not a crime to harm other people if there is no law to say so. At least here on the island, there are only a few things for which a person goes to jail. There's murder, which as I said almost never happens, and that's not for long, since murder is a felony and jail is a brief interlude before being hanged. You can go to jail for the theft of large amounts of money and being caught red-handed with it. But that's rare. Even rape, which may or may not be rare – we don't know – is so hard to prove that I know of no case where someone has been jailed for it. And jail is expensive. So our judges tend not to send too many people to jail. In the case of a theft that is proven, they might ask the thief to give back what was stolen, or to work it off for the person he stole it from. Restitution.'

'Well, now we do have a murder. And an attempted murder. We must establish the connection between the two. But short of hanging McNulty and Aucoin up by their thumbs I don't know how. Why should they incriminate themselves? Just to be nice to us? Or will one of them betray the other? They are intelligent enough to know that betrayal works both ways. So yes, there was attempted murder, to which we can attest since we observed it – as did the intended victim, Mr MacKinnon. But if McNulty and Aucoin keep their mouths shut, I suspect from what you say that if a judge calls a jury it will conclude that there was simply some kind of feud going on, and recommend lenient sentences or even let them go if they say they are sorry. And the murder of Marie Évangéline Harris, née Gallant, will go unsolved.'

'There is some hope, don't you think Sir, if we can find the Cormier twins. They are not very intelligent, and perhaps one or other of them will say if they were involved in the murder of Marie Évangéline Harris, and I-Guess might tell us what was going on in the attempted murder of Calum MacKinnon.'

'Yes, that's the last hope. But with twelve policemen – plus me – on the entire island and both of the Cormiers apparently on the run, how are we going to find them? And if we do find them, we have no grounds even for arresting them. We can only ask them questions. To which they will reply only with their own names!'

I went back to the St Lawrence Hotel – on my own. I was fed up with having a constable tagging along behind me. I was armed, after all. Before I went to bed, I sat down at a small table with a sheet of paper and tried different ways of listing the actors in this drama I was investigating. I was struck by how many pairs there were:

I-Guess	Dunno
Harris	Gallant
Edgar	Modeste
Calum	Madeleine
Marie	Lachlan.

The last two pairs were not – unless I was deluding myself – suspects in either crime. In fact one member of each pair – Marie and Calum – were victim and intended victim. I did not make a pair of Honoré and Madeleine Gallant, as I had made a pair of the Aucoins, since it was clear that the Gallants were no longer a pair in any sense except the legal one of being married. And I saw

Madeleine and Calum as a pair whether the world recognised this or not. So I was left with three suspect pairs.

I-Guess	Dunno
Harris	Gallant
Edgar	Modeste

And I could rearrange the pairs:

Harris	I-Guess
Gallant	Dunno

And there on his own, not paired with anyone:
McNulty

Who did McNulty work for or with? Not Harris – whom he had consistently run down to me. But then he had run down Edgar Aucoin to me too. And he and Edgar were the joint attackers of Calum – but no, I-Guess had been there as well.

Did McNulty work for Gallant? Was he in a trio with Gallant and Dunno? That seemed far-fetched. And after all, Aucoin had some control over the twins. And in the attack on Calum, McNulty and Aucoin had worked together. McNulty and Aucoin moved freely between the columns of my list. Nevertheless, was there a close link between McNulty and Gallant, as there was between Aucoin and Harris?

I had been ordering my thoughts with something like mathematical precision, and still keeping Harris in the equations. But after my recent interview with Harris, he had slipped into the background of my thoughts. Gallant had advanced into the foreground.

I was dog-tired, but when I went to bed I still lay awake for a while shuffling in my mind the names in those columns. By the time I went to sleep I was left simply with two names:

Gallant	McNulty

256

18

Someone was knocking on my door. Light shone between the curtains. Morning. I sat up in bed. 'What?'

'It's me Sir, Armstrong. You'll need to get up! I'll be waiting downstairs.'

I leapt out of bed, washed myself briskly using the jug and basin on the usual marble-topped stand, got dressed, ran down the hallway for a brief visit to the closet, then dashed downstairs into the hotel lobby.

Armstrong was waiting for me. 'They found the Cormier brothers,' he said, 'both dead. At the battery on Fanning Bank.' He led the way out onto the Quay and along the street, walking briskly.

Fanning Bank was only a few streets away, a public park between Government House and the Harbour. I had heard that one of William Robinson's first acts on arriving in Charlottetown a few months ago had been to allow part of the Government House grounds to be given over formally to the citizens. They had already been using it informally for some years. The park of lawns and trees ran along the shore where a few cannons from what was originally a huge battery faced out over the Harbour.

Down near the shore was a small crowd of people. 'Police!' Armstrong called, and they parted to let us through. A police constable was standing near one of the cannons. At the base of the cannon, on the grass, lay the bodies of two men, grappled together. Both were wearing frock coats. Each had the throat of the other in a grip. They seemed to have throttled each other to death. Was that possible? Each had a large bruise and cut on his forehead, and there were streaks of blood on their coats. Gruesomely, each had an eye gouged out and hanging on his upper cheek like a wet marble from a cord. I recognised I-Guess. Dunno was similar in size and build but, as had been described to me, with darker hair. The mouth of each was fixed in a snarl. The open eye of each was staring and of an identical grey colour. The gouged eye-socket of each was a blood-caked pit.

'See if you can get hold of Dr Reid,' I said to the constable. 'Tell him I need his help at once.'

The crowd parted to let the constable through. He ran off across the grass. I said to the crowd, 'If you've had a look, please move on. We'll be investigating here for at least an hour, and we're not going to move the bodies until after that.'

Some people moved off, and others lingered. A few others came up and looked, then after a while moved on. A few people asked each other, 'Do you know who they are?' Nobody did, but I heard some people remark that they had seen one or other of them 'around'.

Armstrong and I looked at the grass. There were signs of disturbance but no objects to be seen. One of the cannons had dark stains on the barrel. We went and looked close up. Sticky, blackening blood. I could imagine the brothers banging each other's heads against the cannon. 'Assault and battery,' I said to myself, but not to Armstrong. I looked down at the grappled bodies and a jingle from school popped aimlessly into my head:

One fine day in the middle of the night
Two dead men got up to fight.
Back to back they faced each other,
Drew their swords and shot each other.

I thought of Calum's description of I-Guess and Dunno as Romulus and Remus – the Roman twins, suckled by the same female wolf, who had hated each other and done all they could to destroy each other. But Romulus had won. He had killed Remus and gone on to found Rome. Here neither had won. And I felt despair at the fact that what Armstrong and I had thought the previous evening was our final hope – that perhaps we would catch up with one or other of the Cormier brothers and they would give us information – was gone.

We waited, without talking, and the crowd began drifting off, although a few passers-by still came up to have a look, most of them exclaiming 'My God!' or 'What happened?' or 'Who are they?' Occasionally Armstrong or I would reiterate that we could say nothing and it would be a while before the bodies were moved. Nevertheless, a two-horse van had drawn up at the edge of the grass, and two men came over to us.

'Undertakers,' one of them said. 'Police business?'

'Yes. You'll have to wait a bit.'

They went back to their van. Shortly a horse and trap drew up and two men jumped out – the constable, and Dr Reid, carrying a black leather bag. He marched over to us briskly, with a sideways glance at the scene.

'Good morning,' he said. 'How can I help?'

'I'm sorry to send for you like this. Thank you for coming. It's just that this is such an unusual scene, it would be helpful to have your thoughts on what happened. These men are Zénon and Zotique Cormier, non-identical twins who are known to have hated each other. But can they actually have strangled each other, both at once?'

Dr Reid went and stood over the bodies. I stood next to him.

'It's unusual,' he said. 'Of course the whole thing is unusual. It makes me think of Romulus and Remus! As you see they are still in rigor. They died some hours ago, during the night. They seem to have battered each other with their fists.'

He pointed to the hands around each other's necks. The knuckles of all four hands were scraped and blood-streaked.

'And to have banged each other's heads against that cannon – you see the blood. And to have grappled on the ground. And each gouged out an eye of the other. They were losing blood and they would have been enfeebled by the blows to the head. But all their effort seems to have gone into that last grip. They may have lost consciousness and died almost simultaneously, and in their death convulsions the grip would have tightened. Rigor has now locked it very tight, of course. We are seeing the moment of death. I don't see how any other person could have arranged this – this "tableau". It would not have been possible, and both are strong fellows. I've never seen anything like it. If you had separated the bodies and brought them to the morgue it would have been more difficult to decipher. Thanks for asking me here. I'll do a post-mortem on each and write a report. But I can see no alternative but to rule that this was mutual homicide. Not that I've ever made such a ruling before!'

'Before we move them, can I ask another question? Can you tell from a body whether or not a man was left-handed or right-handed?'

'Sometimes by callusing of the hands, or increased musculature on one side, but this is not infallible. But now I see what you mean. One has his right eye gouged, and one has his left eye gouged. Ah!' He looked at me and said quietly, 'I won't discuss this here for fear of being overheard, but it does remind me of the last time we met.'

'Furthermore,' I said, 'I can see that each has a fob watch chain to his coat pocket. The one who has had his left eye gouged, as if by a right-handed person, has his watch in his right breast pocket. I am right-handed, and I assume you are too, since we keep our watches in our left breast pocket – as does the other man.'

'Excellent.' Dr Reid knelt down on the ground and looked closely at the hands clenched on the necks. 'I would tentatively say that one has a more used right hand and one a more used left hand. I'll have a closer look at the mortuary. But the watch fobs and the gouging of different eyes are already good evidence. This one was left-handed.'

He pointed at Dunno, and stood up.

I gestured to Armstrong who in turn gestured to the men standing at the edge of the lawn with their undertaker's van pulled by a single black horse. They got up into the seat, one of them flicked a whip at the horse, and the van came lurching over the grass. The crowd, by now only a dozen people, waited to watch the loading of the corpses.

I found myself standing to one side with Dr Reid. 'Do you have another moment, Doctor?'

'Yes, by all means.'

'I have been wondering about Marie Gallant – Mrs Harris. You noted that her hands and feet had been bound, and that they were not bound when she was brought in to the morgue.'

'No, they were not. But I knew they had been bound, because of the abrasions on the skin.'

'Could you tell whether they were bound at the time she was killed? I mean, whether or not she had been released from her bonds before she died.'

'I'm afraid I can't tell for sure. But if she was killed while her hands and feet were tied, the bonds must have been undone very shortly afterwards. If she had lain dead for any more than half an hour or so with her hands and feet bound, there would be the signs of lividity – a discolouration of the skin due to pressure after death. The bonds left abrasions, originally red with the blood from broken skin – like scratches – but by the time we saw them they had turned black and blue. Lividity, as the name implies, is pale, and it's also more diffuse than a scratch or cut. And you'll recall, there was some dried blood under the fingernails, and one broken nail. She might have managed to scratch someone when bound, but it's much less likely than if her hands were free. So although there is a possibility that she was beaten to death while bound, then her bonds were released, it's much more likely that they were released before she

261

was killed. And by the way, as I mentioned briefly earlier, I understand your line of reasoning about the handedness of these dreadful men. If one of them had a hand – no pun intended – in the death of Mrs Harris, it will be the left-hander.'

'Thank you, Doctor. May I ask how your new patients are getting along?'

'As I would expect. Mr Aucoin has lost blood and for a few weeks he'll have to be careful when moving, as he risks opening his wound. As for Mr McNulty, he is in pain but stoical. Lucky he is not a manual worker, since he will never be able to put that shoulder to work again. And lucky he is not left-handed. He has had a low fever but there's no sign of blood poisoning.'

Dr Reid looked at me quizzically. 'What a turn of fortune it is,' he said, 'to have Mr McNulty fallen from grace like that.' He smiled, tipped his hat, and marched off briskly.

I stood for a moment looking out to the bay with its low red and green hills and moving ships and boats. I found myself thinking that if McNulty were here I would discuss some of my thinking with him. What a 'Silly Billy,' as Lucy had said. I now felt much more circumspect. As I walked, I reflected on Dunno's left-handedness and the lists I had made the night before. It had first seemed likely to me that Marie had been killed by Aucoin or I-Guess or both, under the instructions of Harris – unless Harris was also present before going to Charlottetown. Now it seemed she had been killed by Dunno. If so, who else was there? Possibly Aucoin, who knew both the Cormiers. But possibly McNulty. And possibly even Gallant? Dunno was Gallant's man.

On impulse I decided to find out if I could have a word with the Governor. I could see his house across the park not far away. Obviously, one did not barge in on the Governor, but it might save time to make an appointment myself. I asked Armstrong to come with me and we set off across the grass. At the gate of the drive to Government House there was a soldier, as when I had first visited, a corporal in a red coat, standing at ease. I asked whether I could speak to the Governor's secretary about a brief appointment. 'You may be able to slip in before the Levee, Sir,' he said in a Cockney accent. 'It's not the sort of formal Levee that we have on a big occasion, but the Governor makes himself available once a month. The Levee starts shortly and various people will be streaming in all morning, but no one has arrived yet.'

He asked us to follow him, we walked up the driveway, and he knocked on the main door. An attendant looking rather like a butler appeared. I introduced myself and Armstrong, and asked if I could possibly have a brief word with the Governor before the Levee. He asked us to wait and disappeared for a minute or so, then reappeared.

'That will be fine, Superintendent Hobbes, come ahead.' He showed Armstrong a chair against the wall of the hallway. I followed him around to the room where Robinson and I had met before. Robinson was standing there looking immaculate with some sort of Order pinned to his chest. Luckily I was wearing a clean uniform jacket and did not look too scruffy.

'Please excuse me Sir,' I said, 'but I was on business nearby – a double murder down by the battery – and a question has arisen which I think you may be able to answer.'

'Not at all, Hobbes, no trouble at all. I'm so pleased my wife and children are having such a lovely holiday at the Ocean House. I visited them myself the other day, and I met your very lovely wife, and Mrs Gallant whom she and Olivia are helping. The life of a diplomat's wife can be very tedious, and I'm glad Olivia is having an escape.' He remained standing and looked at me expectantly. 'A double murder?'

'Yes, of twin brothers in a fight to the death. One of them may have been involved in the murder we are still investigating. Eventually, I'll be able to report to you about it, Sir, if and when I manage to link it to the other events.'

'I hear that Sergeant McNulty – briefly Inspector McNulty, and now presumably plain Mr McNulty – is under arrest following an attempted murder on the North Shore. Not near North Rustico, I'm pleased to know.'

'That brings me neatly to my question. Mr McNulty is not yet well enough to talk to us, but an informant has speculated that he might have links with the Fenians. For one thing the rifle he had at the scene of the attempt was a new model called the Snider-Enfield which I'm told is popular with the Fenians.'

'It is,' Robinson said eagerly. 'On account of its shortness. It's easier to hide. And it shoots very rapidly. An ideal weapon for the Fenians. I fear it will make them even more of a force to be reckoned with. I know their two so-called invasions of Canada have been repulsed easily enough, and their vicious assassination of D'Arcy McGee has caused no spontaneous uprising among the Canadian Irish. But they are not dead yet. I'm not sure they'll ever die. That burning rage they have is fed by greedy landlords who oppress people in Ireland, and to a lesser extent here. The landlord-tenant question is not yet resolved on this island. The suppression of the tenant riots in 1865 by bringing in troops from Nova Scotia has left particular resentment. There is talk that the Fenians might have infiltrated the Tenant League. However, there was a great Irish Islander, Edward Whelan, who died a few years ago, who condemned the Fenians in his newspaper, the *Examiner*. He was also one of the most powerful promoters of Confederation. Taking all this into account, I don't think the Fenians are playing any role in the case you are investigating.'

'You have answered my question!' I said. 'I really wanted to know, from the horse's mouth as it were, if you'll forgive the expression, whether or not to start investigating a possible Fenian conspiracy.'

'I'll forgive you the horse's mouth, since I am indeed familiar with the Fenians, being an Irishman myself. I'm obviously not of their "persuasion", as they would put it in Ireland, but I have known some of them.

Ireland is remarkably like Prince Edward Island, in that even political enemies – or any enemies – tend to know each other and pass the time of day when "off duty" as it were. Before being on duty the next day and conceivably shooting each other – at least in Ireland. Here they will just cheat or slander each other. I won't embark on a discourse about British policy here, but the Colonial Office is definitely concerned about the Fenian question in British North America. It's part of my job to stay informed about it, and it's what I described to you before as my general mission to encourage the Islanders to choose Confederation. *Parva sub ingenti*, as I often say to Islanders, "The small under the protection of the great", is a loyal description of the relation with the mother country, but British North America will do a lot better as a confederation than as scattered provinces.'

He paused. 'Now what I have said is the official line, so to say. But – between you and me please – having grown up mainly in Ireland, I know how personal political agitation can be, and how it feeds on enmities between families and individuals. Often an act of political terror is an act of private revenge. And apart from their political aims which I disagree with but understand, groups like the Fenians attract fanatics. Their politics is a religion. The word Fenian comes from the Old Irish Gaelic word *Feni* which means "Ourselves". Actually Ireland contains a mass of different selves – Irish speakers, English-speakers, Roman Catholics, umpteen sects of Protestants, Gaelic Irish – and so-called Anglo-Irish like me. And I think that in British North America, as well as in the United States, people from different groups in Europe are learning to rub along together more than they ever could where they came from. Frankly – and this is really a private opinion, not for passing on – I wish a Confederal system could be applied in Britain and Ireland. It might work very well to have the two islands partitioned into provinces or states, each with some autonomy. They could even have a system like the Americans whose House of Representatives is elected on the basis of population, with a

Senate elected on the basis of each state, large or small, having equal representation. Why shouldn't our House of Lords be like that? If people are confident of reform, when fanatics come along urging them to return to a sort of tribalism, people don't like it. They reject the fanatics. But sadly, then the fanatics are angered by the rejection and become more fanatical!

'Let's say that McNulty is a Fenian,' Robinson went on, 'although we are not sure. If he is, he will be a fanatic for the Cause, and even if the Cause is doomed to failure, he will pursue it to the end. And let's say – although again we are not sure – that he is involved in the murder of Mrs Harris and the attempted murder of the Gaelic schoolteacher. I would suppose that the personal and the political in his mind will become very mixed. It's just as in Ireland when a man burns down a landlord's barn and all the livestock in it. Is this because the landlord is thought to be a rack-renter or a slave-master over free people? Or is it because he has in some way brought someone in the man's family to ruin? It can be both at once.'

Again he paused, perhaps aware that he had embarked on a tirade. A quiet and gentle man, I thought, but not without passion.

'I mustn't go on,' he said. 'And you know what you are doing. But if I could give you any advice it would be as I've said: if there are Fenians involved in these crimes, I would not stop at the idea it is *only* political, or *only* personal.'

'I'm grateful for the advice,' I said. 'I hope some time we can meet at more leisure and I can tell you about similar processes in British Columbia.'

'I look forward to that. And I can tell you more about Ireland – in case you ever visit there.' He smiled as if he thought I would. 'In the meanwhile, here I am ready to start a small-scale Levee, and looking forward to it. I like this island. It's a microcosm.'

We nodded to each other, and I left the room.

19

As I walked back with Armstrong to the Brig I came to a decision. Are decisions arrived at by logic? This one came to me without thought. I must make sure that Gallant could not leave the island – 'fly the coop'. Of the list I had once made of four – Gallant and Dunno, McNulty and Aucoin – Dunno was now dead. Two, McNulty and Aucoin, were in custody. One remained: Gallant. At the Brig I sat down with Armstrong and explained that I wanted Gallant to be watched at all times. With so few constables on the island, this would stretch our resources. But two men could be delegated to Gallant, day and night. I wrote the following letter to Gallant:

Charlottetown
20 July 1871

Dear Mr Gallant,

I have decided that for your protection you will be accompanied at all times (except of course in private meetings) by a police constable. He will from time to time be relieved by a colleague, so you may expect to see several constables on this duty. I am instructing each to introduce himself to you at his first appearance, and to make sure his presence is discreet.

Thank you for your forbearance.

Yours sincerely,
Chad Hobbes

It was now Armstrong's task to arrange this 'protection', with constables from one county taking over from those from another as

267

Gallant travelled between his four offices. I issued a written instruction to Armstrong that the constables should be told that in the event Mr Gallant showed intent to leave the island, he should be 'detained'. For his own protection of course.

I had no doubt this was an irregular procedure. I should consult with Mr Brecken. But I reasoned that he would find it hard to agree, or that if he did agree, Gallant and perhaps friends would put pressure on him to rescind the instruction. Anyway, it was best that if I took the initiative and something went wrong, it would be on my head, not Mr Brecken's.

Then I strolled over to Dr Reid's sanatorium. There was a constable in the hallway sitting on a chair from which he could observe both McNulty's and Aucoin's rooms, reading a newspaper. First I visited McNulty. As before, he was sitting up in bed. The constable had told me he had been offered a Bible to read but had refused it with a shake of his head: he remained silent.

When I walked into the cell, he looked at me then turned his head away.

'Is there anything you'd like to say?' I asked.

He made no reply.

'I'll come back later,' I said, and left.

Then I went to see Aucoin. He too was sitting up in bed, reading the *Islander* – the weekly conservative newspaper of the island, the liberal one being the *Examiner*.

'When you read next week's paper you'll see that I-Guess and Dunno are dead.'

He seemed unmoved. 'I knew it,' he said. 'Anyone else hurt?'

'No.'

'That's good.' He put down the newspaper and looked at me.

'You mean you care about people?'

'I wouldn't want to see someone get hurt just because they happened to be passing by.'

'Well, thank you for telling me about the combustion problem. Not that we prevented the explosion. Have you lost a friend?'

'No. Modeste and I looked after I-Guess, and he was a hard worker, and he never hurt either of us as long as I was with him. But you couldn't like him, he was too dangerous.'

'So who unleashed him on Marie Harris?'

'You're leading me on. The evening Mrs Harris was killed, I-Guess was in the house with me and Modeste.'

'I must be mistaken then. So it was Dunno who was unleashed.'

'How would I know?'

'Oh, I'm pretty sure you know. In fact I have a theory. You and your wife were taking care of I-Guess, probably locking him in your house with you, because you knew Dunno was just down the road.'

'As you say, that's a theory.'

'I have another theory too. You were involved with picking up Marie and bringing her back to Harris's house to be killed.'

'I wasn't.'

'I believe you.'

'Then why did you say it? You're leading me on again.'

'What else can I do? You're not telling me anything. Certainly nothing about the murder of Mrs Harris. As for the attempted murder of Calum MacKinnon, I trust what I saw with my own eyes. I saw you, with a "priest" in your hand, about to bring it down on MacKinnon's skull. It would have killed him. Just imagine if MacKinnon had failed to stop you! I was too busy with McNulty, I couldn't have stopped you. You would have killed MacKinnon in front of my eyes. And you would have hanged for it. You're very lucky. When you go for trial for attempted murder, the judge won't necessarily hang you. He'll just send you to jail for a long time. In the Brig, where no one spends much time. So he'll send you "over across" to rot for a few years in some jail in New Brunswick or Nova Scotia or whichever jail is cheapest.

'And here's another theory. That was an odd place to attack MacKinnon – not very good cover. But it was one of the few spots on the road where there is shale on the road. So I-Guess runs out from behind a hillock and drags MacKinnon off his horse onto the shale. You smash MacKinnon's head in with a priest. Then you pour whisky into his mouth from that flask you have with you, and drop the half empty flask on the road. And then you all go away. Eventually someone comes along and finds MacKinnon – lying on the road with his head smashed in by a fall onto the shale, and smelling of whisky with the flask beside him, and his horse grazing by the road-side. An accident. It's obvious that MacKinnon was riding along taking swigs from his whisky flask and on the way to being drunk. And he fell off his horse and was killed. This was a plot. You and McNulty – we don't need to include I-Guess, he was just an instrument, and now he's dead – decided to murder MacKinnon and make it look like an accident.'

'Not to kill him. Anyway then the forces of the law turned up,' said Aucoin. 'You and your partner. How did you know?'

I did not answer.

'Who told you?'

Again I did not answer.

'I'm not admitting to any of this.'

'It doesn't matter what you admit or don't admit. My police colleague and I will tell the judge what we saw. Mr MacKinnon will tell him what he experienced. You have the scar of Mr MacKinnon's dirk to show the judge. Your friend McNulty has had his shoulder shattered by a bullet. And of course there is the "priest" to show, and McNulty's nice new rifle from the police station. You haven't a chance. And by the way we haven't talked to your wife Modeste yet, but we certainly shall. Perhaps she'll have something to say.'

'She won't say a thing.'

'Then, who knows, she may be jailed for contempt of court.' I hated what I was saying, and of course I had no faith whatsoever in the capacity of an Island court to imprison someone for contempt, but it seemed the only way.

Aucoin stayed silent for a while, looking from me to the wall and back. 'All right,' he said. 'How can I make things easier for myself and Modeste?'

'Well, they say in court you tell the truth, the whole truth and nothing but the truth. But I'm not sure you'll do that. I suppose what you have to do is weigh things up. How much truth do you tell, in order to gain what?'

I got up to leave.

'You must be worried,' Aucoin said. 'After all, you don't know who's behind this. You know I work for other people. I wouldn't cook up this so-called plot all by myself. You can get me charged for attempted murder, but you won't have enough proof, you still won't know.'

I decided to take a gamble. 'But I do know who cooked up the plot,' I said. 'It's Honoré Gallant.'

Aucoin's face suddenly lost any tint of pink it had and turned grey-white. 'What makes you think that?' he said, uncertainly.

'Why would I tell you? But you see the position you are in. Mr Gallant is very powerful. He may have some way of sliding out of this, I admit. You'll go to jail for years or life. Your wife will go to jail for a while. Is there a woman's penitentiary somewhere "over across" that the island government can pay for? I somehow can't see this eminent Councilman Gallant going to jail that easily. Let alone being hanged.'

'You're saying these things to lead me on – so I get other people in trouble to save my own skin.'

'That's a very mean way of looking at it. It may be that other people have done things much worse than you have. And they'll get away with it! You won't.'

271

'Mr Hobbes, or Superintendent Hobbes, or whoever you are, I'm not going to tell you what I know of the whole business. I might end up in worse trouble than jail! I mean as dead meat. And you're not even taking notes in the presence of another witness. If you pass on what I say I can always deny it, and who's to know? You're not even going to stay on the island. You'll go home to England.'

'I look forward to it. But for now, Mr Aucoin, throw me a bone – just as you'd throw one to your dog to keep him quiet. Tell me something I need to know that you can always deny you have told me. Something that doesn't incriminate you.'

He thought for a moment.

'OK. Mr Gallant *knows*.'

'That's not enough. What does he know?'

'That Marie was not his.'

'Thank you. I didn't know that. I'm grateful to you.'

And I was.

Aucoin had certainly thrown me a bone. I gnawed on it for a while, taking a walk around Dr Reid's very pretty garden. Gallant *knew*. Leaving aside when and how he *knew*, and why Madeleine apparently did not know he knew, he knew. So he could have killed Marie. Outside Greek myths I did not think a man could kill his own daughter. Or arrange to have her killed. But in fact he knew she was *not* his daughter.

Then there was Calum. If Gallant *knew* Calum was Marie's father, why not have him killed too? Was I looking at a revenge tragedy?

Or, turning the knowledge around, if Gallant knew, did he worry about other people knowing. Who else knew? Madeleine and Calum. Marie herself. Probably Lachlan. Harris? I doubted it: after all the marriage was an alliance.

I suddenly felt worried about Madeleine and Calum. Would Gallant have another try to get rid of Calum? And finally get rid of Madeleine? The risks would be high. For one thing, Gallant must realise that I might know.

Then I was at risk too. But I might by now have passed on this knowledge to many others. The cat was out of the bag.

So what would I do if I were Gallant? I would make a run for it. This was, I suppose, why I had had the sudden idea of having him watched. But he was a cooler customer than I, an intriguer all his life. He would be more likely to limit the damages. He might even, if confronted, say something like, 'Of course I know! I knew all along, but I wanted to protect my reputation and my family's, and furthermore Madeleine agreed we should keep this secret, at least while Évangéline was growing up. And when John Harris and Évangéline wanted to be married, Madeleine and I decided to keep the secret for ever. Now the secret is out, my wife is of course free to go and live in sin with her lover. I can accept this tragedy and continue with my own life.'

This was plausible. Gallant could come out of the story as a martyr – the only principled person in a world of lust and betrayal. The more I thought, the more I concluded that Gallant would be most likely to brazen it out.

But what if he had a hand, at least, in the murder of Marie and the attack on Calum? That must *not* be known. Anyone who knew it would have to be got rid of, or bought over, or frightened into silence. So who would have an inkling of his possible involvement? Me, for sure. Aucoin. And McNulty. Suddenly I could see a way of approaching McNulty.

Two years before, on Vancouver Island, Lukswaas – Lucy – had advised me to get into the skin of the murderer, imagine myself as him, just as the successful hunter of a bear imagines he is in the skin of the bear. Now I had been doing the same thing, with Gallant being the bear. But McNulty was a bear too.

I went back to see McNulty. Again he was sitting up in bed. He had a book under his left elbow supporting the weight of his plaster cast. The book was the Bible he had refused earlier. He looked at me balefully.

'Are you still in pain?' I asked.

He stared back and said nothing.

'Well, if you won't talk, I shall,' I said. 'Perhaps I can even speak for you. I can have a dialogue with myself. Of course there are details I don't know – and which I would like to know – but I'll speak from what I think I know. And although you may stop your mouth you cannot stop your ears, or at least not both of them, given that you can only move one hand.

'I imagine myself as you, Willie-John McNulty – funny, when we worked together I didn't even know your first name – Willie-John coming to this island with a cause. As a young man you were a Presbyterian, then you found Catholicism and became a priest, then you found a woman and… I'm not sure about whether you have lost faith in women or not. If you have, you will have moved on to a new faith. It might be Fenianism, but I imagine there are other names for it, so I'll just call it the Cause. Maybe you are, after all, a triple renegade! Three times you have left one belief and embraced another. And you are yet another person who comes to this island with a mission! Catholic and Protestant clergy from the early beginnings, then various Colonial army and naval officers, and now Governor Robinson has the mission of bringing the Island into Canada! Your mission is the opposite! To do anything you can to keep it *out* of Canada. But it will still be attached to Britain! I don't understand the complexity of all that. The Cause is to liberate the island from the tyranny of the so-called mother country Britain by going against the wishes of the mother-country that the island should become part of a new country – which in turn is loyal to the mother-country. Then the island will be on its own – to be picked off. But it won't, it will still be a British colony. It makes my head spin. But I don't, personally, have a Cause in the light of which I can make sense of all this. I'll leave that to you.

'Anyway, here you are – in disguise, more or less, having joined the island police, where of course you can learn a good deal about any *secrets* that are not already known. It turns out that most secrets *are* known on the island, but that is by the by. And you become allied, as it were, with a powerful man called Gallant who has another powerful friend called Harris, and between the two of them in this microcosm that is the island, they can put themselves up for hire. They are publicly declared friends of Confederation, but if they both changed their minds in a crucial Legislative Council vote, they could reverse it. Of course, there are other involvements too, and for all I know you are allied with more Gallants and Harrises. But you become part of their lives. You do things for them. You help Gallant with, let us say, his "business contacts" over across in Nova Scotia from where you have arrived. And when Gallant decides to deal with a family problem, you help him.

'To tell you the truth, much of Gallant's problem still eludes me', I continued. 'But I know some things. I know that Gallant married Madeleine Poirier in what was in effect an arranged marriage. It may or may not have been consummated. Madeleine became pregnant and gave birth to Mairi – sorry, Marie…'

I had seen McNulty, otherwise still immobile and unblinking, flinch when I said the word 'Mairi'. I waited for him to say something but he did not. 'As you know,' I said, 'although it's a general secret, Mairi is Gaelic for Marie, and her father was a Gaelic speaker by the name of Calum MacKinnon.'

'I didn't know,' said McNulty in a dry voice.

'Then why were you trying to kill Calum MacKinnon?'

McNulty went back to silence.

'Then I've surprised you. And I've let out a secret – to you, of all people. But it seems that, like me, you don't know the whole story, just part of it. You might have known Madeleine and Calum had been lovers, but you didn't know Marie was not Gallant's daughter but Calum's daughter. Anyway, with Aucoin and I-Guess, you were going to kill Calum. It would look like an accident of course. His body would be found, the head broken in where he hit the shale – unluckily falling

275

off his horse on one of the few hard parts of the road, but then he was presumably swigging whisky as he rode along: he would smell of it and a half empty flask would be lying beside him. So if Armstrong and I hadn't arrived, Calum MacKinnon would be dead. I suppose the attack on MacKinnon was a favour you provided for Gallant. Perhaps at this very moment he is rushing to the Attorney General to admit his share in this business, so as to lessen the penalties you and Aucoin will have to pay. But I haven't heard anything about this so far. And isn't it fascinating that you didn't even know MacKinnon was Marie's father? And that in attacking MacKinnon you were simply carrying out an act of revenge for Gallant! By the way, I-Guess is no longer in the land of the living. He and Dunno had their final meeting this morning, here in Charlottetown.'

McNulty's face showed nothing. I did not go on to explain what had happened to I-Guess and Dunno.

'Of course Armstrong and I did arrive as you were attacking MacKinnon. I should have been a long way away in Georgetown, following your message, but there I was on the North Shore road! And when you saw me, just as Aucoin was about to administer the last rites to MacKinnon with the "priest", you raised your Snider-Enfield and were about to shoot me. So I shot you. By the way, if you had shot me, what would you have done then? Fled the island? Abandoned the Cause? I suppose you would have made up some story, or simply suggested that you were elsewhere at the time. Another mystery for Inspector McNulty to solve! The unfortunate murder of the Attorney General's investigator, Chad Hobbes. By McNulty himself! You might have been able to take advantage of the situation without your head spinning too much. The Cause would help you concentrate. Anyway, that didn't happen.

'Now for the other crime: the murder of Marie Harris. I think you were involved in that too. I'm not sure whether you killed her or not. I hope it wasn't you, because when you and I worked together on this case we exchanged various thoughts, and the thought that you might have committed the murder is distressing to me. But if it was you, I'll find out, and you'll hang for it.'

McNulty was looking at me stonily. I did not expect a reply and I did not get one.

'But what a shame,' I said. 'And I don't mean that sarcastically. What a shame to hang for a murder motivated by private revenge – yours or the revenge of someone else you were helping. To hang for the Cause would be better. Your supporters might even make ballads about you. I don't think they'll make ballads about this murder. Willie-John McNulty who threw away his ideals in order to carry out a revenge murder for a corrupt politician – and another attempted revenge murder too!

'But let's assume you did not commit the murder and you were not there when it happened. You did have a part in it though. You will remember Dr Reid's autopsy. Marie had been bound and gagged. The evidence suggests this was before the murder, not during it. The evidence suggests that some people – it would take more than one – bound and gagged Marie at Thunder Cove then brought her back to Stanley Bridge. I'm sure that you were one of those people. Then it becomes legally interesting. Did you know that when you brought this young woman to the person who had commissioned you for this task, she would be murdered? If you did, then you will hang as surely as her actual killer.'

'Hobbes,' said McNulty in that dry voice. 'I did not kill Marie Harris, nor was I there when she was killed.'

'But you know who killed her.'

McNulty raised his right hand, palm upwards, in a gesture of something like frustration, then lowered it.

'I left her with Gallant and Dunno,' he said. 'In Harris's house. And I rode back to the tavern in Stanley Bridge where I was staying the night, and headed back to Charlottetown very early the next day. My task was accomplished. I thought Gallant was Marie's father. I didn't think he would kill her – not that I'm saying he did.'

'Thanks.'

'I'm not saying I would repeat in court even that I left Marie at Harris's house or had anything to do with bringing her back from Thunder Cove. I want you to understand that if I tell you something that may incriminate that despicable and evil bastard Gallant, I may well deny it later. It's too late for me to help Gallant – or Harris. They are going down. It seems I am going down too. But I'm not going to drag them down with me.'

'Why not? The danger is the other way – that they won't go down, but you will. What about how you and Aucoin and I-Guess chased Marie to Thunder Cove and brought her back to Gallant – at Harris's house?'

'Some time I'll tell you if I think I have to. I'm not going to talk about it now because Aucoin is a friend of mine. I've told you enough.'

'Again, Thanks.'

Modeste Aucoin was still in the women's lock-up behind the Brig. I went to see her. She was sitting on a wooden chair in a tiny cell with bare walls and the usual iron-frame bed. Constable Higgins let me in and locked me in with her. There was another wooden chair and I sat down. Mrs Aucoin looked at me. I told her about the death struggle of Zénon and Zotique. She listened impassively, but when I had finished, a smile cracked her usually severe expression.

'Would you believe it? We always said that would happen, and some people said we were exaggerating, but we weren't.'

'It must be pretty grim in here, Mrs Aucoin. I can get some reading matter sent in to you if you like. I noticed various novels and travel books in the police office. I suppose the constables on night duty read them.'

'That's kind of you. Travel books would be just the thing, as I sit here wondering if I'll ever get out of here. As for novels, I don't read them. Reality is good enough for me. And look at Zénon and Zotique! If you read it in a novel you wouldn't believe it! Now Mr Hobbes, can I see Edgar?'

'No you can't. I know you more or less invited yourself here, but it's safer for you. And we can't put you up in the Sanatorium. You aren't ill.'

'That's a dangerous thing to say, Mr Hobbes. How do you know I won't hit myself over the head with a chair and injure myself? Then I could go to the Sanatorium and tap messages to Edgar through the walls, as in *Le Comte de Monte Cristo*. You look surprised. I've read quite a lot in French. I prefer it.'

'I don't know enough about French here. I gathered that Edgar, at least, came from Nova Scotia.'

'We're both from Chéticamp. It's a French-speaking village not far from Antigonish. But don't ask me any more questions. I won't answer them. I'll ask *you:* how is Edgar?'

'*Chagriné* I would guess. I'm not sure if that's correct in French. Chagrined. Not happy with events. Not very talkative. To get the facts straight: when did you and Edgar meet Honoré Gallant?'

'A long time ago – maybe ten years. It's public knowledge. Edgar and I helped get young girls out of the orphanages while they were still open – into employment as domestics.'

'Not only out of kindness of heart, I think. You also got them into dance-nights and perhaps other places where they could meet older men.'

'That's not against the law. They were over twelve.'

'It's against the law if you are accepting payment for these meetings.'

'That's questionable, Mr Hobbes, as you very well know. If a girl is over twelve she's free to do what she wants with a man. He's free to give her a present or money too. And Edgar and I were free to charge admission to dance-nights where music and drinks were provided at a cost.'

'Some girls of twelve are still very young in appearance.'

'I know what you're getting at. And some girls under twelve look quite grown up. We believed what girls said about their own age. Or occasionally we forgot to ask them. That's not a crime, is it? One book in English I've read is *Alice in Wonderland*. A lovely book. Alice is wise and very grown up. What age is she?'

'When Lewis Carroll made up that story for Alice Liddell, she was aged ten.'

'How are you so sure? And I didn't know she was called Alice Liddell. Is that public knowledge?'

'In Oxford at least. Lewis Carroll was a friend of her family. I used to see her walking with her parents in the Meadows at Oxford. When I saw her she was fourteen or fifteen. The story was written four or five years earlier.'

'That's amazing that you saw her. Was she pretty?'

I felt caught. How had I become drawn into this?

'Yes she was pretty. Her sister, a couple of years older, was exceptionally so.'

'At fourteen or fifteen, would you say Alice looked like a woman?'

'She was still a girl, I would say. But then that was the fashion.'

'It's all very blurred, isn't it? One girl under twelve can look more like a woman than another who is over twelve and looks like a girl.'

'Of course.' I thought of a way of getting back the initiative in this conversation. 'If you recall the drawings in the book, Alice wore a pinafore – the costume of a little girl. Did your girls at the dance-nights wear pinafores?'

'Mr Hobbes, you are quite cunning. Yes they did. And I'll bet you that your Alice still wore a pinafore when she was at home baking a cake – if she did such things when perhaps the servants had a day off. Even myself, at my advanced age, I could choose to wear a pinafore. It would indeed be mutton dressed as lamb. Dance-nights are great places for mutton dressed as lamb, as you may know.'

'Where were you when Mrs Harris was killed?'

'I don't mind telling you that. Edgar has probably already told you. He and I were at home, in our house, with I-Guess. R I P.'

'You liked I-Guess?'

'Nobody could like him, but he could be very hard-working once directed to a task, and he always behaved well with me. But then he knew Edgar was around.'

'Did you know Dunno?'

'Of course. Again it's public knowledge that Edgar directed where I-Guess would go, and Honoré Gallant directed where Dunno would go. That way, they wouldn't meet and do harm to each other – as has happened now that Edgar is not able to direct I-Guess.'

'Dunno was in Mr Harris's house that night, wasn't he?'

'I wouldn't know. I didn't know who was in that house! I knew Edgar and McNulty had been away together in a boat that afternoon and early evening. Edgar came home splashed with water. He said he and McNulty had been fishing. I said "Where are the fish?" He said, "We weren't catching anything, so we just took a trip along the shore." I knew he was lying, but I allowed him to keep his dignity. He was off on some enterprise that he and McNulty thought was important. Edgar works for Harris, not Gallant. McNulty works for Gallant. But they sometimes help each other out. I think of myself as a clever woman, but I can tell you that it never entered my head that anyone could hunt down and murder a young woman who had just given birth a week before! And now I've said enough. Mr Hobbes. I enjoy talking to you but I won't answer any more questions. I just want Edgar out of jail. Then I hope you'll let me out.'

'I can only decide about you personally once I know all about what happened that night at Harris's house and that day when Mr MacKinnon was attacked.'

'I expect you'll know very soon, Mr Hobbes. Somehow you will find out. Please don't forget to send in some travel books. And I was only joking about hitting myself on the head. I value my head too much.'

My interview with Modeste Aucoin had been almost agreeable. Such a strange and austere woman, with such a disreputable past. But I liked her. I could also see a sort of beauty in this slim and agile but rather tall woman with those small but glittering dark eyes. The beauty puzzled me. For that matter, even Edgar Aucoin, now I knew him better, was almost likeable in his flashes of honesty. McNulty was intellectually challenging, as ever, but what was he really like? I might never know.

I was feeling a sense of shame, though. In my interrogations of Aucoin and McNulty I had become quite nasty – aggressive, and making implied threats, as well as blurring what I knew of the truth. One thing I had decided as a boy was never to tell lies, never to cover up the truth. This was probably because my parents hid secrets that would have ruined their reputations as a country vicar and his devoted wife. But now I did not like what I was becoming as a policeman, even if I was a superior sort of policeman in command of others. Or was it because of that? Was I becoming a bully? But with people like McNulty and the Aucoins, how could I remain gentle and civilised? Actually, I thought rather ashamedly, I was not a bully with Modeste Aucoin, because she was a woman. But I had always got along well with other men. I had friends in England, and in British Columbia – and now on the island. Calum was a friend. But I had been more aggressive than I knew I was capable of being, when I interrogated Aucoin and McNulty. Was I angry with them? Yes. Or was it that when I got inside their skins, as Lucy had advised me two years before, as a hunter gets into the skin of the bear, I became something like them? In identifying with them, so as to understand them, was I becoming like them – evasive, cold, and above all angry?

20

I got up at six o'clock, and after a huge breakfast together at my hotel Armstrong and I set off to North Rustico, a lovely ride along almost empty roads, although occasionally we had to stop as farmers were moving cattle from one field to another across the road, or carts were crossing each other in opposite directions. I loved the sense of productivity on the island – a sort of huge garden or farm set in the sea bordered by pink and red cliffs and beaches.

At Ocean House we left our horses to be fed and watered in the stables, then took a walk down to the harbour for half an hour. At eleven o'clock we entered the lobby. Madeleine Gallant was sitting alone on a sofa and we went over to her. I thanked her for being there, and introduced Armstrong, but asked if we could speak alone. Armstrong would stay in the lobby.

'I've asked for one of the small drawing rooms to be set aside for us,' Madame Gallant said, 'and for coffee to be brought.'

In the drawing room we each took an armchair. A waiter appeared with a tray and distributed plates of biscuits and a pot of coffee and cups and saucers onto a table, then left. We faced each other. Again I realised that she was an extraordinarily beautiful woman. She was elegantly dressed in summer muslin, but it was dark blue and with a black lace stole to indicate mourning. I felt nervous because I feared it would not be easy for her to open her thoughts and feelings as I wanted her to. But I was wrong.

'I've had an extraordinary time here,' she said. 'With Lucy and Olivia I feel I'm coming back to a confidence in myself I had lost long ago. I'm still mourning my daughter and yet I'm nursing her baby! And her baby, Aline, is doing so well. I can't go into the details of what has been happening among the three of us women and our children. We have been sharing our lives, and at this minute I know Aline is safe with the others. Lucy knows I'm here with you and she looks forward to seeing you later. She's a darling and so is Olivia and the two of them love their husbands so much! I have never loved my husband, but I have never had the courage to leave him and go to another man who can love me as you love Lucy and William loves Olivia. Now I have found some courage, as I think you know. Please ask me whatever you want, and believe me, I'll reply to you frankly. I have learned in the past days what frankness in women is like. And I realise that it suits me.'

'That will be helpful. I have to ask you some embarrassing and difficult questions. I won't be taking notes, and if you say something you regret, you can always deny it later if necessary. Frankly, I've said this to several other people I have interviewed in this investigation. I admit that I can act according to what people tell me, whether or not they deny it later. But people are sometimes worried that what they say will be used against them in a court so they don't say it. Understandably they don't realise that there is very little risk they will end up in a court – especially in a jurisdiction like that of this island – and if they do, their testimony is limited quite narrowly to the case being tried and by the rules in court So first, please tell me how you met your husband Honoré Gallant, and why you married him.'

'Everyone will tell you it was an arranged marriage. Of course we are not in the Middle Ages, but it happened. My parents had the *Magasin Général* – the store – in Malpeque, and Honoré used to visit there to buy this and that. He got to know my father – not least because my father's business was successful, and they shared liberal ideas. We are all Acadians, and Catholics, and we are a very small minority on the island now, although it used to belong to us and the Mic Mac – Île Saint-Jean, or *Abegweit*. You will know about the deportation of 1758. You may even know about what we call the miracle of Malpeque. Through bureaucratic bungling it seems, the village was forgotten about! Its inhabitants and the few hundred Acadians who escaped deportation by hiding in the woods and those who returned after being deported or hiding on the mainland, all assured the survival of Acadians on this island. My Poirier ancestors fled to go and hide near the Restigouche River in New Brunswick and returned to the island only a few years later, then settled in the Malpeque area. Those survivors of the deportation managed to re-establish our society, and what kept us together as we were surrounded by English colonists was the Church. Eventually the Irish arrived, and many of us intermarried with them, as we had a century before with the Mic Mac. The Irish were strong Catholics like us. And we stick to our language, although any of us who have to do with business also speak English. My father and mother were fluent in it.

'I'm proud to be an *Acadienne* when I tell you this story. We made ourselves free, on our traditional land. But we were still under the power of the Church. I was brought up very strictly indeed. I was not even allowed to look at my own body. I wore a chemise even when taking a bath! And my religious education was all prayer and the New Testament, from priests who were narrow-minded and fanatical and who hated women – I mean they were sentimental about motherhood, but the idea of a woman in love with a man was frightening and abhorrent to them. Woman was on earth to serve man – just as nuns were there to serve priests. As a girl I wanted to read books, but I wasn't allowed to! I went to school at the convent, and only a few of the nuns were kind. Most of them were bitter and ferocious and beat us and punished us by making us stay on our knees on wooden floors for hours on end reciting endless rosaries. My parents loved me, but they couldn't show it. I was an only child, I don't know why. Sometimes I wonder if they ever made love! My father was cold and busy, my mother was warmer but also busy. When not at the convent I worked in the store. Sometimes there was talk of when I would be married, and I had crushes on good-looking boys who came into the store, but by the time I was nineteen I had hardly talked to a man.

'As an Englishman you would never understand the mentality I grew up with. The constant expectation to be *good*. To be a saint, even. And the Catholic Church is a universal church. This means that it possesses the only truth, and in the long run everyone in the world will come to accept that truth. There is no room for questions, no room for dissent. I was a good girl. I had to obey my parents in everything.

'When Honoré first came to know my parents he was aged about twenty-five. The young notary. He was always well-dressed and neat, very polite, and he spoke exceptionally good French – which is important to us. He was also quite good-looking. Now he is not. I would say his character has caught up with him. His face and his body and his gait, even, have all become heavy as if he is weighed down by something. He was serious as a young man, but not weighed down. He was energetic and lively and very successful, but with a kind of shyness as well. I liked him well enough. He was such a *good* man – in the sense I have described. He even worked as a lay brother in the orphanages in Summerside. We had no courtship at all, he was too religious for that. He just spoke to my father, and I was called into the room, and he asked me to marry him, and I looked at my father, standing there proud and happy, and I said yes.

'So we were married, in the church at Malpeque, and we went for a honeymoon – a *lune de miel* – to Charlottetown. Honoré wanted to show me off. We would walk all day in the streets, arm in arm, and people he knew would greet us. And of course, in the hotel we shared a bed. I knew the facts of life. You can't grow up in a small town without seeing animals mating and giving birth. Well, you can't even keep dogs and cats without seeing all that. And I expected something marvellous to happen when I first got close to a man. The idea of a man and a woman coupling like a dog and a bitch! – but at the same time the union of two souls before

286

God! We had taken vows to love each other, after all. We had kissed each other a few times – in front of other people. When we first went to bed, we were both in nightdresses, and he began to embrace me and take my nightdress off. He kissed me and caressed me and then he became suddenly horrified! He jumped out of bed, and he took a candle and he looked at me. "You have hair there!" he said as if accusing me. "What's wrong with you?"

"Doesn't everyone have hair there?" I said. I was frightened. "My mother has hair there. It grows when a girl becomes a woman. And after all, men have hair there." "How do you know?" he yelled angrily. "I've sometimes seen men making pee-pee by the road." I said. "Don't you have hair there?" "Of course," he said, "I'm a man!"'

'We didn't touch each other that night or the next few nights. We changed into our nightdresses with our backs turned, and slept with our backs turned. But eventually we did what a married man and woman do. Because I had – I had taken certain steps to make myself seem more like a girl than a woman, and I showed him how much I wanted to be a good wife. Our marriage was consummated. It hurt, since I was a virgin. But when it no longer hurt, he became uninterested. I mean, after the first few times, he could not become excited. Forgive me, I shall be frank with you. Lucy has said I can be. Honoré asked me to do some things to him to get him excited – dirty things – and I refused. So then he smacked me, on my bottom. That made him excited but I told him that if he ever smacked me again, I would go back to my parents. He said that if I ever did that it would be a scandal, and he would ruin my father.

'Mr Hobbes, I hope I'm not shocking you by telling you such intimate things. But Lucy swore to me that you would not be shocked. She was not shocked either. She just said that Honoré was a bad man with no physical power. She said, "Tell Chad that your husband had no *skookum!*"'

I could not help smiling. 'I'm not shocked at all, and I admire your courage in telling me all this. *Skookum* is a word in Chinook, the trade language of British Columbia. Yes, it means power – but not power over other people. Plenty of people with no *skookum* can tyrannise others! Skookum is a magical or emotional power – the power to move other people, and of course the power of sex – in either a man or a woman. It's also the quality of not being broken or worn out – something like "fitness".'

'Then certainly Honoré did not have *skookum*. But he did have power over other people. Over the years I have occasionally met women, usually servants, who were in the orphanages when he "helped" there, and when they learned I was married to Honoré they shrank from me as if I were poisonous. I realised years ago that his experience with women before he met me had been only with little girls in the orphanages, and that he must have beaten them and used them in other ways. If I was not like a grown woman but like a little girl whose bottom he could spank, he could just about act as a husband in the physical sense. Of course he acted very well as a husband in the material sense. He worked hard, he earned a lot of money, we had a big house, and when my father's business faltered, he helped out. I sometimes felt as if I had been bought. But I'm not the only woman to find herself in that position.

'But I'm leaping ahead. There is not much I can say about the first few years of my marriage that is not true for the next twenty years. In the first year, after a few months, I was so unhappy I could have killed myself. And Honoré had lost all desire for me – even that sporadic desire he was capable of under just the right conditions. You see I put my foot down. But I would not do things – I can only describe them as dirty things. He said "Look at all the things dogs do!" and he said that God had created the natural world so that our souls could come together in the light of God, even though the body was foul and dirty – and so on. Even dirty things were divine nature between married people – although of course they were sin between unmarried people. But then any touch whatsoever was a sin between unmarried people. Did I say he had studied

288

at the Seminary of Quebec? That was theology. Then he studied law to become a notary. He knew how to reason. He also reasoned that since the man ruled the woman, the man was allowed to chastise her. But I would not allow him to spank me. So he was no longer excited. And he resumed some of his work in the orphanages in Summerside.

'Now I wonder if I should have gone and told the priests, perhaps the bishop in Charlottetown – to alert them of my suspicions about Honoré and the orphanages. But they were only suspicions. I had no evidence at all. And the scandal would have killed my parents. Anyway I was pregnant. When I saw Calum last week – just before those people attempted to kill him… Mr Hobbes I forgot to say how grateful I am…'

She began to cry, and pulled out a handkerchief to wipe her eyes.

'Madeleine. I would like to call you Madeleine, not Madame Gallant. And I'm sure Lucy when she talks of me refers to me as Chad, so please call me Chad. Thank you for feeling grateful, but if anything had happened to Calum I would feel very sad indeed.'

'I know. You like each other. And he told me last week that he had told you about us. He said you understood. And I spoke about it all with Lucy who of course understood – I don't mean because she is a pagan from the furthest reaches of civilisation, I mean because she is a truly natural woman. And faithful to her man. You know, I think even I was a natural woman some twenty years ago. And I was faithful to my man – I mean to Calum! Once I had been with him, I was never with Honoré again – apart from once. I found I was pregnant from Calum, and I thought I must leave Honoré and go to Calum. Calum wanted me to, and he swore he would protect me and care for me. But I decided not to. For my parents who would have literally died from shame – and who would have had no more help in their business from Honoré. And for Calum who would have lost the school he had just started and become a ruined man whom nobody would either employ or do business with. And for me because I was a good Catholic in spite of what I had done with Calum, and I knew I must at all costs rescue appearances. So I yielded – just once – to what Honoré wanted. Actually, I must be honest: he was no longer coming near me, so I seduced him. I asked him to beat me because I had done a bad thing. I didn't say what the thing was. He beat me. He became excited. I opened my legs to him. A few weeks later I told him I was pregnant.

'I stopped seeing Calum for a long while. A few months before Marie's birth, we had moved to North Rustico. But two years later my father died, and I had the excuse to go to Malpeque without Honoré, to visit my mother, with Marie from time to time. By the way I always called Marie by that name, never Évangéline as Honoré wanted. I would stay with my mother for weeks sometimes. Honoré didn't mind. We were no longer sharing a bedroom, and when I was away he could do whatever he wanted without having to make excuses – "I must go to a meeting in Charlottetown." But as I later realised, he was going to various secret places where he could pay little girls to do what he wanted. We soon had two houses, one in North Rustico, one in Charlottetown, and he had offices there and in Summerside and Georgetown. We managed to spend a lot of time apart – me in one house, he in the other, occasionally trading positions – or "swapping" as you say in England and Ireland. I'm learning new English words these days, from Lucy and Olivia…

'I even managed to bring Marie up in a less strict way than Honoré would have wanted. He wanted to send her away to school, to Nova Scotia. But at least in Charlottetown the nuns were within my reach. Honoré gave the convent school a lot of money, and they were not going to be too harsh with his daughter. And thank God, although she did not look like Honoré she did not look unlike him. We Acadians tend to look similar, but I have blue eyes – my paternal grandmother was Irish. And Honoré has Irish in him too. So she passed as his child. She was not at all like him in personal traits though. She was always adventuresome, and since we were often here in North Rustico, she got to love the sea and everything to do with it – fishing, boating, swimming. Honoré is frightened of the sea, although he doesn't admit to being frightened of anything, and he hates going on boats because he can't swim.

'I suppose Marie was something like Calum.' She paused and wiped tears from her eyes again. 'I cry every time I let my mind dwell on Marie… Although for the first time in years I have a feeling of hope! I was going to talk about Calum. You know him a little. He's a man who can do anything – a farmer, a scholar, a fisherman, a sailor, a school-teacher, a huntsman and a poet. One day I hope to learn enough Gaelic to read his poems. That day will come… When I first met him he was tormented by the loss of his wife, Síle, who had been buried at sea. He was not a broken man – nothing would break him – but he was badly wounded. He was over twenty years older than I. I was newly married to a man I could not love, I was tormented, and unhappy. From time to time I worked in my father's store to help him out. And when Calum and I first met, in the store, we looked at each other, and each saw pain in the other's eyes – I know, because we have discussed it. Pain for such different reasons! Then as we talked, we fell in love. In the sense that when he left the store I felt bereft. I wanted to go on seeing him forever. He felt the same. A few hours later, in the late afternoon – it was October and the sunlight was softer than in summer, and I remember there were yellow butterflies clustering around yellow dandelions by the roadside – I walked out towards Darnley. I had asked someone where Calum lived. And on the road I met him, walking towards me. He had decided to walk into Malpeque and into the store to see me again. And you know what we did? We looked at each other and we fell into each other's arms. There was no one around on the road. There was a clump of oaks on a hillock in a field beside us, and hand in hand we walked over to the oaks and we lay down on the ground, taking off each other's clothes. And when we – when we came to our ecstasy together, we were looking into each other's eyes. Since then we have been – in our minds – man and wife. But with many long gaps! At times we fought that fact. At times I said I could not see him. And at those times I knew he went with other women. So we were not man and wife. Or were we?

'But how is this? An Acadian woman, married and with a child, in another kind of marriage with a Gael, twenty years older? Certainly the age meant nothing to us. It doesn't now either. He is no less active at sixty-three than he was at forty-three. And I'm still a woman in my cycles, if you know what I mean.

'It's funny, in this last week, to talk with Lucy about her marriage with you. How could two people be so different? Yet she says someone once said you two were like two peas in a pod. And so you are. Olivia's case is different again. In terms of background and family she and William are definitely as close as two peas in a pod, but they are temperamentally quite different. She is jolly and bouncy and colourful in the way she dresses. She says this is because she is the daughter of a Bishop, and she is boisterous as a reaction. You can imagine how amused I am, by the way, as a Catholic, to meet the daughter of a Bishop! In contrast to Olivia, William is sober and thoughtful and quiet.

'But I must come back to the hard, dreadful reality… What more can I tell you?'

'I'm sorry to say I must ask you about Marie. When did she learn she was Calum's daughter?'

'I'm not sure when she first thought she was. She confirmed that she knew when at last I spoke with her after her *lune de miel* – her honeymoon – with John Harris in Quebec. She was always Calum's friend when we visited Malpeque. I had told him she was his daughter, but he is sensitive, and he never betrayed that to her. He called her Mairi, affectionately. He told her stories about monsters and ghosts, then when she was older he told her about the history of his people, and the Highland Clearances – all this in English of course. Marie learned good English from Calum. For some years when Lachlan was living with Calum, Marie used to romp around with him, go fishing, go swimming – in bathing dresses of course, very modestly. They were like brother and sister. I'm sure there was nothing of a love affair between them at the time.

'Then for a while John Harris would come to dinner with us when we and Honoré were in Charlottetown at the same time. I never liked him. He was obsessed with power and influence, as Honoré had become. But he had very good manners, and a store of knowledge. In fact I think Marie liked him because she was used to talking to Calum about serious things. You know how so many men either don't talk to women or they listen patiently to the women rattling along about domestic things, but they seem to think women don't have minds. They have no idea of what Olivia, talking about her marriage which is obviously an exception, calls "intellectual companionship". John Harris was not afraid of women's minds. It's no doubt indelicate to say so, but I think because he has no manly desire for a woman, he is ready enough to grant her a mind. The more "manly" men often want to keep women in their place. When John proposed to Marie I was shocked, of course, by the age difference of twenty years. But then I thought of me and Calum where the age difference means nothing! I did object to the marriage, and I told Marie that I thought John was not enough of an out-of-doors man for her, he was like a lily in a greenhouse. Could she imagine going out sailing, fishing or swimming with him? "You mean I should marry someone like Lachlan?" she said. "He can't even read or write!" She had not seen Lachlan in a long while, and she seemed to be avoiding visits to Malpeque, so she saw very little of Calum. He might have put her straight. But perhaps not. She was very strong-willed. And of course Honoré was delighted – just as my own father had been, twenty years earlier – and settled all sorts of money on her and John and their family to be. He has become very wealthy, Honoré.

'So Marie was married. And she and John went for a wedding trip to Quebec. But when she got back she came to me and cried and said it was an awful mistake. She liked John's company when they talked together about books, but she said, "He isn't a man!" I knew what that meant, and I asked if the marriage had been consummated – I was thinking in the back of my mind about annulment – but she said it had, just about.

'I was very upset for Marie. I even told Calum the last time I saw him, about six months ago. In his wisdom, he told me we had to wait and see how Mairi would live her life, especially since at the time she was pregnant with Aline. Little did we know that the father was Lachlan!

'But history has repeated itself! Sometimes I can't believe it. What sort of a fatal coincidence is it that a woman, me, has a daughter by a man who is not her husband but brings up that daughter as her husband's, and then this daughter in turn has a daughter by a man who is not her husband and she perhaps hopes to pretend her baby daughter is her husband's? What a horrible trick of Fate! But of course, if you think of it – and My God, I've thought a lot about it – Marie had the example of me before her eyes! It seemed as if I had got away with my lie, so perhaps she could too! And if she knew I was still, on and off, having a love affair with Calum, perhaps she thought she could have one with Lachlan? Lucy tells me that even among the West Coast Indians who have not converted to Christianity, for a woman to have two men at once would be a dangerous thing! Why should Marie and I think we could get away with such a thing? I did, because Honoré only cared for himself and his business and whatever he was doing with young girls. Marie did not get away with it. Because it could not be hidden. Years ago I read the plays of Shakespeare, and I remember Lady Macbeth is sleepwalking and washes her hands again and again and says 'Out, out damned spot!' That damned spot, the purple patch on Aline's back, betrayed Marie!'

'That's very important,' I said. 'I was going to ask you about it. You were at the birth. So was Dr Kelly. And so was Modeste Aucoin, I gather, who almost certainly used to find little girls for Honoré.'

'I know. I can't see Modeste as an evil woman, but she and Edgar Aucoin have made their living in evil ways. For sure they have sold little girls to various middle-aged so-called gentlemen. Including Honoré. I'm not sure about John. That would involve little boys, which would risk accusations of sodomy, would it not?'

'Only if someone else was in the room. It's notoriously hard to prove. English boarding schools are rife with sodomy. I'm glad I went to a day school. But the authorities leave it alone. As they leave alone the question of the age of consent in girls. It will be the same here. As far as John Harris is concerned, I had a long talk with him the other day and I think it's more as if he's a natural monk. He has no desires for women – although as you say, he likes them – but if he has desires for men, he rejects them. Instead he wants purity. How much agony that involves for him, I don't know. And if he has ever slipped into actual physical relations with men or boys, I suspect he puts the history behind him and tries to forget it. But to get back to Modeste Aucoin, what is her role in all these events?'

'I learned to be a midwife over the years, as some married women do. I helped friends give birth in North Rustico and Charlottetown. Modeste has also worked as a midwife. In Marie's giving birth to Aline, Modeste was there to help me. By the way, Calum has told me that Marie wanted the baby to be called Aline. I had thought of the name Alice. But I am now calling her Aline. I still don't have the whole story from Calum, there was no time when we last met. But I can't believe Modeste had anything to do with what happened to Marie.'

'I would like to know about when the birth started. Did Marie go into labour at the time you expected?'

'No. It was about two weeks earlier. She had said she thought the baby was due in the second or third week of July. But as you may know, a week or two earlier is not what could be called premature, and predicting the date of birth is unreliable. We had arranged what to do if she felt labour coming on. Edgar would ride to Rustico, which would take about an hour and I would be in Stanley Bridge within another two hours, and meanwhile Modeste would be with Marie. And that's what happened. Marie went into labour in the late afternoon on a Saturday. I arrived a few hours later, and Aline was born very early on the Sunday morning, the 25th of June.

'Modeste is very efficient and, believe it or not, very kind. Between us we helped Marie give birth without undue pain, and in fact with joy at the end when this lovely little girl emerged! Dr Kelly was there too, but he was drunk, and quite useless. He sat reading a book. But when the baby was out and we put it to Marie's breast – you know, it helps the afterbirth if the mother suckles, and of course the baby already wants to suckle – Dr Kelly jumped up and pointed, shouting "The spot! This is an Indian child!" He went downstairs, talked to John, and left the house.

'When Marie was settled, I went downstairs. John was sitting in an armchair crying – sobbing. When I spoke to him he raised his head and said, as if in agony, "The baby's not mine! It's an Indian baby! Dr Kelly has just told me about the spot!"

'I said, "Look, John, if this is an Indian baby I'm very sorry for you. But she – it's a little girl – is Marie's baby, and she must not come to harm." I don't know why I thought of harm, but I did. John said vehemently, "I won't harm her! But I thought the baby was mine! And if people know about this, I'm finished!"

'"Look, John," I said again. "I have heard of this Indian spot. I've never seen it before. But I know it turns up now and again among us Acadians. Of course it's associated with Indians – the Mic Mac have it sometimes – so people keep quiet about it. And as I say, it goes away in time. But we all know the first Acadian settlers intermarried with the Mic Mac. Look at us! Our Acadian ancestors are from Normandy and Brittany where some people are as fair as English people and they often have blond hair and blue eyes! But we here in North America are usually very dark. If Acadian babies have the spot it's because they have a great or a great-great grandparent who was Mic Mac. We know in our family that we are part Mic Mac, from long ago – just as we are part Irish too, which can bring back the Norman blue eyes. By our family I mean the Poiriers. But Marie is Acadian on both sides. She is the usual mixture of Gallants, Poiriers, and yes, Mic Mac and Irish. And in any case the spot fades away, and it's always completely gone by the time the child is aged five or so."

'I think this made an impression on John. He became much calmer. I told him to wait for a while, and I went back up to the bedroom and I explained to Marie – who was nursing the baby – and to Modeste what I had told John. "You are great, Madeleine!" said Modeste. There is a genuinely good side to Modeste, I don't know how. And of course she is an Acadian too. And she said, "You may be right about the spot appearing in Acadians sometimes, although I've never seen it! Don't worry, I'll agree with you all the way."

'Eventually I fetched John, and he was very timid but moved. He embraced Marie gently, and admired the baby who was indeed very good-looking and lively. Marie was doing very well. The baby was nursing. Modeste was nearby and came in every hour or two. Marie and Modeste and I did not discuss the issue of the purple spot. We were enjoying the baby! I felt somewhat worried about what revelations might come out, but hopeful that what I had said was true. John had gone to Rustico for a brief meeting with Honoré on the Tuesday afternoon in preparation for a Council meeting later in the month. He also had to go to Charlottetown for a meeting and a dinner on the Friday evening. I stayed until early Friday morning. I would have stayed a few days longer, but Marie insisted I should go back to North Rustico. She said she wanted to be alone with her baby. Modeste would come in on the Saturday morning to check on Marie and the baby, and be near at hand if needed by Marie. It's only when I think back on events that I realise that Marie must have been planning to run away with the baby.'

'Forgive me,' I said, but I still don't understand her character, although you have described her so well. Why do you think she ran away?'

'I have tormented myself with that question. If I can keep my head and think clearly, I see several possibilities. The first would be that she was frightened. John was probably unhappy in spite of my assurances, and perhaps he became threatening – I don't mean he would hurt Marie, but perhaps he would hurt the baby? And Marie was frightened of Honoré. What if Honoré found out about the purple spot? I wouldn't tell him, but perhaps John would tell him. Or Edgar Aucoin would know about it through Modeste and then tell Honoré. I'm not sure Edgar would – certainly I know Modeste would not talk about it – but Marie might have feared that Edgar would tell.

'Another possibility is simply that Marie looked ahead and realised that to continue with John and the lie she was telling him would mean a life of hell. I think she had fallen in love with her baby! I know that sounds odd to a man, but I have discussed it with Olivia and Lucy and I think of myself when Marie was born. Mothers fall in love with their babies! And maybe she had the thought that she could not live this love to the full in the situation she was in. She would have wanted to escape to a more joyful world where she and the baby could be happy. And perhaps when she looked at this little baby she loved, she saw something of its father – Lachlan! I think she must have loved Lachlan passionately. And why not? I see Lucy and I see you, and you are brave enough to love each other in spite of what the world thinks. I wish Marie could have lived to see you both! There are no examples here. I have never heard of an island woman marrying a Mic Mac. They are respected, but white people – some of whom of course are as dark as they are – keep their distance.

'Yet another possibility is that Marie wanted to live with Calum! Again that sounds odd. But having broken the barrier – I mean morally

– of deciding of her own free will to go with Lachlan to conceive a child, why should she not break the other barrier and go to live with or near her own real father? All of this frightens me because I am part of it, and I am the cause of it. I have not lived my life truthfully. Perhaps, facing this little child born into the truth, Marie did not want to live with her in a world of lies. Marie was what the philosophers would call an idealist. She wanted the world to be different, she wanted to *make* it different. So I think all these reasons came together, or at least some of them, so she did what she did!'

'So you don't think she ran away out of fear of being attacked?'

'Attacked by whom? Not John, I think.'

'By your husband, Honoré?'

'He would be too afraid, too prudent. If it became known, his public life would be ruined.'

'But Madame... Madeleine, what if Honoré knew about the purple spot on the baby which could mean she was not Harris's? And what if Honoré knew Marie was Calum's daughter? That surely might have sent him into a rage and caused him to lose all reason.'

'That's my deepest, darkest fear.' Madeleine began to cry again, speaking through her tears. 'Who would have told Honoré about the purple spot? If he knew Marie was Calum's daughter, he never said a word about it to me.'

'But he *did* know Marie was not his. I have been told that recently by someone who I don't think was lying.'

'Oh God! Then no wonder he hated me so much – a cold and relentless hatred. Which no doubt I deserve. But if he knew, who would have told him? Certainly not Calum who was, after all, the only other person who knew apart from myself and Marie... You mean Marie might have told Honoré? My God, I've never thought of that. They used to argue bitterly at times, and he would raise his voice to her. Might she have answered back with that truth? It's not impossible. But I think she would have told me afterwards, she would have warned me. I think it's more possible that Honoré simply deduced it, long ago. When I first told him that lie, he was not very young – he was aged twenty-six – but he was inexperienced with women. Apart from dance-hall girls I suppose. He may not even have known about women's cycles. But if he came to know more as he became older, he might have looked back and come to a conclusion. I have sometimes feared that. But again, he never told me – and after all, he might have enjoyed telling me that, since it would add to his power over me and given him an excuse to treat me as the Whore of Babylon… But thinking of these biblical metaphors, what about the straw that broke the camel's back? As we talk, I find myself thinking with dread that perhaps Honoré did know he was not Marie's father, but he chose to go along with the pretence that he was – out of pride or vanity. She was a beautiful girl! She even attracted the attention of his political soulmate John Harris who is not attracted to women at all! But then the baby being born with the Mic Mac spot, the sudden knowledge that this hoped-for child to seal the political union of Harris and Honoré would instead shatter it – that was the straw that broke the camel's back!'

'And then what happened?' I said quietly, hating myself for having to ask it. 'Do you think that once the straw had broken the camel's back, Honoré exacted revenge on Marie?'

'I knew we would come to that question,' she said – much more calmly than I had expected, but she was for a moment almost numb. 'Yes we would come to that question…' she repeated. 'I don't want to face it, but I must. I have had long practice, dear Chad – and I call you dear because Lucy is already dear to me – long practice in restraining my feelings. So I shall restrain them now. I think it is possible that Honoré could exact revenge on Marie for her having had a Mic Mac child, precisely because he knew also that Marie was not his own child!

'There, I've said it. In my heart – in my heart gone cold – I know it's possible that either Honoré killed her, or caused someone else to do it.'

She was looking straight ahead, motionless, as if frozen.

'I'm afraid that's what I think too', I said. 'But thinking is a long way from knowing. Eventually I − we − shall know. Whether or not Honoré will ever pay for this is another question. I remember my tutor in jurisprudence telling me: "Hobbes, never forget one thing: Justice is not the same thing as the Law." We had been discussing cases in which the perpetrators of crimes had been found not guilty for legal reasons. Law had triumphed over justice.'

'I want Honoré to pay,' Madeleine said, quite coldly. 'Because although I can reproach myself for having gone to another man to engender a child, and having then lied to Honoré in letting him think the child was his, this would not have happened if he had not been who he is in the first place. *Y é l'diable en personne!* I mean, he's the Devil in person. A monster!'

'Thank you for everything you have told me,' I said after a pause. 'I have been keeping back some information that might help at least a little. I asked you what reasons Marie might have had to run away with the baby, and you gave reasons, all of which may be true. But when Calum and I spoke with Lachlan, on Lennox Island, he told us something I found very touching. Marie and he had 'made the baby,' as he put it, on the hillside above that pond behind Thunder Cove where she eventually had to leave the baby in its cradle among the reeds. And she had told him that starting in mid-May about two months before the baby was due, he should go at around six o'clock to the pond every Friday, and wait until sunset for her to come there if she needed to talk to him. Calum can tell you everything Lachlan said. I have a feeling that you had best hear the details from him − and eventually from Lachlan himself. But Marie had told Lachlan that a week or two before the baby was due to be born, she would sail the boat to Thunder Cove on a Friday, and Lachlan would meet her, and they would then go to Calum and ask him to send for you and then she would have the baby − there, at Darnley. She knew she had to leave John Harris, and for a variety of reasons she thought this would be the best way to do it. She would present him, and you all, with a *fait accompli* – a baby that was obviously Lachlan's as well as hers. And she hoped you would accept this.'

'*Oh mon Dieu!* My God! But the baby came early! Lord, what a risk she was taking. Marie! But now I understand. Yes it helps to know. It explains. But it makes things worse to know that she might have succeeded in this plan. Dear Marie!'

Madeleine began to cry. I felt like reaching across and touching her shoulder, but I decided not to. After a while she stopped. She took a handkerchief out of her sleeve and wiped her eyes.

'Lachlan kept his side of the agreement,' I said. 'He went to the pond religiously. And it was he who found the baby, on a Friday at sunset. Only, Marie was gone.'

'So Edgar went and tracked her down and brought her back. Because he saw her leaving?'

Suddenly I realised I had not thought this part through. I was convinced Edgar and McNulty and I-Guess had pursued Marie to Thunder Cove. But why were they all there at Stanley Bridge and able to notice that she and the baby had left? Perhaps Modeste, who was to be available to Marie, had found out and let Edgar know. But why was McNulty there too? Gallant must have sent him there!

'Where was Honoré the afternoon Marie ran away?'

'He was here in North Rustico when I got back from Stanley Bridge at around ten o'clock. He was having his usual break from his office work. At lunch time, he then told me he had business in Summerside in the evening and the next morning, and that he would stay there over night, which he does from time to time. As usual he prepared his travel bag and told me he would leave from his office after his afternoon appointments.'

'And what had you told him when you arrived?'

'Just that Marie wanted to be alone, with help from Modeste, and I didn't need to stay any longer.'

'You say you think Honoré had deduced that he was not Marie's father. He is very clever, or very cunning. I think he must have deduced that Marie had sent you away because she wanted to run away. And he must have sent a message to McNulty to ask him to make sure Marie did not leave the house on that day. Did you realise that McNulty was working for Honoré?'

'Of course. McNulty was Honoré's creature, fawning around, waiting for instructions. And a sergeant in the police too! I know Honoré! He must have been delighted. To have a police sergeant in his pocket!'

'So he sent his pocket police sergeant to Stanley Bridge to keep an eye on Marie along with Aucoin.'

'Oh God! Marie should not have sent me away! I wish she had confided in me and told me her plans. You know something? I would have approved!'

'But she didn't know that.'

'Thank you, Chad. My God, I wish so much she and I had been able to talk openly throughout these events!'

'How could you? If you had been open with Marie, she would have become desperate with worry. As you would have if Marie had been open with you.'

It was time to stop. I almost felt like embracing Madeleine, she sat there so poignantly still.

'Thank you,' I said. 'You have helped me understand the emotional currents in this tragedy. I have a lot of evidence, but not quite enough. I have found it very difficult interviewing Honoré. He defends himself so well. Sometimes in an interview a person will crack. He doesn't crack.'

'That's because he's so evil,' Madeleine said, standing up. 'And now I must go and find my baby. The others will be back shortly.' She paused. 'I still think like a Catholic, although I no longer believe in it. I can't escape

303

it. I find myself thinking: what is the mortal sin behind this tragedy? The mortal sin was not when I committed adultery with Calum. It was when I married Honoré, a man I did not love. Because of my love for my parents! I wonder what I have learned from all this. I suppose it is: "Never live a lie – ever!" I lived a lie with Honoré. The whole world we live in – society, if you want – lies. But that's no excuse. I stayed too long with Honoré. I thought I could live the truth on the side, in my mothering of Marie at least. Then when she married John, I knew this was a lie that she couldn't live. And she didn't. She did what I couldn't do. She left. Then she was killed – for not living the lie! Even Calum who always tells the truth and never lies in words, has been living a lie. Neither he nor I had the courage not to live it. But it's not too late for him and me to live the truth – no matter what others think. I suppose now we are older we can take our punishment better, and live more simply, and if necessary out of sight of society.'

'You'll have your friends,' I said. 'You are not alone. Perhaps there is a circle of truth – not secret, not hidden, just private.'

'Yes. Calum sent me a poem the other day, by mail. I have it here.'

She reached into a pocket of her dress and pulled out a piece of paper which she handed to me. There was a poem, in what I recognised as Calum's handwriting:

Chaidh mo ghaol ort thar bardachd,
Thar mac-meanmna, thar ardain …

I shall not transliterate more of the Gaelic, but it was followed by a translation in English:

My love for you has gone past poetry
Past whim, past pride,
Past sweet-talk, past love-song,
Past skill, past the music of laughter,
Past ecstasy, past beauty,

Past grief, past anguish,
Past thought, past nature,
Past the great world breaking like a wave.

I read it and looked up at Madeleine.

'What kind of man wrote that?' she said. 'What madman? What poet? He used to frighten me with the intensity of his emotions. How could I ruin my world and go and live with a man like that? But look at what he has done! He has built up that farm from nothing, he has set two sons on a good path in life, he has published his books on his own, and he has never told a lie. And those intense emotions have never broken out and threatened me. "The great world breaking like a wave." Calum and I have loved each other for more than twenty years, and we have kept it all in – except for those rare moments together. And our daughter, born out of our love, is dead! I should give up. Calum should give up. We should each curl up and die! But he sends me this poem. And he knows I will come to him. The ruin has gone too far. If Marie were alive, or if she is looking at us from some corner of heaven, she would say to Calum and me "Be happy together" – "*Soyez heureux ensembles*". As she said in that final desperate note. Calum showed it to me. We didn't even need to speak to each other about it. We know what we shall do.'

I found myself thinking of the magic circle of Lucy and me at Orchard Farm in Victoria – cut off from society except for a few friends. We had survived. I asked Madeleine, 'Can you please take a note to Lucy?'

'Of course.'

I pulled out my notebook and pencil and wrote in the clear hand that Lucy preferred:

Darling Lukswaas, dearest love,

I am so close to you, but I cannot see you now. I am so fixed on my purpose, and so agitated in my heart that if I saw you I would bring upset and pain to you and Will – and indirectly to your friends. You'll

understand, I know. I miss you terribly. I promise to see you within a few
days. I'll keep safe.

As ever, your Chad

I tore out the sheet of paper, folded it, wrote *LUCY* on the outside, and handed it to Madeleine.

'I'm telling Lucy that I can't see her now,' I said. 'I have so much to do to finish this business. And perhaps you can add when you see her that I would feel as if I were intruding on your holiday. William Robinson is not here. Calum is not here. It would be more fair if all three of us men were here.'

'I understand, and I know she will too. All three of us women are learning so much from each other. For myself, it's keeping me alive. I have learned how to mother my own grandchild!'

I went and found Armstrong who was rather surprised at my announcement that after a quick lunch at the Seagull Tavern, we must return right away to Charlottetown. Another few hours on horseback.

21

We arrived in Charlottetown at the end of the afternoon. Higgins, who was again on duty, said that Modeste had been making a fuss, demanding to see me the moment I returned. I went to see her. She was sitting on the wooden chair, with a pile of books on the table. 'These are boring,' she said. 'But I've had time to do some thinking, I've changed my mind, and I want out of here. You arrested me, with my agreement, because I was obstructing your enquiries. But now I've told you everything I know.'

'How can I be sure of that? You could be keeping all sorts of things up your sleeve.'

'All the same, I don't think you can keep me here for long unless you charge me. I know things are slack on the island, but we're a British Colony, and there is such a thing as *Habeas Corpus*.'

'You're right, I can't keep you. I thought you wanted to be near your husband.'

'He's in the Sanatorium, and don't worry, I'm not going to hang about hoping to see his face through some barred window. Poor Edgar! He must be hating it. He's an out-of-doors man. Anyway I want to get back to the house and look after the chickens and my dog – and read my own books.'

'You'll have to sign a statement before leaving.' I pulled out my notebook, and wrote in pencil as I spoke:

> '*I, Modeste Aucoin, state that on the evening and all the night when Marie Évangéline Harris was murdered, Friday 30th June, I was in my own house nearby with my husband Edgar Aucoin and with Zénon Cormier. Can I call him a hired hand? All right, Zénon Cormier,*

our hired hand. I heard no sounds of disturbance from Mr John Harris's
house, about fifty yards away. I have refused to answer questions about
other matters, but I am aware that I have not been charged with a crime.
I have demanded to be released. I know this is at my own risk. I shall
make myself available for further questioning by the Police immediately if
required.

'I can give this to the constable to write up properly, and if you sign it you can leave. I said when we detained you that it was for your own safety. Do you feel safe?'

'As safe as I've ever been in this world.'

I ate alone in a tavern around the corner. I no longer needed to have a constable with me. Then I sat in my hotel room writing brief reports of what I had been doing – for Mr Brecken. I should go to see him, but I felt too obsessed with following the investigation through.

The following morning after breakfast I went to see McNulty again. I knew enough, after my interview with Madeleine, to feel more assertive than before. McNulty may have been feeling more assertive too. He was sitting on a chair next to a small table that had been brought in so that he could rest his left elbow on it.

'So, to start with the murder of Marie Évangéline Harris,' I said, 'I know that you and Aucoin and I-Guess followed her when she took the boat from the wharf below Harris's house. I'm not sure of the details. Gallant must have told you to go there, since Marie had sent her mother back to North Rustico, and Gallant would have deduced that Marie was planning to run away. You and Aucoin were keeping an eye on Marie probably starting from the early afternoon, but she slipped away by boat, which must have been a surprise since she had recently given birth. Perhaps you expected her to leave by the front of the house, but then after a while you noticed the boat was gone and you chased her. I don't know if all three of you followed by boat, or whether one or two of you went by land. But you caught up with her at Thunder Cove. She had already hidden the baby and you couldn't find it. You bound and gagged her and brought her back by boat to Harris's wharf. You left her in the house with Gallant and Dunno. Again, a detail I don't know is how Aucoin managed the proximity of Dunno and I-Guess, but I suppose he was used to it. He and Modeste probably locked I-Guess in their house since Dunno was around. Gallant and Dunno raped her – or at least buggered her, which is a form of rape – then murdered her by beating her and by slashing her with an eel spear. Or they buggered her once she was dead! Or maybe just one of them buggered her. That makes no difference legally.'

I paused. McNulty was pale and expressionless.

'How could you do that?' I went on. 'You hunted down a young woman who had given birth to a baby only a week before – a brave young woman who had run away with her own baby – and although you couldn't find the baby, you delivered the mother into the jaws of death.'

'I didn't know they would kill her.' His voice was dry, as in our previous interview, as if the sap had gone out of him and he was now a husk.

'You must have had an idea they would do her harm. You knew it! And now you "regret it". Where's your conscience, McNulty? First Presbyterian, then Catholic, then what I can only call "the Cause". Where's your conscience?'

'Don't preach at me, Hobbes. The Cause is what we call the Brotherhood. Leave it at that.'

'The Brotherhood. All that brotherly love. How about the women in this world? Are they just here to be bound and gagged, and delivered to rape and murder? Or to be loved and married and then abandoned for the Brotherhood? For the Cause?'

'You know nothing about it.'

'Then tell me about it. Do you want to live or do you want to hang? You can hang for the felony of being in a conspiracy to murder, even if you did not strike the blow – or in this case blows, many blows. I hope she died early in the beating. If she didn't, she was tortured to death. Or her murderers committed necrophilia. You saw the evidence of that, at the autopsy.'

'Yes I saw it!' McNulty burst out. 'With that monster Dunno there…' His voice faded.

'And that monster Gallant who enjoyed lashing young women across the bare buttocks with his belt. Or was it you? Maybe it was you who beat her with your fists! Maybe *you* picked up that eel spear and raked it over her backside, slashing and cutting her. I'm told you were not there. But why should I believe anybody's word about that? Still less believe *you*? Anyway all that will be up to a court and jury. You could be charged with murder. You could be found guilty. As I said yesterday, I don't think it will be a very glorious murder from the point of view of the Cause. This Brotherhood I imagine are quite a pious bunch in their personal lives. I bet they go to church every Sunday! But brother McNulty gangs up with a twisted politician he is blackmailing, and rapes and murders a woman who has just given birth to a baby! Perhaps it's just as well for you that you'll hang – or at best spend many years in the Brig with nothing to read but the Bible, until perhaps the other prisoners who are there for a few weeks but know your history decide to get rid of you. At least you won't be out in the wide world cringing and hiding from the revenge of the Brotherhood. You'll be beaten to death!'

'What do you mean by blackmail? You know nothing of my relationship with Gallant.'

'Well, I'm deducing it. And deduction is a logical process.

'A: you are devoted to the Cause and you are a ruthless man. Plenty of evidence for that – for example the attempted murder of MacKinnon – to which there were witnesses: Armstrong and I.

310

'B: Gallant had many things to hide. The beating and possible raping of little girls. The involvement with smuggling. The possibility that his wife could be having an affair with the Gaelic schoolteacher. I'll stop the list there.

'Ergo C: you had a power over Gallant. He was *your* man.'

'That's upside down. I was *his* man. He got me my post in the police! You didn't know that, did you? A few years ago he and I met, in Antigonish where he had business – yes smuggling, and the other business of buying children for himself. And if you have been getting your information from Edgar Aucoin, be aware that he is no angel. The Aucoins buy and sell children.'

'I know that. Did Gallant buy the Cormier brothers by the way?'

'Of course. They were very violent and their mother could not handle them, so they were sent to the Orphelinat where they had to be locked in separate rooms and they kept the house awake all night, shouting threats to each other and trying to break through the walls. Something had to be done quickly. Gallant gave a donation to the Orphelinat, as he often did, and took the boys off their hands. One of them, Dunno, ended up living with a family near Georgetown to whom Gallant paid some money to look after him. Gallant also paid money to the Aucoins to look after I-Guess.'

'Why?'

'Gallant must have realised he could use the Cormier boys. They are very useful indeed – so long as they are kept apart. I mean they *were* useful. They had a reputation. I know that in the past if Aucoin went to collect payment for a bill overdue to Gallant, and he had one of the boys with him, the person would pay up at once. No need even for threats. As you know, these days, Dunno does some work for Gallant. But you can't accuse me of having anything to do with the boys. I didn't.'

'You did. A murder and an attempted murder.'

'I meant, not until recently. And as for the so-called attempted murder, it wasn't that. We were just going to put MacKinnon out of action. Cripple him, perhaps. Give him a very bad bang on the head so he could no longer think straight.'

'And not remember it was you and Aucoin who had attacked him? No, once you attacked him you had to kill him. Otherwise, when he recovered from his injuries, he would be able to say who had inflicted them: you and Aucoin.'

McNulty said nothing. He looked down at his immobilised hand on the table.

'Why?' I said. 'What had he done to you? Or should I say, 'What had he done to Gallant?'

'You know. Remember what you told me the last time you were here. Calum was going to bed with Gallant's wife!'

'When did Gallant find that out?'

McNulty was silent.

'Did you tell him?' This was a horrible thought but there it was.

'Look, Hobbes, why should I admit to something like that?'

'Because it will come out anyway. For example, I'll soon interview Gallant yet again. By the way I have assigned him police "protection" so he can't fly the coop. Perhaps he'll decide to blame *you* for all this. Yes, he'll say, he used his influence to get you a post with the Charlottetown police, but then you climbed and climbed – a sergeant in only two years. And you became full of your own power. You began to blackmail him. He'll say all this. He won't even have to mention the little girls – *that* could stay well under the carpet. But you blackmailed him by revealing that his wife was sleeping with a Gaelic schoolteacher much older than he. And of course you would keep this as a secret if Gallant made it worth your while. Poor Gallant! Where could he turn?'

'Hobbes! You know it wasn't like that. Why would I attempt to kill MacKinnon if I were blackmailing Gallant? Then it would be in my interest to keep MacKinnon alive.'

'Perhaps. But if Gallant was not *your* man, and instead you were *his* man, it becomes clear that it was he who instructed you and Aucoin to get rid of MacKinnon. And I mean get rid of.'

'All right. I won't protect Gallant. He is a swine. The truth is that if I am anyone's man, I am Ireland's man. That is the Cause, if you like. I did think that Gallant was in my hands – that is in effect in the hands of the Brotherhood. He knew next to nothing about how the Brotherhood was formed, but he knew it was our mission to preserve any part of so-called "British" North America from being part of the British Empire, which it would be either as part of a Confederation of Canada, or as a British Colony on its own. But, to put it simply, if Prince Edward Island – in spite of all predictions – stays out of Canada and remains a tiny British Colony, it will be more possible to detach it completely from the British Empire. It's almost bankrupt, for one thing, and the railway project is piling up still more debts. When people are discontented they choose radical solutions. And although the rulers of this island, the 'Family Compact,' are loud in their support of the "Mother Country", I doubt if more than a fifth of the Islanders feel English, or even British. We will have the Island French on our side. They have hated the British since the deportations. Then there are the Irish – twenty-five percent or so. And even about half of the Scots who are another forty percent. Do you think your friend MacKinnon has any love for the English?'

'Probably not. But I gather from him that the people who starved and expelled so many Highlanders in the Clearances were the Scottish Chiefs themselves, after their defeat in 1746. And not all Irish are pro Fenians and against Confederation – in fact the Irish-born owner of the *Examiner* wrote vigorously against the Fenian movement on this island. He was also known for his strong support of Confederation. And your own country, Ireland, is not only part of the British Empire, it has a parliamentary Union with Britain. Are you aiming to make this island free because you can't make your own country free?'

313

'I want both of them to be free,' McNulty said, with an air of dignity.

'But what a way to achieve it! To cultivate an alliance with a man who enlists you in the murder of a woman acknowledged to be his daughter, and the attempted murder – sorry, but that is what it was – of an innocent schoolteacher.'

'I wouldn't call MacKinnon innocent. He makes love with another man's wife.'

'Have you ever been on the other end of that situation?'

'That's personal.'

'Of course it is. Everything is personal. Look at what you call your "relationship" with Gallant. You may tell yourself it's a political relationship, but it's as full of lies and deception as a bad marriage. I was wrong to get into a discussion of whether Gallant was your man, or whether you were his. You each belong to the other and need each other. And you each hate each other. You are like the proverbial two scorpions in a bottle. Or like the Cormiers – Romulus and Remus!'

'Romulus won…' McNulty said.

'And founded Rome. But you have *not* won. Here you are, with a broken shoulder, sitting in police custody. Gallant is still at large, performing his "business", as you call it. *He* has won.'

'Not for long.'

'Yes for long. Unless you tell the truth – not just to me but in a statement for the Attorney General.'

'I am not a betrayer.'

'I agree you are not a betrayer of the Cause – the Brotherhood. You have told me no more about it than what could be found in a newspaper. But it's not betrayal to tell the truth about a suspected murderer – a particularly vile one.'

'You haven't proved that yet, if he is still free and as you say taking care of his business.'

'I'm close to proving it.'

314

'Only through circumstance. On the evidence of Aucoin and me, if I decide to cooperate, and of Dr Reid's findings, you can establish that Gallant was in the right place at the right time, and that he had many reasons to want to kill Marie. But not that he actually did it.'

'This is the kind of conversation we had when we first worked together. We had better stop.' I stood up. 'I'm sorry it has come to this.'

'I am too. But my mind is more clear following our discussion. I'm willing to make a statement of what I have told you – but I can say or write nothing about the Brotherhood beyond what I have told you, which is, as you say, at the level of the newspapers.'

'I don't give a fig. It's not on my agenda. Of course sedition and rebellion are the concern of the police, but I have had no information about either in this case.'

I opened the door and went out into the hallway where the constable was on duty. Going out into Dr Reid's garden felt like getting out of jail.

Although the island was so small, communications were no easier than they had been in British Columbia which is bigger than most European countries. Information was sent by telegram from a few towns around the coast, then was copied or printed out and delivered by a man on horseback or in a horse-drawn trap. Letters went by post through relays of horses. I ascertained that Gallant was now in Georgetown, working at his office and staying in a room he had permanently set aside for him in a boarding house. He was followed at a distance by one constable or another. He knew they were there, of course, and replied rudely when they occasionally checked with him that all was well. They reported occasional meetings he had with another notary, and with various ships' officers: Georgetown harbour was a centre for the island's trade with the mainland, and for the import of coal from Cape Breton.

Modeste Aucoin had left the Brig the previous evening. I had a short telegram from Lucy saying she had received my note, that she and Will

315

were happy, and that she loved me. I did not want to see either McNulty or Aucoin again. They could be left behind bars to think. Or to read their Bibles. Dr Reid reported that medically both were making a good recovery. Aucoin was almost better, although he would have to be careful moving as he risked re-opening his wound. McNulty was no longer in such pain, but would end up partly crippled, unable to move his arm. He was in no condition to move much either.

I worked on my reports, and I took a walk in Charlottetown and along the harbour, in no mood to talk to anyone or to look in the shops. I did like the place though. Apart from its often rickety plank sidewalks, and some areas which smelled of sewage, it was a thriving town and port, with some elegant buildings, and some very well-dressed women and men, along with robust and lively farmers. I too was well dressed in a suit, and did not attract attention.

After dinner at what was now my usual tavern, I walked for a while around the harbour where there were still people strolling and talking. The air was warm and there were lights along the quay. Otherwise it was a dark night with a half moon crossing the sky to the southeast. I went back to the St Lawrence Hotel and to bed. I slept fitfully, as there was not much breeze, and my open window was small.

I kept waking up thinking gloomily that McNulty had been right. All the evidence I had was hearsay, and I could not even establish for sure that Gallant had been in Harris's house at Stanley Bridge on the evening of the murder. The only possible witness was his accomplice Dunno – who was dead. Even if I put police constables to work questioning the drivers of traps or wagons, and eventually established that Gallant had been in Stanley Bridge that evening, or even if McNulty and Aucoin were miraculously ready to swear that they had handed over Marie, bound and gagged, into Gallant's hands, there would be room for him to bluster his way out of it. He could say, perhaps, that of course he had wanted to confront Marie, and indeed he had done so – poor martyr that he was, faced with the immoral behaviour of his nearest and dearest in the form of his adulterous wife and now possibly also his daughter (who had proved not to be his daughter at all!) – or he had cried his heart out in front of Marie and gone on his way to Summerside a broken man. And so on... He would know nothing, poor innocent. When he could not find Dunno, he had set off to Summerside on his own. And the sinister Dunno must have crept into Harris's house – perhaps looking for I-Guess – and violated and beaten Marie to death in a blind frenzy.

I was afraid Gallant would get away with it.

Shortly after six o'clock, as I was lying on my back gazing at the whitewashed plaster walls brightening in the sunlight from the window, there was a banging at my room door. I sprang out of the bed, in my nightshirt, and shot back the bolt. It was Constable Higgins, in trousers and a shirt with no jacket. He handed me a telegram. I moved over to the window to read it:

Honoré Gallant found dead at dawn drowned in Georgetown harbour near Coal Wharf. Note in pocket being taken to Charlottetown Police by Constables Mackie and Jones post haste. Body to follow on ice. Mackie

In other words, this Mackie had sent the telegram before leaping on his horse and presumably galloping with his colleague Jones towards Charlottetown. How long would that take? About three hours. And the body, in a wagon, on ice? About five hours.

Nothing to do but wait. I told Higgins to show the telegram to Armstrong as soon as he arrived at the Brig, and I got dressed properly and left the hotel and took a walk. Without thinking, I found myself walking across the park towards the battery where I-Guess and Dunno had met their deaths. The cannon had been cleaned – no blood marks – although the grass was still flattened where people had stood. I turned and wandered into town where I found a restaurant where breakfast rivalled Ringo's in Victoria. I always like breakfast. I tucked into sausages and bacon with black coffee, and read the week's *Islander* which as usual had extensive bulletins from Europe, and as usual not cheery. The terms imposed by Germany on France in the aftermath of the Franco–Prussian War seemed to make future wars more likely. Oh well, why should I care? I was not in Europe. I did not bother thinking about Gallant's death either. It would be a waste of time to speculate. But as I got up from my table, I did feel a weight off my mind.

When I got back to the Brig, there was another telegram, from Georgetown, the time being given as 6.30. It was addressed to me:

> *Superintendent Hobbes. Am arriving early afternoon with information*
> *re Gallant death. Modeste*

I could not help wondering whether Modeste had been aware of the irony in the phrase 'Gallant death'! She probably was.

22

The two constables arrived first. They looked exhausted and were covered with red dust from riding hard. The horses were taken to the stables, and I gave the constables half an hour to clean themselves up and to have some breakfast. I felt impatient, but I thought I would get more clear information out of them if they had rested a bit.

We sat around the table in the grimy meeting room of the Brig – myself, Armstrong, Mackie and Jones. Although we were all police officers, our clothing varied, from my light brown linen suit to Mackie's blue tunic jacket, a red silk neckcloth, and black-and-white checked trousers, and Jones's crumpled checked cotton suit with a stiff collar and a blue bow tie. Mackie and Jones both had truncheons at their belts, which was police identification enough. Mackie was the younger of the two, and seemed brisk, if not impatient. Jones, an older man, avoided my eyes.

'Since you sent the telegram, Mackie, why don't you start?' I said.

'Yes Sir. As I wrote Sir, Mr Gallant drowned. He was found at dawn floating in the water at the end of the Coal Wharf. A dock-man saw him and fetched us. I should tell you, it was an unusual sight. He was floating face downwards with his head under the water wearing a short coat but seemingly no trousers. His lower part was visible – oh hell! Sir, to put it in our usual island language, he was floating arse upwards and his arse was bare. We got a boat out and heaved him into it. He was in fact wearing trousers, but his belt was undone and they were down to his ankles. We brought him ashore and laid him on the ground. Water poured out of his mouth. We sent for the nearest doctor, Dr Nelson, who pronounced him dead. We arranged for him to be transported here as we knew you would want to see him, and there is a morgue here where he can have a post-mortem.'

'Yes, we'll send him to Dr Reid. Any marks of injury?'

'None. We didn't take any more of his clothes off, Sir. We discussed it but decided not to. We did pull his trousers up. It didn't seem right to leave him like that. We noticed no signs of injury on his lower body or anywhere else. We searched his trouser pockets and found only a hand-kerchief and some small change, in the right pocket. In his right-hand coat pocket there was a spectacle case with the spectacles in it, a wallet with the note we mentioned, and various bank-notes – forty Canadian dollars, and fifty Island pounds. In his left coat pocket was a Smith and Wesson Model One revolver – a short barrelled type, point 22 calibre. It was fully loaded with seven rounds. The note we found in his wallet was soaked but legible. I spread it out carefully and put it between sheets of waxed paper.' Mackie reached into his own pocket and produced a flat, neatly wrapped wax-paper package and handed it to me.

'That was sensible,' I said as I unwrapped it carefully. It was one sheet of paper which had been folded in four. Now it lay flat, damp but not soaking. I could read it without taking it off the wax paper.

Monsieur G,

> *Je suis à Georgetown, en affaire comme d'habitude, et j'ai trouvé une nouvelle et très belle marchandise qui pourrait vous intéresser…*

'I can't read French,' I said. I looked at the Georgetown constables.

'Neither of us does either,' said Mackie.

I moved my chair so that Armstrong, who did know French, could move his chair over to look. He read slowly:

Mr G,

> *I am in Georgetown on business, as usual, and I have found a very beautiful piece of new merchandise of interest to you. It is only ten years*

old and is in very good condition. If you would like to inspect it, it will be
at the storage shed you sometimes use on the Coal Wharf. I see that these
days you always have an associate with you, day and night. Before you
approach the Wharf I can negotiate some business with your associate,
so that you will be free to inspect the merchandise. Can we say 10.00
tonight? I shall assume you will be there.

Your friend ...

'It is signed with an illegible squiggle, as you can see,' said Armstrong.
The word friend is *amie* with an "e", indicating that the writer is a woman
– although the writing is quite childish, as in a school primer. People often
write childishly when they are disguising their own hand.'

I looked at Mackie and Jones. 'So which of you was following Mr
Gallant last night?' I asked, although I could forecast the answer, looking
at Jones.

He bit his upper lip and moustache, and said, 'It was me Sir. I have
failed in my duty.' He looked gaunt and grey, although he was probably
not much over forty.

'Go on.'

'I watched Mr Gallant all afternoon and evening. He sees quite a few
people who come and go to his office. And from time to time boys arrive
with letters or messages. I saw nothing out of the ordinary. At around seven
o'clock he went to dinner in the King George Tavern – it's the best in
Georgetown. I stayed outside the dining room. I couldn't afford such a
place. But I got a sandwich sent back from the kitchen, and a glass – one
glass – of beer. Mr Gallant so far as I could see was reading the newspapers
at the table – the *Examiner*, and the Halifax paper, and the New Brunswick
French paper, it's called *Le Moniteur Acadien*. I was sitting in the hallway
when a lady came up to me. She was dressed in mourning, with a black veil.
I couldn't see her face. She was quite tall and slim. She made a movement
of her head towards the dining room, and said to me, "I see you are looking
after Mr Gallant, poor man. He has had a bereavement, as you may know.

321

I'm a friend of the family – a very close friend of his dear wife – and she has sent me with a message for him. It's not in writing. I must deliver it by word of mouth." She touched my arm and said "I'm so sorry," and she reached into her dress and brought out a handkerchief, a black handkerchief, and turned away and lifted her veil slightly, so that she could wipe her eyes. I couldn't see her face. She turned back to me and said, "I know who you are, you are Constable Jones, and I know you must watch Mr Gallant for his own safety. But he is a very sensitive man. I need some time alone with him. I think when he hears my news, he'll find it very hard to contain his emotions. Please let me meet him when he leaves this restaurant. He knows where to meet me. I sent him a message this afternoon. I think he will have received it, won't he?"'

'"Of course" I said, "we don't interfere with his messages."'

'"I'm staying with another family friend, just around the corner," she said. Sir, I may not be getting this right word for word, but I do remember what she said.'

'Of course, go ahead.'

'So she said, "I know you are not a rich man on the pay of a police constable – although I must say I sleep better at night for knowing that men like you are on duty protecting citizens like me. I want to give you this." And she handed me a small envelope. "It contains sixty American dollars," she said. "Please buy something for yourself and your wife. All I am asking from you in return is an hour with Mr Gallant. I promise you that he will meet you back here by eleven o'clock. Now I am going to leave and wait for Mr Gallant at my friend's house. When he comes out of the dining room, just before ten o'clock, he will go there. You stay here, and he'll be back by eleven, and then you can follow him to where he stays."'

Jones stopped and looked at me anxiously.

'So all happened as predicted,' I said to him. 'The lady left. Mr Gallant came out towards ten o'clock and walked out of the restaurant. You waited. And you ordered another beer or two. I'm not saying you broke the sixty dollars – that's well over a month's salary. But you sat down and waited with a drink or two. And of course Mr Gallant did not return. Nor of course did the lady in black.'

'Yes Sir.'

'Well, Constable Jones, you are now suspended from duty. You are also under arrest for dereliction of duty.' I was making this term up, but it sounded right. 'Armstrong can you please escort Jones out of the room and hand him over to Constable Higgins?'

Armstrong got up, as did Jones, and they left the room. We waited in silence until Armstrong came back.

'Anything to add, Mackie?' I asked.

'No Sir. I'm sorry Jones fell for that story. But he's not a bad man.'

'Perhaps. But we do have to suspend him. And he didn't simply fall for a story, he took a bribe. Do you know who this woman in black was?' I knew.

'No. But mourning is a good disguise.'

'And who was the man who discovered Gallant's body?'

'A dockman, called Cassidy. He was getting ready for work at dawn and as the day brightened he saw the body. It was floating, head down, next to the end of the wharf, and as I said – forgive me Sir – bare-arsed. I was there soon after. When we got the body out I recognised Mr Gallant right away, although he was rather swollen. I went through his pockets, as I described.'

'Was he well liked in Georgetown?'

'Not exactly liked. Respected. I used to see him around in town. He was polite but not friendly.'

'Armstrong, what do you make of the letter in his pocket?'

'Well, Sir, reading between the lines, I suspect the "merchandise" being offered was a ten-year-old child. The choice of the French feminine word *marchandise* along with *nouvelle* and *belle* could suggest a girl child.'

'It seems so in this case. Mackie, did Mr Gallant have a reputation in Georgetown for unusual behaviour?'

'No more than anyone else. There is gossip about everyone. I never heard anything terrible about Mr Gallant. Apart from smuggling of course.'

'Why "of course"?

'Well, Sir, just about everyone in Georgetown is involved with smuggling – what with Nova Scotia just over the water. Mr Gallant was known to be someone you could go to and get the documents straight. Let's say you had brought something in and you wanted to sell it on, he would take an affidavit for you to state it was for personal use, and he would fix it with the Customs officers.'

'How would he fix it?'

'Let's just say there are three customs officers in Georgetown. They are not poor men. They have big houses.'

'So what do you think happened to Mr Gallant?'

'I reckon somebody pushed him into the river.'

'Sorry, I haven't been in Georgetown. It's on the Brudenell River, isn't it?'

'Yes, it's an estuary where the Brudenell River joins the sea in the harbour. It's a wide bay and the deepest harbour on the island. It's usually quite calm, since it's east-facing and sheltered from the prevailing winds. If you're thinking about whether the body would have been swept ashore or out to sea – no. It needn't have moved much if he drowned before midnight. The tide was coming in, by the way, so he would just rise with it.'

'Thank you. I suggest you tag along with Sergeant Armstrong here. He in turn will tag along with me, most of today. Since you've started the case, you should follow it through. You've done well.'

The next event was the arrival of the body – on an open wagon, covered with a canvas sheet, and lying on ice. We asked the drivers to swing the wagon into the yard behind the Brig, and to wait, since we would be asking them to take it to Dr Reid at the morgue. We inspected it in the open air, which was just as well, as there was a stench of tidal water and possibly sewage, in spite of the fact that Gallant's clothes were hard and brittle with ice. He was lying on his back with his eyes staring and glassy although filmed over. His flesh had swelled, and was bluish grey. Rigor had set in: I couldn't move his arm. His face was stuck in a grimace, but that is what rigor does. Armstrong took some official notes, and we sent the wagon on to Dr Reid.

At one o'clock, Modeste Aucoin arrived. She was the passenger in a two-horse trap. She too was covered with red dust. Armstrong provided a clothes brush and she stood in the street brushing herself. She was dressed as always quite strictly, in a plain grey suit jacket over a grey silk dress. But she wore a narrow-brimmed sun hat tied with a red ribbon. She came into the Brig, and headed immediately for the police wash-room and lavatory. After all, she knew where they were.

Armstrong and Mackie and I waited for her in the police room. Higgins escorted her in. She sat down on the opposite side of the table.

'Do they have to be here?' she said to me.

'I'm afraid so.'

'Then I won't be able to say everything I want.'

'In that case I suggest we start with all of us here, and if we reach a point where you would like to tell some things to me alone, the others can leave.'

'All right.' She took her hat off and laid it on the table. Her hair was black with hints of grey, her eyes dark and piercing. 'How's Edgar?'

'He's much better. He can move around, although he'll have to watch himself or he may open the wound again. There's no blood-poisoning or fever.'

'Can I see him?'

'Perhaps you can, after this. Thank you for coming here. What would you like to tell us?'

'I was there when Mr Gallant fell off the wharf in Georgetown and drowned. We were talking and he took a step backwards by mistake, tripped on the edge of the wharf, and fell in. I heard a big splash. I rushed to the edge of the wharf and knelt down and called to him. The tide was coming in and the water was about eight feet below me. I could see nothing of Mr Gallant. Then he came up again, quite quickly, he just floated, face down. I could hardly see him, he was just like a dark log in the water which was black. I know it's just past the half moon, but there are no lights on the wharf. I suppose he may have tripped over the wharf edge because it was too dark to see it clearly. The wharf is held up by huge logs sunk into the mud below the water, and the surface is made of wooden planks with a border along the edges, made of long square beams of wood faced with padded leather, with holes for passing ropes through. Off the wharf there's just a sheer drop of ten feet or so – according to the tide. And by the way Mr Gallant can't swim – or he couldn't. When I was working as a midwife with Madeleine Gallant we used to talk together, and she told me that.

'Anyway, I ran back to the bottom of the wharf and called loudly for help, in case there was anyone working in the storage sheds near the base of the wharf, but there was no one around. So I ran along the road into the town and to the police station to report this to a constable. There was no sign of any light inside. I knocked on the door again and again, but no one answered. So I took a piece of notepaper from my purse and wrote on it that Mr Gallant was drowned off the Coal Wharf, and I looked at my watch and I could just see it was eleven o'clock, so I wrote the time on my note, and I slipped it in under the police station door. Then I walked around looking for people. Georgetown is dead after the taverns have closed, the houses are quite far apart, and in summer everyone goes to bed early to get up early. I was tired, and I was very shocked. I went back to the guesthouse I was staying in – The Eagle's Nest – and everyone had gone to bed. I went to bed and slept a little.

And when I got up at first light I almost ran over to the Coal Wharf. Mr Gallant was still there in the same place, floating, face down – and with his trousers down, or off. I wondered if he had loosened them in his struggle not to drown. The water is very murky there, so I couldn't see any of his body except what was above the surface. By that time there were people gathering to look, and the police came running – this young man here.' She pointed at Mackie. 'And some others. So I knew everything would be taken care of. Shortly after the telegraph station opened, at six o'clock, I sent you the telegram saying I was coming. And here I am.'

'Just a moment, if you don't mind, Mrs Aucoin.' I turned to Mackie. 'You didn't say anything about a note under the door.'

'The police station is not manned at night in Georgetown, unless we have someone in the lock-up, which we didn't last night. And I was first in this morning, and I didn't see a note. We can send a telegram and get them to look again.'

'Good idea. Armstrong, would you ask someone to send a telegram, something like "Please check very carefully for message through the police station front door possibly lost."'

Armstrong left the room and we waited in silence. Modeste opened her purse and took out a little mirror and glanced into it briefly then put it back. Armstrong returned after five minutes or so.

'Mrs Aucoin, you do a lot of reading,' I said. 'You must know you have started this story at the end. When did you first see Mr Gallant yesterday?'

'You must know that. Constable Jones will have told you. I saw Mr Gallant at the restaurant, eating his dinner and reading newspapers. I spoke with Constable Jones, and asked him to allow me some time with Mr Gallant, and he agreed.'

'He has told us about it.'

'What did he say exactly?'

'That a woman in mourning clothes, with a black veil, accosted him and gave him sixty US dollars to stay in the restaurant when Mr Gallant left. The woman was you, then.'

'It certainly was. I don't wear mourning all the time, but I still mourn the death of Marie Évangéline, whom I greatly liked – and for that matter I am mourning the disappearance of my husband, Edgar Aucoin, into your custody. How do I know he isn't dead?'

'He isn't dead. As I said earlier, he's making a good recovery.'

'But what if something happened to him, Mr Hobbes, what *if*?'

'What if you wrote this letter?'

I passed the still-damp letter across to her. She read it.

'My goodness! Who wrote that? Not I! That's not my handwriting, and it's not my signature!'

'But you did what the letter proposes. You met Mr Gallant on the Coal Wharf.'

'I don't want to pick at facts, Mr Hobbes, but I didn't *meet* him on the Coal Wharf. I waited for him outside the restaurant. I had travelled to Georgetown with the intention of seeing him either yesterday evening or today. But at his lodgings I was told he was at the King George Tavern. When he came out, I accosted him – as you might put it – and we talked for a few moments, and we walked together down to Water Street and then along to the Coal Wharf. There was a half moon quite high in the sky and I said I wanted to look at it. The wharf is a few hundred yards, I suppose, out of town and there are no houses nearby, only a few sheds, usually deserted at night. As I say it was dark. The moon gave enough light to walk by, but once we got to the end of the wharf we couldn't see each other well. The moon was more or less behind Honoré, high in the sky. I could hardly see his face. He may have been able to see me better.'

'This wharf. Can you describe it in more detail?' You mentioned earlier there was a wooden edge which Gallant tripped over.'

'I know a lot about wharfs, since my father was a fisherman. This one is a wharf for heavy loads of coal and lumber. As I said, it's held up by very big wooden posts sunk into the ground underwater and it's surfaced with layers of planks. And the ledge along the sides is made of square wooden 'four by fours' lined with padded leather and with holes, as I mentioned, for the ropes of boats moored alongside. Along the inside of the ledge on the wharf there are various bollards and those T-shaped iron cleats for mooring boats. The wharf sticks straight to the south into Brudenell Bay. Along the east side of the wharf, closest to the town, people stack various boxes of tools and equipment along the ledge. We were standing at the end, close to a sheer drop, talking in raised voices – I was angry, but I wasn't shouting, although there was no one around to hear.'

'What did you talk about?'

'I would prefer to tell this to you alone.'

'Please tell us all that you can. At least the basic points. I assure you, it will help.'

'Will it help get Eddy out of jail?'

'We don't bargain in the police. You know that.'

'No I don't know that. It seems police constables can be bargained with. One might say even "bought".'

'Touché!'

I suppressed a smile. How could I like this utterly dreadful and frightening woman so much? Was it because at some base level of myself I found her attractive?

'All I can say, Mrs Aucoin, is that if you can help us solve the two crimes we are investigating, of course we shall be grateful.'

'I won't hide the truth from you gentlemen. Why did I meet Mr Gallant? Why did I use a degree of subterfuge to meet him in a place out of earshot of other people? Because my husband, Edgar Aucoin, is under suspicion of murder, and of attempted murder, and I want to clear his name! Because Edgar was working for Honoré Gallant in the past, and although he may fear being hanged or imprisoned, he fears Mr Gallant even more! Mr Gallant could destroy not only Edgar, but me – and our children!'

'Your children?'

'Two boys, of ten and twenty-one. As I told you, they are living in Antigonish for a while. They love it over there, with cousins of ours. But that is within reach of Mr Gallant. Talk to your colleagues in the Nova Scotia police! That is if you do talk to each other, coming from different countries.'

'We'll talk to them, Mrs Aucoin. To go back to your meeting with Mr Gallant on the Coal Wharf, I suppose you knew there would be no one around at night.'

'There's no gas lighting in Georgetown. Since the wharf sticks out into the bay and is going nowhere, and it's lined with boxes and crates and ropes around bollards, it's not exactly a romantic spot for a walk, and as I said it's some distance from the nearest houses.'

'What did Mr Gallant say?'

'Not very much. I was disappointed. I told him he should admit to the murder of Marie Évangéline, and he just laughed at me. I reminded him that Edgar and your former colleague McNulty had followed his instructions to fetch back Marie who had fled towards the west in her sailing boat, and when they fetched her back they brought her to the library in Harris's house where Mr Gallant and that crazy twin Dunno were waiting. Edgar then came home to our house and McNulty had returned to the Stanley Bridge tavern where he was lodging. I reminded Mr Gallant that he and Dunno were in Harris's house, and that evening or night Marie had been brutally beaten and murdered. I begged him to go to the police and admit to what he had done. When he laughed at that, I begged him to write a letter about it to you, Mr Hobbes, and then to flee the country. He has so much money, in banks not only here on the island but in Nova Scotia and in New England. I begged him not to let my husband take the blame for a murder he had not committed and for which he could hang. He laughed at me. I must avow that I became quite heated. I felt like yelling at him, but I kept calm in case the sound carried over the water to the houses in the distance. I could see their lights.

"'Admit that you killed her – you and Dunno!" I said in a low voice. "She deserved it, the bitch!" he said. "No one deserved that kind of death!" I said. I could have shrieked but I didn't. I can hear my own voice in my mind now. You can call it low and deadly. I said, "You went on mistreating a dead woman! You raped her body!"

"'You know what Dunno is like!" he said.

'I said "You're worse than Dunno because you have a mind. Dunno has none!"

'I could hardly see him in the dark. I was so angry I could have screamed at him but instead I took a step forward, and I said to him "Help my Edgar!" and I raised my hand as if to hit him. Not that I would have dared. I'm tall for a woman, but he was a lot heavier and stronger. He took a step backwards and stumbled over the edge. At least he suddenly disappeared. I heard a big splash. And that was it! I've already told you. I could see nothing in the dark, just occasional glittering of the water in the moonlight. As I said, he couldn't swim. Who on this island cannot swim?'

We sat there, stunned I might say, but not quite. Modeste was trembling with anger, but looking at me with penetrating sparkly black eyes.

'Thank you,' I said. 'If Sergeant Armstrong here, with Constable Mackie's help, writes out a brief précis of what you have said, will you please sign it?'

'If it's accurate.'

'You can check that, and correct it as you wish. We are very grateful.

You do realise that when this goes to the Attorney General and possibly to court, questions might arise about how Mr Gallant fell off the wharf. People may ask, for example, if you pushed him over.'

'Me, push him over? I know I'm quite tall, but he is a heavy man – sorry, *was* a heavy man. Even if I had been so foolish as to try and push him over, there would have been a struggle, and as you can see looking at me, there are no signs I have been in a struggle. I would not have succeeded anyway. No. Frankly, and I would say this gladly in court, Honoré Gallant was a brute. I'm glad he's dead. I suppose my accusations were so intense that he was shocked into stepping backwards. He must have stumbled on the raised edge of the wharf. I couldn't see that in the dark. But yes, he must have been shocked. I am only a woman, after all, and I knew what he had done. I just wanted my husband to be free and not blamed for something he had *not* done! I'm only grateful that Honoré Gallant did not kill *me!*'

'Again thank you. Sergeant Armstrong with help from Constable Mackie will draft a statement which I hope you can sign. You have given us your narrative of events. And if there is anything of a delicate or confidential nature that you wish to discuss with me, we can stay here together while they draft the statement.'

'Yes, there are a few small things,' she said.

Armstrong and Mackie got up and went out of the room. I was alone with Modeste, facing her across the table.

23

'Hats off to you!' I said. 'I don't know how to say that in French.'

'It's easy. *Chapeau!* It just means "Hat"!'

'*Chapeau!* I am not going to put your narrative in doubt. But can I ask a few questions about details – not to be officially noted?'

'Of course. But I need to get up and stand. I've had enough sitting down today.'

She stood up, rather slowly, and moved towards the wall with her back to it.

I felt embarrassed at sitting while she was standing, so I stood up too, beside the table, and we continued our conversation.

'Do you know how to fire a gun?' I asked.

'Certainly. I've often used a shotgun to shoot foxes and skunks. The skunks come up to the house looking for garbage, and if the dog is off his leash he'll go at the skunk and get sprayed, and he'll stink for weeks. So you have to shoot the skunk first. Have you ever washed a dog who has been skunk-sprayed?'

'No. I've never even seen a skunk.'

'Except the human kind, I imagine.'

There was a knock at the door. Armstrong came in with a piece of paper. 'Excuse me Sir, Excuse me Mrs Aucoin, but we already have a telegram from Georgetown Police.' He handed me the paper, and left the room.

Careful examination of entrance hall reveals note slipped under door hidden by inside doormat. Note informs police Honoré Gallant drowned Coal Wharf around eleven o'clock last night. Georgetown Police

I passed it to Modeste – by now I thought of her as Modeste, rather than Mrs Aucoin – to read.

'*Chapeau!* again,' I said. 'Have you ever visited that police station?'

'I must admit I have, once or twice.'

'I find myself wondering if you noticed the inside doormat. It's so easy to slip a letter under a door and have it go under an inside doormat by mistake.'

'My goodness, yes. I should have thought of it. There was no way of seeing it of course.'

'To return to guns. You don't by any chance have a revolver or pistol do you?'

'Goodness, no.'

'I find myself wondering if perhaps you had a gun in your hand. It might have added to Mr Gallant's anxiety on the wharf, causing him to step backwards rather precipitously.'

'Well, I'm not saying that I have *never* had a pistol. But I haven't got one now.'

'Perhaps it fell into the water. I'm sure the bottom in a harbour like that is quite deep in mud and sludge.'

'I'm sure it is,' she said, smiling almost sweetly.

'Can you please tell me any more details you know about the murder of Marie Harris. They are not strictly necessary, you have told us all we need to know. And I attended the post-mortem.'

'McNulty told us about the post-mortem. Can I trust you? I think I can. I like men who like women, and I think you like women. I'm not sure if McNulty likes women. He doesn't respect their minds. He tells himself he doesn't need us. He does need us. All men need us – even someone like Harris needs us. Only he is the opposite of most men: he could love Marie for her mind but not her body. And McNulty could never realise I had a mind. Edgar of course is another reverse case: he loves my body and he is afraid of my mind because he needs it. He's clever but he's lazy when it comes to thinking.'

'I'm becoming confused. You knew McNulty?'

'Yes, but it's a secret. From everyone, except Edgar of course. Edgar knows my elder son is by McNulty.'

'Please explain to me clearly, Mrs Aucoin.'

'I wish you could simply call me Modeste. I can explain. McNulty – let's call him Willie-John, shall we? He hates being called Willie-John. It's apparently the most traditional Irish Presbyterian name there is. By the time he arrived in Antigonish, twenty-four years ago, he had turned to being a Catholic, gone to some awful seminary where the seminarians had to whip themselves every day, and then he emigrated to the New World. Antigonish is a very pious place, and was then served by English and French priests. How did we meet? At confession, I must admit. My French-speaking confessor was ill and Willie-John stood in, and I confessed in English. Not to terrible things, but I did avow that I was not a virgin at the time. He encouraged me to come back to him for future confessions – which I know is not the right thing – but he did encourage me, so I came back. We fell in love. I mean it. From his side I can understand it. I was very pretty, and I was upset and I needed advice – which is irresistible to a man. From my side it was not so easy to understand. Fall in love with a priest? And I couldn't even see him properly through the grille. But I could hear and feel an intensity in him. He burst out that he wanted to see me face to face! We met outside the church. He was not very tall, but quite good-looking, and even more intense. We became close. I could bring him to delights he had never guessed at! Soon I was expecting a child. He left the church – resigned. He was excommunicated too. But he took that lightly. He had concluded that all Christianity was a fraud on the people, to stop them rebelling against authority and governments. And as you know, he's very clever indeed. He began to write articles for newspapers and journals, in Antigonish, and in Halifax. About political questions. He had jumped from saving souls to saving bodies. Willie-John knows how to take what seems to be a cautious position and then to move it gently towards something more radical. A wolf in sheep's clothing. He also started to read avidly in French. He had a friend at Saint Francis Xavier College who would lend him French books which he would devour.'

'But he told me he didn't speak French!'

'*Au contraire!* He could already read it when we met, and he learned to speak it with me. We had many lively discussions! It was a bit less lively in bed, which is one reason I went eventually with Edgar. But by then I was less important to Willie-John His writing was more important. His correspondence with people in Ireland, in England, in the States. I felt neglected. And then I met Edgar. A dancing man, a rogue, a scoundrel if you like, but a man with a heart and a life to him. Not educated like Willie-John, but Willie-John's head was in the clouds when Edgar's feet were on the ground. So I ran off with Edgar. We came to live on Prince Edward Island while my then eleven-year-old son preferred to stay with his father Willie-John in Antigonish. I had not been married to Willie-John, by the way, and although he called me his wife, he had come to despise marriage. Edgar had no great respect for it either. Nor do I respect it when I look at the likes of Gallant and Harris. I'm an unmarried woman! But, you know, I've never been with any other man since I've been with Edgar, and I know he has been with no other woman either. I saw him as my husband.'

'But, forgive me, you and he have spent all these years providing little girls to monsters like Gallant.'

'I wouldn't say "all these years", but I agree we have done some bad things. Not for a long time, I must say. We have procured girls for men. Girls over twelve, for the most part. We may have made mistakes. I've explained this to you before. Don't forget that when an orphan girl with no money receives enough money for a few hours to support her for a month, this may save her life. And let me tell you something else. I'll spell it out for you. What is the one thing a young girl does not want to happen if she goes with a man for money? To get in pod, that's what – to become as you would say politely, "enceinte". So a girl has some stupid beast of a man crawling all over her, knowing he can do what he wants because he has paid for it. And she can have his baby! I used to say to the girls, not very daintily: "Do everything and anything you can to make sure he gets his jollies before he gets inside you. And do it nicely! Let him come into you anywhere except there. Let him hurt you, even, anywhere except there. You'll get over it!" Now that's not the way I lead my own life, Mr Hobbes – or, can I call you Chad?'

'Of course.'

'Chad, if you and I were to get close together I have a feeling we would both not be satisfied with anything except *that*. We would want to seal our union in the closest possible way. Or let me, for delicacy's sake, talk about this at another level: when I feel like being close to my man, Edgar, *there* is where I want him. And there is where he wants me! Dare I say I suspect it's the same with you and your wife who I am told is absolutely lovely.

'The other thing I want you to know is that I learned as much as I ever could about contraceptics and I imparted that knowledge to the girls. Not that the men like that sort of thing. But a little sponge soaked in lemon juice or in default of that, in vinegar, might not be noticed. And then there is the time of the month. I don't want to sound holier than thou. I'm not a missionary. But I took care of my girls. And normally if they got hurt I would find ways of making the man pay – in money or in pain or shame. I could get rumours going about a man if I wanted.

'You'll notice I said "normally". There were exceptions. Let us imagine one very rich man, as an example, who wants to lash a girl's bottom with his belt. And then make her beg forgiveness for her sins, and suck his member. And he is ready to pay a lot of money for this. With no risk of her getting in pod! And the worst after-effect for her is a very sore bottom for a few days, and a sense of disgust. And –

let yourself imagine this – when she goes to the man she loves, and yes there is often a man she loves, there is something she can give him: herself. She can open to him without disgust and let him in without having to bother herself with the memory of some dirty pig violating her insides…

'I won't go on. And I mustn't exaggerate either. Most men I've known actually do want a fairly simple time with a girl. They simply want "this and that". And you know what? She can give him that simple this and that with some warmth and affection. And get paid! And if properly instructed, not get into pod either! Most of our "associates" – I'll use that word, rather than "customers", which is so vulgar – they don't want to hurt girls.

'Honoré Gallant was a special case. He saved me and Edgar from a bad legal situation over in Nova Scotia, and we were grateful to him. That was how it started. It turned out he had become friends with Willie-John too, who eventually also came to live on Prince Edward Island. Edgar and I would see Willie-John from time to time – on business connected with Gallant, or with him paying us a visit when he was in or around Stanley Bridge, as he did on the day poor Marie died. Gallant never knew Willie-John was the father of my first son. And nor did Edgar for some years. If Willie-John knows one thing, it's how to keep a secret. Edgar and Willie became friends, of a sort. But as I say Edgar, though lazy, is clever, and eventually he found out about me and Willie and that my elder son was by Willie. Edgar took it in his stride. After all, he could see and feel every day that I loved him. And we had our own fine boy. Does that shock you?'

'No. It's unusual but it doesn't shock me. It must have depended, though, on you not deceiving either of the two men in the time you were with them.'

'That's astute of you, Chad, although I might modify it to not deceiving either of them about large things. About small things, perhaps. But however it was done, we knew each other and we trusted each other.'

'Do you mean that when you met Gallant in Georgetown yesterday, Edgar and McNulty knew of the plan,'

'Of course not. The woman in black is I myself, and my idea alone.'

'Were you making a point to Gallant, appearing as a woman in mourning?'

'Yes I was. After all, to my mind, he had killed Marie. But… perhaps the mourning was for him! For Gallant who was about to die! I must have had a premonition!'

'And what about the attack on MacKinnon? You describe your husband and McNulty as intelligent men. How could they be so stupid?'

'You only say that because you caught them. You would not have thought they were stupid if you had found MacKinnon dead on the road, reeking of whisky.'

'I might have. I know MacKinnon drinks wine and whisky, but not on the road.'

'Chad, I like the way you think.' She looked at me with what seemed like a glimmer of genuine tenderness in those piercing black eyes.

'I like the way you think too,' I said. 'What do you think about John Harris?'

'Honoré introduced Edgar and me to his friend Harris. As I said, at the time Honoré did not know I knew Willie-John. I've told you that Edgar and Willie and I trusted each other. But Honoré knew nothing of that. He introduced Edgar and me to Harris, but I don't think he introduced Willie-John. He, Honoré, knew that Harris was looking for people to live in that house he owned near his own house at Stanley Bridge.

'Harris is a sad man. He probably needs to go with men, not women, if you know what I mean. But he doesn't go with men. He's disgusted by that idea. Or if he does go with men he's disgusted afterwards, or he has a bad conscience. Or he tries and fails with women. But Gallant? Of course I wrote that letter about the merchandise. Believe it or not there are young girls who are glad to be beaten black and blue by a monster if they can come out of it with some money for the first time in their lives. The ten-year old part was just bait. I've never knowingly introduced a ten-year old to anyone.'

'How did he know the letter was from you? That's surely not your handwriting. He must have known, or he would have been suspicious of it.'

'I always wrote to him about that kind of business using that children's handwriting and that squiggle for a signature.'

'So you and Edgar took some of the money that passed between men like Gallant and young girls.'

'Not so much money as you think. Are we rich? No. Edgar and I live by our wits, you might say. Anyway, to return to Marie. I saw her body and then so did Edgar. We could see that Dunno had been at her. You had to keep even animals − even hens and geese! − away from those boys. We also saw that Honoré had been at her with his belt. And it must have been him who had used that diabolical eel spear to rip gashes down her bottom. Honoré was as much a monster as Dunno! The only way he could be with any woman, I suppose. I don't think he could do anything natural. So yes, when we were on the quay, I confronted him with my suspicions that he was in the room when she died. And he confirmed that he was.'

'Amazing that he told you so much! No, I'm sorry for being sarcastic.'

'It doesn't suit you.'

'All right. Now you can answer another question for me. Through your husband Edgar, you must have learned about Madeleine and Calum MacKinnon. Why do you think Madeleine stayed with Honoré?'

'She was strictly brought up. There was a time when her parents' store was not prospering. She was a good Catholic. So she married Gallant. Edgar came to know that the man she was in love with was MacKinnon and that Marie was his daughter. I suspect that although MacKinnon probably wanted Madeleine to be with him, she knew that would have ruined him in his profession. She wanted the best for her daughter – her and MacKinnon's daughter. She didn't get the best. Look, I'll admit to you, on Edgar's behalf, that the worst thing he has ever done was to attack that man MacKinnon. You don't understand the power Honoré had over us. He could have used the very thing he profited from through us – the fact that we would introduce him to young girls – to ruin us! Remember! You have already questioned me about dance-nights and young girls. But you have been hanging back from questioning Honoré. He is – was, thank God – a very powerful man. I'm very pleased he fell over the end of the Coal Wharf.'

'You have said it all, I suppose. I can see you would be pleased at Gallant's demise – leaving aside exactly how he took that fatal step backwards. Your husband, whom you love dearly, will not be in the position of having Gallant finding some way to make *him* into the accused murderer of Marie. And as we have said, Gallant possessed information about you and your husband which he might have used against you. And, although I don't know for sure, I think you were fond of Marie. Nothing more? No conflict perhaps between you and Gallant alone?'

'No. Nothing between him and me alone. I procured girls for him, I admit it. That was ugly. I don't live easily with a sense of shame. But to come back to your question about Marie's murder. Think of your own wife, Chad. Think of a young woman who had just given birth to a child by a man she loved. By the way I don't even know who Marie's man was! Or not for sure. I can guess though. Perhaps a certain young Mic Mac who speaks three or four languages but cannot read or write a word in any of them. Chad! Remember one thing. I was the first person to go into that library. There she was, slashed and bloody. When I saw her I knew I would not rest until whoever had done that to her was dead. He didn't deserve to be living and breathing on this earth.

'I checked whether the poor darling was dead, although of course I could see that. I felt for her non-existent pulse. I bent down and gave her

341

a kiss on her cheek. And I swore to myself, just as I have said, that I would never rest… Actually, before I went and got Edgar, I swore to her. And I am a woman of my word – usually. I said into her ear, "*Inquiète-toi pas, mon ange, Modeste va s'occuper de ça,*" meaning "Don't you worry, my angel, Modeste will take care of this".

'I looked around at that shambles. It's funny. I think in French, but the word "shambles" actually came into my mind. A few days later I thought of it again and wondered why. I went to our English dictionary and I found that in old English the word "shambles" means not only a mess but a butcher's shop. I suppose from the mess of meat on the butcher's table. It was a shambles all right. My heart had almost stopped beating. But I felt the need to put some order in the scene. First I picked up the weapon – the eel spear – which was lying on the floor. There were dark streaks on the tines which looked like dried blood. I picked it up and put it on a chair. I don't know why, but it was obscene lying on the floor. Then I went and picked up the poor dear's clothes from here and there on the floor. Her shirt, camisole and dungarees were ripped near some of the buttons. There were patches and streaks of dried up blood on the clothes. I folded them and set them in a pile.

'And now see how lucky I am! I can rest. Two monsters killed her. One has died in a fight to the death with his twin. And the other has had an unexpected accident in front of my very own eyes and drowned!'

She looked at me steadily.

'I won't ask you anything more,' I said. 'I'll do my best with your husband, I promise. To start with I'll allow you to see him. I'm sure you can help him to explain his situation in a way that helps him. Your statement on Gallant will also greatly help. And the more clearly the murder of Marie is settled, the more likely the attempted murder of Mr Mackinnon will be seen in proportion.

'With regard to the murder of Marie, I myself will be providing state-ments to the Attorney General. In turn he will provide a report to the

Coroner, Dr Reid. The report's conclusion may well be that Marie was murdered by persons unknown, since the main suspects Honoré Gallant and Zotique Cormier otherwise known as Dunno are now dead.

'As for the death of Gallant, the statements by you and Constable Jones and the Georgetown Police, and a statement by myself, will all go to the Attorney General who will decide if he wants to charge and prosecute you for a felony and bring you in front of a court. But it seems to me very unlikely that the Attorney General would wish to pursue the case further on the basis of what you have said. There is no evidence of violence and what you describe looks like an accident. I shall recommend that you are not charged.'

24

'Thank you,' she said. 'So this is the end of our formal conversation.'

'The only kind of conversation we can have is a formal one.'

'Nevertheless I want to say something more. And I want to show you something. And I want your assurance that you will never mention these things to anyone – in or out of your investigation.'

'As I've said, I can't make such assurances.'

'But our conversation – or call it your interrogation of me – has been concluded. In two stages – one for the statement, and one in which I have clarified some questions. But now I want to go further, to a final stage. Chad, I want you to hear my confession.'

'I'm not a priest!'

'But I cannot make this confession to anyone else. Not even to Edgar. Or, especially not to Edgar. If I don't tell someone who I can count on to understand – and the only such person I can think of is you – I fear that I'll feel tormented for the rest of my life. Please!'

She was looking me almost defiantly, but with something else in her eyes: pain.

'All right,' I said. 'I'm very grateful to you, and if I can help by listening to you, I'll listen.'

'Thank you. The first thing I want to do is show you something. Prepare to be shocked.'

To my surprise she turned her back to me. She hitched up her skirt and petticoat to her waist and held a fold of them in her left hand. She was wearing the usual white cotton drawers stretching almost down to her knees, and below the knees were white silk stockings. With her right hand she reached behind her waist and slowly pulled the drawers down over her buttocks, leaning forward slightly to do so. I gasped – audibly. Her buttocks were striped and zig-zagged with angry red weals, and along the weals the skin was broken in places and there were flecks of dried blood. My God!

Without turning she said, 'Look, Chad. This is what Gallant did to me – with his belt. I know it's ugly. And now you have seen enough.'

She stood up straight, pulled up her drawers with her right hand, then let her petticoat and skirt fall. She turned around to face me.

'I wonder if I dare sit down now. You have seen why I have preferred to talk standing up.'

I pulled out a chair for her and she sat down gingerly, moving to the front of the chair.

I sat down in a chair facing her.

She smiled at me. 'I don't know why my parents called me "Modeste". I've always liked the name. But as you have seen, it's not really my nature. I sometimes think I should be called *Immodeste!* When I was a little girl we were very poor. I found I could get little presents and small change from boys by pulling down my drawers and letting them have a look. Nothing more than that! Thank you for allowing me to show you my injuries. They are evidence, aren't they? Even if they are a secret as part of a confession.'

She paused for a moment, looking at me seriously, almost sadly.

'And now I shall tell you', she said. 'I'm surprised you and your colleagues didn't question me more on certain aspects. For example, how was I able to – let us say – "persuade" Honoré to step off the wharf? You assumed, quite cleverly, that I must have had a revolver. I did. I don't have it with me at the moment. But why assume that by drawing a revolver and pointing it at Honoré I would succeed in making him, as it were, walk the plank? He just meekly backs off the edge of the wharf? No chance. For one thing he has a revolver of his own – the same kind as I do, a Smith and Wesson point 22 calibre. What a coincidence! No. Edgar provided these revolvers to both Honoré and me. So if I pull a revolver out of my purse, Honoré will have his own revolver out of his pocket in a flash. And if he shoots me? Wonderful, since I am armed and he is killing me in self-defence – a respectable man being attacked by a mad-woman with a disreputable history!

'Or let's say I somehow take his revolver away and I do make him walk the plank, as it were. Why would he jump off the wharf? He can't swim. I know that. As I said to you earlier, his wife told me so. Will I have the nerve to shoot him? A bullet from a Smith and Wesson in his body – and that's the kind of revolver I have. It won't stand up to examination as a cause of death. These are light revolvers. Unless the 22 calibre bullet hits the heart or brain it won't even stop a person.'

She paused again, as if waiting for a reply.

'I'm impressed', I said, 'by what you know about revolvers. And I know what you mean. I'm not happy about the evidence such as it is. Most of it provided by you! But it will have to do. Frankly, any coherent explanation will do. Nobody wants to dig deeper into this apparent accident, because as you know absolutely nothing can be proved.'

'I understand that. It's why you are not making much, even, of the note I sent to Honoré. You accept, out of convenience, my first statement that I didn't write it. But I want to give the truly detailed account to you. As I said, a confession. I don't care for absolution. The last time I went to confession, Willie-John gave me absolution! The devil! Then he wanted me for himself. But that was all right, since I wanted him too. But don't you think confession is for the person who confesses? It's a way of getting the story clear in her mind.'

'Yes. In my short career so far I think I have received a number of confessions for that reason.'

'Good. Last night it was very dark on the wharf, at least underfoot, in spite of the moon being just past half. At the entrance to the wharf from the road there are a couple of sheds but there was no light or signs of life from any of them. We walked out into the dark, along the wharf towards the end. As I explained, the wharf is supported by wooden logs and there is a surface of wooden planks, so it's not dangerous to walk on it in poor light, and there are low wooden beams forming a ledge along the sides and end. Near the end we stopped, facing each other. As we talked at least my eyesight became more clear, and I could discern Honoré quite well in the moonlight. Not his face very clearly but he was standing with his back to the end of the wharf and the half moon was in the sky behind him, so his silhouette was clear. The wharf was open to the sea behind him in front of me and on my right, but on my left along the edge of the wharf there were several piles of fishing nets weighted down with stones, and various baskets and boxes. I could see all these dimly as my eyes got used to the moonlight. There was also a bunch of eel spears lying on top of each other – four or five of them – with the points facing the end of the wharf. People spear eels off wharfs and jetties. And poor Marie was slashed and gashed by an eel spear! I thought, well, if the worst comes to the worst and Honoré attacks me, I can always make a dash for the spears and use one to push him away. Poetic justice! But I wanted to placate him. I didn't want trouble, and he is a lot bigger than I am.

'We had the conversation I have just told you and the two policemen about. Only it was in a different tone. Yes I accused him of killing Marie and I asked those questions, and he admitted, sneering at me, that he knew what had happened in the library room at Harris's house and that she deserved what she got. As I've said, I was not angrily shrieking at him. There was nobody around, but sound could carry over water and perhaps the shores along the base of the wharf. I was reasoning with him and pleading with him in a low and submissive voice.

'Honoré began berating me angrily, saying, in French of course: "I don't care about your accusations! All you can say is just hearsay, and who would believe you against me? And I didn't come here just to listen to your crazy stories! Where's the merchandise?"'

'I said, as submissively as I could. "I'm so sorry, but when I went to pick up the girl, just half an hour ago, she refused to come with me. She began to cry. And her Auntie, who is the one who looks after her, and who was looking forward to the money, began to lament that she mustn't betray her dear departed sister and let her niece do this... So I came away, and here I am."

And I apologised to him. I began to cry – or it sounded as if I was crying. As I've said, I could see the wharf and the ledge along to my left and some coils of rope and boxes along the edge, and the eel spears, and Honoré in silhouette against the sea which was black but glittering because of the moonlight and I began to see his face in more detail.

'I said to him, through my sobs, "I know I've let you down. You know me well, and you know I'm proud of being efficient and of carrying out anything I undertake to do. And after all that you have been through in the last few weeks, I can understand you being angry. What can I do to make up for this? I don't want you to get upset at me and Edgar. I've promised you something, and I want to fulfil my promise. All I can think of is, Honoré, let me be the merchandise. Whatever you want to do to me, or whatever you want me to do for you, shall be done!"'

Modeste paused. 'I should add,' she said, 'that I had never given myself physically to Honoré. Yes I provided "merchandise" – but it was never myself. And I knew Honoré would be curious, and he would be gratified. He had once accused me of being "too proud". Now perhaps he had me where he wanted me. I'm not a young girl, but I was taking the chance he would accept my offer. And he did. If it had not been so dark,

I would think he smiled. But I can't be sure. He said, "It's true, Modeste, that you have made me angry. And I shall have to punish you for it."'

'I could vaguely see him lifting up the flaps of his coat and undoing his belt and pulling it free. "Bend over!" I think that's right in English isn't it? In French he said *"Penche-toé!"* I knew what to do. I turned my back to him, lifted my skirt and petticoat, and pulled down my drawers to below my knees. I bent over. And he lashed me with his belt. On and on and on! I put my fist in my mouth and bit it so as not to cry out. I could feel the tears hot on my cheeks. Then I had to crouch down and steady myself with my hands on the planks of the quay so as not to be knocked over by the blows!'

Modeste was looking at me with burning eyes, then she blinked and a tear came down one cheek, then one down the other cheek.

'Chad', she said, crying. 'I suddenly knew the wrong I had done over the years, in making girls do this. I had told them cheerfully that it was nothing, they would get over it. I was thinking of how intense the pains of childbirth are. We all, us women, get over them! I thought a beating on the bottom with a belt could never be so painful! But this thrashing with the belt was not only the physical pain, it was a humiliation. I, *Immodeste*, had thought no one could ever humiliate me. But now I knew. Gallant was humiliating me. And he knew it too! He was panting and grunting. Every now and then he would spit out a word in a low voice: *"Espèce de cochonne! Putain! Salope! Garce!"* meaning "Dirty pig! Whore! Slut! Bitch!" He was putting every ounce of his strength into the beating of a woman. Or a girl. As you may have seen, although I was standing up with my back to you when I showed you the marks of that beating, I had shaved myself down there. Another humiliation. He may not have seen it in the semi-darkness, but I couldn't risk not doing it. I must admit the idea had come to my mind earlier that I should be prepared for anything to happen. I knew I would have to please him. If not he would destroy me in some way. He lives – or rather he lived – in order to destroy people.'

Since she had been standing upright I had not seen lower than those terrible wounds.

'At last he stopped,' Modeste continued. 'His breathing was heavy. "Come," he said. I knew what to do next. I had trained girls how to do it! I stood up and pulled my drawers up and my skirts back down, then I took a pace towards him and kneeled down on the flooring of the jetty in front of him, reaching out to him with my hands.

"Pardon me," I said "I'm begging you to forgive me. Now you have punished me and I see the error of my ways, and I'll do anything for you." He was putting his belt back into the loops of his trousers but he didn't bother fastening the buckle. I reached forward in the half dark, and I began to unbutton his trousers, from the waist downwards. I pulled them down. He stood there looming above me against the sky, dark against dark. The end of the quay was only a few steps behind him. My face was close to his belly and his legs and they were a dim white. His member was sticking forward but I paid no attention to it. His trousers were around his ankles over his boots. And I knew what I had to do.

'I stood up quickly and took a few steps back to my left and I leant down quickly and grabbed hold of the shaft of one of the eel spears. It was heavier than I expected and ten feet long or so – but I held it in both hands out in front of me like one of those poles fishermen use to push boats away from a wharf. The sharp blades of the spear were pointing towards Gallant. I was threatening him with the very weapon he had used on poor Marie! I was about the length of the eel spear away from him. He quickly bent down and tried to pull his trousers up, but I hissed at him: "*Espèce de vieux cochon!*" Meaning: "You dirty old pig!" He straightened up again and I shoved the spear-head towards his chest. He stepped backwards to avoid it, then made a lunge toward me with his hands forward, but he stumbled, then he tried to pull his trousers up again and I shoved the eel spear towards his chest and at last I raised my voice: "*T'es un monstre!*" meaning "You're a monster!" He staggered backwards another step or two, unbalanced because he was trapped by his trousers around his ankles. I gave another stab forward with the eel spear which almost hit him in the chest and this time I shouted *"T'es rien qu'un tas d'marde!"*– You're just a piece of shit! He staggered back another step, stumbled on the ledge, and over he went. With a horrible bellowing shriek – *"NON!"*

'Then a splash – a terrible splash. Then nothing. I dropped the eel spear which made a clatter on the ground, and I stepped forward and looked over the edge of the quay. The water was black but with a silvery glitter from the moonlight. Then there was a sort of swirl in it and Honoré came to the surface. He was floating face down. Of course his backside was bare, and white in the moonlight. In fact there was a reflection of the moon not far from him in the black water. I like the moon, don't you?'

Modeste was standing in front of me trembling, her eyes flashing.

'But what if it had gone wrong?' I asked. 'What it he had not been standing so close to the edge of the quay? You were very brave, but it was a terrible risk if he had succeeded in fighting back.'

'With his trousers around his ankles? And with me lunging the eel spear at him? If he had not stumbled back over the edge, I would have dropped the eel spear, because he could try and grab it and use it against me. Then I would have pulled out my little revolver and shot him – through the head. We were quite close by then, and I wouldn't have missed. And I would then have shot him again, to make sure. And since he would have been lying there dead with his trousers down, I would have said later that I had shot him because he was trying to rape me. You're the policeman, you know these things. Would that have worked?'

'I suppose so. People would wonder, but then they'll wonder anyway. By the way, did you leave the eel spear on the ground?'

'No. I replaced it very carefully to its former place, lying with the other spears along the edge of the wharf. I stood on the wharf listening carefully. No one must have heard that horrible shriek. Then I walked back along the wharf and into the town.'

'You did well. So your official account to me, as of now, and leaving out the eel spear, is what? As short as you can make it.'

'All right.'

She paused for a moment.

'I was speaking quietly in case the sound carried.

'"Admit that you killed her – you and Dunno!" I said.

'"She deserved it, the bitch, and she got it!" he said.

'"No one deserved that kind of death!" I said. "And you went on mistreating a dead woman! You raped her body!"

'"You know what Dunno is like!" he said.

'I raised my hand as if to hit him. Not that I would have dared. I'm tall for a woman, but he was a lot heavier and stronger. He took a step backwards and stumbled over the edge.'

I stepped forwards and gave her a light kiss on her cheek.

'I think Modeste is a lovely name,' I said. 'In Latin *modestus* or *modesta* mean "in due measure" – that is, measuring things without exaggeration. You get the measure of things. You live up to your name.'

She leaned forwards and gave me a light peck on my cheek, in return.

'Can I go now?' she asked, almost meekly. 'Or do I have to sign a statement?'

'I'll review the statement prepared by Sergeant Armstrong. I'm afraid you'll have to stay in the Brig a little while longer, in a separate room. I'll call you when the statement is ready for you to read and sign. I can then send it by messenger to Mr Brecken.'

'Back to the Brig! That little room is at least quiet, but I want to go home and pick up Bo-Bo and collect the eggs. What about Edgar? Will you be sending him and Willie-John to court?'

'It's possible. Again the decision will be Mr Brecken's. The attack on Mr MacKinnon amounts to attempted murder. On the other hand, Mr MacKinnon was not hurt, and his attackers certainly were! And I doubt if Mr MacKinnon will insist on revenge. He'll want to get on with his life. So it's likely that Edgar and McNulty will be released in a day or two.'

'Thank you for telling me. Now, I'll tell you something. I had time to think in that little room in this so-called Brig. I would not want some injustice to happen to Edgar. That is partly why I pleaded with Gallant so to save Edgar from being held responsible for what happened to Marie. But I find that I can't live with Edgar any more. He and Willie-John hunted down Marie and bound and gagged her and brought her back and handed her over to Gallant. I don't know how much Willie-John knew about Gallant. He may not even have known that Marie was not Gallant's daughter but MacKinnon's. That was a very big secret. But Edgar did know it. And that means he knew that Gallant could kill Marie – not only to get rid of her but to drive Madeleine crazy with despair. Knowing that Edgar knew that, I can never let him close to me again. I know that the other day, when he was wounded, I was clinging to him. Now I couldn't even touch him. You understand?'

'I'm afraid so. But what are you going to do?'

'You can help me. Please!'

'How?

'You still have Edgar in custody. I want to meet him and tell him I never want to see him again. And that he will have to leave the island for ever. I don't want to leave. Why should I? He's a man. He can make a new life in Nova Scotia or New Brunswick. But I don't want him here. I want to be free and look after my animals. And, who knows, once I've got over my grief about Marie and about what a pig Edgar has turned out to be, I might even find a new man!'

'I hope you live the life you want. But we can't banish Edgar from this island!'

'Can't you threaten him that if he comes back, you – the police – will make life difficult for him?'

'I won't be here – personally. There will be other police.'

'What about that nice young Sergeant Armstrong? All right you can't banish Edgar, but Armstrong could assure him that if he ever harassed me he would be in trouble!'

'If only! You know what the law is like here. It's like an old hound with no teeth.'

'It will make some difference. Can I talk to Edgar with you and Sergeant Armstrong as witnesses?'

'Of course. I'll do two things apart from reviewing the statement prepared by Sergeant Armstrong and having you review and sign it. First I'll send it with a note to Mr Brecken. Then once I have his reply, I'll send someone to fetch Edgar from the hospital and we can have the discussion you want.'

'I knew I could count on you, Chad.

'Thank you.'

She left the room. I stood thinking.

There had been a meeting of minds between me and Modeste Aucoin. What on earth was that about? I liked her clarity, her humorous way of conveying thoughts without seeming to commit herself to them – her ruthlessness. Yes, I liked her ruthlessness. She knew how to lure Gallant to his death. The woman was a murderess! But I meant it when I said '*Chapeau!*' Had I lost all moral sense? But what was the use of moral sense if I felt that Gallant was the murderer, yet without physical evidence the law would not be able to identify and punish him? Was I also ruthless? I was aware of a compulsion in myself to carry through anything I had started. Could I kill someone? Probably.

Gallant had never raped or beaten Modeste. So long as Edgar and Modeste ran errands efficiently for Gallant, neither of them was at risk from him. Marie was not Modeste's own daughter. But Modeste had told me why she had pursued Gallant to his death: she was the first to see what most probably he and Dunno had done to Marie. And she had decided to put an end to him. After all, it did not look as if anyone else would. As always she was quick and clever. She did not have to murder him in cold blood. She reduced him to a condition, standing on the edge of a wharf at night with his trousers around his ankles – where it only took a threatening movement from her – lunging forward with the eel spear – to topple him off the edge to his death. She had been true to her word and she had avenged Marie. And at some cost to herself: she had partly served this monster's immediate sexual need so as to get him off guard. I found myself ready to help her in anything. *Chapeau!*

25

I sent Modeste's signed statement by messenger to Mr Brecken with a note, and within an hour I had it back with a scrawled note from him:

No need to charge and prosecute Mrs Aucoin. She can be released. Agree, best to keep the two gentlemen in custody for now. Please come and see me tomorrow morning at 10.00 for full discussion. FB

It was now late afternoon. I sent a constable over to fetch Aucoin in a carriage, since I assumed his wound was still at risk of opening. When he was escorted into the room where Modeste and Armstrong and I were waiting, he looked startled and staggered slightly. His face was already pale.

We sat around a table, Modeste facing Aucoin across it, Armstrong and I at the ends. Everyone was looking at me. I had Modeste's statement in my hands, and I passed it across the table to Aucoin.

'This is your wife's statement,' I said. 'I'd like you to read it. Take your time. Then we'll talk about it.'

Aucoin looked across at Modeste, hesitating.

'*Lis-le!*', she said. 'Read it!'

Aucoin took a pair of reading glasses out of his coat pocket and put them on, leaning forward. I could see no sign he was in pain from his wound as he moved.

The statement had four pages, and he read slowly. By the second page the fingers of his right hand were drumming on the table. He turned the pages with his left hand. When he finished, he let out a sigh and looked at the table. Then he raised his eyes and looked at Modeste.

'*Un grand merci!*' he said. '*Chérie!*'

He kept looking at her intensely.

'Keep to English,' Modeste said, quite sharply. 'And I'm not your Dear. And don't thank me. I didn't do this only to save you. I did it mainly for Marie. And I wouldn't have to be writing any of this if Marie were still alive. And why is she dead? Because you and Willie-John delivered her into the hands of the Devil!'

'I didn't know what Honoré would do! To his own daughter!'

Modeste looked at me.

'That won't wash,' I said. 'You remember I asked you to throw me a bone, as you would to a dog to keep it quiet, and you told me that Gallant *knew* Marie was not his daughter. I don't think, by the way, that McNulty knew. But you certainly did.'

'All right, I knew *that!* I didn't know what a monster Gallant was.'

'Of course you did,' I said. You and Modeste had been procuring for him for years.'

'Then she is just as responsible as I am!'

'Bastard!' Modeste said vehemently.

She glanced at me and at Armstrong and I thought for an instant she might apologise for using the word, but that would have been artificial. She was, as always, herself.

'There are two different levels of responsibility,' she said. 'God, I wish you were more intelligent, Edgar! When I met you, I was fed up with intelligence! My own intelligence that tormented me, and Willie-John's intelligence that tormented both him and me. I fell in love with you because you were a man who could *do* things, not only think them. But there you were hunting down a young woman and a newborn child and bringing her back to the hands of not only one monster but two! You *did* it all right! But did you fucking well *think?*'

It was shocking to hear the bad language of the island from a lady's mouth. She went on:

'I'm telling you here and now, formally, in front of these two gentlemen of the police as witnesses, that I am divorcing you! Just as I married you without benefit of clergy and without the law, according to my own will, I am divorcing you according to my own will! I don't want to see you again! If they hang you for attempted murder of Calum MacKinnon, I'll be sorry for the effect on our son, but I won't cry a single tear for you. And if they don't hang you, I want you to clear off, to go somewhere I can never set eyes on you! I'll make this easy, by staying here on the island. I just want you to go off the island and stay there for ever. Do you agree?'

Aucoin looked at me, then Armstrong.

'If I do agree, does this make it easier for me?'

'You mean in the case of the attempted murder?' I said. 'Not at all. And if you hang, then the only way you'll stay on the island is underground.'

'I won't hang,' said Aucoin. 'MacKinnon was not even hurt. And he stabbed me!'

'We'll discuss that later. Or a court will decide. Perhaps you'll simply be sent off island to that new prison "over across" in New Brunswick – to rot for a number of years. Or perhaps, indeed, you will get away with it. A jury may not find you guilty, and Mr MacKinnon is unlikely to press private charges. We at the Police can't banish you from the island, and we can't persecute you or punish you. But we can make life difficult for people in many ways. And personally I won't be here to protect you. I'm on my way home! To England!

'I suspect quite a few people on the island, when word gets around about what really happened in the case of Mrs Harris will be, shall I say, ill-disposed towards you. Modeste has declared in front of witnesses that your common-law marriage no longer exists. She has expressed the wish that you leave the island and leave her in peace. She has at least the moral support of Sergeant Armstrong and myself. And again to use the phrase 'common law', if you declare in front of witnesses that you will undertake to leave the island – *if* not charged – and never to come back, this does have some weight. If you make a nuisance of yourself in the future there are witnesses to what you undertook here and now.'

This was largely meaningless. But in my present frame of mind I preferred the old Common Law of England to any of the varieties of statute law I had so far come across.

'All right! All right!' Aucoin said. 'I can't believe this!'

Now he looked almost tearfully at Modeste, but she stared back icily.

'Just tell me, in front of them, that if you are not charged, you'll leave the island as soon as you can, and not come back,' she said calmly.

'If I am not charged, I'll leave the island as soon as I can, and I won't come back.'

'Thank you,' I said. Sergeant Armstrong can take you out of here again. I'll talk to you tomorrow.'

Armstrong stood up and led Aucoin from the room. Modeste leaned forward, her face in her hands, and began to cry.

I sat quietly, and after a while she raised her head, took a handker-chief from her blouse, and wiped her eyes.

We both stood up.

'Thank you,' she said. 'Can I go now?'

'Of course.'

'Once you have solved all this, will you leave the island?'

'Yes, my wife and I have a way to go – we are not sure exactly where. England to start with anyway.'

'Before you leave, please come and say goodbye.'

'I shall.'

The next morning, a Monday, I met Mr Brecken at the Colonial Building. He was, as before, courteous and straightforward. Sitting across a table from him, I gave him a brief account from my own perspective.

'I won't deny it will be extremely distressing,' he said, 'to read accounts in the newspapers about Honoré Gallant's death. The editor of the *Islander* came to see me just now and said rumours were circulating about Gallant's final meeting with "A Lady in Black", but I asked him not to repeat such gossip. 'Do you think she killed him?'

'Yes and No. I realise that sounds evasive. I mean "No" in the sense that there is no evidence whatsoever of violence against his person, and "Yes" in the sense that she accused him of a crime and this could have shocked him and upset him in both senses of the word – causing him to step backwards by mistake over the edge of the wharf.'

'Well put.' Mr Brecken smiled. 'I find myself wondering if he was made to walk the plank. You know, when a man is forced at gunpoint out onto the plank he will either be shot and fall off, or he will step off and drown. In either case he will be eaten by the sharks. I'm not saying the gun was literal, since we have no evidence Mrs Aucoin had one. She couldn't have pushed him, could she? He was quite a solidly built man. I don't know Mrs Aucoin.'

'A tall but slim woman, certainly not as strong as Mr Gallant.'

'I'm fairly sure that if there was a coroner's inquest, it would rule that the drowning was an accident, don't you think?'

'There's no evidence for anything *other* than an accident.'

'Exactly.'

'As for the murder of Mrs Harris, I would think murder by persons unknown is a possibility since the investigation cannot be brought forward. We found two suspects who died before we could bring them in for questioning. Publicly, this will have to be handled with care.'

'I agree.'

'As for the attempted murder of Mr MacKinnon, there too I am not sure how far a judge can go. Mr MacKinnon has no injuries. Would he be likely to bring a private action against McNulty and Aucoin?'

'I would very surprised if he did. He is most likely to want to keep his own privacy.'

'A lot of things are swept under the rug on this island – all sorts of misdemeanours. But attempted murder is a felony, thus a capital crime. It would seem to me wrong to charge and possibly hang Messrs McNulty and Aucoin for an attack in which the only physical harm done to Mr MacKinnon was the shock of falling off his horse onto shale and sandy ground, from which he has apparently recovered. And the other physical harm done in the incident was the injury to Aucoin from MacKinnon's dirk, and the shattering of McNulty's shoulder by a bullet from your revolver. You were on a special commission from me, and I shall take responsibility for not bringing this further. There will be no charges nor prosecution in court for these two men. I know some retribution should be, from the moral point of view, exacted on Aucoin and McNulty, but I am not inclined to take this any further. What do you think?'

'Again, I agree.'

'Well, there we have it. You have fulfilled your commission. In the space of about two weeks. You have solved the murder of Marie Évan-géline Harris. And although you have not arrested either of the suspected murderers, your enquiries stirred events to the point that one of the suspects had an accident that few people or nobody will regret. As for the other suspected murderer, he died in that fight to the death with his brother. And although the stirring of events will no doubt lead to a spate of stories and rumours, that is nothing new for this island. And there will be an official account – meaning what I shall say myself in answer to enquiries, and what the editors of the *Islander* and the *Examiner* will say.

'In this account, the Police conducted an investigation where suspects were identified. Before it was possible to interrogate them, they died in manners unrelated to the murder in question. If asked, I shall state that police investigation established that Mr Honoré Gallant was found drowned at the Coal Wharf, with no evidence of foul play. My report to Dr Reid, the Coroner, will reflect this.

'Of course there are loose ends. For instance, Messrs McNulty and Aucoin's involvement in this case. For example, they may well have been seen bringing Marie Évangéline back from Thunder Cove. Were it not for the fact that the main suspects have died, we could have pursued this further. But as it is, where would we get sufficient evidence of their involvement to charge them with possible accessory to murder? We just cannot pursue this line of investigation further. I also think about how the baby came to be found cradled on the waves in that pond behind Thunder Cove. And how the baby is now being taken care of by her grandmother, Madame Madeleine Gallant. She and Mr MacKinnon are now free to marry and I hope they do so. All sorts of details of the real story will be talked about. But there will in effect be two stories – the open one and the secret one. Everybody knows, and nobody knows. It's "the island way".

'On balance I suspect that at least some worthy people are happier than they were when your investigation started. I will arrange for a generous fee in pounds sterling to be paid to you – I know among gentlemen we do not discuss money, but you will be satisfied, I am sure.'

'Thank you, Mr Brecken. I'm fairly sure that your version of the 'open story' will prevail. As for the Cormier twins, who knows what was wrong with those two? They acted almost like automatons – to use that new-fangled word for machines which seem to operate on their own. But the really evil person in all this, Honoré Gallant, started in life with all the advantages his family could give him, as well as great intelligence and good looks.

'May I carry on with my commission for the rest of today? I would like to discuss this case with Messrs Aucoin and McNulty before releasing them. Of course if any new information emerges I shall let you know.'

'Gladly. Do feel free to discuss whatever you wish with them.' Mr Brecken leaned backwards in his chair. 'Now, Chad – may I call you Chad? – if you can tolerate it I would like to share some of my own thoughts on this awful business. To get some things off my chest as it were.'

'I'd be happy to hear your informal views.'

'Well, my views chop and change, but I *feel* a certain despair, along with relief. Gallant was never a friend of mine, and I never trusted him. I do, by the way, trust John Harris. I am anxious about how he is going to come out of all this.'

'I would like to see him later today.'

'Please do. He is an unhappy man, and I think he always has been – not only because of what happened to his wife, and in his house too, and the obvious suspicions which many people will have had about him. I fear we'll lose him as a Councilman. But if I put my own interests aside, I almost hope we do lose him, since I think he had best look after himself, take some time to lick his wounds. As for the loss of Gallant, it removes a risk. His private life was a sort of simmering cauldron that might have boiled over at any time. There are few secrets on this island, as I'm sure everyone tells you. A few large secrets, I am sure, buried in the sludge at the bottom of the cauldron, but such matters as Madeleine Gallant's relationship with Calum MacKinnon will be already bubbling away beneath the surface. By the way, thinking of sludge, I suppose it is too deep in Georgetown Harbour to make a search for fallen objects worthwhile? Yes, I suppose it is.'

I could not help smiling. 'Whatever might be there must remain buried, as I'm sure it's quite irretrievable.'

364

'Good. I do appreciate how you have managed to contain any discussion of the political aspects of these murders to discreet hints. Island politics must be hard for a man "from away", as we say, to grasp, but from what you have mentioned you seem to be grasping them well. In the next year or two there will be a decisive vote on Confederation, and it could go either way. But your investigations have been of great benefit, in spite of the horrors they have revealed, since it seems that both Gallant and Harris were more susceptible than I knew to possibly switching their allegiance away from Confederation. To be sure, this would be a betrayal of the people who voted for them, but such betrayals happen frequently. You might think I would rejoice at such a switch, since I am myself against Confederation, but the double-dealing is disconcerting, and the switch would cause more bad feeling than it was worth. I'm not unhappy with the opportunity to have two new people elected to the Legislative Council. Those eight-year terms are ridiculous.

'As for the issue of the "Cause" – meaning, in effect Fenianism – I think there McNulty has been quite carried away. I have no idea whether or not Fenianism is dead in Ireland – Mr Robinson could tell you more about that – but it's dead in Canada. And it has never come alive in Prince Edward Island, since our Island Irish are becoming prosperous, and almost to a man in favour of joining Canada. "Poor McNulty!" I might almost say. But I cannot pity such an able man. I was happy to promote him to Inspector – only ten days ago. I thought he deserved it, didn't you?'

'Yes, I was pleased and I did think he deserved it, but in retrospect it becomes clear that at least some of his apparently helpful knowledge of the murder didn't come from our investigation but from the fact that he had been involved in Gallant's plans! I don't know whether he feels shame at having delivered Marie to her death, but he should do.'

'I'm afraid there is more of the Jesuit in him than I knew. And of course he was educated by them! He could reason himself both into and out of a bottle. But it's all in the premises, isn't it? If he gets something wrong, he pursues it to the end against all evidence – or rather he reasons the evidence out of the way. I think he will want to leave the island. I hope so. This place is ruled by pragmatism, not big ideas. There is no "Cause". Survival will do. And eventually, we hope, prosperity. What do you think of it, our island?'

'It's one of the most beautiful places I've ever been in. Coming over the hills with their emerald green fields to that view of the sapphire Gulf is astonishing each time I take one of those roads to the North Shore. The imagery of jewels comes to mind because the colours here are like those of jewels and precious stones. And my wife and her new friends have been so happy at the Ocean House. I hope we can stay another while before we take our way – perhaps some months, although I have not had time to discuss this with my wife.'

'Would you consider staying longer? You could make your home here, and I know you would do very well. My goodness, I could see you as a judge, or as creating a new Island Police service. I would do everything I can to help you.'

'That's very kind of you. Again, I'll discuss it with my wife. We are on a journey "home" to England. But in a sense it's a wider journey to look for an unknown home. My wife Lucy is a native Tsimshian from British Columbia and her people are being slowly destroyed. And Victoria is associated for us with the terrible deaths of people we loved. We couldn't stay there.'

'But if in England you decide it's not home after all, please remember us here, and come back. We'll remember *you*. In any case, if you stay here another while, we'll see each other again, and I'd very much like to meet your wife.'

'Thank you.'

'We both stood up and shook hands.

Back at the police room, I asked Higgins to find out if John Harris was in Charlottetown and if I could visit him later. Then I walked over to the Sanatorium to see McNulty.

Again he was sitting in a chair. He had been scribbling on a notepad with the pencil allowed to him. He attempted to stand up, but winced, and I gestured to him to stay seated. I took the other chair.

I had thought of interviewing him again, under pressure, without telling him until the end of the interview about either the death of Gallant or about the decision not to pursue the case of attempted murder against Mackinnon. But this seemed to me a low and mean way of proceeding. So I gave him a brief summary of Modeste's presence at Gallant's death, following the lines of her official account.

He listened without much expression in his face other than attentiveness, but by the time I had finished, I could see that his body was less tense, and his breathing easier.

'Good for her,' he said.

'Yes, Good for her. By the way, she told me of your relationship and how you are the father of her eldest son.'

'Did she?' He smiled. 'That woman is not short of daring. And did she tell you of the strange and unconventional friendship that still persists among her and me and Aucoin? And that I visited them from time to time when in the Stanley Bridge area.'

'She did. But that friendship is no more. Modeste wants nothing more to do with Aucoin.'

'I'm surprised.'

I let this pass, and said, 'I want to question you further about a number of things that are not clear to me. But since I don't want to play cat and mouse with you, I can tell you that I discussed the attempted murder case with Mr Brecken this morning, and we agree that it will not be brought to court. The only people physically hurt are you and Aucoin. And I'm fairly sure MacKinnon will not bring any private charges.'

'I'm relieved. Thank you. So I am free to go?'

'Not quite. I am still employed by Mr Brecken, and I can detain you here to ask you questions about the murder of Mrs Harris and anything arising from it.'

'All right. But this is not related to a statement? It's a conversation between us?'

'Yes.'

'Good. Again I'm relieved, and I'll be frank.'

'As a man of principle, which I know you are, how could you take Marie away from her daughter near Thunder Cove? And how could you deliver her into the hands of Gallant? You knew what he might do, especially as he would have Dunno with him.'

'You can ask the same question of Edgar Aucoin, and of course you will. For me, and I suspect for him, it was not a clear situation. I had paid a social visit to Gallant at his North Rustico office in mid-morning on my way to see the Aucoins. That's when he told me to hurry up and go along with Aucoin to watch Marie's house in Stanley Bridge, and make sure she stayed there until he arrived after his work, around six o'clock. He wanted to talk to her on her own while her husband was in Charlottetown on business. I half thought he wanted to have some kind of reckoning with her. He had told me she could be quite determined and opinionated. Dunno was often around with Gallant, so his presence at the house meant nothing in itself. As for the baby in Thunder Cove, since we could not find her, we thought Marie had given the baby to somebody she had gone to meet there. She refused to tell us where the baby was but she was fighting us off and beginning to yell. We had to gag her and tie her up. Believe me, I have been thinking a lot about this. You once asked me if I had a conscience and I told you not to preach at me. I do have a conscience, an acute one. I think a lot about what is moral and what is not. What does the Cause, as you would call it, justify? I was educated by Jesuits after all. It profoundly marked my way of thinking. And sometimes

I'm a fool when it comes to understanding people. I thought I understood Gallant. As we have discussed before, he was a dealer in people, he bought and used them. I knew he was an evil brute who liked to beat the bottoms of little girls with his belt. But did I think he could do that with his own daughter?'

'But she wasn't his daughter.'

'I know – now. I had been thinking of her as his daughter. He had brought her up – although he was not much at home. He still had his wife, and although I wondered if she was entangled with MacKinnon, they did not see each other often. And I didn't know Marie was MacKinnon's daughter. The outward appearances of Gallant's marriage were intact. You see what I mean? I just didn't foresee that Gallant could bring the monster Dunno into his plans, and that the two of them would brutalise and kill Marie. I've been sitting in here thinking about my own thinking, if you know what I mean, going round and round in my head. All I can conclude is that I understand ideas, not people. I know that seems as if I'm eating humble pie, but I'm more angry with myself than anything. I pride myself on my strategy, and my tactics. By the way, I've done a lot of reading about military campaigns.

'But as Modeste has often told me, I have no idea how women think. I accept that. But Gallant was a man. I thought I knew his thinking. I was wrong. Perhaps one of the only good things about the Jesuits is that they believe that by reason any man can be brought to the truth. The truth as defined by them of course. And certainly not the truth as women see it. For Jesuits, women don't have minds at all. But look at Modeste! She thinks like both a woman and a man. It fits her name. She sometimes frets that she was not christened with an entirely female name. In French, Modeste can be a man's name or a woman's name. And she has a mind which is as strong as any man's.'

'That sounds like a compliment to her,' I said. 'But it demonstrates precisely that you are right when you say you have no idea how women

369

think. Yes, she has a strong mind, but it's a woman's through and through. She sees everything at once. Then she acts. Action and feeling are one. By comparison we men are fragmented. Or we tie ourselves in knots. If Modeste had not thought clearly and acted clearly I would still be wondering how I could bring Gallant to justice. And you would be wondering how you would ever get out of here.'

'Don't rub it in. Yes, I'm grateful to Modeste. Gallant could not be brought to the truth. I now see that. God knows what went on in his twisted mind, but it was not reason. In terms of reason, he should not have murdered Marie, and unleashed Dunno onto her. Under orders of course. I knew I-Guess better than Dunno, but Edgar has told me they are the same. They would do terrible things to people, but only under orders, only when told to. The only thing they would do without orders was attack each other! So whatever Dunno did to Marie, he was told to do by Gallant. But surely she must have been dead before some of those things were done. I hope so.'

'Well, as you say, and I won't rub it in, it's on your conscience. And what about the attack on MacKinnon? It was only, you say, to warn him off, on Gallant's orders. But you could easily have killed him, by accident. And you could have damaged his brain. You've seen that kind of thing – people who have fractured their skulls and who can never again think straight, or talk straight. What were you doing?'

'I'm not proud of it. Yes, I took Gallant's orders. But then there was the Cause… And although you are not making much of it, I could have shot you and killed you. Actually, I was just pointing my rifle at you in order to stop you in your tracks. If you had stopped, I don't know what I would have done, but I would not have killed you. As it was, when you drew your revolver, I might indeed have killed you – instinctively. But you were quicker than I. And of course I've been thinking of that too. Not least because I know that having aimed a rifle at you, I can never again be trusted by you. I had hoped – in spite of the double life I was leading – that you and I could eventually be friends.'

'I also assumed we would be, since we could talk so easily, and I enjoyed our dinners together. Even now, I enjoy talking with you. But you're right. I can't be friends with a man who has aimed a gun at me with at least some intent to kill me. Actually, more than some intent. We have discussed this before when you maintained you only meant to injure MacKinnon, not to kill him. Which made no sense, because if he remained alive he could tell others who it was who had attacked him – you and Aucoin. It's just the same with shooting me. It had to be fatal or I would live to tell the tale.'

'All right. I agree. I'm not proud of it.'

'Do you like this sort of intrigue? The deception? From the very first evening we met you were deceiving me. The pretence that someone was following us in the street in Charlottetown. The constant emphasis on smuggling – which even I, ignorant as I was about the island, sensed was a red herring. The constant under-mining of Harris, so that I would suspect him more than your boss, Gallant. And you told me you couldn't speak French, but Modeste tells me you read and speak it very well. We interviewed French-speaking people in English. And there you were, interview-ing Aucoin and Gallant alongside me, pretending you had never met them before, and with them pretending the same thing. And what were you telling Gallant about your discussions with me? You must have been keeping him abreast with events. He knew from you what our plans were.'

There was a silence during which we looked at each other, rather warily.

'I can't deny it,' said McNulty.

'And one more thing,' I said. 'It was you who shot the horses from under MacKinnon and me. Nice work with the new Snider-Enfield. That must have been very satisfying. I suppose you don't care about horses, but you did kill two of them, and one of them suffered particularly badly. Calum and I got the point. It was a warning. Keep off! But who was the warning to? Both of us? Calum? Or me?'

'More to MacKinnon than to you. Gallant wanted him dead. He wanted me to shoot MacKinnon as he rode beside you. Which might scare you off, of course. But mainly it was revenge. Surely he knew MacKinnon had been fucking his wife. Sorry, the bad language of this island is getting to me. I don't know how he knew. I didn't tell him. I didn't know for sure myself until you told me. His wife won't have told him. Or his putative daughter Marie. I think he must have simply worked it out. He was cunning and clever. He had no illusions about people. He once told me that everyone on earth was evil – with no exceptions. He said it went back to the serpent in the Garden of Eden. Christ! The man was as bad as a Presbyterian. A bloody Calvinist! Sorry, I'm getting carried away.'

'So is everyone evil? What do you think?'

'Of course not. Even I am not evil. Bad, yes. Foolish, yes. Dangerous, yes. But I have values. All right, that sounds mealy-mouthed. It's all pride! I'm proud of my ideals. I'm also proud of my cleverness. As I said, I didn't know at first whether Gallant really wanted to kill Marie and MacKinnon. At least I could understand he might want to kill MacKinnon, as I said – out of jealousy and revenge. But why Marie? Why not Madeleine? I have only realised why in the last few days, thinking about it. It was to make Madeleine suffer – to die of grief and pain, not quickly in a murder. He would have killed her lover and the daughter she had by her lover. And she would have died of pain.'

'But it was you who would have killed MacKinnon for him!'

'Yes, and that would have put me in Gallant's power of course. If I was caught, then he would wash his hands of it. I thought of all that. Once I had killed MacKinnon I would have told Gallant I had written an account of all my dealings with him and put it in a bank deposit box to which only certain friends had the key. So then he would have been back in my power!'

'There you are again – two scorpions in a bottle. You and Gallant would have ended up like I-Guess and Dunno! Dead with your hands around each other's throats. And you still burble about values!'

'I may do evil, but not because I want to. I'm capable of love. I loved Modeste. Don't you see that? When she left me for Edgar, my heart broke. And I loved her so much that I moved to the island here and became friends with her and Edgar. Anything to be able to see her from time to time. Of course I pretended I had come to terms with her leaving me. But no! I could not come to terms with it. And I'm not like Gallant. I don't think the world revolves around me. I loved Modeste, and I'll tell you what: I still love her. I love her body and her mind. And now you tell me she has had enough of Edgar. Why?'

'Think it through. Normally I would say, if you want to know "why", then ask Modeste. But I'll say the opposite. I don't want you to go anywhere near her. And I'll take the liberty of telling you why, since she will not want to see you anymore than she wants to see Aucoin again. In any case he is leaving the island. But use your moral sense, if you've still got one after all that self-flagellation at your seminary. It's simple: she cannot endure the sight of Aucoin any more, given that he hunted down Marie, the young mother of a week-old child, and dragged her back to her death. And you did the same thing! Is that enough reasoning?'

McNulty became agitated more than I had ever seen him.

'Yes! It is!'

Neither of us spoke for a minute or so. I broke the silence.

'May I ask what you will do next?'

'Given that I am out of the Police and my reputation here on the island is ruined, *and* – to be frank – the Cause has not much hope in the island… Given all these facts, I'll have to leave. I'll go back to Antigonish and see my son, then I'm not sure where. The States? Back to Ireland? Somewhere in Canada? England?'

'I hope you're joking.'

'Half joking. But there is work to be done in England.'

'For the Cause you mean.'

'For the Cause, if you want to put it that way.'

'So I'm freeing you to a further life of subversion and sedition.'

'Possibly. But that's what freedom is, isn't it? I may do terrible things when you set me free, or I may do good things.'

'There speaks the Jesuit!'

He smiled. 'You're right. But I truly thank you for not being vindictive towards me, and I wish you good fortune. You and your wife are remarkable. I hope you find a home.'

'Thanks. I won't wish you good fortune, since it may include sedition and so on. But I won't wish you bad fortune either.'

'In Ireland we use the word *cess* in these situations. No doubt it comes from the Latin *succedere* – to happen – in the past tense *successit*, "it happened". Successfully. To wish a person the opposite of success, we say "Bad cess to him". You and I are not wishing each other bad cess. That will do.'

This time he actually succeeded in standing up, although he staggered a little to find his balance. We did not shake hands.

'I assume you have somewhere to go,' I said. 'As soon as Dr Reid agrees, you can leave here.'

My interview with Edgar Aucoin was shorter. He was restlessly walking around his cell when I arrived. He stopped and looked at me. His expression was both angry and sad – perhaps just confused.

As with McNulty I was not going to play cat and mouse, and I told him he would be free. Which in his case meant that he would be free to leave the island as soon as possible.

'I'm in the shit,' he said. 'I've lost Modeste. With your help! But I'm not blaming you. I've never felt you were out to get me. Some Peelers

374

are – you know, they are going to take pleasure in crucifying a man if they can. You're fair. And as for MacKinnon, he's a man, and he has guts. I wish him well. I'm just worried about Mr Harris. His wife was beaten to death, and now it turns out to be probably by his closest friend, that swine Gallant, and with all the rumours flying around he'd surely be best to resign. I've known him for three years – since before he married Marie – and he can go into a melancholy state, he stops talking, goes off his food, can't sleep.'

'Thanks for warning me.'

'He's not like me,' Aucoin said. 'I bounce back. Even without Modeste I'll bounce back.' Now he looked defiant.

'I'll go now,' I said. 'You'll be released right away – and assuming that Dr Reid judges that you are safe to move about, as it seemed you were yesterday – I hope you'll be on your way.'

I left him standing there. In truth I was feeling sorry for him at having lost Modeste. Then I remembered what he and McNulty had done.

I had lunch with Armstrong – sandwiches and a glass of ale brought in from a tavern around the corner from the Brig – and I summed up my conversation with Mr Brecken.

'I'll write him a formal recommendation, while I'm still in post, that you continue in your rank of sergeant and that in the event of an expansion of the Island Police you should be part of any discussions and plans. Actually, fetch me a piece of paper and a pen and ink and I'll do it now.'

I did this and we finished our lunch. We shook hands, and I walked out into the street. I did not want to return to the Brig now. But before I left the island I would do so, to say goodbye to Armstrong and the other police. And I would send a note of thanks to the efficient Mackie in Georgetown.

I was feeling quite happy by now, and planning to send a telegram to Ocean House and to arrive there that evening. But I felt a certain gloom as I approached Harris's Charlottetown house, a rather grand one on the corner of a street facing the park. I was admitted by a maid in uniform and ushered into a library – smaller than the one at Stanley Bridge, but impressive. Harris was dressed in a suit and looking not as down in the dumps as I expected. We shook hands and sat in facing leather chairs.

Again I told the story of Modeste and Gallant, in its official form. He had already heard rumours, and he listened patiently. Then I summarised my conclusions about how Marie had died – leaving out the story of Lachlan. When I had finished, he sat quietly for a while, his head bowed. He took out a white handkerchief and wiped his eyes, then put the hand-kerchief back in his pocket and looked at me.

'I can still hardly believe it,' he said. 'Poor dear Évangéline… Now I think about it, there is one thing that bothered me at the time about Honoré Gallant. Soon after the birth of the baby, I had a meeting with him in North Rustico and I told him about the birth, and that all had gone well. I mentioned that the baby had a purple spot in her lower back, suggesting Mic Mac ancestry. I had been nervous about that spot after the birth: I thought it was some kind of blemish! But Madeleine reassured me that it could be found in some Acadian babies and that it would fade and disappear over a few years. I even felt proud that this child of mine had Mic Mac ancestry. They are, after all, some of the most civilised Indians in North America: they interbred with the Vikings! But when I told Honoré about this purple spot, he became agitated and angry, although I told him what I knew about it. "That's just an excuse!" he said. "It's hogwash!" Then he seemed to get a grip on himself. But now I wonder if rage about the purple spot moved him to inflict what I saw on Évangéline's body.'

'You didn't report this to me before!', I said. 'But yes, it could have made Gallant angry.'

I then remembered my conversation with Madeleine at the Ocean House and our discussion about the breaking of the camel's back.

Gallant's back! And her wondering how her husband could have learnt about the purple spot. I could see how Gallant was driven to destroy Marie.

'I didn't think it was important!', Harris continued. 'I knew Honoré was a bad man. I mean he visited brothels whenever he was off island, and he took bribes from smugglers. I never did, by the way, in case you are wondering. He also, when he visited Antigonish, compiled false manifests for cargoes. I kept hearing these things. But we were political allies. And his wife and daughter were so lovely. They were everything he was not. He was a monster, I suppose – like the Cormier brothers, but in a different way. I still can't believe he would have been capable of beating and raping his daughter. I mean, she was not his flesh and blood daughter, but she was brought up as such.'

'She was not exactly raped,' I said.

Why should Harris not know the truth?

'She was sodomised,' I said.

'My God! But surely that would have been Cormier. It runs in the family.'

'I know. But by Modeste's account, Gallant was also in the library, knew what happened there and approved of it. It becomes his crime as much as Cormier's. I don't know who did what. If it's any consolation, she would almost certainly have been unconscious by that time.'

'Necrophilia. It's like a medieval catalogue of sins. Except that to commit a sin you have to know you are doing it. If it was Dunno – meaning Zotique – I doubt if he would have known it was a sin. Honoré would have known. And I won't deceive myself. I know very well it would have been Honoré who lashed her with his belt. I've heard he did that to girls.' He looked at me. 'It's a nasty little world we have on this lovely island.'

'It's nasty everywhere. When I lived in Victoria, on Vancouver Island, it was often described as a Garden of Eden. But there were plenty of snakes there too.'

'That's hardly a consolation. And what about Aucoin and the attack on MacKinnon?'

'Resolved. Aucoin is a free man. However, he is leaving the island. Modeste refuses to have anything more to do with him.'

'That heroic woman! I was going to say I didn't know she had it in her, but actually I think I did know. I know she didn't kill Gallant, but she stood up to him, and he lost his judgement I suppose, and his balance as well, then had that accident.' He paused. 'So is Modeste going back alone to the house up the road?'

'I assume she's there now. With her dog, Bo-Bo.'

'And what about me?' Harris said. 'What am I to do? Where am I to go? I know I'll have to resign my seat in the Legislative Council. I've been scuppered by this scandal. What's next for me in the world?'

I had heard this almost hysterical tone from him before. But before I could reply to these rhetorical questions, he answered them himself.

'Your news confirms me in a decision,' he said. 'Have you heard of the Oxford Movement?'

'Of course. Anglo-Catholicism, then Cardinal Newman. And I went to Oxford. But I had no religious involvements there and I didn't go to church.'

'Newman, sadly, gave up on Anglicanism and turned to Rome. I couldn't do that. But now Edward Pusey, who is still in Oxford, is working towards setting up monastic orders. Would you believe it? It will be possible to be an Anglican monk – to take vows, to find brother monks and sister nuns, and to go among the poor and the sick and to help them, and still be an Anglican!'

I found myself thinking of elaborate services in gilded chapels with long almost mesmeric rituals in a haze of candles and incense – 'Smells and Bells', as this High Church ritual was called in Oxford. At least it was by people like me who disliked it.

'So that's what I'll do,' Harris said. 'I'll rent out my properties here and voyage to England and go to Edward Pusey and throw myself at his feet and offer myself to his mission!'

'It's a good idea,' I said, and in his case I almost believed it.

'Thank you. And I've just had a thought – about Modeste. If she's at the house in Stanley Bridge again, then perhaps she can look after my own house until I decide whether to sell it or not. I can employ her as a caretaker!'

'Good idea,' I said. 'She is amazingly capable.'

'I shall also need to visit Madeleine Gallant who is taking care of Aline. I am terribly indebted to her for taking on that darling baby. But what could I do with a young baby? It might seem selfish on my part to leave Aline in the care of somebody else, but Madeleine is her grandmother and I simply cannot see myself in charge of a child and staying much longer on the island for now. Although I will be away, I do want to help with the care of this child.'

I would leave it to Madeleine to tell him who the true father of Aline was.

I stood up, and we shook hands.

'Bon voyage!' I said.

I walked out into the sunny streets of Charlottetown in the late afternoon, often the best time of day on the island, when a fresh breeze rippled the leaves of the shade trees.

EPILOGUE

Calum and I were walking into the westerly wind, our heads bent forward. The wind was not cold but it was brisk and fresh, with occasional gusts. We were both wearing rubber boots, which occasionally sank into the rust-red sand of Thunder Cove, although we were now keeping on the harder sand where the waves were advancing in white lines, each line rising gradually then turning over and breaking with a thump followed by a sucking, swishing sound. I narrowed my eyes as the sun setting in front of us on the azure gulf sent out dazzling shafts of light. It still had some warmth in it, in October, and the day had been warm, but we were dressed for autumn, Calum in a lilac-grey tweed shooting jacket, myself in a light tweed coat. Neither of us wore a hat. We always walked quite fast, both of us being rather quick by nature, and I was enjoying the sparkle of the end of the afternoon, a sort of tonic in the air.

We reached the west end of the beach where a low red sandstone cliff created a barrier between the shore and the next stretch further west. We stopped for a while to look at how the water was coloured red outwards, in spite of the breakers, by the constant erosion of the cliff into sand. The whole island was being gradually eaten away by the sea. Perhaps in a few million years it would all be gone.

Now we pounded eastward on our way back along the shore, not talking – the sound of the wind was stronger than our voices. I thought of poor Marie, parallel to this shore, most likely in mid-afternoon on the last day of June, sailing into the wind, tacking as she knew how, aware that she was being followed by another boat perhaps a mile or two behind, distantly in sight.

We were approaching the headland with its red arch. Gold rays from the sun as it descended shone through the arch dramatically and sparkled on the waves. We crossed the beach where a miniature delta of rivulets flowed down to the waves from the creek which drained the pond, cutting a channel in the sand closer to the dunes a hundred yards or so to our left, the grey-green marram grass flowing with its own waves in the wind. Calum had told me that marram grass was common in the Western Isles of Scotland, facing North America across the Atlantic. He felt at home with it.

Suddenly the wind seemed to drop, but this was because we had entered the lee of the headland with the arch. We stopped for a moment. 'Here is where she would have pulled in the boat,' Calum said. 'Or just about. She would not have been able to get it very high on the shore, although the tide was coming in, and she couldn't wait. It was still here when they arrived, and they must have pulled it up higher to retrieve it later. Or perhaps Aucoin and McNulty left it to I-Guess to pull up both boats as they ran after Mairi. And they must have seen her waiting for them at the top of the beach.'

We turned inland and walked towards the angle of headland and beach across another delta from another creek, and across a low ridge of softer sand behind which there were saltwater pools in which the pinkish white cumulus clouds above were reflected, the reflection shimmering and distorting in the breeze. 'She would have been around here', Calum said, 'nursing her baby in haste, scribbling the note to hide in the wicker basket, and then running to the pond to hide her baby. She would have come back to wait for them. Brave lass. And they would have come up to her and seen she did not have the child. God knows what they said or did then. Perhaps one of them ran up into the reeds behind, or even up to the pond, but could see nothing. Perhaps they tied her up there and then, with rope from their boat or hers – there is always rope in boats – and left her lying on the sand while they looked again for the baby.'

'I didn't ask them about those details,' I said. 'They simply confirmed they had bound and gagged her, and could not find the baby.'

We forged ahead across the soft sand and around the saltwater pools, then through the beds of thick reeds, our boots squelching in mud, until we reached the pond. We had come around it on our way to the shore, by the usual path, as we had done many times before on our walks. Now with the sea behind us, the slope of the headland rising to our right, and flatter ground on the other side, the pond looked huge. It was several hundred yards across, surrounded by reeds, its shore raggedly indented and probably changing from year to year. Somewhere in an inlet in the reeds, Marie had left the baby in its cradle. She knew it would not sink, the wickerwork being so tightly woven, and the cradle with the tiny baby in its blanket so light. She had probably jammed it into the reeds, but in a place which Lachlan could see from their usual courting place somewhere in the clumps of low trees on the slope behind. She must have given a last kiss to the baby, then turned and run back to the beach and her fate. She knew Lachlan would soon be here and would see and take care of the baby. She knew, I suppose, that she would not see Lachlan for a while. The baby was safe from harm. She was going back into harm. How deep a harm she surely could not have known.

We continued on, around the pond, not talking, both of us grim-faced. We reached the top of the ridge and looked ahead down to the muddy shore of Darnley Basin which was now in the light of the setting sun like a vast pool of molten gold, with the sea where it opened between low headlands to the north now streaked with light blue as well as gold. We walked for twenty minutes or so down through scrub and grass on muddy sand until we were on the bay shore, then we turned left towards the row of fishermen's huts. We walked up to Calum's hut and we found the basket we had left there earlier, full of the oysters we had collected in Darnley Basin in the early afternoon at low tide. We stooped down and each took a handle. With the basket between us we walked along the path and then onto the road of hard-packed mud that led eventually to Calum's croft.

'Not every outcome is bad,' Calum said as we walked. 'John Harris came to visit Madeleine before leaving the island. She told him about the baby's real father and although it was painful for Harris to come to terms with this, he decided to leave a fund to help in the upbringing of the child, in memory of his Évangéline. As for Lachlan, he has really come into his own, now he is not only a *L'nu*, a native, but a true "Mic Mac", meaning a member of the tribal family. At the same time, he is still working in my sons' printshop. He is also visiting us every week and becoming the true father of Aline. And I am the grandfather. And Madeleine is both mother and grandmother!'

'Another good outcome is with Modeste,' I said. 'We visited her the other day. She finds she cannot live any longer in Stanley Bridge. It's too painful. So she is buying Harris's house in Charlottetown, and plans to make it into a Guesthouse. She has, it turns out, some money she has saved over the years. Her two boys want to come over from Antigonish to live with her in Charlottetown to help her out with this new business. Harris is becoming an Anglican monk in England, and he is not holding out for a high price for the house. Cables are buzzing back and forth across the Atlantic.'

'Modeste is a fine woman,' Calum said. 'You know what? In all this, we men have done nothing compared to the women. You and I did our bit, as men – on the side of life, not of death. But it was the women who saved us all!'

Now the sun was truly setting, the air was damp and chilly, the ground darkening in the shade. The fields looked almost grey. The golden light from the windows of Calum's house cheered us on. We mounted the wooden steps side by side and set the basket down. Calum raised his hand to knock, but the door opened. Lucy stood there smiling. 'We heard your footsteps,' she said – meaning that *she* had heard them: I sometimes joked with her that she could hear footsteps a mile away.

I stepped into the light and embraced her. We kissed on the lips briefly and she stepped aside. Calum, following me in, kissed her on the cheek, as I kissed Madeleine, holding her baby. Then Will came running 'Papa!' he called, and I picked him up and swung him in the air.

'Oysters!' Calum announced, pointing to the basket.

'We'll bake them,' said Madeleine. 'And I'll put some potatoes on.'

Will wanted to show me the scribbling he had been doing with pencils on some of the sheets of paper Calum got from his sons at the printers in Summerside – paper scrapped from the proofs of books, printed over, but good for packing and for lining drawers, and now for scribbling on.

After I had become a free man again at the end of July, I had gone to Ocean House and stayed with Lucy and Will. I only saw Olivia and her children for a few days, as they had to return to Charlottetown. William was missing them, yet he could not take a holiday in North Rustico, staying in a public hotel. It would have been considered beneath his dignity as Governor, although he would have loved to have done it – as he told me when we spent a few days at Government House some weeks later.

So Lucy and I had some days at Ocean House with Madeleine and Aline. Then, after an exchange of letters between Madeleine and Calum, he had come to North Rustico to fetch them – in a two-horse trap whose woodwork he had newly varnished, and actually wearing a suit. Lucy and I had not been there when Calum and Madeleine met. It was private. We went to the beach, to be out of their way, and when we got back, they were gone.

Now Lucy missed that time with Madeleine and Olivia. What Calum and I had called 'the Court of Women'. Like any court they had talked. They had walked too, and they had held each other's children. They had all pitched in to play with Olivia's two elder children. When I arrived Madeleine – it seemed miraculously to me, although not to Lucy and Olivia – was nursing her own granddaughter, putting her to the breast, although turning away and covering Aline with a blanket when I was present. It was as if she was Aline's mother. And Lucy told me that although in some cases when an older woman suckles a child who is not her own the milk only partially comes through, for Madeleine it came through fully. The baby needed nothing more than Madeleine was giving her, and she was thriving.

When Madeleine had left, and Lucy and I and Will were alone together, we took our usual delight in each other. But Lucy missed her friends. It seemed to me that they had all changed each other. Madeleine was still sad for Marie, and she had lived through two decades in longing and pain – except from those few ecstatic interludes with Calum – but she had come through to a calm confidence, as if she had been through everything and could now do everything. Olivia, although I did not know her well until our later stay with her and William, had been able to break out of the constraints of her necessarily self-conscious and careful life as a Governor's wife, when she had to welcome the citizens who poured through Government House at various receptions. She even had to give tea parties for the wives of Assemblymen and doctors and the professors at Prince of Wales College. As she put it, she was always on show. But at Ocean House, although she was careful to behave herself properly in public, which was second nature anyway, with Madeleine and Lucy she had for the first time since coming to the island been able to let her hair down and be herself – a jolly, informal, very active woman who liked to go with the others for a day on the beach far from prying eyes, where whatever servants were with them would wait on the side of some sand dune while the ladies walked further on and took their outer clothes off and lay in the sun or climbed the sand dunes and rolled down them with the children, or splashed into the waves.

For Lucy herself, after two years of life with me at Orchard Farm, missing and mourning the Tsimshian girls she had grown up with, and her closest non-native friend Aemilia who had died with her man and her son in a massacre by another tribe, she found a part of herself again with Madeleine and Olivia in that idyll at Ocean House. Not least, her English, which she had learned almost all from me, had gained new vocabulary in what I might call 'women's areas', but were simply human areas of experience as lived by women. And she had come into more confidence. She had always been very sure of her own thoughts and perceptions, and took none of them second-hand. But she had been shy in society, and now she was no longer shy.

I watched Lucy with joy as she and Madeleine bustled around together making dinner. Calum and I were sitting in front of the fire, where he had stoked up some logs, since the evenings were now cooler, talking idly and passing Will between us. Then Lucy came over to me and gave me a peck on the cheek and said, 'Supper will be ready in a few minutes.' Calum jumped up and said, 'I'll have to get those bottles of champagne I have in the ice house.' I put Will down again, some way from the fire – but he knew how to keep away from it – with his pencils and paper. Lucy was over at the wood stove. Madeleine was standing with Aline at her breast, rocking slowly from side to side.

'Chad,' she said, 'Would you mind reaching me the cradle.' She made a sign with her head towards the nook near the fire where the cradle lay on a chair. I went and picked it up. The wickerwork cradle made by the Mic Mac. The cradle that had floated, if not on the waves, at least on the steady waters of the pond below the slope where Marie and Lachlan had made the baby. I held the cradle as Madeleine laid Aline gently in it, tucking her under her blanket. The little girl was lovely – like a sleeping Indian Princess. I passed the cradle back to Madeleine who stood rocking it gently.

AFTERWORD

Although Sir Robert Hodgson, Governor William Robinson and his wife Olivia, Frederick de St Croix Brecken, and Chief Joseph Snake are historical characters, no one else in this story is, and its events are fictional.

The Prince Edward Island railway was officially started on 5th October 1871, when Olivia Robinson ceremoniously dug the first sod. As predicted, building the railway almost bankrupted the island, and the Dominion of Canada had to bail it out. The island joined the Dominion in 1873, and Sir Robert Hodgson at the age of seventy-five at last moved into Government House as Lieutenant Governor of the island where he had been born. William Robinson and his family, after a period of leave in Britain, went to Australia – at last not another island, or if an island also a continent – where he became known as not only a first-rate Governor of Western Australia then Southern Australia, but as a composer of songs and even an operetta.

Some of the statements and comments on the Highland Clearances attributed to Calum MacKinnon come from the essays of one of the greatest poets of the 20th century, Sorley MacLean, who wrote in his mother tongue, Gaelic. The poem translated by the present author in Chapter 20 is no. 61 of MacLean's poem cycle *Dàin do Eimhir*. The last native speakers of Gaelic in Prince Edward Island died in the 20th century. Now about 5,000 Islanders have French as a mother tongue. A minority of the Mi'kmaq people on Prince Edward Island currently can speak their original language, and efforts are being made to widen its use by teaching it.

In 1997 the longest bridge in the world over a sea that freezes, Confederation Bridge, was opened to connect Prince Edward Island to New Brunswick. But the island is still an island, and some people there still talk of 'over across' and refer to the mainland as 'Canada'.